Wartime Wishes for the Land Girls

BOOKS BY ELLIE CURZON

A VILLAGE AT WAR SERIES
The Ration Book Baby
The Spitfire Girl
The Wartime Vet

ELLIE CURZON

Wartime Wishes for the Land Girls

Bookouture

Published by Bookouture in 2024

An imprint of Storyfire Ltd.
Carmelite House
50 Victoria Embankment
London EC4Y 0DZ

www.bookouture.com

ISBN: 978-1-83525-253-6
eBook ISBN: 978-1-83525-252-9

This book is a work of fiction. Whilst some characters and circumstances portrayed by the author are based on real people and historical fact, references to real people, events, establishments, organizations or locales are intended only to provide a sense of authenticity and are used fictitiously. All other characters and all incidents and dialogue are drawn from the author's imagination and are not to be construed as real.

For the adorable and adored Pippa, who would've loved the Land Girl life.

PROLOGUE

DECEMBER 1943

'Daisy!' Lottie called desperately, her voice echoing in the freezing air.

The deep, wintry woods were a dark maze of leafless trees. Snow falling from the night-time sky was blown through the canopy of branches overhead on icy blasts of wind and lay in patches that crackled under Lottie's heavy boots. This was no weather for anyone to be out in, especially not a lost and frightened little girl.

Lottie tightened her gloved hand around Matthew's. His precious niece, the girl he'd promised to protect, was out here, somewhere, in the dark, looming woods, where scratching brambles choked the paths and branches reached out like clawed hands. Lottie's heart rushed at every sound she heard; every crunch of snow underfoot, every sigh in the freezing wind. Blossom, Lottie's faithful dog, was just ahead, sniffing her way through the undergrowth, and Lottie prayed she would find Daisy's trail soon.

By her side, Matthew's call was firm and clear despite his obvious distress and the midnight woods rang with urgent cries from other voices too. The whole of Bramble Heath village seemed to be out searching for the lost girl.

If the man who had taken Daisy could hear them, would he hand her over and give himself up? Surely he wouldn't do anything desperate and unimaginable – would he?

Lottie tried not to let her thoughts spiral, but the village had been whipped up into a frenzy by a heady cocktail of war and fear. People had become scared of shadows and sounds in the dark, haunted by the spectre of Stefan von Brandt, the German who had been hiding among them in Bramble Heath, moving silent and unseen by night. They saw him on every corner, this man who had the blood of a monster in his veins, who was so closely connected to the worst of humanity.

Lottie and Matthew had to find Daisy before she came to harm or succumbed to the freezing cold.

More than ever before, Bramble Heath needed a miracle.

ONE

Lottie was on the platform at East Grinstead station, wrapped up against the cold, as she waited for her train. She'd just been home to visit her parents, who lived in the town, her last chance before Christmas, and she was keen to be getting back to the farm in Bramble Heath village. Although she'd miss her parents, she couldn't wait to spend Christmas there with her dearest friends, the other Land Girls. They couldn't all go home, because the war was raging and the country needed to eat.

The sound of the Salvation Army band playing Christmas carols gave her a warm glow despite the chill and she hummed along to 'Once in Royal David's City'. The cattle shed in the lyrics brought to mind the farm she had grown to love and the animals who she cared for there. The jangle of the Salvation Army's collection tins mingled with the hiss from the steam trains and the hurrying footsteps of the passengers.

Blossom, her faithful shaggy-haired terrier, with chaotic spots of brown, black and white fur, stood beside her. The little dog glanced curiously at the bustle of young men in uniform carrying their kitbags. Some of them would have managed to get precious leave over Christmas, while others were leaving their loved ones to head back to barracks for the festive season.

Signs pointed to the nearest air-raid shelter and the station was full of posters warning travellers to *Beware the Squander Bug!* and to *Make Do and Mend*. Even the adverts for Christmas couldn't escape the war; on one was a man in khaki offering his sweetheart a tiny box of chocolates, while other posters warned the public not to take up space on the trains by sending too many parcels. Not that there was much in the shops to buy.

The war had been going on for so long now that Lottie barely remembered what it was like to live in a world without government information posters everywhere, or uniforms on the streets. She was in uniform, too; anyone who passed her would know that the young woman with rosy cheeks and large blue eyes was a proud member of the Women's Land Army. Or Land Girls, as they were also called, even though Lottie wasn't exactly a girl any more – she was heading for thirty.

Over the sound of the band and the trains, she heard a sudden commotion and, tucking an escaped length of her dark blonde hair under her felt hat, she turned to see what was happening.

There, on the opposite platform, she saw a tall man standing in the open doorway of a carriage. The milling passengers had stopped and were cheering him as one.

With a start of surprise, Lottie realised that she recognised him. This was Sidney Gastrell, the man who had been on the front pages of all the papers and in all the newsreels at the cinema after catching a would-be traitor.

The story had been in the news for weeks: a gunner made contact with a German spy, offering to provide targets for Nazi bombers. But the airman hadn't realised he was not in fact talking to a Nazi but to someone with British interests at heart; Sidney Gastrell himself. The would-be Nazi who had carried out his traitorous correspondence with Gastrell could now look forward to a life sentence in prison.

That Gastrell found time to perform such heroics in between raising money for war orphans, welcoming the refugees who had fled occupied Europe and visiting casualties of the conflict who were shipped back for treatment made it all the more remarkable. But Sidney Gastrell didn't look remarkable at all. He was in his fifties, with greying temples and the air of someone who was surprised to see such adulation.

Lottie enthusiastically joined in with the cheering and Blossom wagged her tail excitedly. Seeing someone like Gastrell arrive at the station in a second-class carriage, travelling like any other ordinary person, touched her deeply, reminding her of how everyone in Britain from all walks of life was united against their common enemy. While bombs rained from the sky, Land Girls like Lottie worked in the fields, making sure that the nation wouldn't go hungry. And men like Gastrell did their bit by catching traitors.

How anyone could betray their own country during wartime, Lottie couldn't understand – especially as she knew all too well the despair and the pain of losing a loved one to an enemy bomb.

Lottie blinked back the tears that sprang to her eyes as she recalled her visit earlier that day with her parents to the grave where her sister had been buried. They had laid a wreath on Martha's grave, made from holly picked from the garden, and they had talked to her. Lottie, her words catching with sadness, told her about life on the farm and how everyone there still missed her. It was comforting, in a way, to think that maybe Martha was listening.

Once he had given a bashful wave of acknowledgement to the crowd, Gastrell turned his back to the platform and helped a man down from the train. He was dressed in khaki, one sleeve of his overcoat empty, his step unsure. Lottie realised that he must be one of the many injured servicemen who Gastrell devoted himself to helping. As the first man reached the platform, Gastrell was aiding another, a man in an RAF greatcoat, his face a patchwork of different skins. He must've been a patient at the pioneering hospital in East Grinstead, where so many badly burned pilots were being given back their faces.

Watching him, Lottie was struck by the fact that there was nothing grand about Gastrell, even though the whole country regarded him as a hero. He risked life and limb chasing down traitors who had stayed one step ahead of the law. He'd even run a few Germans to ground after they'd come down in their planes and gone on the run. Lottie hadn't read any of the books he'd written about his escapades, but every other person she knew seemed to have. The newsreel had even said there was a film in the works about him.

Then a woman appeared in the doorway of the carriage and took his outstretched hand. Lottie had seen her in the newsreel too – she was Gastrell's wife, Rachel, and unlike him, she was as glamorous as a film star. She had to duck as she stepped out of the carriage to avoid bending the long feathers on her velvet hat. Her earrings twinkled in the winter sunlight and her fur coat looked expensive.

'Three cheers for Mr Gastrell!' called a young officer, sweeping off his cap.

Lottie cheered even louder and Blossom barked with glee, jumping up, carried away with everyone's excitement.

'Hip-hip, hooray!' Lottie shouted. 'Hip-hip— ooof! Watch out!'

She nearly lost her balance as one of the other passengers blundered into her and she looked up, annoyed.

TWO

Lottie spotted his dog collar at once; the tall man who looked barely over thirty with slightly unruly chestnut hair was Matthew Hart, the new Bramble Heath vicar, with his adorable little orphaned niece, Daisy. She was just eight years old, a perfect age to enjoy Christmas. Lottie hoped that, despite the war, it would be a magical one for her.

Lottie hadn't met them properly yet, but she'd heard about their arrival in the village and she had seen Matthew on his rounds, making sure the families who had fathers and sons away fighting knew that they could call on him, should they need anything. As the weather grew colder, she had seen him dropping off rations for the oldest residents of the village so they could stay warm before the hearth and didn't have to keep venturing out for supplies. He was a quiet young man, who bowed his head and got on with the job of ministering to his flock.

'Sorry, I— sorry,' he said distractedly, his head still turned away as he watched Gastrell. He held Daisy's hand protectively, but her attention was all for Blossom.

'What a brilliant dog!' the little girl declared, stretching out her mittened hands towards Blossom, who sniffed at her with interest. Her light blonde curls popped out from beneath a hand-knitted bobble hat. 'Uncle Matthew, come on, you've got to see this dog!'

The young man finally tore his gaze from Gastrell and looked briefly down at Blossom. 'That's a nice doggy, isn't it?' he said vaguely, and gave Lottie a nod of greeting, but she didn't think he recognised her.

'Uncle Matthew, *look!*' Daisy demanded again, waving at Blossom. The dog had tipped her head to one side and was staring at the girl. Then Daisy grinned toothily at Lottie. 'I really love dogs.'

'I do too,' Lottie replied, smiling at her. Then she asked Matthew, 'You're from Bramble Heath, aren't you?'

On the other platform, the Gastrells were making their way out of the station, followed by a tide of cheering passengers. Some even seemed to have forgotten their own trains and to want instead to stay close to the unassuming hero of the home front, the man who kept them safe in their beds, just as surely as those in uniform did. Lottie wondered what he was doing in East Grinstead, but his new book was in every bookshop window, so perhaps he was here to meet his readers. He'd have quite a turnout if so.

Matthew finally gave Lottie his full attention.

'Yes, Bramble Heath is my new parish,' he said. 'Are you from the village too?' Then he narrowed his bright blue eyes and remembered: 'From one of the farms?'

Lottie nodded, pleased that he recognised her after all, although perhaps her Land Girl uniform, with her brown felt hat, green jumper, brown breeches and socks with clumpy shoes, gave away where she worked. 'Yes, I'm at Goslings' farm. I've seen you around. I'm sorry I haven't been to any of your services...'

The fact was that Lottie *had* been to his church in the

village, but that was before Matthew had started there. Before the death of her sister, she had gone every Sunday, but her attendance had tailed off as she wrestled with her anger and grief, and now she couldn't bear the thought of going back into the ancient medieval building again. The truth was, she was angry with God for taking her sister away. How could a loving, merciful God allow someone so young to die? Why couldn't He stop the horrors that were taking hold, the deaths and murders, the people chased out of their homes, only to die in camps that were beyond anyone's worst nightmare? How could she sing His praises?

Just then, a loud hiss of steam announced the arrival of the train to Bramble Heath. Some airmen, who were no doubt travelling to the RAF base just outside the village, lifted their kitbags onto their shoulders, ready to board the train.

Among the passengers who were climbing out, Lottie recognised Mrs Pearson, a young mother from Bramble Heath, who beamed at Matthew as she helped her little twin boys onto the platform. She wore her hair in huge victory rolls at the front of her head, with a velvet hat decked in wax fruit balancing just behind. A large brooch sparkled on the lapel of her darned coat.

'Good afternoon, Vicar, and hello, Daisy! Oh, and Lottie and Blossom, too,' she greeted them, looking as jolly as ever. 'We're off to visit Father Christmas in the market!'

'That's where we've been,' Matthew told her. He was friendly enough, Lottie thought, but he had big shoes to fill. The late Reverend Ellis had been like everyone's cheery grandpa. Matthew, despite being less than half his predecessor's age, seemed older than his years and much more introverted. Matthew's friendliness seemed forced, like it took effort. 'Daisy visited Santa's grotto, didn't you?'

Daisy nodded, her red cheeks dimpling. 'I did, and he was very nice. He gave me Bunny!' She proudly held out a small toy rabbit and Mrs Pearson's boys gazed at it with wide eyes. Toys, like everything else, weren't in plentiful supply.

'Mummy, can we have a rabbit, too? *And* another dog?' one of her boys pleaded.

'You never know what else might be in Father Christmas's sack,' Mrs Pearson said with a smile. 'Maybe you'll get a little soldier in a uniform like Daddy wears where he's off fighting. Now, I'd better let you get on,' she added and bustled away, dragging her sons with her. 'Lovely to see you!'

'Bye-bye!' Daisy said, waving her rabbit after the boys.

'Daisy loves animals,' Matthew said matter-of-factly. Lottie waited for him to say more, but he didn't. Instead, he looked after the departing Pearsons, then turned his attention back to Lottie.

'She's welcome on the farm any time,' Lottie replied, trying to find something to say to him, although she would enjoy showing Daisy around anyway. 'Oh, where are my manners, honestly? I'm Charlotte Morley, although everyone calls me Lottie.'

'Reverend Hart,' he replied. A moment later he seemed to realise that more was required and added, 'Everyone calls me Vicar. But when I have a name, it's Matthew.'

'Pleased to meet you, Matthew and Daisy,' she replied. The little girl beamed at her. 'If Daisy likes sheep and pigs, cows and chickens as well as dogs, I'd love to show her around the farm.'

'Oh, yes, I love all the animals,' Daisy replied excitedly. 'I like deer, too. They come into our garden and eat the grass. Uncle Matthew says they're looking for Father Christmas.'

Matthew gave a nod and said, 'Well, they know where Father Christmas is, but they're just checking that all the houses have chimneys so they can let him know. And if they find a house that doesn't, they just check the doorbell is working instead.' He glanced to Lottie. 'Yes, we'd love to visit the farm, if it's no trouble.'

If he was business-like when addressing Lottie, the same couldn't be said for when Matthew spoke to his little niece. Instead, his eyes shone with affection, his tone warm.

'How about the day after tomorrow, say eleven o'clock?' Lottie suggested.

'We'll see you then,' Matthew assured her in that stiff way of his, as Daisy beamed excitedly. 'Thank you.'

All the other passengers had left the train by now and they were among the few still on the platform.

'Time for us to get back to Bramble Heath,' Lottie said, and added, 'Do you need a hand with Daisy?'

Too late, she saw Matthew bristle as his gaze darted to the walking stick that he held in one hand. Lottie cursed herself, but she really hadn't meant to suggest he couldn't manage. She'd heard that he'd been injured in the war and she knew that veterans didn't want to be treated as if they were helpless, she was just trying to make the new arrival feel welcome.

'Helping a wounded soldier?' Matthew asked in a somewhat curt manner, letting Lottie know that he had taken her offer just as badly as she feared. She wondered what Matthew's life had been before he came to Bramble Heath, how he had ended up a country vicar after fighting on the frontline, but it was hardly the sort of question she could ask. His brisk reply hung in the air between them for a second until he looked at Daisy, who was smiling towards Blossom. Something about the little girl seemed to change his mind and he nodded. 'Thank you, yes.' Then he rubbed the tip of his nose against Daisy's and asked her in a very serious voice, 'Ready for take-off, Captain Hart?'

Daisy nodded and cried out, 'Wheeeeeee! I'm a Spitfire plane going after the Germans!'

The guard reeled off the list of stations that the train would pass through on its way to Bramble Heath and Matthew leaned his stick against his leg and lifted Daisy high into the air, mimic-

king the sound of an aeroplane's engine as he flew her straight
into Lottie's waiting arms. Daisy was a trusting little mite,
clearly delighted to be making a new friend – especially a new
friend who happened to have a very cute dog. Yet Lottie didn't
get the feeling her uncle felt the same.

Juggling Daisy and Blossom's lead, Lottie made her way
towards the train.

'Come on, Uncle Matthew!' Daisy said and Lottie glanced
away, not wanting injured Matthew to feel uncomfortable with
her staring as he struggled onto the train. But when she looked
back, he was watching the tail end of the crowd that was
following Sidney Gastrell into town. Then he turned back to
the train.

'Right,' he said, business-like. 'Home, Miss Daisy, in time for
tea!'

THREE

After saying goodbye to Matthew and Daisy, Lottie walked up the hill, following the lane towards Goslings' farm. The hedgerows that bordered the fields on one side were studded with red rosehips and draped in lacy cobwebs that were jewelled with ice. Blossom strained on her lead as they neared home and Lottie was keen to get home too; the afternoon was very chilly and ice was in the air, and the woods that ran along the other side of the lane were full of shadows.

It had been an odd journey back from East Grinstead, Matthew barely saying a thing while Daisy had filled their compartment with her merry chatter. She was clearly very taken with Blossom and had told Lottie all about her trip to see Father Christmas.

Lottie had to keep reminding herself that she'd seen the rather moody Matthew play aeroplanes with his niece. It wasn't something she'd expected from a quiet young vicar, especially one who hadn't seemed very friendly. A bachelor taking on a young child was certainly unusual, although Lottie knew that he wouldn't be short of women in the village keen to help him care for her. And despite his manner towards her, she wanted to help too.

She heard the sound of horses' hooves up ahead and Blossom barked.

'I know that bark!' came Nicola's merry call through the gathering shadows. The Geordie Land Girl was always upbeat, even in the freezing cold. 'It's a bit nippy to be out!'

'Yeah, I'm freezing!' Lottie replied, as the trap carrying the Land Girls rounded the bend. 'Thanks so much for coming out to rescue me!'

What a welcome sight it was. Her friends knew how hard it had been for her to go back home to East Grinstead and visit her parents, and had promised to meet her on the way back. Since Martha's death, her family had pleaded with her to give up being a Land Girl, or at least to move to another farm that wasn't so near to an airbase, a clear target for enemy bombs. But she had refused.

She understood why they wanted her to leave the farm where Martha had lost her life, and where Lottie nearly had been trapped in an inferno when a barn had been torched, and yet she didn't want to leave her new friends behind, or the memories of Martha that were still there. And, more than anything else, she was certain Martha would've wanted her to stay at the farm. They had talked so often about doing their bit for the war effort, just as their father did as an air-raid warden. Her friends from home had gone to the four corners of the country, as Land Girls on other farms, or were working as nurses, or in the women's auxiliary groups attached to the military. She'd be letting them all down if she gave up and went back home.

And she'd be letting the country down, too. The only way to win the war was if everyone made sacrifices and that was exactly what Lottie was determined to do. She had to stay, she had to do what she could to keep the country fed during its darkest hours.

Nicola and Shona were huddled together, wrapped warmly. They had swapped their uniform felt hats for bobble hats that they'd knitted by the fire in the farmhouse's kitchen and were tucked up in large fluffy scarves and overcoats. Nicola's dark curls popped out from under her hat, which framed her cheerful round face. Shona's nose was red from the cold, standing out from her pale face. With her gloved hand, she patted her auburn hair back into place under her woolly hat.

The two bay Shire horses harnessed to the trap whinnied, steam escaping their flared nostrils in the cold air. As soon as the vehicle rolled to a halt, Blossom bounded up into the blankets piled in the back. Nicola reached her hand down to Lottie and said, 'Up you get, pet.'

Lottie grasped it and heaved herself up to sit beside them. They were a tight-knit bunch, the closest of friends, brought together by working on the same farm throughout the war. Together they'd faced the worst of times. They were the kindest companions Lottie could have wished for after Martha was taken from her and she had come to regard them as her family. From all over the kingdom, they'd been thrown in at the deep end and they'd kept the home fires burning, digging the crops and tending the cattle that were so vital to the people not just of Bramble Heath but of the whole country. They were their own sort of army.

'I had the most bizarre trip back from town,' Lottie told them as the trap set off. 'I saw a celebrity and met a vicar!'

'Let me guess!' Nicola laughed mischievously. She glanced back at the dog, by now snuggled down happily and already snoozing. 'A celebrity, eh? Well, little Blossom looks very pleased with herself, so... Lassie!'

The papers had been filled with articles about Lassie for months and Lottie did wonder if she could smuggle Blossom into the pictures so that she could see the film when it was finally released. But she shook her head, laughing. 'No, sadly not Lassie! It was Sidney Gastrell. I saw him get off the train with his wife. Everyone was cheering – it was so exciting! He's such a hero, but he just seems so ordinary, really. His wife's *really* glamorous, though. She looks like a film star!'

'Oh aye!' Nicola said excitedly. 'Some of the lads from Heath Place were saying he's giving a talk tomorrow. They're going over to get their books signed, they're like daft lasses chasing after Humphrey Bogart, them RAF boys!'

The girls all laughed and the sound rang in the frosty lane as the horses' hooves clip-clopped against the road. Lottie loved moments like these. It didn't matter how hard the work was on the farm, how muddy their shoes got or how tired they were, the Land Girls always managed to find time to enjoy each others' company.

'You're right, they are!' Lottie chuckled. 'He's such a hero, but so unassuming. And he's got fans everywhere. Even vicars – because that's how I bumped into Reverend Hart, you see. Or should I say, he bumped into *me*, because he was so busy staring at Gastrell.'

'Even vicars like Sidney Gastrell,' Shona observed in her broad Yorkshire accent.

'He's a quiet one, that lad. I always thought vicars were the sort you couldn't stop chattering on,' Nicola replied. She was right, Matthew didn't say much at all. Yet, as Lottie knew to her cost, everyone had a story in wartime and he was a young man who relied on a walking cane and was caring for an orphan. 'Keeps to himself, don't he?' Nicola went on. 'His niece is a bonny little thing though... No mam nor dad, but she's got her uncle, bless her.'

Lottie didn't reply at once. She'd sat on the train, watching Daisy happily natter away, and wondered what the little girl's story was. It was all too common to hear about children orphaned during the Blitz; tragically, even some of the evacuees in the village had been. Lottie had wanted to say something to Matthew, to tell him that she too carried that same secret pain of wartime loss with her. And yet she hadn't wanted to intrude on his grief, or make a blunder.

There were, of course, any number of ways that someone could lose their life. She had to stop assuming that, because someone had died during this dreadful war, they had met the same awful, sudden end as her dear sister Martha.

'He's very brave, raising her alone,' Lottie told them, even though she was sure they'd already be thinking the same thing. 'And it was so funny, I saw a different side to him with her that I hadn't expected at all. He lifted her into the air and pretended she was a plane!'

'You're sure we're talking about the same lad?' Nicola laughed. 'Every time I see him, he's got a face like a slapped backside on his birthday.' Then she shrugged and a mischievous smile crept over her features. 'So, ladies. Youse remember that I told you I was going to knit myself a right canny pair of gloves for winter? And I never was a knitter, me. More at home with a shovel than a needle and thread!'

Lottie chuckled. She and the other girls had been doing their best to teach Nicola how to knit. Lottie and Martha used to have at least three knitting projects on the go at a time. 'Have you finished them yet? Let's see!'

'I'm wearing them!' Nicola gathered up the reins in her left hand and held up her right hand for her friends to see. She was wearing the bright red gloves she'd been toiling over for weeks, dropping stitches and muttering oaths here and there. 'Spot the deliberate mistake, lasses!'

Lottie couldn't spot any obvious holes and the gloves seemed to be a good fit. She nudged Shona, who seemed rather distracted. Maybe she was missing her family; Christmas made it all the harder to be away from their loved ones, never knowing if they were safe.

'They look bonny, as you'd say,' Lottie replied. She was proud of the bits and bobs of dialect she'd picked up from her friends who'd come down from the north of England to work on the farm. She'd never met anyone from Newcastle before meeting Nicola and she'd only seen Scarborough, the Yorkshire seaside town where Shona was from, in a postcard. 'I'm actually very impress—'

Then Lottie saw it, at the same moment as Shona did. Dangling beside Nicola's little finger.

'An extra finger?' Lottie roared with laughter, helpless with mirth, and clutched on to her friends as they laughed too. 'Oh, Nicola, however did you manage that?'

'Same reason I always save odd socks,' Nicola deadpanned. 'You never know when you might need a spare!'

Lottie and Shona laughed even harder.

She was sure she worked with the best Land Girls in the country. They always managed to find some way to have fun. She suspected someone like Matthew would disapprove of them being so jovial during wartime because it seemed that he thought such levity was reserved solely for children. But Lottie felt that they had to find joy wherever they could and that it might not last for long. Even out here in the countryside, with Nazi planes flying overhead and an airbase nearby, they weren't safe.

FOUR

Lottie was quiet that evening; visiting Martha's grave always wore her out. It was hard to be reminded that she had lost her and yet she felt compelled to visit that small space in the cemetery where her sister rested. If she didn't visit with her parents, who else would? She hated to think that Martha was alone, while life carried on without her.

That night, she went to bed in her little room overlooking the fields. At the end of the bed, Blossom curled up on the home-made patchwork quilt, a reassuring weight across her feet.

Before she turned off the lamp beside her bed, Lottie looked over at Martha's photograph. The farmland of Bramble Heath rolled into the distance behind her smiling sister, whose arms were outstretched as if she was trying to embrace the whole of the countryside that she had come to love so much. It was how she liked to remember her, not cold in the ground, but happy and free.

Martha had been so full of life. She hadn't deserved to die and have her dreams torn from her. But so many lives had been taken in this dreadful war. None of them had deserved to die, either.

'Goodnight, Martha,' Lottie whispered to the photograph. 'Sleep tight.'

She snuggled down under the blankets, thinking of the ride home in the trap with her friends, and how they'd laughed. Martha would've loved to have been there, she was sure. She'd certainly have had something to say about Nicola's knitting. If she'd still been here, she might even have spotted Nicola's mistake before her project came off her needles and stepped in to remove the extra digit without making Nicola feel silly. She was kind like that.

Then her thoughts drifted once more towards Reverend Hart, or Uncle Matthew as she had heard Daisy call him. She couldn't help but feel some concern about him, he'd been so subdued. She'd make sure she said hello to him the next time she saw him in the village. And Daisy too. She wanted to make sure they felt welcomed. Matthew was busy supporting his flock, but who was looking after him? Although she wasn't sure he'd take kindly to her help. Well, she would give it anyway, no matter how gruff he was. It was what Martha would've done.

She must've fallen asleep, because the next thing she knew was that Blossom was barking. The little dog was usually so placid. Lottie was immediately awake, a jolt of fear running down her spine as she clutched her quilt.

Moments later the air-raid siren split the night with its hellish wail. She couldn't help the jarring panic that rushed through her and the temptation to freeze to the spot. Whenever the siren sounded, it took her back to *that* night, the horrible night that took her sister from her.

She tried to fight her fear with practicalities. She couldn't think about the enemy planes flying over, the bombs they carried, just waiting to drop. She had to move, and fast.

She got out of bed and switched on her blackout torch. Its thin light illuminated her room enough for her to find her coat hanging on the hook on the back of the door and her shoes under the iron bedstead. Then she pocketed Martha's photograph.

'Off we go, Blossom,' Lottie called to her constant companion, trying to keep her fear from her voice. 'Don't be scared, girl, we'll be in the shelter in a jiffy.'

Blossom was no longer barking, but she was on edge, her dark, bright eyes staring up at her owner. Lottie picked her up, held her tight and did her best to reassure the little dog even though she was trembling too.

She left her bedroom and joined the other Land Girls, who were similarly half asleep, curl papers poking out from under their headscarves. She was too frightened to speak, too scared of the tremor they'd hear in her voice, but her friends gave her encouraging smiles. They knew what she went through each time the siren sounded.

They stumbled along the landing in torchlight, before heading down the stairs past prints of old views of Sussex with women in elegant crinolines wandering down country lanes where nowadays tractors thudded by, driven by Land Girls in breeches.

They trooped through the farmhouse kitchen, the range still giving its warm glow in the darkness. The huge wooden table that seated everyone at the farm was scrubbed and ready for breakfast, the places already set. Lottie ignored the taunting voice in her head that cruelly asked her if anyone would be missing from breakfast tomorrow morning.

The back door was open to the farmyard, where Alastair, Lottie's good friend and the Goslings' lodger, stood sentry to make sure everyone made it safely out of the house. He was a kind, trustworthy man, who had once been in the Royal Navy but had exchanged it for a life on dry land and a job in the Ministry of Agriculture. His quiet, confident presence, along with his tall, military bearing, distinguished strands of silver hair and neat moustache, made her feel safer as they filed past him.

'All counted out!' Alastair called as he pulled the door shut behind Lottie and Blossom, leaving the house empty.

'Oh, thank goodness,' Lottie said. She knew Alastair had his reasons for being so keen to make sure everyone got to the shelter and it was a story as heartbreaking as her own.

Though he had found happiness again in Bramble Heath, Alastair had known immense grief too. While he was away at sea, risking his life to command a Royal Navy destroyer in the Atlantic Ocean, a German bomb had claimed the life of his wife, Vicky, as the Luftwaffe subjected London to the Blitz. He understood what Lottie had suffered when Martha had died and in him she had a friend she could talk to about even the bleakest times, when no sun seemed able to penetrate the clouds of grief.

It was freezing out, without a trace of cloud, and a three-quarter moon hung above them, turning the world silver. The sound of aeroplane engines beating against the air and the rat-a-tat-tat of guns joined the racket of the siren. Lottie shivered, not just from the cold but from the return of the memories of that dreadful night.

Her heart rushed in her chest as she clung even more tightly to Blossom with her clammy hands. That moment, that awful moment when she realised that Martha wasn't there, that she wasn't running to the safety of the shelter but out into the field, came back so vividly to her that she could smell the smoke and the scorched earth.

She tried to slow her hurried breathing, to bring herself back to the present.

Soon it'll be Christmas. Soon we'll all be standing around the Christmas tree, singing carols and giving out presents, and we'll all be happy and safe.

'Nearly there,' said Frances, one of the Land Girls, and took

Lottie's elbow as they hurried down the familiar path to the shelter.

All over the village, people would be rushing for their shelters, from Sarah, the evacuee who loved to come up to the farm and help, to Matthew and his niece, and the Poles who had fled the invasion and found a welcoming home in Bramble Heath.

Please be safe, all of you. Please get to your shelters, Lottie thought, wishing she had the power to rescue them all. And only a mile or so away, at the airbase, brave young men were hurtling along the runway, into the sky where there was nowhere to run and hide.

She glanced at Shona, who was silent as she made her way towards the shelter. Her brother was a pilot, flying from a base in Cambridgeshire, and Lottie wondered what went through her thoughts each time the engines roared at the airbase. Was she worried about him? She had never really talked about him and Lottie wasn't sure how to ask.

In the torchlight, Lottie saw Mrs Gosling standing by the shelter's open door, counting everyone in one by one, and it instantly took her back to that one night when Mrs Gosling had noticed one of them was missing.

And that one had been Martha.

She smiled gently at Lottie as she went into the shelter. Mrs Gosling was thinking of that night too, she knew.

The girls had helped Mrs Gosling to make the shelter as nice as they could, so that it felt more like another room of the farmhouse, albeit one that didn't have any windows. There were patchwork cushions and a chair for everyone, and a stock of soft, warm blankets and quilts. And soon it would be decked out for Christmas, so that if – God forbid – there was an air raid at Christmas, they wouldn't miss out on the festivities.

One by one the girls each took a seat, some of them leaning their heads against their neighbour's shoulder, others intent on knitting or reading. They'd all found ways to cope. Lottie, for

her part, cradled Blossom on her knee and the little dog eagerly
licked her face.

Frances chuckled. 'You must taste delicious!' she teased, as
she found her place in the book she'd brought.

Lottie grinned. 'Maybe I taste of sausages?'

As their laughter filled the shelter, the atmosphere changed.
They'd be all right.

Alastair came in with Farmer Gosling, who was wearing a
dressing gown and an overcoat over his pyjamas, his flat cap at
an angle. He ushered his wife Agnes in, then closed the door
behind them. 'That's us all settled, then. Let's hope this isn't a
long one! I'm missing my nice warm bed.'

'They sound close tonight,' Shona observed with a shudder,
lifting her head from her knitting to look up as if she could see
the planes passing above the roof of the shelter.

She was right, they did sound close.

Shutting her eyes, Lottie listened to Shona's clacking
needles combined with the roar of the planes, and for a moment
it almost stole the breath from her lungs. She and Martha used
to sit down here knitting too, talking about what they'd do after
the war.

They'd planned to open their own knitting shop in East
Grinstead and sell wool from the sheep on Goslings' farm.
Martha, who had worked at a department store, was the one
with the business head and had talked of rents and rates and
wholesale prices. Lottie, who'd been on the staff at Woolworths,
had daydreamed that she was walking around inside, gazing at
the shelves filled with wool in a rainbow of colours and racks of
patterns showing the latest designs and needles of all different
sizes. There'd be a counter with a brass till and a sign over the
door proudly saying *The Morley Sisters*. It didn't matter that
everyone said women wouldn't get any help setting up a business, especially girls under thirty. It had been the dream that
had got them through as the planes had moaned overhead.

But that could never happen now.

'Maybe it's just because it's a clear night,' Lottie suggested, hoping the others didn't hear the tremble in her voice, 'and the sound travels?'

'Maybe, love,' Mrs Gosling replied, even as the throbbing of the engines vibrated through Lottie's feet. 'Maybe they're quite far away.'

Lottie nodded. As Blossom settled on her lap, her gaze wandered to Frances, her blonde hair secured under a scarf and a warm shawl round her slender shoulders. She was sitting opposite her, absorbed in a book, her long fingers turning the pages. *The Humble Hero*, its title declared. *By Sidney Gastrell.*

Sitting beside Farmer Gosling she saw Paddy, one of the lads who worked on the farm as they waited until they were old enough to go to war, take his own copy of the book from the pocket of his battered coat. As soon as he opened the volume and took out his woven tapestry bookmark, Farmer Gosling was peering over his shoulder, reading along with him.

'Have you got to the story yet about the soldier who works with him, the one who survived Dunkirk? It's astonishing,' Frances said. Her south-east accent was flecked with a bit of cockney when she got excited. She flicked back a few pages. 'I love the way he tells us about his boys. Here it is:

> *Luke Williams is from an army family, and, as soon as he was old enough, he joined up. When war broke out, he was proud to go to France as part of the British Expeditionary Force and fight against the Nazis, in the very same region that his own father had fought in the Great War. These men fought bravely to bring liberation to Europe, but they were routed. Luke was one of thousands of men – some three hundred thousand – who had to be evacuated as the Nazi forces advanced.*
>
> *They were cruelly trapped, the Nazis throwing their fire-power at them as they waited for the Little Ships to come*

valiantly to their aid. Luke's comrade-in-arms, his friend Arthur, was injured. But they had to get to the ships. Luke would not leave the side of the man who had come to be like his brother. He wouldn't abandon him. He carried Arthur in his arms even as a hail of Luftwaffe bullets chased our brave young men to the boats that promised them their voyage to sanctuary. Luke was struck, but still he went on, still he carried Arthur.

I had the honour of meeting Luke a week after Dunkirk. He was recovering in hospital, on the same ward as the friend who he would not abandon. Luke lost his arm, but, he joked, he didn't lose his friend. This brave young hero, I am proud to say, serves with me now, to bring down the Nazis in our midst.

Frances had stopped reading and even though the planes' engines still rumbled overhead, there was silence in the shelter, quiet respect. They could sit out an air raid in a shelter, couldn't they? After men like Luke and Arthur had risked their lives?

Lottie wiped her eyes with the back of her hand. She thought of Luke, who wouldn't abandon the man he regarded as his brother, and she thought of Martha.

Oh, Martha, I didn't abandon you. I would've done anything to save you.

She thought of Gastrell helping the injured men down from the train. Glad to find something to take her mind off the air raid, Lottie told them, as the sound of the planes grew ever louder and her panic rose, 'I saw him today, Sidney Gastrell! He'd just arrived in East Grinstead. He seemed ever so—'

But she never got to finish her sentence. A sudden, ferocious, mechanical whine tore apart the air, moments before everything violently shook with a tremendous, terrible crash.

FIVE

Dust fell from the ceiling and everyone in the shelter was jolted half off their seats. Blossom barked in alarm, writhing in Lottie's arms as she held the dog as tight as she could, her eyes jammed shut.

'Don't leave me, don't leave me, don't go!' she begged her little friend. She couldn't bear it, she didn't want to be left alone again.

She felt an arm round her shoulders, then heard a woman gently hushing her, soothing her as the sudden, awful panic that had gripped the shelter's inhabitants began to settle.

'It's all right, pet.' It was Nicola, rocking Lottie gently like a sobbing child in their mother's arms. As Blossom softly licked Lottie's hand, Nicola hushed her again and whispered, 'Me and Blossom have got you, Lottie, don't you fret.'

Lottie didn't reply but let herself be held by Nicola as her terror slowly subsided. That wasn't a bomb, it sounded like a plane. One of the Luftwaffe, perhaps, brought down by one of the young men from the airbase.

'Everyone all right?' Farmer Gosling called. 'Still got our fingers and toes?'

Lottie forced herself to open her eyes and, as Farmer Gosling lifted the hurricane lamp, she looked from face to face. Everyone was pale, shocked to the core.

But they were all right. One by one, they nodded.

Thank goodness.

Blossom put her paws on Lottie's leg and lifted her head to lick her cheek. The little dog, protective and loving and silly all at once, who had been her constant companion since Martha's death, was never far from her side. She couldn't just sit in her room and weep herself away, because Blossom needed her. She needed to go out, to play, to be fed and exercised. When Lottie wept, Blossom curled up beside her or clambered onto her lap. She simply wouldn't let her owner fall into a well of despair, even when it got so bad that Lottie thought that she'd never smile again. With Blossom to care for, she had something – *someone* – who gave her a reason to get up every morning.

'You okay?' Nicola asked gently.

Lottie sniffed back her tears and looked up at her. 'I think so. Yes, I am... as long as everyone else is all right, I am. Thank you, Nicola.'

But it had sounded so close. Lottie's stomach twisted with fear. They might be safe, but what about everyone in the village? What if it had hit down there? Had everyone made it to their shelters? What about the evacuees who had fled the cities to Bramble Heath to be safe?

She thought of Matthew trying to calm Daisy and Mrs Pearson's boys curling up against her in the dark, waiting for the raid to end. Children who, only hours before, had met Father Christmas and enjoyed a snatch of festive light in the grim darkness of the war and who now trembled in terror.

Everyone in the shelter was looking at her, their expressions darkened. Martha had been the only resident of the farm to fall to the German air raids and her death had shaken them all.

When the sisters arrived in Bramble Heath they'd

wondered if they would fit in and make friends, but there had been no need to worry. The Land Girls here were all sisters. Well, mostly. Nicola was a mother to them somehow, despite being no older. She was the one who cared for them, who made sure they were all safely at home when the blackout started, and the one who listened to their worries and guided them at work.

'All right, love?' asked Farmer Gosling. He held out a dented hipflask and said, 'Have a nip of this. You'll be right enough.'

Lottie took the flask with a trembling hand. 'Th-thank you,' she said. She took a tiny sip and the whisky burned a path down her throat. She wasn't sure if it made much difference, but the kind gesture meant a lot to her. She passed the flask back to him and hugged Blossom. 'I do feel a little better now, thank you.'

'Good girl,' Mrs Gosling said kindly.

Frances closed her book. 'We should go and get the tree tomorrow,' she said. 'What do you all think?'

Lottie smiled gratefully, her spirits lifted; Frances knew how much she loved Christmas. A celebration of hope, light and love in the darkest of times; just the ticket for a country at war.

'I say a big yes to that!' Lottie beamed and Blossom wagged her tail.

Nicola gave Lottie's shoulders a squeeze. 'Aye,' she agreed, 'it's time we got trimmed up for Christmas!'

SIX

After the all-clear had sounded, it was at last time to go back to bed. Wearily, Lottie got to her feet and everyone filed out, shuffling and yawning.

Despite their tiredness, Lottie and the others walked around the edge of the farm buildings, checking to see if they were all in one piece. Even though it was dark, they'd definitely know about it if one of the barns had been hit and was on fire, and they would have to act right away, or the farm would be lost.

Lottie sighed with relief when they realised that there wasn't anything amiss and if the animals had been disturbed earlier, they were sleeping soundly now. Surely whatever had come down wasn't as close as it'd seemed, even though she could smell the scent of smoke. Morning would come all too soon and they would find out what had happened then.

As she went back to sleep, she wondered again about the plane that had crashed out of the sky.

What about the pilots, did they bale in time? And was it one of ours, or theirs?

She felt a pang as she thought of George, the pilot who had

been Martha's sweetheart. Before Martha's death, he'd been so full of life and he was haunted by her loss. And Lottie couldn't bear to think of the number of friends he'd flown with, who he'd lost; yet they all had to keep flying, swallowing their fear to get into their Spitfires every time the scramble bell rang. For Martha's sake, she hoped against hope that George was safe; George, and everyone he loved.

But she was so tired that her thoughts dissolved into dreams of Christmas trees glistening with lights, transporting her back to her childhood as she and Martha knelt among boxes and wrapping paper, playing with their new dolls.

As soon as the first light crept in around the blackout curtains, Lottie was wide awake and she got out of bed as fast as she could without disturbing Blossom, who was snoozing on the patchwork quilt. But there was nothing to be seen from her window, other than the mist hanging in the air above the frost-covered fields as the weak winter sun rose behind the hills.

She needed to know, with an urgency that was lodged deep inside her, what had fallen from the sky last night. The crash had been so loud that no one could have survived it and yet she needed to know; she needed to *see*.

Martha's smiling face drifted in front of her as she threw on her clothes and she swallowed, trying to contain the wave of panic that was rushing up inside her, that awful feeling of dread that she'd had when Mrs Gosling had asked, *'Where's Martha?'* moments before the bomb fell that had killed her.

Blossom yawned herself awake and must've picked up on Lottie's urgency as she hastily jumped off the bed and stood by the door. Lottie opened it and the pair hurried downstairs.

Mrs Gosling was in the kitchen, stirring a huge saucepan of porridge, as Lottie ran past her.

'Lottie, what's the hurry?' Mrs Gosling asked her, but Lottie didn't stop.

'We'll be back in a minute!' she assured her as she dashed out of the back door with Blossom.

Once outside, Lottie realised she had no idea where to start looking, but then she noticed something she hadn't last night when she'd been too scared and tired. She could smell smoke and now, just beneath it, the scent of fuel.

Her stomach lurched. The plane couldn't have crashed so far away from the farm after all.

Blossom had pricked up her ears and was starting off towards the lane that led to the main road.

'Is that where it crashed?' Lottie whispered to herself with a shiver of horror.

Perhaps she shouldn't go and look after all. And yet she thought of it all again. The ambulance driving across the field. Constable Russell, the local policeman, hurrying after it. Martha's Land Girl hat lying fallen on the grass. The acrid smell of smoke and fire. Nicola clinging on to her, stopping her from running to her dead sister's side. Nicola saving her from a sight she'd never have been able to scrub away.

I have to go.

Lottie ran across the farmyard with Blossom, their footsteps crunching over the frost as they headed for the lane. The smell of smoke and fuel grew stronger and Lottie coughed, but still she kept running, her gaze darting left and right through the weak sunlight as she looked for any sign of the crashed plane in the fields.

And then, finally, there it was.

SEVEN

The wreckage of the enormous plane was so twisted and jagged that at first Lottie had trouble understanding what she was looking at. A crater had ripped open the muddy grass and the smell of smoke and fuel was overpowering. She clasped her hand over her mouth, but she couldn't look away. The dark green of the fuselage – what was left of it – was soot-smeared and, where it had torn away, snapped steel ribs caught the watery light.

But even so, she could make out the livery on what was left; the large black cross of a Luftwaffe plane, even though there was no tail section in sight that would have displayed the hateful swastika. And yet knowing it was an enemy plane didn't rob her of her shock. She felt no sense of triumph or pride. The violence of the scene horrified her. No one could've survived it. She was looking at a tomb.

But then something moved. Lottie gasped in alarm and Blossom barked in warning.

Someone was there, appearing from the other side of the wreckage through the last of the smoke. A figure dressed in black.

'Who's there?' she called sharply. But her fear vanished as she saw the tousled chestnut hair and the dog collar. Blossom recognised him too and wagged her tail. 'Reverend Hart?'

Matthew was swathed in a heavy coat. He gazed at the remains of the stricken bomber as he leaned on his walking cane. He looked as though he was carrying all the cares of the world on him. How he had come to use that cane, just as how his niece had been orphaned, was the subject of much village conjecture but, as far as Lottie knew, the new reverend had chosen not to disclose whatever tragedies had befallen him.

At the sound of Lottie's voice, Matthew started as though someone had fired a gun. He blinked and shifted slightly, just enough to peer at her through the morning mist.

'Is that Lottie?' he called with a note of cheer in his voice that Lottie knew must be forced; his expression was anything but light. She noted too that he had that talent for names that certain professions – though he'd likely call it a vocation or a calling – seemed to lend to those who served in them. Matthew had heard her name on the platform at East Grinstead and, like any good parish vicar, he had stowed it away neatly for later. 'And Blossom too!'

'Yes, it's us,' Lottie said. She took a hesitant step forward, a shard of glass that must've come from the plane's windscreen shattering underfoot. 'I heard the crash last night, I knew it was close. I just... I wanted to see.'

She realised she must've sounded like a grim voyeur and yet it was true, she *had* wanted to see. As dreadful as the sight was.

Blossom didn't hesitate. She bounded over to Matthew and hopped up, trying to lick his hand.

'She's saying hello,' Lottie explained.

'Hello, little miss.' Matthew lowered himself carefully to one knee, his gloved hand tightening on the handle of the walking stick. He fussed Blossom, murmuring gently to her as he did.

Something about Blossom's unrestrained friendliness touched Lottie as she stood there, surrounded by the hellish wreckage, and she could see it had touched Matthew too.

'I... I wasn't expecting to see you here,' Lottie said. She swallowed. 'Do you think... no, they couldn't have survived, could they?'

And as she said that, she knew that the bodies were still there, somewhere in the twisted wreckage; young men who'd woken up yesterday morning in Germany, only to die in a field in England last night.

Matthew shook his head. Without looking away from the little dog, he replied, 'No. They would have needed a miracle.'

At Matthew's words, a dam broke inside Lottie. They'd died, just as Martha had died – not even all that far away from where a bomb, most likely dropped from a plane just like this one, had robbed her only sister of her life. She tried not to sob, yet the more she fought with herself, the harder it was to hold it back.

I shouldn't have come to look, I should've stayed away, and now I look like a fool in front of the reverend. Oh, what's the matter with me?

As she cried, she felt a familiar paw against her leg and glanced down to see Blossom, who had returned to her side. She knelt down in the frost to stroke her dog, the little friend who had helped her heal, and her sobbing began to subside.

She heard Matthew's careful tread as he navigated the debris-strewn grass to circle the wreckage. Then he was beside her, kneeling on one knee as he told her gravely, 'I'm sorry you had to see this.'

'I *wanted* to see...' Lottie explained through her tears, as Blossom licked them from her cheeks. 'Not to be ghoulish, only... my sister was killed, you see. And when I heard the crash last night, it all came back to me again.'

'I'm sorry,' Matthew said again. Then he cleared his throat and said, 'We should say a prayer for these men.'

A prayer? Lottie bit her lip, unsure. 'But they've killed people, our people. I don't think I can pray for them. They're murderers.'

'Each one of them was somebody's son.' Matthew was almost sharp, his mouth set in a tight line. He bowed his head and began to recite a prayer that Lottie recognised. It was the prayer for remembrance, which she had heard at the funeral of her sister. Reverend Ellis had gently intoned it in the little church in Bramble Heath.

Lottie tried to follow the prayer, but she could see the coffin at the front of the church, which contained all that was left of her sister. She could hear her mother's sobs, could see her father's sombre face, and she felt the sting of salt tears against her sore eyes. If it wasn't for a bomber like this plane, Martha would still be alive.

'Forgive us and take away our fear, through the dying and rising of Jesus your Son,' Matthew went on, before finishing with a sombre 'Amen.' Then he said, 'We can't do more for them than that.'

Would that make the dead men rest more easily? She looked up at Matthew and wondered once again what had happened to Daisy's parents. Had they been killed by a Nazi bomb too, like Martha had been? If so, how could he stand here beside the wreckage of their plane and pray for them?

Lottie nodded. 'Do you think they'll go to heaven?' she asked him. She wished he wasn't so stern. She knew he had an inner core of softness, she'd seen it when he'd been with Daisy. But he didn't seem to share it with anyone else.

'I don't know,' Matthew replied. 'Perhaps.' Then he dusted his hands together. 'A higher authority will make that decision.' He lifted his head and met her gaze. Like everyone else in Bramble Heath would today, he looked tired. His blue eyes were heavy with the lack of sleep, his expression sombre. 'May I ask your sister's name?' he enquired carefully.

'Martha,' Lottie said quietly. She smiled just saying her beloved sister's name. Then she remembered that she still had Martha's photograph in her pocket, so she took it out to show Matthew. 'She was taken from us last year, just before the lambing started.'

Blossom tipped her head to one side. She knew the name Martha, even though she had never met her.

Matthew didn't take the photo, but instead reached into his pocket and withdrew a pair of spectacles. He put them on, then peered down at the picture and smiled.

'She looks like she was a very happy young lady,' he observed. 'You must miss her dreadfully.'

Lottie wrinkled up her nose as she nodded, doing her best not to start crying again. 'We wanted to run a shop together, but then the war came along, so we decided to do our bit and we turned up here at the farm together, you see. Both Land Girls. We had such a happy time, and then... But you see, that's why I'm still here. My parents are desperate for me to leave and if they hear about this' – she gestured to the twisted remnants of the crashed plane, as Blossom wagged her tail – 'they'll be even more insistent. But I can't go, because... it sounds silly, but it feels like she's still here. I don't mean like a ghost, but...'

Lottie swallowed. She didn't know Matthew and she'd never admitted that to anyone before. And yet she sensed that, of all people, he would understand. He must've heard stranger things in his time as a vicar.

'Martha will always be with you,' Matthew said, trotting out the professional words that were expected of his profession. 'Wherever you go, you'll be surrounded by her love.'

Lottie nodded. She wanted to say something to him, something about *his* loss. And yet it seemed like a forbidden subject. Vicars existed to listen to the woes of their parishioners, it didn't seem to work the other way round. But she still wanted to say something, to acknowledge that she was aware of his grief.

'And I hope you're surrounded by love too,' she said.

For a long moment, Matthew was silent. He put out his hand and stroked it over Blossom's back, then said, 'I believe Daisy is. I hope she is.'

Lottie nodded and yet she'd noticed that Matthew had skipped around the question.

'I'm sorry for what happened to your family, truly I am,' she told him. Perhaps she had gone too far saying something and yet it didn't feel right to stay silent.

He gave a small nod of acknowledgement, his gloved hand ruffling Blossom's fur again.

'There's no sense to it,' he whispered. Lottie got the feeling he was talking to himself as much as to her, his voice flat and resigned. Despite his youth, there was a tiredness about him that seemed to belong to someone much, much older.

'No sense at all,' Lottie replied. There was so much death, too much, but all they could do was struggle along as best they could through their grief and their fear.

'There was a prisoner-of-war camp in my first parish, up in Yorkshire,' he told her. 'I spent a lot of time with the inmates. Young men, very few like you might expect. Just ordinary people, really, dragged into a war they didn't want any part of.' Matthew gave a slight smile. 'They worked on the farms, just like you. It was quite the thing, seeing them welcomed bit by bit into the villages. It took a lot of time to build that trust.'

'I wonder what it would be like if we worked with prisoners of war here on the farm?' Lottie said, trying to get her head around it, but it was hard. If it wasn't for them, her sister would still be alive. Hundreds of thousands of people still would be. How many people had these young men, who died last night in Bramble Heath, killed? And all the others like them? But from what she'd seen in the newsreels about Hitler's Germany, it wasn't as if they could refuse to fight. She looked at the wreck again and that thought made it even sadder. 'They never had the chance.'

And neither had Martha.

She shook her head. 'It doesn't matter. They're monsters,' she told Matthew. Even if they hadn't wanted to fight, they still had. They'd put on a uniform and climbed into a plane. Couldn't they have ditched their planes in the sea rather than bring their bombs to British shores? How could they fight on the side of the Nazis, with all that Hitler and his ilk were doing, bullying their way across Europe? How many innocent people had they slaughtered because they weren't Germans, or because they had been singled out for their faith and forced to wear a Star of David? 'They're killers.'

They'd all heard stories of airmen coming down and being beaten to a pulp or worse by the locals, alongside stories of the Germans who were settled in the local pub with a pint as they waited for the police. Bramble Heath seemed more likely to do the latter, but with so many of the lads from the airbase near the village lost as they flew so selflessly in the defence of everyone's freedom, that was by no means guaranteed. And for her part, Lottie certainly wasn't planning to invite any of them in for a cup of tea.

Blossom barked at the sound of an approaching engine and Lottie looked up to see an ambulance and a jeep from the airbase turn in to the lane.

'We should leave them to their work.' Matthew watched the vehicles approach, then touched his hand to Lottie's elbow and asked, 'Should I see you home?'

Lottie turned slowly away from the wrecked plane, shaking her head. 'No, thank you, I'm sure you need to get back to Daisy.' With Blossom at her side, she headed back to the farm-house without Matthew, a bad taste in her mouth.

EIGHT

As Lottie joined the other Land Girls round the breakfast table, she felt rather guilty that they'd milked the cows without her while she'd been off looking at the crashed plane, but she knew they understood how much last night had affected her.

After they'd finished their porridge, Mrs Gosling said, 'There's bits and bobs for you girls to do around the farm, as ever, but why not go and find us a Christmas tree first? And make sure you get one for the church, too. The jobs can wait until you get back.'

She smiled gently at Lottie as she said that.

'Thank you,' Lottie said, grateful for the opportunity to take her mind off the painful memories of her lost sister and the thought of the young men who had died last night. But she reminded herself that if their plane hadn't been brought down, they might have taken many more lives. Tens, hundreds of people could be killed with one plane-load of bombs.

'I'll grab the axe and some rope,' said Nicola, bounding from her seat at the opportunity to head out on a mission. 'Shona, you and Frances fetch the big handcart. We've got a job to do!'

Frances got to her feet, brushing her hands together, and Shona pulled on her gloves.

'Off we go!' Lottie cheered as the four of them strode out of the kitchen, Blossom marching ahead of them, wagging her tail.

Once they'd collected everything they needed, the Land Girls, wrapped in home-knitted woolly scarves and gloves, bumped the handcart over the frosty meadow, heading for the woods that ran around the edge of the farm. They were going in the opposite direction from the crash site and although Lottie noticed Frances and Shona glancing towards it, they didn't say anything out loud. They hadn't quizzed her about it when she'd mentioned to them that she'd gone to see the wreck and met Matthew beside it, but they were clearly curious about it.

Shona most of all, perhaps. Surely the wreck was a reminder of the danger her brother was constantly putting himself in? But maybe, Lottie thought, she didn't connect the two things. After all, it was an enemy plane that had come down, not one of theirs.

As they reached the woods, some rooks took flight into the chilly air, cawing noisily, which sent Blossom into excited, rapturous barking. Up in the frosty, leafless branches, Lottie saw thick clumps of greenery – not the nests that the rooks built, she knew, but bunches of mistletoe.

'We'll have to find a way to get up in the tree and bring down some mistletoe,' she said, her breath escaping in icy clouds. She knelt beside Blossom, stroking her to calm her down.

'Find a way?' Nicola laughed. 'You're talking to the lass who was building her own tree house when all the other bairns were out at Brownies!' With that, she reached up to grab hold of a heavy bough and hauled herself into the tree.

Frances made a dash to stand below Nicola, her arms spread, clearly ready to catch her. 'Careful, Nic!' she called. 'Take it slow, don't slip!'

'Howay!' Nicola called brightly. 'Catch the mistletoe instead!'

As everyone, even Blossom, watched Nicola climb up the tree, Lottie couldn't help but picture herself and Martha, side by side in their Brownie uniforms. Her parents had a photograph in an album somewhere. They had earned badges together, they had slept in a tent, they had put on a pantomime to raise money for the local dogs' home and had proudly worn their uniforms to school on Baden-Powell Day.

They'd had such fun, hadn't they? They'd climbed trees, too, and slipped and laughed. Nothing had seemed dangerous or frightening back then. And, like all sisters, they'd had fights over stupid things – clothes and boys, as they'd grown older – but they always made up and had been stuck together like glue.

Lottie glanced at Shona, who had moved to Goslings' farm a little while after Martha's death to fill the place left by her. Her sister would've loved this, watching Nicola climb the tree. Instead, it was Shona who was watching, smiling at her friend's antics.

Lottie stroked Blossom, trying to think of Martha without crying. Matthew had said that Martha's love was around her and perhaps it was. She would think of the happy times they had together and not the awful moment that had snatched Martha away from her for ever.

'Lottie, pet!' called Nicola, holding out a bunch of mistletoe. 'Catch!'

Lottie jumped to her feet, holding out her arms, as Blossom barked. The green and white bundle flashed through the air and she just managed to catch it in her gloved hands.

'Phew!' she gasped. 'Now we just need to find someone to kiss underneath it!'

A memory of Martha with George swam into her mind. They'd adored each other. Lottie had found a bridal magazine under her sister's pillow; they'd been thinking about getting married and had joked about the idea of Martha knitting her own dress. It was no wonder that Martha's death had hit George so badly. Afterwards, she would see him around the village sometimes and they'd say hello, but a sad shadow lingered between them.

Nicola climbed down from the tree, nimble as a cat. She dusted her gloved palms together and gave Lottie a smile that she knew meant, *all okay?*

She nodded. Martha wouldn't have wanted her to spend the rest of her life in despair; she'd loved life and would've wanted her to carry on. And perhaps, if she listened hard enough, she would hear Martha's giggle when the Land Girls were together.

She carried the bundle over to the handcart, then the girls continued on through the woods. Even though the branches were bare, it didn't feel bleak; the wintry blue sky peered between the trees and there were patches of shiny deep green where holly trees grew.

'A robin!' Frances called, as she spotted one landing on a branch just up ahead. It watched them approach, its bright, dark eyes taking them in.

'Now all we need is snow,' Shona said and chuckled, 'and we've got a Christmas card!'

'It's perfect!' Lottie replied, taking in a deep breath of the crisp air. It was so clean and fresh, nothing like the stench of smoke and fuel she'd smelt earlier where the stricken enemy plane had crashed.

They took one of the wider tracks that wound through the woods and Frances glanced down in surprise. 'Looks like someone's brought a van or something through here,' she said, pointing to the tyre tracks in the soft earth. 'I wonder if there'll be any Christmas trees left!'

'A van?' Lottie gasped. 'That's cheating, you can't load up all the trees in a van!'

'There'll be a riot in the pub if somebody's poaching trees!'

Nicola joked, striding on ahead in the tracks of the unknown vehicle. She turned a corner in the path, then suddenly spun on the heel of her boot and hurried back towards the other Land Girls. 'There's no good trees here, we'll look back along the path.'

'Are you sure?' Shona asked her. 'That's where we found the one we had last year. There were all those little ones still growing... Oh, rats, a bunch of spivs *have* come up here and nicked them all in their lorry, haven't they?'

'What a shame.' Lottie sighed. But she didn't want to give up. 'Why don't we just have a look anyway? There might be a good one hiding!'

She marched off, not registering Nicola's pale expression. Blossom panted at her side as they walked. Past the bare sycamores there was a thick holly bush speckled with red berries and on the other side of it, Lottie knew, there was a grove of firs, and—

She stopped, her eyes wide as she stared at the dreadful sight in front of her.

NINE

There, in the grove where Christmas trees had grown, was an enormous piece of battered, ragged metal with a huge swastika, the symbol of such unimaginable evil and violence, painted on its side. Lottie was so shocked that it took her several moments to realise that she was looking at the missing tail section from the wreck she'd found in the field.

The rudder on the tail fin had been partly ripped off and just below it, Lottie saw the shattered windscreen of – not the cockpit, it was the wrong end of the plane. Surely this was where the rear gunner had sat. The man who would aim the guns, which were now bent and twisted by the crash, at the brave men from Heath Place in their Spitfires and Hurricanes as they fought to bring the bomber down. And they had succeeded, that much was clear.

Blossom stood beside Lottie, shivering, and she bent to pick her up, cradling her in her arms. She heard footsteps behind her and turned to see her friends, their faces ashen and their eyes wide as they took in the appalling sight before them.

'I knew the tail section was missing when I saw the wreck,' Lottie said, trying to still the tremble in her voice. She glanced at Shona, who was hugging herself as she stared at the torn remains of the bomber. 'And here it is...'

That explained the tyre marks, at least. Someone from the airbase had evidently been out to search for the tail section and had found it. It would only be a matter of time before they returned with lifting gear to take it out of the woods, leaving a scar of broken trees in its wake.

And now she knew why Nicola had tried to turn back. She had wanted to protect the girls from the sight that now greeted them, of the twisted metal and ruined earth; from the reminder of the horror that threw a shadow over all of Europe.

'Come on.' Nicola gave Lottie's arm a gentle squeeze. 'Let's find a tree and leave this for the folks whose job it is. There's nothing we can do.'

Shona took Nicola's hand. 'I should've listened to you, shouldn't I? Those poor boys... It makes me think of my brother, flying into Europe night after night. And Lottie—'

'Don't worry about me,' Lottie said, swallowing. 'Shona, your brother's trying to free Europe of Hitler and the Nazis. These pilots, they're doing his bidding.'

'They'll send word,' Nicola assured Shona gently. She squeezed her hand. 'You keep faith in him, Shona. Don't count him out yet.'

'I will, don't you worry,' Shona replied, and even though there were tears building in her blue eyes, she gave Nicola a smile. 'He was born under a lucky star, our Jack. That's what Grandma used to say. The Luftwaffe's bullets just bounce off his plane.'

Lottie glanced back at the piece of wreckage and her attention fell on the shattered windscreen. To think that a man had been strapped in there, all alone at the back of the plane as it had flown through the night from somewhere in war-torn Europe. It was hard to think of anything more terrifying. What a horrible, lonely way to die. But did they deserve anything better?

'Nicola's right, we can't do anything,' Frances said, her no-nonsense tone pulling Lottie away from her gloomy thoughts. And Shona nodded, no doubt thinking of Jack's good luck. 'Let's find our tree.'

'All right, let's go,' Lottie replied and, as one, they turned and left the grove and the wreckage behind them and took another path through the trees.

Blossom wriggled down from Lottie's arms and trotted alongside her happily. Lottie began to forget what she'd seen, pushing it away from her thoughts as she tried to think of other things; like spending Christmas at the farm with her friends. She'd seen Mrs Gosling flicking through a pamphlet of Christmas ration recipes and wondered what she'd be rustling up. The woods looked festive as another robin watched them from a branch and holly grew wild along the sides of the path, in the gaps between the bare tree trunks.

'It's nice being surrounded by nature, isn't it?' Shona observed as she pulled the handcart along with Frances.

'There's more fir trees!' Lottie said gleefully, pointing further up the path, where the dark, evergreen branches stood out against the leafless, wintry trees. There would be plenty for everyone.

Nicola took the axe from the handcart and approached the firs, sizing them up. After a moment she gave a nod of approval.

'Stand back, gals,' Shona said, laughing, as her friend gave the axe an experimental swing. 'The woodcutter's here to slay the big bad wolf!'

Nicola chuckled, then took a step back, raised the axe and swung.

'Timber!' she shouted, laughing.

The tree groaned and lurched sideways, and everyone

cheered as Blossom barked and ran in an excited circle around the girls. It really felt like Christmas now.

As Lottie came forward to help catch the tree she spotted something glinting in the mud. She stopped and knelt down to look at it, and realised that it was a wristwatch.

'Look what I've found,' she gasped. 'Someone's lost their watch.'

It looked like the sort of thing a pilot would wear, with large, luminous numbers on its face. The glass was cracked and smeared with blood and, with a lance of panic, Lottie realised that it must've come from the wreckage: she was holding the watch of a dead man. But she didn't drop it in alarm; she was fascinated, because it didn't look like any ordinary watch. Certainly, like nothing she had ever seen before. The ring of metal around the watch's face had been engraved in near-illegible Gothic Germanic lettering, but Lottie could just about make out the words *von Brandt*. Painted on the watch's face, in red, black and gold, was a design of an eagle, head proudly aloft, wings spread, its claws gripping a swastika.

Her mind whirring, she turned the watch over. Something was engraved on the back of the case and she wiped away a gobbet of mud to read it:

Zu mein Patensohn, von Onkel Wolf.

Lottie stared at it, her hand shaking. Even though she didn't know what it said, she knew what she was holding.

'Oh, heck,' she whispered, as she looked up at her friends. 'I've just found a Nazi's watch.'

TEN

After loading the trap with the Christmas tree that Nicola had felled for the church, Lottie and Shona set off for Bramble Heath with Blossom. Lottie had never worked so closely with horses until she'd moved to the farm and was still a bit unsure of them, especially the Goslings' powerful Shire horses. But Shona was a natural, with a calm confidence that the horses seemed to take to without any protest as she tapped the whip and set them off on their journey.

It hadn't grown any warmer; the frost still lingered, crisp under the horses' hooves. As they headed up the lane towards the main road, Lottie tried very hard not to see the wreck. The twisted, burnt metal hadn't been taken away, but one day it would be and all that would remain to show that the once-ferocious bomber had been there would be scorched earth. The pilot's watch was in her pocket, ready for her to hand over in the village. She wasn't going to keep it as a souvenir.

She shivered as she fussed Blossom and rested her head on Shona's shoulder, but she didn't say a word. The grass would grow back in the spring, the earth would heal. Somewhere in

Germany, families would mourn. Lottie would never meet them and yet their sadness, their loss, was just as painful as her own.

But they're the enemy.

'I loved my first Christmas on the farm last year,' Shona said, breaking the silence, as they trotted towards the village. She smiled at Lottie for a moment, before returning her attention to the road. 'That big fire roaring in the grate and everyone merry on Mr Gosling's home-made sloe gin!'

Lottie did her best to put away her sombre thoughts and chuckled. 'And being with friends – the best company anyone could ask for!'

She knew her parents would have loved her to come home for Christmas, but life on the farm didn't stop. The cows still needed milking on Christmas morning, the chickens were still laying eggs. Her parents knew, reluctantly, that she had a job to do, a vital role to play in the war effort.

The high street was busy, the shops open and doing their best to make sure the people of Bramble Heath had the happiest Christmases they could. Bob Knapp was standing in the doorway of his greengrocer's shop and waved hello as Lottie and Shona rode past. There were crates and sacks of food outside his shop and bunches of carrots hanging in the window like unconventional decorations. Ernie Hewson waved to them from inside his butcher's shop, the window of which contained what meat he had found to stock. There would be food on everyone's tables this Christmas, even if they couldn't all have turkey or goose.

The village green, just off the high street, already had its ten-foot-tall Christmas tree in pride of place. Before the war it used to have lights, so Mrs Gosling said, but the locals still decorated it, each family in the village donating something to hang on its branches. It was a riot of colour and variety, with traditional metal and ceramic ornaments, as well as some that had been handmade from wood and painted. There were baubles, stars, angels, trains and sleighs. But this being Bramble Heath, with an air force base on its doorstep, there were planes, too, bearing the liveries of the RAF and the Polish air force to represent the airmen who flew from its runway.

As they neared the church, Lottie saw the George and Dragon pub, decked out for Christmas with paper chains and mistletoe in the windows and a huge holly wreath on the front door.

Two figures in RAF greatcoats were just leaving the pub. She knew one of them very well; it was George, the handsome, square-jawed pilot who'd been Martha's boyfriend until she'd been— Lottie swallowed. *Don't think about it. Not now.* She recognised his friend, the boyish, smiling Freddy Carr, who'd been a famous stunt pilot before the war but like everyone, had given up his peacetime life to do his bit.

'Hello, you two!' she called. 'Merry Christmas!'

Shona pulled on the reins and the trap came to a halt, the horses scuffing their hooves against the cobbled road.

'Merry Christmas! Here's trouble!' called Freddy towards the Land Girls, glancing back as his little terrier, Wilbur, came out of the pub. 'Wilbur wants to know how his lass's doing on the farm!' He stooped to gather the dog into his arms and asked, 'Isn't that right, eh?'

Blossom gave her father a yap of greeting, wagging her tail even more energetically, as Lottie replied, 'She's having a wonderful time. She's even been trying to round up the sheep!'

George tucked a length of his blond hair behind his ear and smiled, although it didn't meet his eyes. There was that look again, that sadness, that Lottie knew so well.

'Friendly little girl, isn't she?' George said.

'She takes after her dad,' teased Freddy, whose mischievous dog had fathered a litter of puppies, including Blossom, not long before Martha's death. 'You girls all right? That was a sorry

business down by yours last night; should all be cleared away
soon enough.'

George set his jaw, as if holding something in. Lottie met his
gaze, then quickly looked away because the pain she saw there
was too much.

'I saw Reverend Hart up there,' she told them. 'He said a
prayer for them – the pilots, I mean.' Perhaps she shouldn't have
told them that. What would they think of the new vicar now?
That he felt sorry to see the enemy killed before they had the
chance to take dozens, hundreds, of innocent lives, with their
plane loaded with bombs? That he'd prayed for the souls of men
that George and Freddy might have shot down themselves?
'Then when we went into the woods to get the Christmas trees,
do you know what we found? The tail section. It's just... well,
it's horrible how such a huge plane can look like it's been
snapped like a matchstick.'

Freddy scooped Wilbur up and chuckled as his dog and
Blossom exchanged a merry bark of greeting.

'I came down myself over France,' he told the girls, as
though it was nothing. As though young men fell out of the sky
every day and somehow found their way home. 'Those poor
blighters last night; it's a rotten thing. It was one of his own took
him down; he must've lost his head, thought he was shooting at
one of us and did for his pals. He came screaming out of
nowhere and cut the thing in two.'

Their own? Lottie tried to suppress a shudder. She'd
assumed it must have been an RAF pilot like Freddy or George
who'd shot it down, or one of the Polish. Never for a moment
had she thought it was one of their own. But then, that was
Nazis for you. All they had was blood and murder on their
minds; they'd kill their own just as soon as they'd kill their
enemies.

'We've given Jerry a kick in the pants and sent him scur-
rying right back to Berlin a time or two, but one of their own...'

said Freddy, shaking his head, 'There's no wonder the Luft-waffe's falling apart when they can't tell our Lanc from their own Heinkel!'

'Makes you wonder what the heck they're doing,' George said, shaking his head. 'In some ways those Luftwaffe pilots are just like us, but when you hear what the Polish chaps tell us about what's happened to their families, their homes... It makes it easier, I'll tell you that much.'

'My brother Jack says the same thing,' Shona agreed sadly. 'All those awful things.'

There was a lump in Lottie's throat that she couldn't swallow. *All those awful things...* Martha, lying cold in her grave. The bridal magazines that Lottie had hidden at the back of a cupboard. The shop that would never open.

'I always say, it's an honour to have the Polish refugees living here in Bramble Heath,' Freddy enthused. 'And you've heard some of the things they went through. Adolf likes to bang the drum about his honourable Luftwaffe, but he doesn't say so much about them opening fire on refugees who were running for their lives, does he? That glorious air force of his treated those poor blighters like targets at the fairground.'

George nodded in agreement. The Polish pilots who flew from the airbase at Heath Place all had a story to tell. Some of them had managed to find sanctuary with their loved ones, but not all. Everyone had been touched by the war in Europe, by the march of the Nazi jackboot. That was why they had to win this war.

'We were just talking in the pub to the chaps who went up to look over what was left of the plane. Good old Dad's Army, keeping an eye on it so the scrap grabbers can't get to work,' George said. That was a job Lottie didn't envy, but someone had to do it. He glanced at Freddy and Lottie saw a wariness in his expression that she hadn't noticed before. She wondered what on earth he was about to tell them. 'I'm not sure they all got the message from Churchill about careless talk, but it'll be all around the village soon enough.'

Freddy slapped his hand to his friend's elbow. 'Probably a good thing,' he said. 'We'll need everybody keeping an eye open.'

Then George continued, 'There's something not quite right about the wreck. You see, they think one of the airmen is missing.'

Freddy shrugged one shoulder. 'He's probably scared witless or nursing a broken bone or two in the woods,' he said. 'But he'll hand himself in soon enough. The war's over for that fellow; he'll be spending what's left of it eating three square a day and digging up tatties with his comrades!'

Lottie blinked at the airmen in surprise. Was this the pilot who'd owned the fancy watch she had found in the woods? The watch that at that very moment was carefully wrapped in wax paper in her coat pocket. She thought of the wreck, how no one could've survived it. If one of the pilots was missing, he must have baled just in time.

He'd want his watch back and would swagger about wearing it, the proud Nazi. Once he was captured –*please God, make it soon* – he'd lounge about in the prisoner-of-war camp, gloating at the good British folk who fed him as he bragged about the cities he'd left burning and destroyed.

'It boils my blood,' George admitted. 'We look after them, but I suppose they look after us in a way when we come down over Germany. It's hardly a holiday camp, but at least our boys are fed and watered. We can thank the Red Cross for that.'

Lottie hadn't realised that. She hadn't, in truth, known much about it at all. Martha used to say that she hoped George would get home safe, in one piece. The next best option was an injury, something that just required some patching up. After that, it was the hospital in East Grinstead, where young men went when the flames took away their faces.

Then there were the prisoner-of-war camps or, worst of all, death. And Martha had been terrified at the thought of either happening to George.

'So, the Red Cross are making sure the prisoners are looked after over there?' Lottie asked him. 'A prison camp run by Nazis... it just sounds so awful. They're so full of hate. I remember all those Jewish children who came over in the Kindertransport... Poor little things, they must be beside themselves with worry about the family they had to leave behind in Europe.'

Freddy assured her, 'It's not a good way to sit out the war, but they have to look like they're following the rules, even if they'd rather do anything but.' He gave a long sigh, then said, 'It's a different story for the Jewish folk and anyone else those monsters in Germany don't like the look of.'

And the world knew it. The world had known it ever since news of the Nazi atrocities in Europe began to appear in the papers the previous year. Suddenly there was talk of one million dead, of inhuman transport trains and concentration camps where innocent people were packed together to die like animals in a slaughterhouse. A place where innumerable victims were being murdered on the whim of a madman and his followers.

Hot anger shot through Lottie.

Because somewhere in the village – in a barn, or in the woods, or who knew where – one of the enemy was at large.

ELEVEN

As they said goodbye to George and Freddy, and Shona drove the horses on, Lottie couldn't help scanning every face that she saw in case it was the missing German airman. Despite the shortages, everyone she saw on the village high street was smiling, excited for Christmas, and yet Lottie could no longer see their joy. Instead, the street had turned grey. She felt the weight of the Nazi's fancy watch in her pocket, suddenly as heavy as lead, pulling at her, dragging on her heart.

What if he'd flown in the plane that dropped the bomb that had killed Martha? He could be her sister's murderer, the Nazi who, without a care for the lives he'd take, had flicked the switch and sent the bomb spiralling down through the darkness. And here he was, a proud, unrepentant killer on the loose somewhere in the village, hiding away from capture. Lottie pictured the watch again, with its Gothic script spelling out his name:

von Brandt.

'Wherever he's hiding, I bet he's bruised and in need of a

good meal,' Shona said, her words breaking in on Lottie's thoughts.

'I'm glad he's bruised, I'm glad he's hurt,' Lottie declared. 'I'm glad he's hungry! What those people have done, he can't suffer enough. He's—'

'Careful!' Shona yanked on the reins, pulling up the horses, as a gang of children ran across the road right in front of them. She recognised them at once, a motley crew of local children and evacuees who played together in the village. They were aged from three to fourteen, the smallest carried on the hips of the older children, the others on foot or riding on battered bicycles, their nimble friends balancing on the handlebars.

The longer the evacuees had been in the village, the harder it was to tell them apart from the locals. They all had rosy cheeks from healthy outdoor living, the grey pallor of the cities washed away by years in the countryside. Their shoes were scuffed, despite the best efforts of their parents and hosts to keep them polished. The clothing ration couldn't keep up with how fast they grew; their hems were never quite long enough and their cuffs never met their wrists. But at least they were dressed for the winter weather, having found scarfs and hats, mittens and gloves from somewhere.

'Have you heard?' Sarah, one of the London evacuees, stopped in the middle of the street. From inside her cosy winter coat peeped the head of a tortoiseshell cat, regarding Blossom with suspicion. 'There's only a German running round Bramble Heath!'

Like all the evacuees in Bramble Heath, Sarah was well cared for by her host family, but she always looked rumpled from her adventures running through the village or the fields and woods surrounding it. She wore her brown hair in a ponytail, but strands escaped the ribbon, and even in the cold weather she didn't stop to pull up her socks, which were forever falling round her ankles.

'We've just heard,' Lottie said. 'He won't be around for long, though. He'll be in a prisoner-of-war camp before dinner time.'

'We're heading up to the woods to patrol!' Sarah announced, to a chorus of agreement from the other children. Lottie wasn't sure she liked the sound of that; the children might think they were immortal, but they were still only children. Besides, this war didn't spare any lives, young or old. 'He'd better not go anywhere near our secret clubhouse, or there'll be trouble!'

'We'll bring 'im in if we find 'im,' said Bill, one of the older evacuees, in his cockney accent. He had shot up like a beanpole and was now several inches taller than when he had first arrived. A bright yellow scarf was wrapped round his neck, keeping him warm, and Lottie wondered if it was a gift from his family back in London. He wrinkled his freckled nose, clearly gleeful at the thought of capturing the missing Nazi. 'Won't that be a brilliant Christmas present? A German in the slammer!'

'Just be careful,' Lottie warned them. 'He might do something desperate.'

'Lottie's right, you need to take care,' Shona added.

'Don't let him see you,' Lottie warned them and the children turned to look at her, taking in her warning. 'And definitely don't try to speak to him. Run back and for goodness' sake, watch out!'

'We'll take care,' said Sarah with a laugh. 'It's him who'd better watch out! Come on, gang. See you later, Blossom!'

Sarah turned to leave, but then performed a neat spin on her heel and was looking at Lottie again.

'What do you think of the vicar?' she asked, catching Lottie by surprise. 'He's a bit of a misery, isn't he?'

'Not the cheeriest of men, no,' Lottie agreed. 'Maybe he'll warm up a bit once he's settled in?'

'We went and called on Daisy so she could come out Nazi-hunting with us, but he said no.' Sarah pouted. Then she shrugged. 'Never mind. I'll make sure I tell her all about it, so she won't miss out!'

And with that, Sarah and the other children dashed away in search of adventure. Lottie watched them go, her fists clenched. Did they have any idea how much danger they were in? Shouldn't someone insist that they be kept inside, so that they'd be safe? Should she have done more to stop them?

She could understand why Matthew hadn't wanted to let Daisy go with them and yet she didn't want the little girl to miss out on playing with her friends either.

Shona tapped the horses' backs with the reins and they set off again. 'I hope they don't cross his path. It's going to worry me all day. It's dreadful to think he's out there, putting us all at risk.'

TWELVE

Shona pulled up the trap in a lane by the churchyard wall. Lottie glanced at the frost-covered grass that grew around the gravestones and wondered how cold Bramble Heath's late residents must be in the frozen earth. She couldn't help but think of Martha, in the ground Lottie had stood on only the day before.

'Let's unload this tree,' Shona said cheerfully, pulling her out of her thoughts, and between them, with Blossom's enthusiastic barks of encouragement, the two Land Girls lifted the tree down from the trap.

Huffing and puffing with the effort, they carried it round to the gate in front of the church, where Constable Russell was talking to Matthew.

He was grey-haired under his regulation helmet, Lottie knew, and looked warm in his dark blue greatcoat with shiny buttons. The bobby who'd replaced him after he'd retired had gone off to fight, so, despite the fact that he was heading for seventy, Constable Russell had returned to his beat. He was the sort of man who had a smile for everyone and was devoted to the village he served. He had come up to the farm within minutes of Martha's death and in the face of such tragedy he had been a calm anchor for them all.

Lottie hadn't really thought of it before, but a vicar like Matthew was the spiritual version of Constable Russell, caring for his flock. And Matthew had his own uniform, too, with his unmistakable dog collar.

They both looked very serious and Lottie suspected that the policeman was passing on the news about the missing German pilot.

'Let's give Constable Russell the watch,' she whispered to Shona.

The two men looked up from their conversation as Blossom ran over to them and sniffed the hems of the policeman's trousers before turning her excited attention to Matthew.

'Here's Daisy's favourite villager,' Matthew observed dryly, leaning his weight on his walking cane so he could stoop to stroke Blossom. Sarah might think that Matthew was a misery, but Lottie could understand why he might not want his little charge running around looking for a Nazi. The young vicar might not be the friendliest person she had met in Bramble Heath, but she couldn't argue with his decision. 'I already have a dozen drawings of this little one.' He glanced up at Lottie. 'She's very excited to come and see you tomorrow.'

Lottie smiled, imagining Daisy's drawings of Blossom, a four-legged blur with a little red tongue.

'And how are you, Shona?' Matthew asked, turning his attention to her friend. His tone had changed, softening, as he addressed her.

'Not too bad, thank you,' she replied, fiddling with the fringe on the end of her stripy scarf. 'Just carrying on, you know how it is.'

Lottie stared in surprise, then quickly looked down at Blossom, hoping no one had noticed her reaction. When had Shona met Matthew? She hadn't mentioned it earlier, when Lottie had told her that she'd gone to look at the wreck and found Matthew there. They couldn't be secretly dating, could they, and that was why Shona hadn't said anything?

Well, aren't you a dark horse, Shona!

'Now that's a fine tree you've got there! Do you need a hand with it, ladies?' Constable Russell asked.

'Oh, it's for the church,' Shona told him and the girls put the tree down, leaning it against the wall.

Constable Russell added, his tone becoming grave, 'I suppose you've heard the news, by the way? There's a pilot missing from the plane that came down last night.'

'Yes, we've heard.' Lottie reached into her pocket and pulled out the waxed paper parcel. 'I found this in the woods, near where the tail section came down. I reckon it must belong to our missing Nazi, don't you?'

She held out the parcel on the palm of her hand and tentatively peeled back the paper. The low winter sun caught the cracked glass of the watch and it glinted in the light.

'Look at that,' Constable Russell whispered, leaning forward to peer at the watch. He carefully took it from Lottie, his expression a mixture of fascination and distaste. 'I'll take this, if you don't mind. And you found it in the woods, you say?'

Lottie shuddered as she remembered the twisted, broken metal that they'd found where there should have been a grove of Christmas trees. 'Yes, that's where it was. See, it looks like the sort of thing that pilots wear and it's got that horrible swastika and the eagle on it so it must've belonged to a German pilot.'

To her surprise, Matthew shook his head as he looked down at the watch. 'Not if it came from the tail section,' he said. 'I believe the missing man is the rear gunner.'

Lottie pictured again the smashed windscreen of the gun turret at the back of the plane. 'But how could he have survived? We saw it, didn't we, Shona?'

Shona nodded, her face pale. 'It was such a mess, all broken and twisted, like it'd been shorn off and just fell to earth.'

'Why wouldn't he surrender?' Matthew wondered aloud. 'It doesn't make any sense to try and survive on the run. He should hand himself in, he must know that.'

A look passed between Matthew and Shona, but Lottie couldn't decipher it. Maybe they weren't dating. Maybe Shona had just been helping him collect the hymn books after the Sunday service. But there was something about that look, something secretive.

'Exactly, the nasty blighter should surrender,' Lottie said. 'Do you think he's got something to hide?'

Matthew shivered and said, 'I don't know.' Then he added, 'Daisy lost so much to them. If this man comes to my church seeking sanctuary, it won't be easy for me to give it.' The young vicar drew in a deep breath, then looked from Shona to Lottie. 'But I will. And I'll report his presence to the proper authorities too.' He gave a stiff nod, satisfied with his decision.

Seeing the wreckage had brought so many painful memories back to the surface for Lottie and she now knew that, as she had suspected, Matthew had lost his loved ones to Nazi bombs too. How could he find it in himself to give sanctuary? Maybe he felt he had no choice, but while that was what a vicar had to do, Lottie couldn't bring herself to do the same. There was absolutely no way. If she saw the Nazi, lurking about, ready to pounce, she'd attack, teeth bared, fingers like claws. She'd run her pitchfork right through him.

'Well, I'm not going to the authorities,' she declared. 'If he crosses my path, he'll get whatever I can throw at him!'

'My little niece will never see her parents again,' Matthew said softly. 'When I had to visit the prisoners of war in my old parish, it took a long time for me to be anything but just about civil with them, but they all have stories. I didn't meet any monsters, though I don't doubt they exist.'

'But Matthew, he's a Nazi! They're smashing shop windows one minute and shipping the shopkeepers off to die in a camp the next,' Lottie reminded him. 'You might not be a sympathiser, but you certainly sound sympathetic. Do you think he would be? No, he would just bludgeon us in our beds!'

'I'm no sympathiser!' Matthew snapped suddenly, his face pale with anger. 'I walk with this cane because of a Nazi bomb. Daisy lost her mother and father to them, so don't you dare accuse me of sympathising! But anyone who seeks sanctuary in my church will receive it, whatever they've done!'

Lottie glanced at the cane. She couldn't help it. Had the same raid that had killed Daisy's parents injured him too? And yet he spoke of treating the Nazi kindly. Lottie couldn't bend her thoughts around it at all.

'As if a Nazi would care about a church!' she retorted. 'I read in a newspaper that they go into churches, throw away the Bible and replace it with a copy of *Mein Kampf*. And they chuck priests into prison camps. That's what they think of churches!'

'What do you suggest I do, Miss Morley?' asked Matthew hotly. 'Drown him in the font?'

'No, but—' Lottie struggled to find the words to reply. Reverend Ellis would never have been sarcastic but then again, she'd never argued with the old vicar. 'But surely you'd have to get the bishop in to bless the church after a monster like that had been inside it?'

Matthew's mouth fell open and he asked in disbelief, 'Bless the church?' Then he shook his head and said, 'I've never heard such rubbish!'

'I don't want to go to a church that's had a Nazi—' But before Lottie could finish, Constable Russell interrupted.

'Traditionally, folk ask for sanctuary at a church,' he explained, brushing an invisible speck of dust from his sleeve. 'There was a burglar once, we chased him up to the church and he claimed sanctuary. Put the good vicar in a bind, I can tell you.' He glanced at Matthew and Lottie realised that Constable Russell was struggling with his own feelings about the missing airman too. He'd seen some dreadful sights over the course of the war – the fallen bombs, the crashed planes, the families he'd had to visit to tell them that their loved one wasn't coming home. 'But at least I know that, should Jerry turn up here, Reverend Hart won't act the vigilante. I know you'll do the right thing too, Lottie.'

Lottie shook her head. The right thing? Nazis didn't deserve to be treated with kindness. Had everyone gone mad?

Matthew nodded. 'And that's what I'll be advising the residents of the village to do as well.' He glanced up at the sky, then shivered in the cold. 'Anyway, let's leave the searching to the Home Guard, that's what they're there for. If he comes to me, I'll sit him beside the fire and call for Constable Russell.' He gave the policeman a polite nod of acknowledgement, then turned to Lottie. 'I do understand why you feel so strongly but we have to live with the decisions we make, just as they do. If he needs sanctuary, he'll have it.'

Reverend Ellis would have done the same, Lottie thought. He'd have given the airman sanctuary and would have had his housekeeper cook up the best meal he could spare, before encouraging the young man to give himself up. He'd have risked his own safety for a monster. And he would have kept everyone in his village safe, too. Reverend Ellis's grave, currently under a thin blanket of frost, where he lay with his late parishioners, was only a few feet away from them.

Perhaps it was what vicars had to do, but it didn't mean that Lottie had to agree.

'Yes, if you wouldn't mind advising the locals to take care,' Constable Russell said. 'I don't want them going after the man with pitchforks. I won't have vigilantes in Bramble Heath, that's not how we do things here.'

'They won't need pitchforks if he doesn't hand himself in,' said Matthew, looking up at the sky. 'It's freezing after dark. If he has sense, he'll make himself known before nightfall.'

'I hope he does,' Constable Russell said, rubbing his hands together as he glanced up at the iron-grey clouds that were rolling in. 'I hope he does.'

THIRTEEN

That evening, Lottie sat in the kitchen by the embers of the fire, alone save for Blossom, who was curled up in a basket at her feet. There was no sound apart from the embers crackling and the occasional soft, contented sigh from the dog.

Lottie wasn't ready to go to bed yet, even though she was tired from her broken night's sleep. She kept thinking of the crashed plane and the missing airman. She thought of Martha, and of Matthew, injured by Nazi bombs, and Daisy, orphaned. She thought of the two men from the Home Guard, heroes from another war, standing guard by the wreck in the darkness with their Thermoses of tea, to put off any looters.

She tried to push her thoughts away and focus on Frances' copy of Sidney Gastrell's *The Humble Hero*. The book fell open on a story about another of Gastrell's men:

> *Thomas Jeffreys was the son of a bus conductor and he grew up thinking he'd join the ranks of clippies too. But Mr Hitler had other ideas. Tom had never been in a plane before, so that decided him, and in the early days of the war he signed up to fly in the RAF. He answered scramble after scramble, fear-*

lessly heading into the heavens while the rest of us ran for our air-raid shelters.

That Spitfire Summer of the Battle of Britain was a time that none of us will forget. The bravery and sacrifice of the few who defended our realm will always remain in our hearts. So many men were lost, so many families still bear the wounds of sons, husbands, fathers, brothers who will never come home. And among those whose lives were mercifully spared are men like Thomas Jeffreys. Men who did not lose their lives, but lost their faces.

The pioneering work of Dr McIndoe in his hospital in East Grinstead had shown the world that it's not just medicine and surgery that puts men like Tom back together. It's wearing their uniforms, not hospital pyjamas. It's a sense of camaraderie, and treating them not as patients, not as figures of pity, but recognising that in them still are the brave men who risked all for our freedom, our very lives. The men who rushed to the call and headed up into the air, never—

The words danced and circled on the page, turning into a frenzied slideshow of images. Her dead sister. The twisted wreck. A Nazi hiding in the shadows. The brave Home Guard hunting for him.

In the still, silent night Lottie heard a sound that set the hairs on her arms on end. Footsteps, crunching across the frosty yard outside. Heading towards the house. She frowned.

What if it's him? What if he got past the Home Guard? How dare he!

Her heart pounding loudly, she carefully put aside the book and, trying not to make the slightest sound, reached for the poker that hung beside the fire. The heft of it reassured her. If he tried to break in, she'd be ready for him.

Blossom seemed to sense Lottie's fear and hunkered down in her basket, her ears flattened against her head. The footsteps were almost at the door now and, as Lottie heard them stamping lightly on the ground to kick off the debris of the farmyard, she and Blossom relaxed as one. Fugitive Germans probably didn't clean their shoes when they broke into a farmhouse, but one particular gentleman from the Ministry of Agriculture did: Alastair was home.

Blossom jumped up from the basket and hurtled over to the kitchen door, excitedly barking her greeting. And Lottie, feeling rather ridiculous now, hung the poker back up, hoping that Alastair wouldn't know how scared she'd been at the thought of the German airman.

She remembered now that he'd been out on a date with Laura, his fiancée. She was the local vet and lived in the village. The last thing he needed was Lottie walloping him with a cast-iron poker.

'Well, Blossom, so much for me trying to be quiet so I didn't wake the house!' Alastair chuckled as he stepped into the kitchen. The air that blew in with him was frigid and cold and he was swathed in a greatcoat and hat, muffled in scarf and gloves. He bent and scooped up Blossom to fuss her as the door creaked shut behind him. As he stood, he saw Lottie in the light that the fire still cast. 'And Lottie too!'

'Evening!' Lottie greeted him. She was beaming now, her frown gone. 'You must be freezing out there. There's some tea in the pot, I could warm it for you. How's Laura?'

'Well and busy. Vets never rest, it seems.' Alastair smiled as he set Blossom down with great care, then took off his hat. 'I'd love a cuppa, thank you!'

Lottie put the kettle on the range and thought of Laura, driving through the countryside in her battered old car to her next call. What if the German tried to flag her down?

'You've heard, I suppose,' she asked Alastair. 'About the missing airman?'

If Alastair had taken Laura to the George and Dragon, as he

usually did, then there was no way he could've avoided finding out.

'It's the talk of the pub. Everyone has an opinion,' he admitted, hanging his coat on the pegs. As he did, he glanced across at Gastrell's book. 'Ah, Mr Gastrell! One or two of the villagers went along to have their books signed today and filled him in on our own fugitive.'

'He's tracked some of them down, hasn't he?' Lottie said with a shiver. She was very glad she'd handed over that watch. It seemed to have been freighted with shadows. 'You know, it's really frightening to think he's just out there somewhere, don't you think? We could do with someone like Gastrell coming to Brambles to winkle him out!'

Alastair took up the poker and went over to agitate the fire into life. As he did, he replied, 'I don't think he's big enough for Mr Gastrell. His last catch was some sort of traitor ring, wasn't it?' The man from the Ministry glanced over his shoulder towards Lottie. 'Our missing German isn't so much of an active threat, so I don't think there's any call to be afraid. If he isn't injured from the crash, he must be physically very weak. This is no weather to be outdoors.'

'But I *am* scared,' said Lottie. 'He's out there. What's he waiting for? You don't know he's weak and injured, we can't be sure of that. He could strike at any moment!'

Alastair knew what it was like to lose someone to a Nazi bomb and had been there for Lottie in the terrible days that followed Martha's death, first with a kind letter, after which he had quickly become a close friend. She knew she could confide her fears in him.

He'd also saved her life – not once, but twice, because, just days before Martha had been taken from her, Lottie had been trapped in a barn that had been set on fire. She would have died in the smoke and the flames if Alastair hadn't bravely, selflessly, run into the inferno to rescue her. He was such a brave man and such a good, wise friend.

Alastair replaced the poker beside the now-healthy fire, then came over to the range to help Lottie assemble the tea things. He was a steady presence in the house, a man who was seemingly shaken by nothing – after all, he had once commanded a battleship before he was invalided out and sent by the Ministry here, to Bramble Heath. As Alastair scooped out the carefully measured tealeaves into the pot he said, 'It brings it back, I know.' He looked at Lottie with a gentle smile. 'Every time the siren blares, I think of Vicky. It's taken me a long time to think of her with love, rather than anger at what happened to her. Seeing that wreck must've been wrenching.'

Lottie nodded keenly, thinking of Alastair faithfully standing guard by the back door while the siren shrieked until everyone had left the farmhouse. She tried to concentrate on the tea things, but she couldn't.

'It really was,' she said. 'Martha... Vicky... they died because a plane like that flew here and...' She couldn't finish her sentence, but Alastair would know what she was trying to say. 'But I couldn't help but think of those dead men, and their families weeping, because they'd never...' She wrinkled up her nose, trying to hold back the tears that were threatening to fall.

Alastair nodded, then put his arm round Lottie's shoulders and gave her a brotherly sort of squeeze.

'I don't think many of the men in those planes enjoy what they do, whether they're our boys or theirs,' he said. 'But I didn't think that when I first lost Vicky. I couldn't even think of them as human then.' He sighed. 'But they are. And that chap out there must be as frightened as he is cold.'

Lottie swallowed her tears. 'I just have a feeling about this, Alastair. I really don't think he's scared at all, you know. I think he's enjoying it. He knows he's frightening us. I can feel it, something is wrong in Bramble Heath, ever since he arrived. I'm scared. I can't help it.'

Did she sound feeble, admitting to a fear that she couldn't fight? And yet, if it came to it, if it *had* been the Nazi who'd come through the kitchen door, she knew she would have gone for him with the poker and not hesitated at all.

'There's nothing wrong with being afraid. It's just part of what makes us human,' Alastair said softly. 'But you're not on your own. We'll all look out for each other.'

Alastair had made sure, from the moment he'd heard of Martha's death, that Lottie wasn't alone. She'd had her friends at the farm looking out for her, too, of course, but Alastair knew what it was like to lose someone so swiftly, so mercilessly. He understood her pain.

As the kettle on the range began to whistle, Lottie picked it up and brought it over to the teapot. She poured, glad of something to busy herself with, and looked up at Alastair through the steam. 'And if he comes here, what should we do?'

'We'll swallow our feelings. We'll make him a cup of tea, sit him beside the fire and, if the Home Guard patrol doesn't get here first, go into the village to fetch Constable Russell,' said her friend. 'And if our chum has any sense, he'll be glad of it.'

Lottie nodded, but her gaze wandered to the poker again. She wasn't going to argue with Alastair. But if the Nazi did come back to the farm, she would grab the weighty piece of metal and make him regret he'd ever pulled his parachute's cord.

FOURTEEN

Milking wasn't a bad job, apart from how early they had to get up to do it. There was something soothing about the rhythm of the milk squirting into the buckets. Sometimes, Lottie would close her eyes and half doze, her head leaning against the warm flank of the cow as her fingers worked.

After milking, the next job for Lottie and her friends was to load up the wagon with the large metal cans of milk so they could be taken down to the station. Despite the icy mist that clung to the farm this morning, the girls carried on working. They hitched the wagon to the tractor, Blossom helping by barking excitedly from her position on the tractor seat, then the hard work really began.

'I'll have muscles like a strongman at the circus if this war goes on much longer!' Shona joked as she and Frances hefted one of the full cans into the back of the wagon.

Nicola climbed down from the tractor, pulling on her gloves as she came to help. That extra finger she had knitted was tied off in a neat knot, *so I don't forget where I put it*, as she had explained.

'It gets right on my wick that they won't let us get in among the fighting,' Nicola admitted brightly as she picked up one of the cans. 'But so long as they won't give me a rifle and ship me off to join the boys, I'll keep on hauling milk churns for the war effort!'

'Funny to think of the cups of tea and the babies' bottles this'll end up in.' Lottie grimaced as she strained to lift the can. 'I never really thought of how the milk for my porridge got to the shops before I was a Land Girl!'

Nicola nodded, already on her way back for a second can.

'Aye, turns out it's got something to do with cows!' She laughed her hearty laugh, then hefted up the can with none of the effort that Lottie was having to put in. 'And turns out us girls can work hard too! We're not just about smelling salts and lacy frocks!'

'Mr Gastrell said the same in that newsreel,' Frances said, as she went to fetch another can. Lottie remembered; they'd sat in the cinema, beaming with pride because Mr Gastrell, who was so full of praise for the armed forces, was telling audiences up and down the country about the hard work of the Land Girls. 'How good was it to hear him appreciate our efforts?'

Nicola paused for a second to let out a puff of breath, then reached out and took the can that Lottie was struggling with and hefted it up onto the wagon as though it weighed no more than a bag of flour.

'Folks listen to what he says,' she agreed. 'And I'll tell you what, when this is all over and done with I'm not going to give up this life. I'm a farm girl now, war or no war.'

'Thanks, Nick!' Lottie stood up and rubbed her back. 'You're made for a life on the farm. I can't really say the same about me. Maybe I'll still open that wool shop after all this is over and I can sell wool from your sheep. I don't know if I'll hang about in Bramble Heath, though, not with the new vicar around. I can't seem to get on with him at all. Do you know, yesterday, he was talking about giving the Nazi sanctuary in the church, and when I protested, he asked if I thought he should just drown him in the font. Honestly!' she tutted.

Nicola hooted with laughter. 'Oh, he's a feisty one!' She chuckled. 'Going toe to toe with our Lottie!'

Before Lottie could say anything in reply, a bicycle bell rang and she looked around to see their postlady – their postman had gone off to fight – arrive. She leaned her bicycle against the farmhouse and approached with an envelope. She was in her mid-twenties, like the Land Girls, and looked impossibly well-groomed for someone who rode around the muddy lanes of the countryside.

'Morning! Which one of you is Miss Shona Thewlis?' she asked, holding out an envelope.

Shona pointed to herself. 'That's me,' she said as she took it. 'Oh, it must be a Christmas card from my Auntie Mags. I haven't had one from her yet. She only ever remembers at the last minute!'

She slid it into her pocket with a shrug and the postlady got back on her bicycle and headed off, lugging her bag of letters and cards to another farm.

'That's the last of the milk cans,' Frances gasped, her face red with effort as she pushed hers onto the wagon.

'A job well done!' Lottie said, brushing her hands together.

An unwelcome thought wormed its way to the surface and took away her smile. Matthew had told her about the farms where prisoners of war worked. Just at that moment, there were Nazis doing exactly the same job as she and her friends, loading up wagons with the morning's milk.

But meanwhile, in Bramble Heath, there was a Nazi at large. Someone who wore a swastika on his watch with pride. And she had a feeling he was no ordinary German, just a victim of the war machine. There was a reason why he hadn't handed himself in. He was watching, waiting. Ready to strike.

FIFTEEN

After Nicola and Frances had set off with the tractor and its cargo of milk cans, Lottie got on with her next job. She had to load her wheelbarrow with bales of hay to take to the barn where the cows were spending the winter.

Blossom didn't seem bothered by the cold and was busy patrolling the barn, sniffing here and there, before returning to Lottie's side, peering at her quizzically.

She was glad to keep busy. It kept her thoughts away from all the memories of Martha's death that the crashed bomber had resurrected. It stopped her dwelling on her fears of the faceless missing man who was lurking who knew where. And it kept her mind away from the terror she'd had to fight every time she worked alone in the barn, her terror that it might catch fire again, trapping her in the blaze.

It had taken her a while to get her nerve back, to go inside a barn and not feel the hairs on the back of her neck pricking up. The stench of the smoke had stayed with her, the sensation of it, thick and cloying in her throat as she tried to breathe, tried to call for help.

She'd told herself over and over again that if only she'd

checked first before going inside, she would never have been caught in the blaze and Alastair wouldn't have had to risk his own life to save hers. She'd blamed herself, even though she wasn't the one who had struck the match and set the barn on fire, not caring who they might kill.

Suddenly Blossom's ears pricked up. The little dog bounded over a stack of hay, barking for all she was worth.

'Blossom, what's up? Is it a rat?' Lottie called after her. Blossom's terrier blood often sent her running after the rodents that were drawn to the warm, dry farm buildings. But then her throat tightened and her heart raced. Had Blossom found a fire? Was she going to be trapped in the flames and smoke again?

Gingerly, she lifted away the bale of hay. If there was a fire, she'd stay calm, raise the alarm and run for buckets of water. She wouldn't be afraid, she wouldn't be trapped.

She turned back to see what Blossom was barking at – and stared in utter disbelief.

There, hidden away, was a bed. Someone had used a piece of canvas tarpaulin as a blanket and had stuffed an old feed sack full of straw for a pillow. The sack, Lottie saw, was smeared with blood.

Blossom, standing on the piece of canvas, went on barking and Lottie shivered violently, but then forced herself to stop. She wasn't going to be cowed and afraid.

Yesterday evening, as she had sat alone in the kitchen with Blossom, the Nazi had been only feet away. And through the night, while she had been tucked up in bed, only on the other side of the farmyard the enemy had been sleeping among the hay bales in this very barn.

What if he's still here?

Lottie tore her gaze from the bed and glanced around. Where was he? She clenched her fists, ready to fight.

'Morning, Lottie!' said a cheery voice. 'What can I crack on with?'

Lottie jolted in alarm, then clasped her leaping heart and forced herself to smile as she saw Sarah standing in the doorway of the barn. As usual, her socks had fallen down round her ankles and her hair was doing its best to escape from its ponytail under her lopsided bobble hat.

Should I tell her about the bed, or will it just scare her?

'I'm just... erm... loading up some hay to take to the cows,' Lottie explained. Blossom was still barking and Lottie knew she had to say something further. 'Sorry, Sarah, you made me jump. All this business about the missing airman, and... well, look what I've just found.'

She gestured to the space among the hay bales.

Sarah trotted over, pausing to pat Blossom's head as she did. She tucked her escaped ponytail back beneath her bobble hat, then, at the sight of the disturbed bedding, her mouth fell open and she gasped. 'Blimey!'

'He must've been here last night,' Lottie murmured. She glanced around the barn again. 'And everyone was asleep in the farmhouse.'

'If he's got a brain in his head, he won't hang around.' Sarah always sounded very confident for her eleven years. Lottie envied her that and hoped she'd stay that way. She'd fallen in love with Bramble Heath, this girl from Stepney in London's East End, and was forever around the farms or out on calls with Laura. 'Word down in the village is that Sidney Gastrell's going to come and have a look. If he does, he'll soon have that toerag in handcuffs!'

'Mr Gastrell's coming here, to Bramble Heath?' Lottie gasped.

The blood on the pillow was making her think of the watch, with the bloodied smear across its smashed glass. While it was likely the Nazi was long gone by now, Lottie felt as if something of him still lingered. Something cruel and dark. She felt it as clearly as the winter chill outside; it was unmistakable.

'He'll find him,' said Sarah. 'And then Jerry'll wish he was back in Berlin!'

'Is that young Sarah I can hear? Our little East End farmer!' Farmer Gosling poked his head round the barn door. 'And talk of Mr Gastrell? I'm just about to start on that book of his.'

'He's coming to Bramble Heath,' Lottie explained as Farmer Gosling strode over. 'Which is just as well, because—'

Farmer Gosling stared at the makeshift bed that had been put together among the hay. 'The airman's slept in my barn! If he's still here, he'll be having a nice chat with my pitchfork!' he snapped angrily, his gaze suddenly wary. He glanced this way and that, up at the rafters and around the stacks of hay. 'Are you hiding, Fritz? Come on out!'

'He'll have took off if he's got any sense,' said Sarah, peering around the barn. 'Especially now Gastrell the Nazi-catcher's coming to the village!'

That seemed to focus Farmer Gosling's mind. 'Right,' he said, looking up into the rafters again, as if he thought he might see the German perched there like a nesting sparrow. 'I'm away to tell the constable that we've had a guest. And then I'm going to tell Mrs Gosling to make sure the kettle's on; we may be getting a hero to tea.'

SIXTEEN

Lottie tried to fight through her shock and finish her task, working with Sarah to take the hay to the cows in their barn, but she couldn't get the vision of the airman's bed out of her head.

Sarah seemed to sense her tension and, though she had been excited by the discovery in the barn, once she was working there was no more said about it. Nicola and Frances hadn't got back yet with the empty milk cans from the station and she couldn't find Shona. And besides, there was nothing she could do. If she ran into the farmhouse kitchen and told Mrs Gosling, it would only frighten her. They'd just have to wait until Farmer Gosling came back from the village. And Sarah was right, wasn't she? The airman couldn't still be here. As soon as the farm had woken up that morning, he must have fled, and found somewhere else to hide.

But if he did jump out on them, Lottie would be ready. And he'd regret landing in Bramble Heath.

A Nazi. Spending the night just a stone's throw from where we sleep. From where Martha once slept.

And not far from where she died.

Lottie winced, trying to push the thought away, but a

surge of scalding-hot anger shot up inside her. How dare he skulk about here! It felt like sacrilege, like he was coming to deface her sister's grave. Judging by the blood on the makeshift pillow, the airman was clearly injured but Lottie felt no compassion for him at all. Not when she thought of her sister and everyone else who had been lost to Nazi brutality. The Jewish people hunted down and murdered. The refugees shot as they fled.

I hope he's in pain. I hope he's suffering.

'Lottie.' She didn't know how long she'd been standing, nor how long Sarah had been at her side, the girl's hand gently resting on her arm. 'Reverend Hart and his niece are looking for you. Well, Daisy's looking for Blossom, I'd say!'

Matthew and Daisy!

Lottie had forgotten that they were coming today; Matthew had annoyed her so much the day before that she'd put it out of her mind. She hurriedly put down her pitchfork. 'Thank you, Sarah. I was miles away.' She whistled to the dog. 'Come along, Blossom, your little friend has come to visit!'

Lottie tried to smooth back her hair, which had escaped from under her Alice band, even though she knew it was futile; it was impossible to look neat and do hard, physical work on the farm. She supposed their arrival was a welcome distraction from what she had just discovered, even if it meant having to spend time with Matthew.

She emerged from the barn with Sarah, Blossom by her side, and saw Matthew in the farmyard, holding his niece's hand as she walked beside him. Daisy stared about, her eyes like saucers. Blossom made a dash for her, barking with excitement.

'Hello, you two!' Lottie said, doing her best to smile as she came over to them. She didn't want Daisy to know that she didn't get on with her uncle and today's visit was about the little girl, after all. 'Sorry I'm such a mess. Just been shovelling hay—'

'Uncle Matthew's been with loads of ladies,' Daisy

announced brightly as she opened her arms to Blossom. 'He's been out all morning!'

'The Women's Institute!' Matthew clarified quickly, casting a fond look at his niece. The little girl was bundled up tight in a coat and wellies, muffled warmly in a hat, scarf and gloves of bright blue wool. She took off with Blossom to run a lap of the farmyard. 'And Daisy's been with my housekeeper, Dorothy, chattering about farms, all morning.' He drew in a breath of cold air, then said, 'Hello, Miss Morley.'

'Hello, Matthew,' Lottie replied rather stiffly. She tried to be polite, at least, and said, 'I expect the Women's Institute were very pleased to meet you and plied you with their Christmas treats.' She wondered if they'd have been as keen if they knew what he'd said about the missing Nazi haunting the village. And what would he think about the man having slept in the barn? But she wouldn't tell him, not with Daisy there. She didn't want her to be frightened. 'Oh, and Sarah's here. We'll show you around.'

Sarah had joined in with the race around the farmyard, Daisy's hand safe in hers as they ran.

Good, Lottie thought. *Daisy needs some friends in the village.*

'You stick with me,' said Sarah gently. The evacuee hadn't lost her parents – she had left a mother in Stepney and a father serving in Europe – but she knew what it was to have to make a start in a new village. Sarah and her friends had a couple of years on Daisy, but they all knew the struggles of war. 'Wait until you see the pigs!' And Sarah gave a spirited *oink*, to Daisy's obvious delight.

'Sarah came to the house to call for Daisy,' Matthew commented. 'But I thought she was a little too young for playing in woods.'

'Never too young for that!' Sarah grinned. 'But I'll come and call again, don't you worry!'

'Have you got deer on the farm?' Daisy asked, bouncing on her toes.

Lottie shook her head. 'I can't say that we do, but there are some that live in the woods. They're very good at hiding, so you don't see them very often.'

Daisy nodded.

'But we've got lots of other animals for you to meet. Come and say hello!'

As Lottie showed Matthew and Daisy around with Sarah's help, she saw the farm with new eyes and it was enough to stop the thoughts of the missing airman intruding. If the Nazi was going to spring out at them, he would have done so while Lottie was on her own in the barn. He wouldn't dare try anything now. They were cowards, the lot of them.

The farm was a fascinating place for Daisy, an unexpected delight around every corner. Here were the cows in the barn, ready to lick her hand with their wide, rough tongues, and there were the pigs in their styes, rushing up to meet their visitors. Here were the ewes, round with the promise of next spring's lambs, and there were the chickens, fluffed up against the cold as they sat in a row on the goats' pen. Lottie let them peer through the door of the milking shed, with the stools where she and her friends sat each day, squirting the cows' white jets of milk into the buckets. She opened the door of the barn to show them the wagons and ploughs that the Land Girls hitched the horses up to. Finally, they went to the stables, where the farm's two Shire horses lived. The huge creatures towered over Daisy, but she wasn't afraid and giggled with joy as one of the horses ran his soft, whiskery mouth across Daisy's hand.

Lottie watched her carefully, leaning down to explain everything and ensuring that none of the animals posed any risk. Sometimes, as they made their way around the farm, Daisy let go of Matthew's hand and, with a grin, clasped Lottie's instead. And Lottie didn't mind at all. She liked feeling the orphaned girl's small, mittened hand within her own, holding it tight, protecting her.

Even if Matthew didn't seem impressed that his niece was holding her hand.

Matthew and Lottie might not get on, but there was no question that he adored the little girl who was in his care. Just as he had been on the platform at East Grinstead, in the presence of his carefree niece he was once again transformed whenever he spoke to her. If the walking stick he used caused him any difficulties, Lottie wouldn't have known; he was as merry as any of them, sharing in Daisy's joy as she discovered the wonders of her new home.

It was a world away from the towns and cities; there was little sign of the war that was raging. But Lottie knew that if they went into the fields around the farm they would find the wrecked plane and the scar in the earth where Martha had been killed.

Lottie heaved open a heavy door on a small, hexagonal-sided building, made from the same stone as the farmhouse. It looked like something from a fairytale, maybe the home of a helpful witch. It had a tiled floor and was cool inside. *As cold as Matthew*, Lottie thought.

'This is the old dairy,' she explained, gesturing towards the clean, scrubbed pans and the wooden butter pats. 'Mrs Gosling still makes her own butter and cream in here sometimes. She uses milk from the farm's own cows. You can see—'

Lottie had taken a step forward and now slipped on the shiny tiles. Her feet shot out from under her. But before she could hit the hard floor, she felt a strong hand grip her arm.

'Oh... thank you, Matthew,' she said in surprise as she found her footing again. Her gaze had locked on to his and she stared back at him, into those large blue eyes. It was like staring into a cloudless summer sky.

Matthew cleared his throat, his hand still holding on to her. 'That would've been quite a spill,' he said. 'All right?'

'I think I've turned my ankle,' Lottie mumbled, still gazing at him. Then she shook her head. What was wrong with her? He'd been rude to her yesterday, making sarcastic remarks. She had no right to be staring at him as if she was a sighing heroine in a film. Rather coldly, she said, 'But I'll be all right, it doesn't really hurt. Thank you, Matthew. The floor's a bit slippery in here.'

Daisy nudged Sarah and whispered, 'Uncle Matthew saved Lottie's life just like he saved mine.'

Sarah's eyes widened and she gasped, 'Did he?' Daisy's only reply was a proud nod.

Lottie swallowed and her gaze was caught by Matthew's again. Did Daisy mean that Matthew had saved her life by taking her in and looking after her? But what about the stick? Maybe it wasn't a war injury. Had he selflessly thrown himself in the way of danger to save the life of his little niece?

'I just slipped, that's all,' Lottie said, but she was still staring at Matthew. There was a mystery there; she could see it, but not quite grasp it.

He matched her gaze for another moment, then turned to Daisy and Sarah and said, 'Let's get on with our tour, shall we?'

Lottie closed the door to the old dairy and carried on, relieved that her ankle wasn't bothering her at all. She led the way to the store where Farmer Gosling kept the tools that the Land Girls used every day, a motley collection of shiny scythes, spades and pitchforks.

'And this is the weapons store,' Lottie teased. She glanced at Matthew as she said, 'In case any Nazi airmen make the mistake of coming to the farm!'

'We'll give them Germans what for if they show their faces!' Sarah cheered and Daisy gave a cry of excited agreement, then frowned and turned to her uncle, blinking up at him.

He shot Lottie a sharp glance and assured Daisy, 'They're not weapons, don't worry. They're for looking after the farm.' Then he added, 'There's nothing to worry about in Bramble Heath. Isn't that right, Sarah?'

And Sarah gave a firm nod. 'Nothing at all,' she assured her new friend. 'It's brilliant here. We've got a clubhouse in the woods and everything. Blossom plays there sometimes and you can too. I always bring my cat, Winnie, and you can bring Bunny if you like!'

'Brilliant, I'm definitely bringing Bunny,' Daisy replied.

Lottie smiled. Sarah was a sensitive girl under her swagger. She had recognised that Daisy, who had been through so much, carried her toy rabbit with her everywhere. And she knew that none of the children who played at the clubhouse would think any the less of her for bringing it with her.

Once again, Sarah's reply was a firm nod.

'Everybody's welcome.' She beamed. 'Come and see the tools.' As the girls wandered over to the farm implements with Blossom, Matthew dropped his voice to a whisper and said, 'I'd rather you don't try to frighten my niece, Miss Morley. I'm trying to teach her forgiveness, not fear.'

'Forgiveness? Matthew, you can't be serious. We're at war. There's a Nazi among us. None of us are safe in our beds!' Lottie retorted. 'If he comes creeping up on me while I'm doing my work, I wouldn't think twice about running to the tool store to grab the sharpest thing in there.'

'Like the poor blighter whose plane took a nosedive into Victoria station back in 1940?' asked Matthew harshly. 'I wonder how the Londoners who beat him to death feel now when they remember what they did?'

Lottie glared at him. She didn't want to accept that civilians had killed an already injured man. 'He'd just crashed his plane and was horribly injured. It would've taken a miracle for him to have survived that. And besides, can you blame the Londoners who set on him? They're watching their city go up in flames around them, their homes reduced to rubble, never knowing if they'll see the next morning, and then Fritz crash-lands in the middle of it. Should they really feel guilty? What else could they have done?'

He rolled his eyes. 'Do you know who dragged him away from the lynch mob? Soldiers. British soldiers, men trained to kill Germans, saved a German from British civilians.' Matthew shook his head. 'But if he did survive his injuries from when the plane came down, Miss Morley, then he died because a bunch of frightened civilians beat him to death. Don't you see? We need to be better than the likes of Hitler. Better than murdering people because of where they come from.'

'This isn't the time to make peace, Matthew. We're at war, we have people to defend, our livelihoods to protect. And the Germans picked a fight with us,' Lottie reminded him. 'A plane with a big swastika on the side of it dropped the bomb that killed my sister so pardon me if I don't want to welcome the missing Nazi with a hug and a bunch of flowers.'

'Can we just get on?' he asked. 'I don't want the girls to hear.'

Lottie didn't reply. She went over to the tool store and stopped Sarah and Daisy just before they reached for a scythe, then closed the door.

'So now you've seen all over the farm,' she said brightly, for their benefit. 'You're welcome to come back whenever you like,' she told Daisy. 'Maybe we can go for a ride in the trap with the horses one day. Would you like that?'

The little girl nodded keenly. 'And Blossom can come too?'

'Blossom will love to,' Lottie assured her.

'You're going to love living in Bramble Heath,' Sarah told her new friend, as the sound of a car engine drifted across the winter air, its wheels crunching on the lane.

That had to be Farmer Gosling, back from the village, with

whoever was coming to look at the place where the Nazi airman had spent the night.

Good. Perhaps it won't be long now until they find him. Because if they don't, I will.

Lottie said to Sarah, 'Why don't you take Daisy to the kitchen? I'm sure Mrs Gosling has some lovely Christmas treats for you both.'

'Come on, pal!' Sarah beamed, squeezing Daisy's hand. Then she clicked her tongue and called, 'You too, Blossom!'

'Not too many,' Matthew told his niece indulgently. 'And don't forget your thank-yous!'

'Yes, Uncle Matthew!' Daisy replied and the two girls headed towards the farmhouse kitchen, with Blossom leading the way, her tail a blur.

Lottie looked after them for a long minute.

'I couldn't tell you earlier,' she said finally to Matthew, her smile fading. 'I didn't want to frighten Daisy, despite what you think. Only last night, the missing airman was *here*.'

'Here?' he asked, eyes wide. Lottie couldn't help but wonder if he would have brought Daisy over to the farm had he known. That would've been the true test of the forgiveness he was so fond of preaching. 'I assume you didn't see him since he hasn't been run through?'

'No, I didn't see him,' Lottie retorted. 'He's lucky that I only saw where he slept. He'd made a bed in the hay in the barn, just over there.'

She pointed towards the barn, its door still open, her pitch-fork leaning against it.

'Like a rat,' she added.

SEVENTEEN

Farmer Gosling's car pulled up in the yard, a much-used workaday sort of car with mud spattered up its sides. And sitting beside him in the passenger seat was a face Lottie and so many people up and down the country knew very well.

'He's here, it's Mr Gastrell!' Lottie said excitedly. Her heart soared. Here was the man who'd capture the Nazi. He would take the threat seriously, she knew he would. 'Oh, thank heavens, we'll be safe in our beds again in no time!'

'*Him?*' Matthew's reply was a sneer of disgust. 'He's a menace. His sort raise lynch mobs.' The young vicar shook his head. 'I'd better go and collect Daisy, I don't want her around the likes of him.'

'What on earth do you mean, raise lynch mobs?' Lottie challenged him, her hands on her hips. How dare he judge Gastrell and be so self-righteous? Hadn't he read the man's book? Hadn't he seen the newsreels? 'He's a good man, he's caught traitors, murderers, the sort of people who'd sooner we died in our beds!'

Matthew said nothing.

Farmer Gosling climbed out of his car and, for such a large man, displayed a surprising turn of speed as he lumbered around the vehicle and opened the passenger door for Sidney Gastrell. No such service was provided for Constable Russell, who was left to extricate himself from the straw and tools that littered the back seat of the jalopy. Gastrell, however, once he'd stepped out, hurried to hold the door wide for the constable and offered him a hand as he struggled from the cramped rear seat. Constable Russell beamed at him, as if he couldn't believe his luck that such an important man was helping him out of the car.

'We have to do something,' Lottie told Matthew in an undertone. 'We can't just pretend that everything is fine, you're living in a dream land. There *was* a Nazi on the farm last night, and he's still out there, and I really don't think we should underestimate him.'

Constable Russell had put on his helmet and smoothed down his uniform. He nodded hello, smiling proudly as he walked at the side of Gastrell. He was no doubt relieved to have the help of such a man to track down the Nazi on his beat.

Matthew shrugged one shoulder and replied, 'Thank you for giving Daisy such a lovely morning. I'll let you get on.' And without waiting for her reply, he turned his back on the new arrivals and headed towards the farmhouse.

'Now then, Mr Gastrell,' said Farmer Gosling, puffing out his chest with pride. 'Welcome, Sir, to my farm. It's been in the family through three generations and I hope to see three more!'

Gastrell was looking around the yard, his expression stern beneath the brim of his dark hat. He looked like a man who meant business, Lottie decided, a man who would know what to do.

'And this here's our Miss Morley,' said the farmer, sweeping off his cap and kneading it in his hands. He looked like a starstruck teenage girl meeting her idol. 'Come on, lass, come and meet Mr Gastrell.' Then he turned to his guest again. 'Miss Morley found the watch and the bed. She's a proper little detective, this one!'

Sidney Gastrell took off his hat then and smoothed down his greased hair with his free hand as he strode towards Lottie.

'Miss Morley.'

Just like practically everybody else in the country, Lottie had heard Gastrell on the wireless. She knew his no-nonsense soldier's way of speaking, the London vowels and the strident manner. What she hadn't expected was quite how loud he would be, as though he was addressing one of his public rallies.

He held out a large hand. 'Sidney Gastrell. I applaud you for your efforts on behalf of king and country.'

Lottie wiped her hand down her jumper first, before taking his. 'Sorry, I've been working. And it's nothing, really, just what anyone else would do. I really hope we can catch the blighter!'

She'd known he was tall, as she'd seen him in the railway station, but close up, Gastrell towered over her. She was glad she wasn't a runaway German or a traitor, otherwise she might have felt afraid of him.

'Several villagers from Bramble Heath came to my talk in East Grinstead yesterday and told me about the criminal – the *killer*, because mark me well, Miss, they're all killers – who's running loose,' Gastrell told Lottie. 'My men and I go where we're needed. And Bramble Heath needs us.'

'Hear hear!' exclaimed Farmer Gosling, raising his cap in salute. At the sound of Gastrell's voice, other farm workers were beginning to appear in the yard and Shona came to stand beside Lottie. They looked just as starstruck as the farmer, gazing at this mountain of a man who had brought down escaped foreign villains and homegrown traitors, bringing them to justice without any care for his own safety.

The Land Girls and young farmhands took up Farmer Gosling's cheer and the farmyard rang with their voices. Lottie's heart flooded with hope.

Gastrell was so imposing, everyone was drawn to him, approaching as close as they dared as they cheered him on.

Even Constable Russell had joined in. Why Matthew had taken against him, Lottie couldn't imagine. Perhaps it was just that, as a bastion of the establishment, he had no time for men like Gastrell who just rolled up their sleeves and got things done.

Gastrell turned to address the growing crowd. He nodded an acknowledgement, then gestured with his hands to quieten their cheers. Once the noise had died down he addressed the gathered workers.

'You're good, honest, hardworking folk. British folk!' But not all of Bramble Heath was, Lottie thought. The Polish aircrews who flew into danger from Heath Place every time the sirens blared had given up their homes to come here, to lay their lives on the line. As though reading her mind, he added, 'And not just British! We all owe a debt to the Polish Air Force who fly from the village and the refugees who have joined the community too. But you farming folk know that sometimes a fellow sees a rat – and when a British fellow sees a German rat, he gets rid of it!' He slammed one meaty fist against his other palm. 'If there's a rat in these parts, friends, I give you my word that Sidney Gastrell will trap it!'

Lottie shouted, 'Hurray for Mr Gastrell! We don't want the likes of that airman in Bramble Heath! There's no room for Nazis here.'

The cheering started again, but Lottie was aware of Shona beside her, who hadn't joined in this time and instead was shaking her head.

'Lottie, don't,' Shona whispered, but Lottie went on cheering.

'I'll carry out my investigations today and speak to the eyewitnesses about what they've discovered!' Gastrell told his audience, casting a glance towards Lottie. *She* was an eyewitness, wasn't she? She'd do her bit by helping capture the Nazi, just as Martha would have wanted her to. 'And because this isn't Nazi Germany, because it's England, a place where we don't keep secrets, I'll make sure all of you know what I've discovered! Because every man' – Gastrell gave a little smile – 'And every woman, of course, who does their bit to bring down Herr Hitler and his mob, is the real hero.'

He lifted one hand, jabbing a finger skywards. 'And if you're listening, Jerry, if you're hiding in your rathole like the pest you are, believe me when I say: woe betide you. Woe betide you, Nazi vermin, because decent folk don't want your kind breathing the same air! We'll flush the blighter out, won't we? We'll give that hateful Nazi murderer what for!'

And across the farmyard voices rang out, cheering on their hero.

From the corner of her eye, Lottie noticed Matthew leaving the farmhouse, Daisy's hand safe in his once more. He had turned up the collar on his coat against the cold and, without glancing Gastrell's way, he got into his car with his niece.

EIGHTEEN

Nearly everyone wanted to shake hands with Gastrell, although Shona walked away, heading back to her work without giving him a second glance.

It wasn't like her to wander off when so much was going on. Why wasn't she joining in?

Lottie stood close to the man who had been so impressed by her own discoveries that might lead to where the Nazi was hiding.

Once everyone had got to meet Gastrell and the furore had died down, Lottie said to him, 'I'll show you the barn.'

Through the door she could see Constable Russell, already inside.

'And where you found the watch, Miss Morley,' he said. 'I have reason to believe we're dealing with a very important, very dangerous man.'

'You do?' Lottie asked him. She'd known the airman was dangerous, but she hadn't thought of him being important as well. He wasn't just any Nazi airman, then. 'I found that fancy-looking watch in the woods, where the tail section came down. It'd snapped off from the rest of the plane, you see.'

'Now then, Lottie,' said Farmer Gosling as they approached the barn. 'Tell the gentleman everything you know. Don't you be shy just because he's famous!' Then he told Gastrell, 'We've seen you in the newsreels, Sir. You'll catch the toerag!'

Gastrell gave a sharp nod. 'I intend to,' he replied. 'We'll run the rat to ground.'

Lottie's heart was racing, but she knew it was impossible for the airman to still be inside. If he had any sense, he'd be long gone.

But what if he came back tonight, when no one could see him in the darkness?

But Bramble Heath was defended by its Home Guard, the men who were too young or old to join the forces, or worked in reserved occupations and couldn't go to fight. Instead, they had come together to defend the towns and villages that were their homes. Oh, some might make a joke of 'Dad's Army', as they were called by some, but they were one more line of defence against the German who had found his way into this little corner of England. Whether they were barely old enough to shave, or snowy-haired and filled with memories of wars and battles from long ago, the determined local volunteer soldiers would hold the line against the airman.

'Before we begin, Miss Morley,' Gastrell said, 'I want to offer my condolences to you. Constable Russell told me you lost your sister. It's a rotten business, I'm sorry for your loss.'

Lottie was surprised to hear these kind words about Martha. She hadn't expected a man like Gastrell to take an interest in an ordinary Land Girl like her, especially when these cruel deaths happened every day. And yet, she thought, what was his book about? Ordinary people, called on to do their duty, whatever the cost.

'Thank you, Mr Gastrell, I really appreciate it,' Lottie replied, choked with emotion. 'S-she died not far from here. In that field on the other side of the yard. And to think a Nazi airman has been here, where she worked, where she died...'

'And yet here you are, turning out to work every day in sight of the place she died, for the good of this country of ours,' he replied. 'The papers call me a hero, but it's the likes of you and the lads who work with me who should be on the front pages. Folks who have lost family, lost a limb, still giving everything they've got to show Jerry that we don't put up with his sort of nonsense. You've got my respect, Miss.'

This, Lottie knew, was why Gastrell was famous, why he was adored. Because he cared about ordinary people. It was why he took the risks he did, to capture traitors and downed enemy airmen, because he wanted to protect the nation and everyone in it.

'Just doing my bit,' Lottie replied and managed to smile, even though thinking about Martha awoke her grief. 'I can't leave. Martha wouldn't have wanted me to. We were happy here. She loved this place and everyone in it.'

She started to think of Matthew's words of comfort at the wreck, but what use were they when he'd proudly give sanctuary to a Nazi? She could never agree with him.

'And you'll honour her name all your life,' Gastrell said gently. 'Now, you tell me exactly what you found this morning, Miss.'

'So, I was loading some bales of hay onto the wheelbarrow,' Lottie began, gesturing to the towering stacks that surrounded them. 'And my dog Blossom started barking. I thought she'd found a rat – well, she *had*,' Lottie went on. 'Because I moved a bale and suddenly I found this bed.'

Constable Russell peered over Gastrell's shoulder and shook his head sadly. The sacking, the hay, the feed bag with a smear of blood. 'The fellow's injured and he's sleeping in a barn? Ought to be in a hospital.'

'If he's the person I suspect he is, he ought to be on the scaffold, never mind hospital,' Gastrell told him firmly. 'And this is just as you found it?'

Constable Russell's expression changed; the sympathy he had felt for the injured man had clearly fled. He knew what these men were capable of. After all, his daughter was engaged to a pilot who'd been shot out of the sky by Nazi airmen and badly injured.

Lottie nodded eagerly. 'Yes, I haven't touched it at all. Who do you think he might be?'

'He's a careless sort, dropping his watch. But I'm glad that he did,' said Gastrell. He knelt beside the makeshift bed and peered closely at it. 'I'll call a public meeting; it's for the good of everybody that we let folks know when there's a dangerous man at large. May I see the watch again, Constable?'

'Of course, Sir,' Constable Russell said and reached into the pocket of his overcoat. He produced a wrap of paper and passed it to Mr Gastrell. 'You did well finding that, Miss Morley. Horrible thing, it is.'

Gastrell carefully unwrapped the watch and weighed it in his palm. Then he drew his fingertip lightly over the glass, tracing the words *von Brandt*. 'This name here on the watch, it's a name I know well.' He closed his fist round the watch.

'Otto von Brandt was a thug who brandished chair legs for Adolf Hitler when he was still a nobody trying to convince folks he was a politician. The two of them went to prison together, back in the twenties. Peas in a pod, fired up by hatred of anybody they didn't like the look of. Anybody who didn't believe the disgusting nonsense their lot spout.'

'Went to prison with Hitler?' Lottie gasped, barely able to say the words. 'And now he's flying a plane? We've got one of Hitler's thugs on the loose in the Bramble Heath? I knew it, I had a feeling this was no ordinary airman. I knew something horribly dark had come right here to Bramble Heath.'

'This watch belongs to one of Hitler's inner circle?'

Constable Russell asked Gastrell, as if he couldn't quite believe it. 'No wonder it's such a horrible-looking thing.'

Gastrell opened his fist again and settled his gaze on the watch as he shook his head. 'No,' he replied. 'Von Brandt was a nasty piece of work; Hitler gave him a title and a flashy uniform and all the power he could wield. They called him the Butcher of Breslau for what he did to the Jewish folk. The villain's dead now; car crash. They gave him the sort of funeral we'd give to a king.'

Lottie hadn't realised she'd been holding her breath. But, hearing the monster was dead, she finally exhaled. 'So how did that ugly watch get here?'

'He had two boys, both Luftwaffe,' Gastrell replied. 'Our lads did for the eldest during a dogfight. I think this watch belongs to the second, by the name of Stefan.' He turned it in his palm, revealing the engraved inscription. 'This inscription, you see, it's from a godfather to his godson – his *patensohn*.'

'So, this missing pilot, the Nazi who slept in this barn last night – he's the son of von Brandt, this evil man?' Lottie stared at the engraving on the back of the watch. 'So who gave him such a fancy watch?'

'Stefan von Brandt's godfather is Adolf Hitler,' Gastrell said. He wrapped the watch up again, hiding it from view once more, as Lottie took in what he had just said. 'Known to the children of his cronies as good old Uncle Wolf.'

Silence fell in the barn. The usual background sounds of the farm – the cows and sheep settling in the barns, the chickens busy in the yard – had disappeared. The world had stopped turning. Everything was focused down to that watch in Gastrell's grip.

Patensohn. *Uncle Wolf. Adolf Hitler.*

Lottie swallowed before she was able to speak. 'Y-you mean that Hitler's godson, the child of a butcher, is in Bramble Heath? We all spent the night mere feet away from him! There are children here, innocent people. We have to find him, stop him, before he –!'

Gastrell nodded. 'He's dangerous all right. And Stefan von Brandt is good as family to the Nazi High Command. The sort of information he'll have would be invaluable to our war effort, so that's another reason why we need to nab him,' he said. 'And we will! Before the war, me and my lads were running escaped convicts to ground and handing them over to the police before they'd even managed to lace their boots. Now we're bringing in traitors and Nazis instead. And we'll bring this one in too. We have to, so he can tell Mr Churchill everything he knows about his murdering godfather.'

So, the missing Nazi could be an incredible source of intelligence. He could know all sorts of secrets; maybe what he knew could even bring an end to the war. But would he talk? What damage would he do to prevent himself from being captured?

'I'm glad you're here, Mr Gastrell,' Constable Russell said. 'Back before the war, I could look after my village quite easily, as the only policeman in Bramble Heath. But not now. One man can't track down a Nazi like this on his own, even with the Home Guard to help.'

'And we won't get under your feet, Constable, the Home Guard's neither,' Gastrell assured him. 'We're all on the same side.' He handed the watch back to the policeman, then reached out and rested one hand on Lottie's arm. 'Miss Morley, keep this under your hat until I hold my meeting later. I'd like to see where you found the watch too, if I may. And don't you worry, we'll grab him.'

'I promise I won't tell a soul,' Lottie replied. 'We must catch him. For the sake of everyone in Bramble Heath. And the whole country.'

NINETEEN

It was cold in the woods behind the farm, patches of frost still lying in the shade between the bare trees. An icy breeze trembled the high branches, which scraped against a cloudy sky.

Lottie had wrapped her scarf round her neck and was glad of her woollen gloves. She glanced at Gastrell as they followed the path through the silent trees, fallen twigs and pine cones crunching underfoot. Blossom trotted alongside, sniffing the air as if she was trying to pick up the airman's scent. How different it was from her last visit; now she was searching for a Nazi instead of a Christmas tree, the brutal reality of the war threatening Bramble Heath once again.

The path took them past the tail section of the wreck.

'It was just up here,' Lottie told him as she pointed towards the little grove of fir trees. 'My friend Nicola had just chopped down our Christmas tree and I saw something glittering on the ground.'

'The youngest von Brandt's a gunner,' Gastrell said in his strident voice. He paused and looked around them, as though he might see something even now. 'Takes a certain sort to be a gunner. Sitting out there in the tail all alone, waiting to put a bullet between one of our lads' eyes. Queer sorts, gunners.'

Lottie hadn't thought of it like that. The rear gunner was like a sniper. And not just any sniper, but a monster from the centre of Hitler's regime.

And now he was somewhere in the village. Waiting. Watching.

Gastrell nodded her on. 'Now, you show me exactly where you found our friend's watch.'

They reached the fir trees and, with all the care of a detective, Lottie scanned the ground for the spot where she'd found the watch. Footprints had churned up the mud and old autumn leaves and pine needles had scattered here and there.

She saw the stump left after Nicola had taken an axe to the Christmas tree and pointed to the ground.

'It was about here,' she told Gastrell, then knelt down and brushed the leaves and needles away with her gloved hand. Blossom sat beside Lottie, looking up at Gastrell as if she, too, was pointing out where the watch had been found. 'Yes, it was about here. So it's slightly off the path. Maybe it fell off when he was going to hide in the fir trees?'

'Perhaps,' her companion said thoughtfully. He didn't kneel beside Lottie, but peered into the darkness of the trees. 'Or maybe he put it there on purpose, because he wanted folk to know *who* they were dealing with. And he might have watched you ladies, seen you scared when you picked up his trinket. Just like them, wanting to see good folks scared.' Gastrell dropped his gaze to Lottie and added darkly, 'Then he followed you back to the farm.'

Lottie shakily got back to her feet, scooping Blossom into her arms.

'Scaring us on purpose? Well, I had wondered why he'd taken his watch off. It didn't look cheap and the strap's not broken or anything, so I suppose it can't have just fallen off and dropped onto the ground.' She knitted her hands together as she went on, 'You're right, he must've followed us. And we had no idea – we led him home!'

'Oh, don't you worry about that, Miss, he would've found his way anyway,' said Gastrell in a fatherly tone. 'I'll be honest, I get letters every day from well-meaning folk telling me there's so-and-so up to such-and-such. Most of the time they come to nothing. I had an idea this'd likely as not come to nothing too, but that watch tells me otherwise. Mrs Gastrell and I won't leave until he's apprehended; I'll have my helpers come down and we'll flush him out.'

He looked around again, lifting his chin to call, 'Do you hear us, Fritz? You'll soon be wishing your parachute hadn't opened at all!' Then he gave a nod. 'By blackout tonight, everyone in Bramble Heath will know who's hiding out in their village. This isn't Nazi Germany, we don't play secrets here.'

'Airmen have pistols, don't they?' Lottie asked, staring into the depths of the woods. Was that a branch moving? 'He could start shooting at us at any moment.'

'He could. This one's a nasty piece of work,' Gastrell confided. He added kindly, 'But don't you worry, Miss, my lads will catch him soon enough. We'll even have some Fleet Street blokes along to the meeting and get the word out far and wide. If I can use what little fame I have to keep my country and the decent people who live here safe, then I'll put up with the cameras and the flashbulbs without a grumble.'

There came the sound then of thundering feet snapping twigs and churning up the woods. But as the sounds grew louder and she heard childish voices and a dozen pair of feet, she relaxed.

'Mr Gastrell, Mr Gastrell!' Sarah's face was red with cold and exertion, her eyes bright with excitement, as she and her friends burst through the trees. She held up a tattered square of sackcloth, the dark bloodstain on its surface still glistening. It was fresh. 'He's only been hiding out in our clubhouse!'

TWENTY

Lottie's heart was racing as they reached the children's clubhouse and she wondered what on earth the monster had done. He could at any moment step out in the gloom under the trees, a sneering smile on his face, a gun pointed towards them. Towards the children. He'd slept on the farm and now he'd been here too: the children's clubhouse, the innocent site of their games.

The simple clubhouse had been built out of fallen branches, scraps of wood and pieces of metal by the evacuees. It was a place they had created for themselves to compensate for being taken away from their families. The local village children had joined in and had brought up from the village all manner of odds and ends that the scrap merchants couldn't use for the war effort. A much-patched but brightly coloured curtain, which no one could have turned into clothing, hung over the doorway and a row of cracked bottles along the window doubled as vases, filled with holly and small branches spotted with tiny yellow flowers. Old doors, too cracked for any house, and the lid of an old trunk acted as walls, and a bent and rusted bicycle wheel leaned beside the entrance, its spokes tied with narrow lengths of colourful fabric, no doubt a prop in one of the children's games. The clubhouse in the woods had become a place for the children's shared adventures. It was an innocent place, some-where for games and fun. Not a hiding place for a cold-blooded killer.

'We reckon we probably didn't miss him by much!' Sarah said with a mixture of excitement and disappointment. The evacuee nodded to the sackcloth that Gastrell now held as he looked down at the humble wooden structure. 'His blood ain't even dry!'

'You've a fine little den here,' said Gastrell. He stooped and went into the clubhouse. 'He's been having his breakfast, has he?'

Shirley, whose parents ran the greengrocer's in the village, nodded. She was one of the older children and wore her long blonde hair in neat plaits tied with ribbon.

'We found the crumbs, and the packet too, and I know exactly where they came from and all,' she told Gastrell.

Lottie could see the evidence all too clearly. There on the earthen floor of the clubhouse was an empty packet of Huntley and Palmer's rich tea biscuits.

'We sell them in the shop,' Shirley explained. 'I know because I help behind the counter sometimes. And we had a delivery come yesterday afternoon. The driver was late, he'd skidded on some ice on the lane not far from here and thought he'd punctured his tyre. And while he was busy sorting that out, someone got into his van. Three packets of biscuits they swiped from my dad's order!'

'What's the name of the shop, young Miss?' asked Gastrell. Lottie was impressed that he was taking the children so seri-ously. 'I'll call in and talk to your people; it all goes together to solve the puzzle.'

'Knapp's, the greengrocer's,' Shirley said proudly. 'Oh, Dad was fuming. Someone stealing biscuits when they're rationed and taking more than their fair share. A Christmas treat for someone in the village. And to think it was some grotty German that nicked them as well. Dad'll be furious!'

'Looks like he moved from the farm to the clubhouse,' Lottie said to Gastrell. The hairs on the back of her neck had stood up.

Sarah knelt to fuss Blossom, scratching behind the dog's ears as she cooed, 'You'd soon sniff him out if he was nearby, wouldn't you?' Blossom licked the girl's hand in reply.

Gastrell plucked up the litter and put it into the pocket of the dark overcoat he wore, then shook his head and asked as he exited the clubhouse, 'You seem like the sort of villagers who know what's what. Who would I talk to about holding a meeting in the village hall?'

'The vicar,' Lottie replied, remembering how Reverend Ellis had often been asked for the keys by the various groups in the village who used it. But as soon as she'd spoken, she recalled how Matthew had reacted to Gastrell's arrival at the farm. He'd called him a menace and rushed back to the village, deliberately avoiding the man for some reason she couldn't fathom. Lottie wasn't at all sure he'd let Gastrell use the village hall. But maybe, as Matthew's friend, she could convince him. 'Don't worry, Mr Gastrell. I've got things to do on the farm, but I'll come down to the village later and ask him.'

'Mrs Gastrell and I will be lodging at the pub,' he replied. 'Come and find us there; I'll go with you and meet the vicar. It pays to know the fellow with a direct line to the man upstairs, eh?'

'I'd say! A very useful man to know,' Lottie agreed, trying to sound enthusiastic even as she dreaded the conversation with Matthew.

Sarah asked Gastrell, 'Will you write about us in your next book?' She gave him a winning smile. 'Junior Nazi-Hunters?'

Gastrell chuckled warmly. 'I might just do that,' he replied. 'You don't sound like a local lass.'

'Not me,' she confirmed. 'London! I was evacuated out here, but we're all just one big gang, doesn't matter where we come from. We've got some of the Polish kids in the gang too, so we're not going to let a German mess about in our clubhouse.'

Gastrell beamed at the children. 'My wife did a lot of work with the Kindertransport, do you know what that is?'

One of the Polish children, a little boy with bright blond hair, nodded so eagerly that his knitted hat almost slid off. 'It's the Jewish children, Sir. They've come here to be safe. Like us!' He gestured at the other children, and Lottie realised he was including the evacuees from London along with his friends who had escaped the brutal Nazi invasion of Poland.

Safe. They've come here to be safe, not stalked by the son of a Nazi butcher.

'Mrs Gastrell's a Jewish lady,' Gastrell explained. 'And though she was born here, she wanted to help the people who share her faith and have been treated so badly. She sets up penpals for the Kindertransport children, so if any of you want to make a new friend, I can ask her to talk to your teachers about joining in.'

'Oh, yes, please!' Shirley replied.

'We'll be their friends,' the Polish boy said, beaming with delight.

Lottie, caught up in the children's joy, nearly volunteered to join in as well.

'What a wonderful idea, Mr Gastrell!' she said. 'See? Nazis don't belong here. We know which side we are on in Bramble Heath.'

And Lottie and Gastrell, and everyone else they could call to their mission, would track down the Nazi. They wouldn't be short of volunteers, Lottie knew. Nobody in their right mind would stand idly by while Hitler's godson was on the loose in Bramble Heath. She just hoped they could catch him before another life was lost to the Nazi war machine.

TWENTY-ONE

Back on the farm, Lottie carried on with her work, going from pen to pen in the cowshed, shovelling hay into the troughs for the hungry animals. The cows eagerly ate up.

'Now, now, Rita Hayworth,' she told one cow, a red Jersey, who was particularly enthusiastic and had shouldered a young heifer out of the way. 'Let Miss de Havilland have some too!'

She wondered what would happen if the Hollywood stars found out that they'd had cows named after them. But really, it was a tribute to the women who looked so glamorous and unobtainable on the silver screen, who gave their audiences a couple of hours of escape from the reality of air-raid shelters, make-do-and-mend and endless meals made from carrots.

The work on the farm, which helped to keep food in Britain's stomachs, never stopped. There might be a Nazi nearby, but Lottie was still a Land Girl and the cows still needed to be fed.

Besides, even now, Constable Russell and the Home Guard were out hunting for him. It wouldn't be long before he was captured, would it?

And yet, as Lottie worked, she couldn't shake the sensation that she was being watched.

She paused and raised her pitchfork. 'If you're here, Fritz, if you've come back, then you must be a fool!'

He was waiting for something, that was for sure. But what? Why wouldn't he show himself? Was he sizing up the farm, deciding who he'd take hostage?

Well, I'm not going to let him. He's not harming a hair on anyone's head if I have anything to do with it, Lottie decided.

Her work finished, she brushed down her uniform and set off with Blossom to the village. They had to walk past the burnt-out wreck of the enemy plane to reach the road. There was only one member of the Home Guard there now; all the others would have been sent off to look for the missing man. He nodded to Lottie, touching his hand to his cap, and she did her best to smile in acknowledgement, though she knew it was a smile that wouldn't reach her eyes.

The wreck was a dreadful reminder of the horrors of the war, the sudden, horrific violence, and she trembled, thinking of Martha again; Martha's last moments as she ran through the dark, the thrumming of the bomber's engines overhead.

Lottie couldn't hold back the sob that rose up in her throat. For Martha, she would help Gastrell find the missing Nazi. For Martha and for everyone else the Germans had slaughtered.

She strode down to the village, fists clenched; if the Nazi jumped out on her, he'd be seeing stars before he had a chance to raise his hand. She went into the George and Dragon to find Gastrell. It was as warm and friendly as ever. A Christmas tree stood by the fire, busy with decorations, and cards decked with snow scenes and robins had been pinned to the wall. Candles on the tables were sprigged with holly and a home-painted banner saying, *Merry Christmas, Bramble Heath!* was tacked across the chimney breast.

She didn't have to look far. Gastrell and his wife were at the bar, with an audience of farmers and airmen. Mrs Gastrell was elegantly dressed, with perfect make-up and a long, thin feather stretching up from her hat bobbing each time she nodded in agreement with her husband's words.

Lottie, suddenly self-conscious in her Women's Land Army uniform, hung back, listening, as Blossom sat close to her feet.

'Now, I don't summon the gentlemen of the press lightly,' Gastrell was saying, not even pausing as he nodded his thanks for a pint that one of the young airmen put on the table in front of him, 'But what I have to tell you all today needs to be on every front page. That's why I'm calling the village together, to get the word out.'

Lottie clenched her fists in her pockets, holding on to the secret that Gastrell had imparted to her in the barn where Hitler's godson had slept. He was here, in the village she had grown to love so much. The village her sister had died for.

Gastrell tapped the ash from the tip of his cigarette into the ashtray beside his glass and went on: 'And for those who ask what harm can one Kraut do, I'll tell you. One Nazi is a link in a chain... With the likes of the Mosleys and their fascist chums out of prison, who knows who our unwanted guest might have in his address book? You're good folks, but not everybody in this country wants to keep Britain the brave, kind place it should be!'

Lottie couldn't suppress her shiver of revulsion at the mention of the Mosleys. She couldn't understand why they'd been freed. It had been all over the papers and on the wireless too. They were fascists, they had supported Hitler. And fascism was exactly what everyone here was fighting against. It was fascist bombs that had killed Martha, as well as Alastair's wife, and left Daisy an orphan. Mosley would gladly ride in an open-topped car with Hitler past Big Ben and Buckingham Palace if the Nazis ever toppled the nation and yet the man had been let out of prison and was only under house arrest. As if staying at home was much of a punishment.

Sidney Gastrell had been to Parliament to lobby for the detention of Sir Oswald Mosley, his socialite wife and their supporters. He had spoken to Churchill himself about the shameless upper-class sympathisers, speaking on behalf of everyone who had been denied a voice by the Nazis. For the people they had murdered in Europe, Gastrell begged the prime minister to put even the most well-connected British-born fascists behind bars.

'Put them back in jail! They're a bunch of traitors!' one of the airmen called and the pub was filled with nods and shouts of agreement.

'Now here's one of us, a warrior on the home front!' announced Gastrell, rising to his feet to greet Lottie. 'Miss Morley didn't let the rat frighten her this morning; she didn't let him stop her doing her duty to keep the home fires burning bright!'

The pub suddenly erupted into cheers and whistles, and Mrs Gastrell's feather bobbed with even more enthusiasm. Lottie grinned at everyone, embarrassed to have become the centre of attention, while Blossom wagged her tail.

'Oh, it was nothing, really,' she said. 'And honestly, I was frightened; I thought he might still be there. But I had my pitchfork – I'd like to see who'd come off worse, a Nazi or a Land Girl with a pitchfork!'

The adulation made her feel brave. She hadn't been *very* frightened, had she? After she'd watched *Went the Day Well?* at the pictures, she had decided she'd be brave too, if the Germans invaded Bramble Heath. And now, one of them had.

'A drink, Miss Morley?' asked Gastrell. 'Or shall we go and meet this reverend?' He looked to his audience and added, 'And once I've got the time for my meeting straight, I hope you'll all spread the word. We want a good turnout!'

Lottie was tempted to accept Gastrell's offer of a drink, but she didn't want to rest on her laurels. Matthew needed to be convinced and she was the woman to do it.

'Perhaps we ought to see the reverend first and you could buy me that drink later,' she suggested.

But Ted, the landlord of the George and Dragon, shook his head. 'Mr Gastrell's tab is on the house,' he said proudly. 'It's the least we can do. You come back in for your drink once you've sorted out the meeting and we'll make sure everyone hears about it.'

No vestige of Lottie's embarrassment remained. She was a friend of Gastrell's now and everyone in the village knew. She stood taller and smiled broadly.

And in a few hours' time, Gastrell would reveal to the village who exactly the missing Nazi was, why he was so dangerous and why it was vital that he was caught.

TWENTY-TWO

The vicarage was in a lane near the church and was a lovely old house built from mellowed stone, the roof a mosaic of mossy terracotta tiles. In the summer, the front garden burst with lavender and roses; mallows and tall hollyhocks would sway in the warm breeze as bumblebees wandered from one bright flower to the next. Sunflowers would peer over the garden wall at the villagers passing by. There were even tomato canes and beanpoles; all the garden's spare space had been taken over to grow food.

All summer long, the front face of the house would be concealed behind a rambling beard of purple wisteria. Now, in the depths of winter, the foliage was reduced to bare branches garlanding the stone walls. But a home-made holly wreath had been hung on the front door, tied with tartan ribbon, and gave it a welcome dash of colour.

Flanked by Mr and Mrs Gastrell, Lottie headed up the path with determined steps. She knew Matthew didn't seem to like Mr Gastrell, but the only way to get the vital message out to everyone in Bramble Heath, as soon as they could, was to call that meeting in the village hall. And the only way to do it was to get the key from Matthew.

'Beautiful house, isn't it?' she whispered to the Gastrells.

'A proper gentleman's residence,' Mrs Gastrell said, with a nod of approval.

Lottie rapped on the front door with its shiny brass knocker. The sound echoed inside the house.

As they waited for someone to answer, Blossom sat neatly on the step, looking up at the door.

'We usually find a sympathetic ear among the clergy,' said Gastrell. 'They care deeply for their country and for ordinary folk.'

Lottie heard footsteps approach on the other side of the door and it was opened by Dorothy Jenner, Matthew's house-keeper. Over her dress she wore a housecoat with a floral print and her greying hair was styled in curls.

'Good afternoon,' she said, staring in amazement at the Gastrells. 'Are you here to see the vicar? Goodness, I'd heard you were in the village, Sir, but I hadn't expected to meet you.'

Lottie smiled at her. 'Hello, Dorothy. Yes, we'd like to see the vicar, if he's not busy. It's very important. This is Mr Gastrell, as you probably know, and his wife.'

'It must be important!' Dorothy stepped aside, gesturing for them to enter. 'Please come in. I'm sure the reverend will be pleased to see you.'

They went into the hallway, which was decorated with Christmas cards on strings of ribbon and sprigs of holly on the picture frames. A large old grandfather clock ticked away the minutes and Daisy's chatter drifted towards them from some-where in the house. Blossom's ears pricked up at once and she strained on her lead.

'Come this way,' Dorothy said and led them down a corri-dor. The rather gloomy Victorian pictures of melodramatic biblical scenes that Reverend Ellis had favoured were gone and

had been replaced with watercolours of the area around
Bramble Heath and a large photograph of Daisy as a baby. She
was sitting on a furry rug, beaming at someone who was lost
over the edge of the frame. With a pang, Lottie realised it
must've been one of her parents she'd been smiling at; someone
Daisy would never see again. But Matthew had evidently done
his best to turn the vicarage into a family home for the little girl
he'd taken on.

Dorothy stopped outside a half-open door and knocked as
Blossom peered round it, her tail wagging. 'Reverend Hart,
sorry to disturb you, important visitors for you. It's Mr Gastrell
and his wife.'

Lottie couldn't help but smile at Dorothy's words. Helping
Gastrell made her important too.

'Hart?' Gastrell said. It wasn't a greeting, it was a question.

As he spoke, the housekeeper pushed the door open,
revealing a room decked for Christmas with holly and paper
chains. There was an advent candle on the mantelpiece and a
small Christmas tree stood in a red felt pot by the French
windows. It was decked with shiny baubles and a pile of
presents waited underneath. Lottie suspected that most, if not
all, of them were destined for Daisy on Christmas morning.

On the table by the sofa were colouring pencils and a
drawing of a tall, long-legged deer wearing a red and white
Father Christmas hat. The wooden bookcase was filled with
what had to be Matthew's books on the Bible, with ribbon book-
marks that dangled over the edge of the shelves, as well as cream
and orange Penguin paperbacks. The lower shelves were filled
with Daisy's; book after book by Enid Blyton, along with *A
Child's Garden of Verses*, *Winnie-the-Pooh*, *When We Were
Very Young* and *Now We Are Six*. None of the books' spines
were shiny and unread; this little family evidently loved to read.

Matthew was sitting on the carpet beside the roaring fire,
Daisy at his side. On the rug in front of them was a jigsaw made

up of large pieces of painted wood. Each bore part of a cheery farmyard scene, the whole cut for child-sized hands. It was perhaps the most relaxed Lottie had ever seen him; but, on the arrival of his visitors, his head snapped up. He reached out and took Daisy's hand, saying nothing. The little girl stared at the visitors, evidently trying to decide what to make of them.

'Reverend Hart,' Gastrell said. 'Hello.'

'Go with Dorothy,' Matthew told Daisy gently. Then he asked the housekeeper, 'Would you mind?'

'Of course not,' Dorothy replied, glancing between the vicar and his visitor. 'Come this way, Daisy. You can help me roll the pastry.'

Matthew kissed Daisy's cheek and she told him, 'We'll make something nice, Uncle Matthew.' Then she scrambled to her feet. 'Can Blossom come too, Lottie? I'll give her a biscuit.'

'I don't see why not,' Lottie said brightly, unclipping Blossom's lead as Dorothy took Daisy's hand. 'She likes baking!'

Dorothy led the little girl from the room, Blossom trotting after them, her tail wagging. Lottie smiled as the trio went out. A smile she wasn't going to lose, even in the face of Matthew's cold reception.

Matthew and Gastrell were looking at each other, each man weighing the other as Matthew reached out for the walking stick that rested beside the fire. As he closed his hand round it, Mr Gastrell finally stepped over the threshold into the sitting room, reaching up to sweep off his hat as he went.

'She's a bonny little girl—' But at the fierce look on the young vicar's face, Gastrell fell silent.

'I'll give you a hand, Vicar,' Mrs Gastrell said, as she hurried towards Matthew. She leaned down to loop her arm through his, evidently trying to help him up. He shrugged her away as though her very touch was fire, jerking his arm out of her grasp and away.

A hostile atmosphere had suddenly invaded the room,

emanating from Matthew. The fire now seemed too hot and the cheery room was stuffy. And Mrs Gastrell's attempt to help had seemed to make it worse.

'I can manage,' Matthew said curtly, levering himself to his feet. 'I don't want you in this house, Mr Gastrell.'

And Gastrell, who had not been at a loss for words until he came into this cosy house, stared disbelieving at the younger man. Lottie could hardly blame him; she'd scarcely believe such rudeness if she hadn't seen it with her own eyes.

'Reverend Hart, I'm sorry for intruding like this,' she intervened. 'I said I'd help Mr Gastrell, and it *is* very important.'

'Get out!' Matthew snapped at Gastrell. He took a step forward. 'You're not welcome here.'

'Please, Reverend,' said Gastrell politely. 'Let's not—'

'Out!' And to Lottie's horror, Matthew raised the stick in warning. Only then did Gastrell replace his hat on his head and give a nod of consent.

'Very well,' he said calmly. 'Very well, Reverend Hart.' He nodded with unflinching politeness. 'Good day, Sir, we won't trouble you any further.'

Lottie wished the parquet floor would open up and swallow her. What had she been thinking, marching into Matthew's home like this, bringing with her a man he clearly despised? But what Sidney Gastrell had to announce to the villagers was so important. And Matthew was deliberately standing in his way. How could he be so selfish? What was the matter with him?

'Matthew, please,' Lottie said. 'We've come to ask a favour, for the sake of the village. We just want to borrow the village hall later, for an hour or so, that's all. Mr Gastrell's got something he needs to tell everyone about the missing Nazi and it's very, very important!'

'Oh, he's good at that,' Matthew spat, his gaze fixed on Gastrell. 'And do you know why? Because he likes people who

fall at his feet. All he wants is to be famous, he doesn't care
about this country or the people in it!'

Gastrell shook his head and murmured, 'I'm sorry,
Reverend.' Then he stepped out of the room and into the hallway. Lottie was impressed by his calm in the face of the vicar's
appalling rudeness. Was Matthew jealous, somehow, of
Gastrell and his courage? 'Well, we'd better find somewhere
else to hold our meeting.' He reached out and took his wife's
hand. 'Come along, Mrs Gastrell, we'll not tarry.'

Mrs Gastrell squeezed her husband's hand. 'Of course.
Perhaps Ted would let us use the pub instead?'

Lottie stood her ground.

'Matthew, please, it's just for an hour or two,' she pleaded.
'The airman's been on my farm and the kids nearly met him in
the woods. People are frightened and it's only right they know
what's going on in their own village!'

'No, no, Reverend Hart doesn't want the likes of us in his
village,' said Gastrell calmly. 'That's his right. But think of your
flock, Matthew; think of Daisy. This has nothing to do with
fame, I promise you. I don't care about all of that.'

'Matthew, Daisy could've been in the woods today with the
kids when they found out the airman had been in their clubhouse,' Lottie challenged him. 'How would you have felt if he'd
still been there, if she'd actually met a Nazi? What if he'd—' She
couldn't bring herself to even imagine what Hitler's godson
would've done to innocent British children.

Matthew regarded Lottie with an expression close to
disgust. His lip curled with distaste and he replied bitterly,
'He'd what? It seems to me that all he's done is try to find somewhere to sleep and some way to dress his wounds.'

'And what of the scum who drop bombs on this country
every night? On little kiddies like that little girl?' asked Gastrell
as he nodded towards the door through which Daisy had trotted

with Blossom and Dorothy. 'Don't be naive. This Nazi isn't an innocent lad, Vicar, he's the worst there is.'

'Oh, he is, make no doubt about it,' Mrs Gastrell joined in, her face pale under the powder she wore. 'Reverend, really, your parishioners need to know. And besides, my husband was capturing escaped convicts before the war. I well remember him out on Dartmoor, in the rain and fog, day after day, after that jailbreak. And who was it who found the men? It was my husband. And ever since the war began, he's been tracking down traitors and making sure the Mosleys and their friends get their due. He's captured airmen who won't hand themselves in. He's been keeping the entire nation safe.' She glanced at her husband and drew in a shaky breath.

'Mrs Gastrell's right, the people in your parish need to know,' Lottie appealed to Matthew. 'The church is the heart of the village, that's what Reverend Ellis used to tell me. I think he would've let Mr Gastrell use the village hall, just like Father Piotrowski's allowed to use the church for the Polish airmen and their families. In fact, I'm sure of it.'

Through the open door, Gastrell and Matthew's gazes were locked on one another. A moment passed before Matthew shifted his attention to Lottie.

'You've been hoodwinked,' was all he told her, then he gave a resigned nod. 'Use the hall, Mr Gastrell, and if the press want to know what I think of you, I'll be happy to tell them.' Then he smiled bitterly. 'But you wouldn't want them putting anybody else's name on *your* front page, would you?'

Gastrell gave a nod of understanding, but no thanks. Lottie couldn't really blame him though; he had endured insufferable rudeness in reply to what was nothing more than a reasonable request. And it made perfect sense for Sidney Gastrell and his dedicated followers to command the headlines. They were hardly lapping up the publicity like film stars, they were using it to draw the public's attention to the dangers on their own doorstep. They'd captured Germans, apprehended escaped prisoners of war and even handed over some British traitors who had been working from within to undermine the home front. It was only right that they were given gratitude for it. The work they did made them famous, but they never sought the lime-light. Their only thought was for their country.

For the sake of their friendship, she smiled at Matthew as amiably as she could. 'Thank you, Matthew. I really— Mr and Mrs Gastrell really appreciate it.'

'We do, we do,' said Gastrell as he held out his hand to Matthew, whose only reply was to turn away. Instead, Gastrell lowered his hand to rest it in the small of his wife's back so he could steer her towards the door. Then he lifted his hat. 'Good day, Reverend Hart. And thank you, Miss Morley. You're a young lady after my own heart.'

Lottie beamed proudly.

As Gastrell addressed Lottie, Matthew turned back towards the room and asked her, 'Would you mind giving me five minutes, Miss Morley?'

'Yes, of course,' she said, and turned to the Gastrells as they headed out of the room. 'Goodbye, Mr and Mrs Gastrell,' she said. 'I'll see you later at the village hall.'

TWENTY-THREE

'I'm sorry,' Matthew said, glancing down towards the walking cane. 'For losing my temper. I shouldn't have.'

'Perhaps *I* ought to apologise,' said Lottie. She was, after all, a guest in his house. And she had hoped to make him feel welcome in the village. So far, they'd done not much more than bicker. 'I know you don't like Mr Gastrell, that much was clear even if I don't understand why, so it wasn't very kind of me to bring him into your house with no warning. Right into your living room, where you were just playing with your niece. I'm not surprised you're angry with me.'

But as she spoke, she realised that Matthew hadn't been angry with her. All his rage had been aimed squarely at Gastrell.

'I've encountered Mr Gastrell before,' Matthew admitted. 'And the only person he's out to help is Mr Gastrell. Oh, he might hunt down escaped criminals and play the man of the people, but he does it because he likes the fame and the money it brings in. *Donations for the cause.*'

'You've met him before? Was that where you were a vicar

before moving here?' Lottie asked. 'Was he trying to catch someone in your parish?'

Matthew shook his head and said, 'Just don't let him take you in. Because after he's wrung out the headlines and moved on to another story, Bramble Heath still has to live with itself.'

'You said I've been hoodwinked.' Lottie lifted her head, catching Matthew's gaze again. 'But I think you're wrong about this. Mr Gastrell is going to help us. Look what he's done, up and down the country. We need him.'

If not for the German bombs and the men who piloted the planes that carried them, Martha would still be alive and they would be living a different life, a life without sirens and death. Without the airman huddled in that lonely station at the tail of the bomber, how many British lads would have come home safe?

'I've no love for the German who came down,' the young vicar said honestly. 'But what reason has he given us to be afraid? What reason other than because Sidney Gastrell says we ought to be?'

'It's the watch I found,' Lottie explained. 'There's a name on it and an inscription. It means we know who this Nazi is. I promised Mr Gastrell not to tell, but believe me, he's really dangerous. A monster.'

'Even so, what harm will he do on his own?' Matthew asked. 'I know what they stand for is evil, Miss Morley, but he belongs in the hands of the authorities. I'm just afraid that people will take matters into their own hands, that's all. But I hope Bramble Heath is better than that.'

'Everyone in this village needs to know what sort of man is out there,' Lottie warned him. 'It's sheer luck that he didn't attack any of us on the farm last night. It's only a matter of time before he hurts someone – or worse.' Why couldn't he see that?

Nothing seemed to get through Matthew's stubborn crust, his determination to be passive in the face of the Nazi threat.

And his rudeness towards Mr Gastrell and his wife really wasn't what Lottie had expected from a country vicar.

'What has Mr Gastrell done to deserve the way you spoke to him, Matthew? What happened when you met him before?' she asked him. 'You loathe the man. I just don't understand why.'

'Nothing happened,' he replied curtly. 'But I know enough about him to know that he doesn't care about anything but himself. And he's very good at convincing people otherwise.'

That simply wasn't the Mr Gastrell who Lottie knew. It wasn't the man in the newsreels, or in his book. It wasn't the man who'd taken a moment to give her his heartfelt condolences, or who did everything he could so that the injured servicemen he worked with could still do their bit.

'We'll have to disagree, I'm afraid,' Lottie told him. 'I honestly don't think he's selfish at all. Quite the opposite.'

Matthew gave a sharp nod. Then, to Lottie's surprise, he asked, 'How's your ankle now?'

'It's fine, thank you for asking,' she replied, lifting her foot and turning it this way and that, demonstrating that all was well. 'Thank goodness you caught me, or I might've cracked my head open!'

When Matthew managed a smile, Lottie was more surprised than ever. It was small, the very ghost of a smile, nowhere near the warmth he reserved for Daisy, but it was a change from his usual glowering presence.

'I was going to make a joke about it knocking some sense into you, but I'm not sure you'd find it very funny,' he admitted. 'And you might decide to knock some manners into me instead.'

Lottie spluttered with laughter. 'I've got quite enough sense, thank you very much! Although not when it comes to bringing someone you don't like into your own home, I'll grant you that. Look, I am sorry about that. But Daisy had a good time up at the farm, didn't she? I hope you enjoyed it, too.'

'Daisy's only stopped talking about it to badger me about playing in the woods with the other children, but I admit I'm too protective to let her do that just yet. When she's a little older. Anyway, how are you feeling now? About the wreck being so close?'

'I'm trying not to think about it,' Lottie admitted. 'Although I do wish they'd take that dreadful heap of mangled metal away. It's not easy having to walk past it every time I leave the farm, it's a horrible reminder of...' *what happened to my sister.* Lottie thought of Daisy, who was at that moment playing in the kitchen with Blossom. That poor little girl. At least Lottie had spent years with her sister; Daisy might not remember much of her parents at all. 'But Commander Seaton thinks he can ask them to hurry up and take it away soon. And... how are you?'

'Muddling through,' he said as the door opened and Daisy and Blossom dashed into the room. Flour dusted the little girl's rosy cheeks and where Blossom ran she left floury paw prints in her wake. 'I was just telling Lottie what a good morning we had at the farm,' he said to Daisy, and then to Lottie, 'Daisy wants to be a Land Girl when she grows up.'

'Oh, I do! I'd love to work on the farm,' Daisy agreed. 'And I want a dog just like Blossom, as well.'

That made Lottie beam with joy. She was so glad to have given the orphaned girl some happiness.

'I'm sure you'd make a wonderful Land Girl!' she said, although she hoped that by the time Daisy was old enough to be a Land Girl the war would be long over and that there would never be another one like it. 'And you know, you two are welcome to visit the farm whenever you like.'

Matthew leaned his weight on the cane and stooped to ruffle the little girl's mop of hair. Daisy grinned up at him. 'Can we go now?' she said.

'I don't know about that.' Lottie chuckled, Daisy's enthusiasm was adorable. 'But you can come another day. When we trim the farm for Christmas, you'll have to come and help. I'd love you to visit us again, and so would Blossom!'

The atmosphere in the room had changed so much, it was almost as if the Gastrells had never been there.

'We'd love to help,' Matthew assured her. Then, as Daisy returned her attention to Blossom, he dropped his voice to tell Lottie, 'Thank you for being so kind to Daisy. She doesn't have anyone besides me, you see.'

And that meant that Matthew didn't have anyone besides Daisy either. What a lonely life his must be; no wonder he could be taciturn.

'It's all right, really. She's got me now, too.' She meant it; it took a village to raise a child, didn't it? And she would gladly help. Lottie smiled at Matthew. 'And so have you.'

She glanced away at Daisy and Blossom, worried she had overstepped the mark. Did that sound too familiar? Would he want her friendship, seeing as they didn't agree on very much at all? But for all that, she felt so drawn to him somehow...

'Thank you,' Matthew said, a smile in his voice at last. 'On behalf of both of us.'

She knelt down to stroke Daisy's soft hair and the little girl's smile of affection melted her heart.

'Anything,' Lottie said. 'Anything at all, just let me know. I'd better leave you both in peace now.'

'Blossom loves you,' Daisy told Lottie as she continued to fuss the dog. 'You're like her mum, aren't you?'

Lottie felt a tug of sadness, to think about how Daisy had lost her mother. But she had her uncle to look after her and he was more affectionate than some parents she'd known.

'And Blossom and her mum have got to go home now,' Matthew said gently. 'But you'll see them when it's time to put the Christmas decorations up.' Then he asked Lottie, 'Will you let us know when?'

'Oh, of course I will,' Lottie assured him as she clipped the lead back onto Blossom's collar. 'It might be tomorrow afternoon, actually, if you can make it?'

'I'll make sure we can.' There was certainty in that answer. It didn't surprise Lottie, because Daisy was obviously her uncle's first priority in life. 'Come on then, Miss Daisy,' he went on, 'let's say goodbye to Lottie and Blossom. Only until tomorrow though!'

Daisy patted Blossom's head, then leaned towards Lottie, who was still kneeling beside her, and planted an enthusiastic kiss on her cheek. 'Bye, Lottie! See you tomorrow!'

Lottie was taken by surprise by Daisy's innocent show of affection and she gave her a fond kiss in return, on the top of her curls. Then she got to her feet. 'Take care, both of you. Until tomorrow!'

TWENTY-FOUR

Later that afternoon, Lottie and her friends led the Shire horses out into the farmyard and harnessed them to the trap. Shona fed them a handful of carrots while they stamped their huge hooves in the cold, the sound of their metal shoes ringing on the cobbles.

Lottie stroked Blossom and told her to be a good girl and look after the farm while they were away. Although she knew that her little dog would just contentedly loll in her basket by the kitchen range; she wasn't much of a guard dog.

Farmer Gosling got into the trap beside his wife and took the reins, while Lottie and the other Land Girls climbed into the back of the trap. It was snug, but at least it meant they'd be warm as the horses jogged them through the lanes, plus by using horsepower Farmer Gosling could save his fuel ration.

The Land Girls had been given pride of place on the trap, but the farmhands and workers were following, some on foot and some by bicycle, all of them keen to be part of Bramble Heath history. The air was filled with excitement and anticipation, and Lottie did her best to smile and join in, but she kept thinking of Matthew's anger when Gastrell had confronted him. And Shona hadn't seemed to be his biggest fan either; yet she had decided to come too. At least then she, and the rest of the village, would hear what Gastrell had to say about the missing man, the information on which he'd sworn Lottie to secrecy.

And once they all knew that Hitler's own godson was hiding in Bramble Heath, they'd be more than glad to have Gastrell in the village to help Constable Russell and the Home Guard track him down before he could do anyone harm.

'He could be in the woods, couldn't he? Or on another farm?' Shona said as they bowled along the wooded lane. She seemed watchful, but more curious than afraid.

Lottie nodded. 'Oh, I'm certain he's still around here some-where. And he needs to be caught and stopped. We're so lucky that Mr Gastrell's here – but Reverend Hart told him he wasn't welcome, and he told *me* that I've been hoodwinked by Mr Gastrell! What's so wrong about wanting an expert on the case, for heaven's sake?'

Nicola shook her head. 'Has he run up against him in the past? I wonder what went on!'

'Reverend Hart did some work with prisoners of war in his last parish,' Lottie explained. 'There was a camp there, you see. I wouldn't be surprised if Mr Gastrell captured some of them and there was a bit of a ding-dong between them. I just can't understand why he's so sympathetic toward Nazis. I imagine he thinks he's doing the Christian thing, but it doesn't sit right with me.'

'He's a daft lad,' Farmer Gosling concluded. 'I saw Mr Gastrell on the front page of the paper last year when he collared that Kraut who ditched up north and pulled a gun out on the locals. If the vicar had had a German pistol pointed at him, he might be a bit less soppy!'

But Lottie wasn't sure about that; something had already happened to Matthew's family at the hands of the Germans.

Something that had left him and his niece with nobody else in the world.

'No, he's lost loved ones, like I have,' she replied. 'But he doesn't think like I do. I think it's more because he's a vicar, isn't it? They're supposed to forgive everyone.'

Although once Matthew knew that this wasn't any ordinary German, perhaps his attitude would swiftly change.

'Happen as the papers'll be there,' said Farmer Gosling, his breath a cloud on the frigid air. 'Mrs Gosling might make a cover girl yet!'

His wife chuckled. 'A cover girl for old farmers, maybe. I could pose like Betty Grable in dungarees!' she teased.

The village hall appeared up ahead. A crowd of people was waiting outside, wrapped up against the cold, flanked by reporters with notebooks and cameras.

'Looks like half of Bramble Heath's here!' Frances observed, clutching her copy of Gastrell's book in her gloved hands. 'It's not every day we get a celebrity come to the village.'

There was a pop and a flashbulb split the air, snapping a shot of the crowd. Night drew in early in December, but people had closed their shops or lodged their children with babysitters just to be here before sunset, to hear what Gastrell had to tell them and still be home in time for the blackout. Even a single flashbulb here in the darkness of Bramble Heath could summon an enemy plane to the village or the airbase on its outskirts, after all.

'Howay, it's like being at one of them Hollywood film premieres,' said Nicola laughingly, glancing back at the farmhands behind them. 'We should've put on our best mink coats, not our duffles!'

'If only I'd worn my sequins!' joked Paddy from his bicycle, and they all laughed, except Shona, who was distant again, lost in her thoughts.

'I dunno though,' Nicola said, pretending to be grave. 'Being rich and famous must get boring eventually. Give me the pigs and a pitchfork any day!'

Constable Russell was standing by the door of the village hall, nodding to everyone as they went in. Captain Spencer, the elderly headmaster of the village school who now led the Home Guard, approached the policeman in his khaki uniform, a swagger stick tucked beneath one arm. It was funny to think that this portly, cheerful man was in charge of the troops who were patrolling the village each night in a so far fruitless search for the downed German. Brave they might be, but most of Bramble Heath's Home Guard were collecting their old age pension and, though the RAF and Polish Air Force boys from the base would help where they could, it seemed as though the fugitive was going to stay one step ahead of them. But not ahead of Sidney Gastrell and his men, surely?

There were men she didn't recognise, cheerfully ushering the crowd into the village hall. Some wore eyepatches, others wore coats with pinned-up sleeves where they'd lost an arm. There was another man in a wheelchair.

'Gastrell's followers,' Frances whispered to Lottie and Nicola. 'All the brave men who were injured fighting – and Gastrell's given them another fight now!'

'Some of the men from his book must be here!' Lottie replied, starstruck. 'The men from Dunkirk, and the Battle of Britain, and the Atlantic convoys. Here, in Bramble Heath.'

Lottie watched as Ewa and her Polish friends went in. After escaping the Nazis' brutal invasion of their country, they had found a sanctuary in Bramble Heath, their husbands fearlessly taking to the skies with the RAF from the local airbase. Ewa nodded to the wounded young men who came wherever Gastrell went. They were all united in the same fight.

'Come on, ladies!' said Farmer Gosling as he pulled back on the reins to halt the horses. 'Let's go and listen to what the gentleman has to say. I feel like I'm in the presence of the king himself... or even Mr Churchill! A true Great Briton is our Mr Gastrell.' He touched the brim of his hat and called, 'Wouldn't you say so, Vicar? A hero in Bramble Heath!'

Lottie was stunned to see Matthew standing at the corner of the village hall, his head bowed as he huddled into his coat against the searing cold. At the farmer's call he looked up, raising the hand that wasn't resting on the handle of his walking cane.

'There are heroes in Bramble Heath every day, Mr Gosling,' he said politely. 'From the Land Girls to the lads who fly from Heath Place. And you too, Sir, keeping the country fed. One doesn't have to be in a newsreel to be a hero, you know.'

Farmer Gosling puffed up a little and said, 'Well, I do my bit, now that I will say.' He gave his wife a nudge and teased, 'A hero, says the reverend, and if the reverend says it then a hero I am. You remember that when you're doling out the porridge portions of a morning, Mrs Gosling!'

'Of course you're a hero,' Mrs Gosling replied. 'You're a regular Errol Flynn, you are!'

Paddy and the other farmhands helped the Land Girls down from the trap. Lottie smiled over at Matthew. Surely he would know that she was wondering why he had come, given his views on Gastrell. Perhaps he just wanted to hear first-hand what Gastrell was telling the parishioners of the village he looked after. And so he should. He needed to know just how dangerous the missing Nazi was.

One of Gastrell's followers, a man in an army greatcoat with an empty sleeve and an eyepatch, came over to them, a swagger in his step.

'Hello, heroes!' he said, evidently having overheard the conversation between Farmer Gosling and Matthew. 'Are you the party from Goslings' farm? Only I've been told to look out for you. Well, with one eye, at least.' He pointed to his patch with a grin. 'Dunkirk, in case you're wondering. Mr Gastrell's reserved Miss Morley a seat in the front row.'

'The front row?' Lottie gasped. Her gaze wandered guiltily over to Matthew. What would he think of her being favoured by Gastrell?

He gave a nod of acknowledgement, then resumed his watchful and impassive manner, silently observing the crowds.

'Dunkirk, eh?' said Nicola with obvious respect for the man. 'Is it right that Mr Gastrell only has veterans on his staff? So's you can all still do your bit here at home?'

The veteran beamed at her. 'That's it, yes! What else are we going to do with ourselves? We've got blokes who were nearly blown to kingdom come, or pulled out of the sea half-drowned, or shot out of the sky. But none of us wanted to just sit back. So here we are, fighting Jerry when he turns up in places like your lovely village!'

'Come on in, Miss Morley, you can jump the queue,' he went on, gesturing for her to come forward, and with a nod of encouragement from the other Land Girls, she hurried into the hall. She was keen for it all to get started. It was time for everyone to know the truth, about who was in their midst. They needed to come together, now more than ever before.

TWENTY-FIVE

The village hall had been decorated for Christmas. A small tinsel tree stood on one of the windowsills and paper chains garlanded the walls, their cheerful aspect contrasting with the serious messages of the government information posters: *Never was so much owed to so many by so few, Careless talk costs lives,* and *Dig for victory!*

The room was packed and the excited audience were already in their seats, keen for Gastrell's talk to start. Lottie looked up at the stage, which was only inches away from her seat in the front row, and then turned to glance back at the rest of the crowd. They were quietening down now, the various excited conversations that had rung through the hall falling into whispers of anticipation. In the audience, she could see people from other farms around Bramble Heath, as well as the blue of RAF uniforms and all the ordinary people who lived in the village too. They all deserved to know what Bramble Heath was up against.

Waiting at the side of the stage were several press photographers. Some were men in heavy overcoats, while others were women who had clearly stepped into the shoes of men who'd gone to war and were now toting cameras and notepads.

How can this be happening in Bramble Heath, our quiet little village?

A murmur of excited expectancy ran through the crowd and Lottie glanced back to where her friends were sitting. She caught Nicola's eye and received a cheeky salute. Reverend Hart was at the back of the hall, seated in a corner, as far from the stage as he could possibly get. His arms were folded firmly across his chest and his face, so boyish when he was entertaining the niece who he cared for so deeply, was hard and tight. Among all of those who filled the village hall, nobody else looked so unhappy to be there as the new reverend.

After a minute or so had passed, the door opened again and Mr and Mrs Gastrell came out into the light. The cameras popped and the audience cheered as Gastrell took his wife's arm and escorted her to a seat on the edge of the stage. She settled elegantly and joined in the applause as her husband stripped off his dark suit jacket and hung it over the lectern. Then he rolled up his sleeves and told the gathered attendees with his characteristic stridency, 'It's good to be among honest, hardworking folk again!'

A loud cheer went up and Lottie was reminded, oddly, of the time she'd gone to the football with her father. Gastrell was the star striker, lining up for a goal, and everyone in the village hall had turned out to cheer him on.

'Good ol' Gastrell!' shouted Farmer Bishop, who was sitting beside her. 'You'll catch that rascal!'

'Yet it's my men who are out patrolling in the cold,' said Captain Spencer pointedly.

'*We'll* catch him! Working with Captain Spencer's Home Guard and Constable Russell and every single one of you,' Gastrell corrected himself benevolently. 'Oh, my name might be the one on the book cover and in the newsreels, but if I could make the publishers and the newsmen do it, every single person who's ever lifted a finger against these rats would have their names there with mine. Believe me, friends, I take no pleasure in being lauded in the headlines! I'm only one man and I need all of you at my side. Not behind me, but beside me!'

Lottie had never heard anything like it. It wasn't the stirring, bulldoggish belligerence of Churchill, nor the ranting, spitting fury of Hitler, but a driving, hard-headed certainty that she knew men like Farmer Gosling would appreciate. Sidney Gastrell on screen was a powerful speaker, but there was a magnetism to him in person that she wouldn't have credited. It was an odd sort of charisma, but a charisma that the people who worked every day on the home front had flocked to in their thousands.

'And with you beside me, we'll give the Nazi what's coming to him!' Gastrell made a fist of his hand, punctuating his words with that fist as he spoke. 'Isn't that right, Bramble Heath? Aren't we fighters, one and all?'

Everyone cheered and whistled again. Lottie was almost on her feet with the force of her applause.

Yes, we're fighters! Even if all I have is a scythe or a pitchfork, I'm a fighter too!

'Let me tell you a bit about why I'm standing here on this stage. Because you've every right to ask what makes me think I can catch the Nazi who's hiding out round these parts,' said Gastrell. 'When I was a lad I always thought I'd be a soldier, but a gas attack in the trenches put a stop to that, so I ended up working in the jails. I was the fellow with the big bunch of keys!'

A cheer went up in the hall, though it was a story that everyone there likely already knew. There was something about hearing Gastrell tell it himself though that gave it a new power.

'And one day, when I came on my shift, I got some bad news,' he went on, all amusement gone from his expression now. 'One of the toerags had coshed a colleague of mine round the back of the head and escaped. He split my pal's skull, killed him. Just an honest man, doing his job, who didn't go home ever again.'

Lottie stared up at Gastrell, impressed that a man who had gone through so much was now standing there right in front of her. A gas attack, a murdered work friend... no wonder he had been galvanised into action.

'But I knew a thing or two about the villain who'd escaped, because I made sure to get to know the lags on my wing,' Gastrell explained, his voice booming across the packed hall. 'And when they get to see you as a mate, not a screw, they'll tell you a few stories. And because he'd bragged about what he'd got up to, the sort of no-goods he ran around with, I knew where he'd be hiding out. Now, maybe I should've told the coppers, but I've never hidden behind anybody else. I went to that filthy corner of south London and I dragged him out of there myself.' Gastrell pounded his fist into the palm of his hand. 'And I was proud to take that scum off the street!'

'And I didn't stop there!' he thundered. 'Before the war, I was bringing in the criminals and no-goods that the coppers couldn't catch – some of them that the coppers were too lily-livered to catch. No offence, Constable, you're one of the good lads. And folks would say to me, "Sid, how come those rascals have more rights than us?"' Gastrell looked around as though waiting for an answer and earned murmurs of agreement from some of the audience. 'Well, I'm here to tell you that no man has more rights than decent, honest folks! I fought for freedom in the trenches of World War One and when I turned out to fight for freedom against Adolf, they said to me' – and here he assumed a toffee-nosed voice – '"Sorry, old-timer, we don't want men of your age, we don't want men who've been gassed." And they said to the men who work with me today, "We don't want you either, with your wooden leg or your glass eye". Well, I do!

We all do! Everybody in this nation of ours can do his bit! And when we're not catching Krauts, we're digging fields or helping families who've lost their houses find a warm place to lay their heads, we're clearing bombsites and watching for fires. Every single man can do his bit, whether he's on the home front or the frontline!'

As the cheers went up again, he bellowed, 'Man, woman and child, you're all heroes to me!'

From the back of the hall rang out an enthusiastic volley of shouts and applause, and Lottie glanced round to see Sarah and her friends, some bouncing in their seats with excitement. Mrs Gastrell smiled benevolently at them, then shone that proud beam on her husband.

Gastrell was full of praise for everyone and Lottie wanted to think of herself as a hero too. But then she thought of Alastair, who occasionally told stories about his time in the navy. There was no doubt that *he* was a hero – he'd run into a burning barn and saved her life – but he hadn't come to Gastrell's meeting, and he'd never stand on stage like Gastrell. Everyone was different, though. Alastair was a quiet hero, but Gastrell's work required a public face.

'And now we come to the reason we're all here,' said Gastrell. 'A few nights ago, while you good people sheltered from Adolf's bombs, one of his planes came down beside Mr Gosling's farm. A farm that people rely on for their food and crops. A farm where decent folks put in a day's toil. A farm where kiddies, evacuated from the city or even from over in Poland, can come and see what life's like in the British countryside. A farm where, not so long ago, a poor lass lost her life.' He settled his gaze on Lottie and said, 'And we all honour her for that sacrifice, Miss Morley.'

Lottie hadn't expected Gastrell to mention Martha. She swallowed back her surprise and nodded to him. 'Thank you, Sir.'

Farmer Bishop inclined his head and whispered, 'We was all very sorry for your loss, Miss.'

Lottie nodded, her heart too full to reply. Gastrell, honouring her sister in front of this huge crowd! She would write home and tell her parents. They needed to know that Martha's death hadn't been forgotten.

'When that plane came down, it claimed the lives of most of its crew. But not all. One of them survived. And he's out there now, running around loose.' He reached into his pocket and withdrew something. From her seat, Lottie could see the watch that she had found, the watch that had been given as a gift by Adolf Hitler. It seemed to carry some sort of evil aura with it now she knew that, as though it somehow contained within its workings some of that malevolence that was stalking Europe even now. 'Sometimes their sort are cowards, yellow-bellies who can't wait to throw up their hands and get three square meals and a comfy bed courtesy of you paying your taxes! But some of them are nasty swine, stealing, terrorising communities, doing what they're told they should do over in Germany. They're not told to hand themselves in, but to make as much mischief as they can. Make no mistake, they'll slit your throat soon as look at you!'

'Then why aren't the newspapers full of tales of downed airmen slitting innocent throats?' Every head in the hall turned, every eye fixing on Matthew as he asked his question in a steady, placid voice. But that voice was strong too, clear and firm as he addressed the hero in their midst. 'I worked with prisoners of war in Yorkshire, Mr Gastrell, and they were more than happy to surrender once they realised they weren't likely to be lynched.'

'We don't like the Bosch, but we're gentlemen, after all,' added Captain Spencer, nodding his agreement. 'Ladies and gentlemen, I should say.'

Gastrell nodded to acknowledge the question and replied,

'Because think of the panic if they were, Reverend Hart. I know what I've seen and I understand why our leaders in Whitehall might not want it splashed across the front pages.' He raised one finger, pointing it skywards. 'But my men and I know what we've seen. And we know the sort of vermin we've hauled in by the scruffs of their sorry necks!'

A murmur of astonishment ran through the audience. There was tutting, too. A cold finger of panic ran up Lottie's spine. It wasn't the threat of the Nazi. It was Gastrell's words. As much as she didn't want to agree with Matthew, he had a point. There was never anything in the newspapers about marauding, downed Luftwaffe pilots.

Gastrell was making the audience doubt the truth. And that was a very dangerous game.

'But this one, this nasty rat, accidentally left us a clue.' Gastrell looked at Lottie again and smiled warmly. Everyone in the hall must have seen it too, she thought, and be wondering what part she had to play in the story. 'Miss Morley, I'm not the sort of fellow who steals someone else's spotlight. Will you join me on stage to tell your tale?'

Lottie froze. *In front of all these people?* She didn't like standing up in front of everyone; she'd hated it at school. But didn't this give her the chance to tell *her* story? To stand on the stage in front of the village and tell the truth. She'd talked so much about doing her bit and now she could do more. She would put aside her nerves because this wasn't just about her, or even just the village. It was about the whole country, and she would do anything she could to protect everyone in it.

TWENTY-SIX

Lottie climbed the stairs to the stage, the applause of the audience ringing in her ears. She stood beside Gastrell and looked out at the people of Bramble Heath, who were staring up expectantly at her. She could see her friends from Goslings' farm, beaming with pride to see her on stage, but her legs felt like jelly and her stomach was filled with butterflies.

'Hello, everyone,' she said, her voice small. She gave a shy wave to the audience. 'I-I found the watch. In the woods.'

Gastrell nodded. 'And this morning, Miss Morley, when you went out to do your bit for the war effort along with all the other hard workers on the farm, what did you find?'

At the back of the hall, Matthew shifted in his seat and folded his arms. He was staring at Gastrell with ill-disguised disgust.

Not far away from Matthew stood Constable Russell, his policeman's helmet held neatly under his arm. He, for his part, was looking over at Gastrell with respect.

Lottie swallowed. 'I-I found a bed. In one of the barns. A makeshift bed made of sacks and hay. And there was blood on the pillow. So it looks as if the airman was sheltering up there.'

'A Nazi!' spat Gastrell. 'Here in Bramble Heath, skulking in the dark, watching the Land Girls as they go about their work. And just this morning, he was in the woods around the den where the kiddies play. *Your* kiddies!'

A gasp of dismay went up in the hall, but Gastrell wasn't done yet. He briefly touched Lottie's elbow and said, 'Thank you, Miss Morley,' before holding up the watch.

Mrs Gastrell rose from her seat at the edge of the stage and took Lottie by the arm. She nodded down to the front row and Lottie realised that Gastrell was finished with her. She didn't protest; she'd never wanted to be on show. She willingly let Mrs Gastrell guide her back to her seat.

As she went, there was a ripple of applause for her from the audience, but she was barely aware of it as she thought over Gastrell's words. Perhaps, if the airman had still been in the barn, he'd *seen* her working, but saying he'd *watched* her made it sound like the man was spying on them, ready to pounce. Even though at the time Lottie had felt as if he had been, now she thought about it, the airman must have been gone from the farm by the time she'd found the bed. He hadn't been watching her at all.

She took her seat again, her hands clammy after her unexpected moment on stage. If only Gastrell had mentioned it before, she would have had time to prepare. She didn't like being forced in front of an audience without any notice.

She looked up at Gastrell. He held up the airman's watch again and the light glinted against it.

'When that plane came down, the tail-end Charlie found himself with a bit of luck,' said Gastrell. 'Because while his mates came down with it, his tail snapped off and hit the trees before it hit the ground. It would've been a bumpy ride, but not a fatal one. And when he made his escape, he dropped his watch. A watch on which there's an engraving.'

The sense of anticipation in the hall was almost physical, as though Lottie could reach out and touch it. On the stage Sidney Gastrell declared, 'Von Brandt!' Lottie shuddered. The Butcher, Hitler's right-hand man. But no one else in the village hall, other than Constable Russell, would know what that name meant. Freddy Carr cleared his throat, filling the silence that had settled. Gastrell turned the watch in his palm and read out, '*Zu mein Patensohn, von Onkel Wolf.* Any German speakers here?'

In the rear of the hall, Matthew replied, 'I have some German. I picked it up when I was ministering to the prisoners of war in my last parish. None of whom had slit anyone's throat.' Then he added, 'But I suspect you know what it says, Mr Gastrell. Stop this grandstanding, tell these people and then go home and leave us all alone.'

Heads had turned to look at Matthew and whispering started up as, Lottie suspected, the good people of Bramble Heath discussed their vicar's animosity towards Gastrell.

'What's the time, Mr Wolf?' some wag in the audience shouted, which cut through the atmosphere and made several people laugh. Then they settled again, the attention on Gastrell once more.

You won't be joking once you know who that watch belongs to, Lottie thought.

'Von Brandt was one of the rottenest apples in the regime; they called him the Butcher because of the sort of things he did for fun,' Gastrell told them. 'He's long gone to meet his maker in France, but he left two sons, each as foul as the father. The first followed his dad to hell last year when one of our brave lads shot his plane out of the sky, but the second... well, this watch tells me that the second son is in Bramble Heath. His name is Stefan von Brandt. And do you know who gave Stefan von Brandt this watch? Who had it engraved, *To my godson, from Uncle Wolf?*' He looked around the room, seemingly picking out each individual member of the audience with that penetrating gaze. 'Do you know who these von Brandt scum call "Uncle Wolf"?' He fell silent for a moment. 'Adolf Hitler himself!'

And all around Lottie swelled the alarmed and horrified gasps of the people of Bramble Heath. The air in the room was suddenly stifling. And they had every reason to panic. A young man who knew Hitler personally, whose father was called the Butcher, was in their midst.

'Hitler's godson? Bloody hell!' Farmer Bishop whispered beside her.

She looked up at the stage, where Gastrell was still holding up the watch. Inside, she was wrestling with a torrent of emotions. She was terrified, yes. But Gastrell was bending the truth when he insisted that the Nazi had been watching her in the barn and he'd never told her she was getting up on stage. Why couldn't he have asked her? There was no way she could have refused, not in front of the whole village, and not when so much was at stake. He'd deliberately put her in an impossible position.

Lottie flinched. The lights were too bright; they made Gastrell look like an actor up there on the stage, playing a part and speaking lines that he knew weren't all true. She didn't trust Gastrell completely. Not any more.

A chair squeaked against the wooden floor. Lottie turned to see Mrs Knapp, Shirley's mother, on her feet. 'Why didn't you tell us before? I would never have let my kids go running about in the woods if I'd known there was some Nazi butcher up there! My little girl was one of the children who found out he'd been in the clubhouse!'

'Now, Madam, don't hold it against the constable or the captain,' said Gastrell benevolently. 'They can only do as their bosses tell them. But in my world, *I'm* the boss and I promise you this: me and my lads will be here in Bramble Heath working with the police and Home Guard every single day until von Brandt is caught. And because I don't believe in keeping secrets from good, honest working folks, I'll be filing reports on the front page of the *Morning Mail* every single day, for all the country to read. What I know, I promise you, everybody in Bramble Heath will know. Everybody in England will know! Let's run this Nazi rat to ground, eh, so he can tell our lads in the War Office all that he knows about Hitler and his cronies!' He turned towards the reporters as the camera shutters clicked and bellowed, 'Let's show him and his devil of a godfather what Bramble Heath's made of!'

TWENTY-SEVEN

The village hall rang with applause and feet drummed against the wooden floor. Lottie found herself clapping, but without the enthusiasm of everyone around her. She felt, suddenly, like a fraud, sitting in the front row. Mr Gastrell's assistant, Mr Gastrell's special Land Girl. But she couldn't get Matthew's words out of her head. He was right. There was nothing in the papers about Luftwaffe pilots slitting throats and even if the press had been told to keep such stories off their pages, wouldn't rumours go round?

It was easy enough – the population was so mixed up, with families split hundreds of miles apart, that if it happened in Yorkshire a Land Girl working there would write home to her family down in Devon and let them know. Even though everyone was warned that *careless talk cost lives*, news like that would spread.

And yet it hadn't.

She looked up at Gastrell, who was so sure of himself, so convinced that what he was doing was right. He believed completely that he had carte blanche to step in and do the work of the authorities and obviously he'd collared traitors and convicts galore. But should he have? Why couldn't he let the police catch them without his help?

Constable Russell and the Home Guard knew the village like the backs of their hands. What help were outsiders who were new to the place, who didn't know the farms, or the woods, the outhouses and the empty barns? And yet the threat of Hitler's godson was real. He was out there, and now the whole village knew, and they wanted action. They wanted to be safe. They wanted Gastrell.

Gastrell raised his hand and motioned the crowd to quieten down. He waited patiently until he could be heard before speaking again. This time, the fierce anger was gone from his voice, replaced by a gentler tone.

'Last year, almost to the very day, our Members of Parliament took to their feet and stood in silence for one minute in memory of all those who had been slaughtered by those butchers from Germany,' he said.

Mrs Gastrell bowed her head and Lottie wanted to reach out and take her hand. To show her that, although she couldn't stop the murders, she had her sympathy for what was happening to her people. The word *murder* couldn't encapsulate the horror of it; Churchill had called it *a crime without a name*.

'Innocent people have been killed in numbers that we can hardly even comprehend. Man, woman or child, it makes no difference to the likes of von Brandt and his sort,' Gastrell went on. 'So I ask you, friends, to stand up and join me in one minute of silence in memory of every decent person whose life has been lost to those gangsters in Germany!'

No one spoke. The only sound was of chairs squeaking against the floor as they were pushed back as the village got to their feet. Lottie stood too. Even if she was beginning to doubt Gastrell's methods, she wanted to show that she cared about the people who had been killed, the people who lived in fear that they or their loved ones would be next.

Lottie stared down at her feet, then she closed her eyes and she saw Martha. She was knitting by the kitchen range, just an ordinary young woman trying to get through extraordinary times. There had been so many other Marthas across Europe, Lottie knew. They would never see peace. Their lives had been stolen from them. And elsewhere in Europe whole towns had gone, memories, history; a whole culture was being wiped from the face of the earth.

Everyone in the hall stood, their heads bowed, as the clock on the hall ticked away sixty seconds. It was the only sound in that little hall until Sidney Gastrell said, 'Thank you, all.' As the villagers resumed their seats he asked, 'Before we close our meeting for the blackout, would anybody like to ask a question?'

Matthew would say something, wouldn't he? Lottie turned in her seat to look his way.

But suddenly Shona was on her feet, in the middle of the hall. Her hands were balled into fists and her blue eyes were wide in her blanched face, staring wildly at Gastrell up on the stage. Around her were the surprised faces of everyone from Goslings' farm. Frances tugged Shona's sleeve, but she ignored her.

'Me. I've got something to say,' Shona announced, almost in a shout. 'I've got something to say to all of you.' She swallowed and glanced around the room as if she was surprised that she hadn't been told to pipe down. 'My brother Jack, he's a pilot. He flies bombers. He's been on raid after raid. And it does something to a man. I've seen him change. He was brave at the start of the war, but the longer it's gone on... he doesn't say it, but he feels guilty. I can *see* it. I *know* him. He's closed up. God only knows how many lives he's taken. I've been worried sick about him.'

Lottie had no idea that Shona had been so worried. Why hadn't she said?

Shona licked her lips before continuing, the hall silent save for her voice, every eye fixed on her. 'Except he doesn't have to worry about that any more. He won't be taking any more lives. He... he...'

Frances held up a handkerchief for Shona, her face ashen, as Lottie rushed her hand to her mouth.

Oh, Shona, whatever is it? Why couldn't you tell us?

'He's been shot down. Over Germany. He's... he's a prisoner of war, in a camp.' She pulled a letter from her pocket and Lottie suddenly realised what the postlady had passed to her that very morning. It hadn't been a Christmas card at all, it had been awful news from home. 'I only found out this morning. I'm out of my mind with worry, my family too. And... and...'

Nicola reached up and touched Shona's hand. 'It's all right, pet,' she murmured gently.

Shona held up the letter, her arm lifted high. 'He was no different from those boys who died at the farm where I work. There's a war on, they get called up, they can't say no. Jack's plane is just a useless heap of scrap too. But he survived. Like the lad who's on the loose. Except my brother's safe. He's in a camp. I know it's hard to understand, but they don't treat the downed pilots like they do all those poor Jews and gypsies, and everyone else the Nazis hate. They're not going to murder him, because he's a prisoner of war and we have to do the same, we just have to, otherwise it all falls apart. But you – all of you...' She held out the letter, pointing it at everyone in the room in turn. 'All of you, you say you want to capture him, but you'd tear that young man limb from limb if you could, I know it. But not me. I don't care who his father is, who his godfather is. I won't have blood on my hands.'

A cold hand seemed to close around Lottie. Shona was right, she would've run at the Nazi airman with her pitchfork without a second thought. And now that everyone in the village knew that he had a monster for a father, wouldn't they do the same?

And yet what if the missing airman wasn't like his father at all? What if he was just a boy, like Shona's brother?

She'd seen the photo of Jack that Shona kept in her room. It wasn't a uniformed portrait taken in a studio. He was standing in front of a shed – an aircraft hangar, Lottie suspected. He looked just the same as the smiling young men in the poster on the wall of the village hall, celebrating the heroes of the Battle of Britain.

He'd pushed his goggles back, on top of his leather helmet, and he was smiling for the camera. He was wearing a lifejacket, a horrible reminder that he might ditch at sea, but his grin didn't show an ounce of fear. His feet were clad in warm, sheepskin-lined leather boots and on the ground beside him was a parachute. The parachute that had saved his life as he drifted down from the sky over Germany.

The other night, in Bramble Heath, another young airman's life had been saved. Slowly, Jack's image in Lottie's mind began to change. The RAF insignia on his uniform merged with that of the Luftwaffe. But that was all. He was still a smiling young man, with hopes and dreams, caught in a war that neither of them had ever asked for.

Freddy nodded and turned in his chair to address Shona. 'The Red Cross keep an eye on them,' he said kindly. 'Your brother'll be all right.' Then he nudged George, who was sitting at his side. 'Isn't that right?'

George gave a brief nod. Lottie was hardly surprised that he didn't have much to say. He must be thinking about Martha too, the girlfriend whose life was taken from her by a German bomb. But George turned to look at Shona as Matthew added, 'That's right, they do. Well done for speaking up, Miss Thewlis.'

Shona nodded and sat down again, the fire that had sent her

to her feet now extinguished. Lottie wished she had been able to sit with her friends as Nicola and Frances hugged her.

'And I'd be happy to talk to you too, Miss,' Gastrell assured her. 'And I'm asking nobody to commit murder, I'm just telling the folks here that he's someone we all need to be very careful of! He's no innocent ordinary German, I can promise you that. Men like Stefan von—'

'You're frightening them.' Matthew rose from his seat as he called out to Gastrell. 'And frightened people lose their heads. We know nothing about this man other than the fact that his father was a monster. His *father*. Not him. Because if you had proof that Stefan von Brandt was a monster too, you'd have told us.' He looked around the hall, at the villagers, who had all turned to watch the young vicar say his piece. 'If you see him, tell Constable Russell, tell Captain Spencer. You can even tell me. I know you're afraid and I understand, but this is a village full of honest, good people. Please don't do anything you'll regret with a cooler head. That's all I have to say. Let your conscience be your guide.'

Everyone was talking at once, voices raised over each other. Bramble Heath was pulled in two different directions at once. Lottie lowered her head and clamped her hands over her ears as she tried to think. Gastrell, on the stage, his voice filling the room, the audience in his thrall, shouting and cheering at every word he said.

And what was that like? Where had she seen it before?

At the pictures. Watching the newsreels. The Nazi rallies in Germany. Thousands of people, riled up with hatred as Hitler ranted and raged. And where had that led? To people being slaughtered by the thousands. Couldn't Gastrell see what he was doing? Was he so determined to get his man, no matter what it took, that he was stirring people up with fear and rage?

No. This is Bramble Heath. We don't hate people. We're better than that. Aren't we?

TWENTY-EIGHT

Lottie was dazed, buffeted by a torrent of people pushing to get to the stage; the whole village, it seemed, was desperate to speak to Gastrell. But she didn't want anything to do with him, not any more. She stumbled through the chairs, desperate to get away.

She barely saw the government information posters on the walls of the village hall, or the paper chains hung up for Christmas. All she saw in her head, on a loop, were the shouting, waving crowds at a Nazi rally, energised with hate.

In the crowd of people she saw Shona, surrounded by everyone from the farm. Lottie wanted to talk to her, but she knew she wouldn't be able to push through the crowd. If only Shona had said something earlier, if only she'd told them how worried she'd been. What a burden for her to have carried in silence.

Matthew was approaching her. He held out his hand and rested it on her elbow as he said, 'Come and get some air, you look ready to keel over.'

Lottie grabbed his sleeve, then let go. She'd refused to

believe him, but now she saw that he was right about Gastrell. 'Yes, some air. It's stifling in here.'

The crowd at the back of the hall was thinning and Lottie let Matthew guide her out through the door into the gathering winter twilight.

'It's all right,' he said soothingly as the cold air hit her. The door opened again and Freddy hurried past, moving at a clip on his way back to the airbase from which he flew Spitfires to defend their freedom. Freddy had survived behind the lines and come back to his girlfriend, Sally. But Freddy wasn't the son of a monster.

She wished she was back at the farm with Blossom, away from all of this, away from talk of Hitler and Gastrell's furious ranting.

'I know it's what vicars always say, but would you like to come and have a cup of tea at the vicarage?' Matthew ventured. 'Nobody needs a humble parish priest with the *hero* and his journalists commanding the stage.'

Lottie had drunk several cups of tea at the vicarage in Reverend Ellis's time. It was a comforting place and Matthew's gentleness was welcome after the anger and fear that Gastrell had drummed up in the village hall.

'I'd love to have a cup of tea, if it's not too much trouble. And *I* need you, even if everyone else is running after Mr Gastrell at the moment,' she replied. 'I'm not. Oh, I *have* been hoodwinked. I feel like such a fool. And Shona... poor Shona!'

'Come on,' Matthew replied kindly. 'Let's go and see what Daisy's been up to. She's the best tonic I know.'

Daisy, that dear little girl, full of joy and innocence. 'I'd like that,' Lottie said. Frances and Nicola had stopped by the door of the hall and were looking back for her. Lottie waved, then pointed to Matthew. Her two friends nodded and Frances gave her a thumbs-up. They understood. She wouldn't be coming home with them in the wagon.

'Your Daisy is a lovely girl,' Lottie told Matthew.

He smiled and nodded as they began to walk, his stick tapping a percussion on the ground with each step.

'Every day, I see her mother and father in her more and more,' he told Lottie with pride and, she could hear, wistfulness too. Daisy had lost her parents to the war, she knew, just as Lottie had lost her sister. 'Daisy's mum was my little sister and she looks just like Emily did when she was her age. And just like her father, Daisy laughs all the time. I don't know what I would've done without her.' Then he shook his head. 'Sorry, that can't bring any comfort to you. It was unthinking of me.'

Matthew knew how she felt, because he had lost a sister too. They had more in common than she had thought.

She laid her hand on his sleeve and this time she didn't jerk it away. 'I don't mind you talking about them. It helps, I think. We can't just stop loving them because they're not here to love any more. I still love Martha. We looked alike, you know, and to begin with, after she first... first was taken from me, I'd look in the mirror to brush my hair and I'd see her. Just for a moment. Just a flash. It made me sad to begin with, but then I realised that part of her was still here, and that's a lovely thing, just as you see Daisy's parents in her.'

The vicarage was just ahead; the wooden gate leading to its garden was never closed. 'Besides, why *shouldn't* you find comfort?' Lottie asked him. 'Why should you be worrying about everyone else?'

'I don't have any family beyond Daisy, you see,' Matthew admitted. 'Emily and I lost our parents a long time ago and Daisy's grandparents on her father's side... well...' And somehow, Lottie just knew. Even before he said it, she knew. 'They were killed in the air raid with Emily, the same air raid that left me relying on this stick. I was in the army before that, doing my bit.'

Lottie glanced at him. The air aid sounded appalling. Three

deaths and Matthew left badly injured, reliant on his stick; three deaths that she realised he must have witnessed. And yet Daisy had survived unscathed.

'I'm so sorry, Matthew, that's awful,' she whispered. 'It's horrible, isn't it – if you don't mind me saying so – when they're taken from you, and you're so close that you could've... I kept thinking I could've done something to save Martha. I felt so guilty.'

Her parents had told them to look after each other; she was sure Matthew would have been told to look out for his younger sister, too. Lottie had felt for a long time that she had let Martha down; that she had died because Lottie had broken her promise to look after her. It had taken her time to realise that it wasn't her fault.

As they made their way up the path to the front door of the vicarage, Lottie realised something. 'But you... you must've saved Daisy.'

'I was out in the garden with her when the siren went. Emily had just gone back inside to help bring lunch out. It was a picnic, to welcome me back,' Matthew replied. 'I'd only got home that morning. I still had my uniform on.' He took a deep breath and blew out a long, shaky sigh. Lottie recognised that sound because she'd made it herself so often; it was the expression of someone trying to keep the grief and memories held in, afraid to let the dam burst. 'The plane came out of nowhere, or that's how it seemed. It can't have been a minute after the siren started – none of them even had time to get out of the house. I told Daisy to run for the shelter when...'

Lottie couldn't imagine it. That something so simple, so unfair as being in your own home rather than in the sunlit garden could mean the difference between life and death.

'I tried to get to them through the flames, but the wall came down on me.' Matthew's voice was small and a long way away. 'And Daisy was there in the shelter. Thank God the neighbours shared it with us or she would've been alone. One of the nurses said it was a miracle that she hadn't been in the house, but I don't think it was. I don't think God would've played a nasty trick like that on a little girl.'

'You were under a wall? Oh, Matthew... but you're right, I don't think God would have either,' Lottie said. She'd asked Reverend Ellis why God had taken Martha from her; he'd told her it wasn't God who'd done it, but Hitler. Lottie suspected that Matthew thought along the same lines and that was, perhaps, why he hadn't lost his faith. And yet Lottie had found it so hard to agree. She was still angry with God, she couldn't help it. 'And... Daisy's father?'

She wasn't sure she should ask, but Matthew was opening up to her and she knew that being able to talk about what had happened helped. It wasn't a secret sadness to be locked away.

'The telegram came while I was in hospital,' he replied. 'He'd been killed on the Maginot Line a few weeks before the air raid. At least they're reunited now.'

'They are,' Lottie whispered, her voice hushed with sympathy. Daisy's father had lost his life with thousands of other British troops, trying to help the French stop the Nazis invade their country. As awful as his death was, at least he had never known that his wife and his parents had been killed. 'It's dreadful, what's happened to your family. But Daisy's lucky, in a way. Because she has a wonderful uncle like you.'

'She had nightmares about the bomb for a long time. She still does, but not as often now. I make sure we talk about her mum and dad and her grandparents. I want them to be a part of her life, even if they can't be here,' Matthew said as they reached the front door. 'But how they died... that's only a little part of it. Because I want her to know that they might not have had long to get to know her, but they cherished her from the first second. From before she was ever born, she was loved. And she's still loved, whether her family is in this world or the next.'

Then he smiled and added, 'That's how I know that Martha's always watching over you too.' His words were filled with gentleness. 'Don't ever doubt it, Lottie, even in your darkest hour. That loving bond that you and Martha share is stronger than anything else, even sorrow. It always will be.'

'I know,' Lottie replied, as another thought came to her. 'Oh, Shona and her brother... I had no idea she was going through all that. I wish she'd told me, but she hadn't told a soul.'

'She did confide her worries in somebody,' Matthew said gently. 'And I don't think she would mind me telling you that she's very glad of all her friends here. She thinks of you all like family.'

Lottie remembered taking the Christmas tree to the village and noticing that it seemed Matthew and Shona already knew each other. She sighed. 'She came to see you about it, didn't she?' she asked. 'I wish she could've told us. She's been so good to me about Martha, I would've listened.'

'And you can all be there to support Shona now,' Matthew replied. 'Just as you have for each other all the way through.'

As they went into the vicarage, the hallway decorated with holly sprigs and Christmas cards and the sound of Daisy's laughter drifting from the sitting room, Lottie turned to Matthew and smiled.

'I'm so glad you've come to Bramble Heath,' she admitted, gazing up at his blue eyes with a lock of his chestnut hair falling into them.

TWENTY-NINE

Lottie was glad to be in Matthew's lounge, with its Christmas tree and decorations. After Gastrell's rebel-rousing speech, it was a comforting reminder of a kinder world. The Christmas cards lined up along the mantelpiece reminded Lottie that this was the time of year for kindness and warm wishes.

As she sipped her tea, sitting beside Matthew on the sofa, Daisy, on the rug, proudly held up her drawing. A girl in a stripy dress with a lollipop head represented Daisy herself and a furry, four-legged character with a pert red tongue was Blossom. Beside them was a reindeer, standing next to a pink present with a purple ribbon.

'I did it for you,' Daisy explained to Lottie. 'Look, that's me, and Blossom, and we're meeting one of Father Christmas's reindeer.'

'That's a beautiful drawing, Daisy,' Lottie said. She put her cup aside to perch on the edge of the sofa and look more closely at the drawing.

'Blossom decided to stay at home today,' said Matthew with a smile. 'It was a bit too cold on her paws.'

Daisy took all this in, nodding, as she listened to her uncle.

'Tell her Daisy says hello,' the little girl told Lottie. 'We're friends, you know. And you're my friend as well.'

She leaned her head against Lottie's knee in a show of affection. What a big-hearted child she was, so friendly and affectionate despite the losses she'd had so early in life. Lottie gently stroked her feather-soft curls.

'Yes, we're friends too,' Lottie assured her, with a smile for Matthew. She was very fond of Daisy and surely Matthew couldn't fail to be pleased that his niece was finding such a welcome in the village.

'Daisy's got more chums than anyone I know since she started going to the village school,' Matthew explained fondly, his tender gaze settling on his niece. 'She's constantly getting invitations to go out for tea. Isn't that right, Daisy?'

Daisy lifted her head and pouted. 'But I'm not allowed to go to the clubhouse in the woods.'

'Maybe in the spring,' said Matthew. Lottie wondered how much of that was to do with the escaped German, but she suspected that in any case Matthew might not feel ready to let his little niece quite so far out of his sight just yet. 'Bramble Heath's welcomed us both. That's why I don't want Gastrell to drive a wedge through the village. Especially tomorrow.' He darted his glance towards Daisy, who had picked up her drawing pad and pencil again, then mouthed, '*The funerals.*'

Lottie hadn't thought of that, but of course the airmen who'd been killed needed to be laid to rest decently. Gastrell probably wouldn't agree.

'Is he trying to stop them from going ahead?' she asked. 'But where else could they go?'

'He hasn't said a word about it,' Matthew admitted. 'Hopefully he doesn't know. It's not something that I've put out around the village beyond the regulars at the church. St George's has some very forgiving worshippers, but I know this sort of thing can provoke strong feelings.'

Lottie sighed. She lowered her voice in case Daisy was listening. 'We've had to do this before, of course, being so close to an airbase. Reverend Ellis told me he'd had a couple of complaints, people saying they didn't want their loved ones lying in the same churchyard as the enemy. But he pointed out that if our boys who don't get back are treated decently out there, then we should do the same here. Besides, they're still human beings. What makes someone an enemy? Lines on a map.'

But what if they were Hitler's godson? What if they really believed in the Nazi poison?

Lottie shook the thought away. It didn't belong in this friendly room where a little girl was playing.

Matthew nodded but when Daisy glanced up at him, he said nothing more on the subject. Instead he slipped down from the sofa to sit on the floor beside the little girl and peered down at her drawing pad.

'What're you drawing now, D?' he asked.

'You and Auntie Lottie,' Daisy told him, as she drew with her colouring pencil.

Lottie got down from the sofa too and knelt on the other side of Daisy. She saw a man with a white dog collar, evidently Matthew in his priestly attire, holding his cane. And next to him was a smiling woman in green and brown, holding a spade. Beside them was Blossom making another appearance, this time balancing a red ball on her nose. A horizontal oblong of green ran across the bottom of the paper and at the edges were buildings that looked like sheds and barns.

'See? You're at the farm!' Daisy explained, gesturing towards her drawing. 'And Blossom's with you!'

'Well, you've made me look very happy,' Lottie chuckled, pointing to herself in the picture.

'You *are* happy,' Daisy replied. 'Because you're with Uncle Matthew.'

Lottie was taken aback. Did Daisy think...? But she was Matthew's friend, nothing more. They hadn't known each other very long. Perhaps that was all Daisy meant. Lottie told herself not to jump to conclusions, especially about an innocent drawing.

'Of course – I'm always happy when I'm with my friends,' she said, and smiled at Matthew.

He returned her smile, his eyes twinkling as he told Daisy, 'And so am I.'

'When I have bad dreams, I get out of bed, grab my pad and pencils, and draw pictures,' the little girl told Lottie, matter-of-factly. 'And it doesn't matter what I draw, it makes me happy again.'

Lottie knew what that meant. Sometimes, at night, the contentment of this little girl was shattered by nightmares of the day her family was taken away from her.

'When I have nightmares, I take Blossom for a long walk in the woods,' she told Daisy. 'And then I feel better.'

Daisy looked at Lottie with surprise, as if she hadn't expected a grown-up to admit to having nightmares. Then her surprise changed to understanding and she patted Lottie's knee.

'Can I walk Blossom in the woods with you too?' she asked.

'Of course,' Lottie replied. 'Just name the day!'

Lottie gladly lost track of time, sitting on the rug with Matthew as they watched the little girl draw. It was a fascinating insight into her life and what was important to her, and it touched Lottie deeply that she and Blossom featured so much in Daisy's drawings, along with Matthew, Dorothy and the children from the village.

At one point, Daisy insisted that Lottie and Matthew help her draw the animals on the farm. Lottie couldn't remember the last time she'd had so much light-hearted fun as they populated the sheet of paper with the animal residents of Goslings' farm.

The harshness of the world outside had retreated, for a little while at least.

Dorothy had already come in to draw the blackout curtains and she reappeared now to let Matthew know that it would soon be time for Daisy's bath.

'I'd better get home,' Lottie said, reluctantly getting to her feet. 'It's been lovely.'

'Let me drive you,' Matthew offered. Lottie was glad of it, with darkness drawing in and the airman out there somewhere.

'That would be smashing, thank you, Matthew,' she replied. 'I really appreciate it.'

She knew he had to be careful – petrol was rationed – but the farm wasn't a long way off. As Matthew stood up, he plucked Daisy up from her perch on the rug and into his arms, lifting her effortlessly even as he put his other hand on the sofa to lever himself to his feet. When he did, Lottie was reminded that, despite the disability that the bomb had left him with, the vicar was still a young man. And a fit one too, it seemed.

'You be good for Dorothy,' he told the little girl indulgently. 'And when I get home, we'll have a story and then it's bedtime. I bet if you ask Lottie, she's going to be doing the same for Blossom. A bedtime story, then all tucked up!'

'Every night,' Lottie told Daisy, grinning because she knew he was teasing her. 'I'm reading *The Tailor of Gloucester* to her at the moment!'

'I liked that one, too, when I was little,' Daisy replied, and with a giggle she buried her face against Matthew's shoulder. 'And we're reading *The Children of Cherry Tree Farm*. It's brilliant.'

Lottie stroked Daisy's curls. 'Goodnight, Daisy. Thank you for showing me your drawings. I'll see you tomorrow at the farm, just like the children in your story.'

Daisy turned to smile at Lottie, beaming. 'I can't wait! Goodnight, Lottie!'

Matthew kissed Daisy's cheek and said, 'Let's hand you over to Dorothy and get Lottie home to Blossom!'

He stooped to put his niece safely back on the floor so she could trot over to the smiling housekeeper, who took her out into the hallway and closed the door behind her. It was just Lottie and Matthew in the room now, the fire crackling in the hearth, the lights low. She caught his gaze and she felt it again, just as she had on the farm when she'd slipped and he'd caught her before she could fall. A connection.

'I don't know what I would've done without Daisy,' Matthew murmured. At the sound of a creaking floorboard from above, he glanced up and smiled. 'She lost her whole world the week before her fifth birthday. Her happiness... her resilience... It humbles me every single day.'

Lottie wondered about this man, what he thought, how he managed to carry on each day after everything that had happened to him. She'd never met anyone quite like him, someone who had been a soldier and now wore a dog collar. Who had taken on his orphaned niece.

'And you care for her, you've given her a home,' she said quietly. Instinctively, she reached for his hand and her fingers trembled as she touched him. But she didn't draw her hand away. 'I don't know if you want to talk about it, Matthew, but you lost your sister and you rely on a cane to get about. It must make things so difficult, things that everyone else takes for granted. You've gone through so much and yet, despite it all, you won't let Daisy down.'

Matthew looked down at their joined hands, then curled his fingers very slightly around hers as he admitted, 'People treat you differently, you know, when you're a soldier. A young man, fighting for his country.' He smiled sadly. 'And now I'm a cripple in a dog collar. And it's not easy to be looked at that way. The sympathetic glances when they don't think you're looking; but the walking stick hasn't changed who I am.'

'You're still brave,' Lottie said, feeling the strength in his hand. 'The way you stood up to Mr Gastrell in that packed hall earlier, full of his adoring fans; that's brave. And moving to a new place to become the new vicar, with Daisy to look after, that's brave too. You're still a soldier inside, you're just fighting in a different way.'

He shook his head and sighed, 'Perhaps I'm wrong about the young man whose plane came down. I don't know, Lottie. But the fear Sidney Gastrell's stoking in this community... frightened people do things they wouldn't otherwise.' Matthew looked to Lottie, meeting her gaze. 'Even if he's the monster Gastrell says he is, I don't want somebody to run a pitchfork through him. We have to be better than those creatures we see screaming hatred in Berlin.'

Lottie tried to swallow her guilt. Hadn't she been all too ready to attack the German? Wouldn't she have grabbed a scythe and run at him?

'You're right, we must be better than them.' She shook her head. 'And I feel dreadful that I got sucked in. That I was a ball of rage and hate. It's not like me, Matthew. It's not. I told myself that of course you could forgive, because you're a vicar. It's what you have to do. But it's not that simple, is it? You've lost your sister to a Nazi bomb as well. But you didn't lose sight of God, like I have. You decided to serve him instead.'

'We have to make a better world than this one,' he said simply. 'And communities like this one are too precious to lose.'

'And that's why you became a vicar.' Lottie realised this only as she said it and her gaze drifted to his snowy white dog collar. 'To make the world a better place. All the fighting, the death... the world feels godless, but then *you* can make people see that God's been there all along.'

She looked up at Matthew again. His simple statement of faith seemed to make him glow in the firelight. He was the voice of a power far stronger than hate.

'It starts here.' Matthew patted one hand to his chest. The other hand was still holding Lottie's. 'And it's more powerful than any weapon. I'd rather this be a world where children play in the woods for fun, not patrol for downed Nazi airmen.'

'I want that too,' Lottie replied. 'More than anything. They've had their innocence taken away, and it's not—'

Just then, somewhere in the street beyond the vicarage, the peace was torn apart by shouting.

'What on earth is going on?' Lottie gasped.

Matthew was already heading through the hallway, Lottie's hand still held in his as they went. When he pulled the front door open, a blast of freezing-cold air flooded the hallway, but that wasn't what made her shiver. Daubed on the wall of the church opposite, the fresh white paint still trickling over the stones, was a monstrous swastika.

THIRTY

There were figures outside the churchyard, the weak beams of their blackout torches dancing in the gathering dark. A chill ran through Lottie at the sight of that appalling symbol of evil, its crooked arms seeming to scrape and dig at the wall it had been painted on. And to think that someone could have painted it onto the side of a church, a place of hope and goodness. She felt sick to her stomach.

She held Matthew's hand tightly as they went through the garden gate and into the street, Matthew hurrying as best he could with his stick. As they got closer, she could make out who the figures were. Constable Russell was standing back, staring up at the streaks of paint, and beside him was Mr Knapp from the greengrocer's and Ted, the landlord of the George and Dragon.

'Reverend Hart!' Constable Russell had turned round and seen Matthew and Lottie arrive. 'I don't know what to say to you, this ugly graffiti on your church.'

'I saw it,' Ted explained, aiming his torch at the swastika, before darting the beam away in disgust. 'I came outside the pub and there it was.'

Matthew was staring at the graffiti, his face stricken. After a moment Lottie saw him draw himself up and he said, 'This is a disgrace. How dare anyone do this?'

Lottie held his hand even tighter. 'Nobody from Bramble Heath would ever do it, I can promise you that.'

'I agree,' Ted said. 'But some blighter did. And they broke into my outhouse and all. One of my regulars told me they'd seen the door hanging off the hinges. Out I go to take a look and someone's nicked my paint. Then I look up and there it is, that revolting scrawl on the bloody church!'

Constable Russell shook his head. 'I don't like this at all. A break-in, graffiti... we've got a Luftwaffe gunner on the loose to deal with and now we've got a vandal on top of that.'

'No, Constable, that's not what you're dealing with!' The voice was that of Sidney Gastrell, who strode round the side of the church with the press pack at his heels. At the sight of the swastika a murmur of astonished anger went through the men from Fleet Street and they all immediately began scribbling in their notebooks. Cameras clicked, but in the blackout, they could use no flashbulbs to illuminate the scene. 'This is no vandal, this is the work of Stefan von Brandt,' Gastrell declared. 'He's not hiding in the woods, he's here with a plan. He's brought Nazi hate right here to Bramble Heath. This is a threat, there's no mistake about it.'

Lottie looked up at the hateful graffiti again and saw, in her mind, the blood on the makeshift bed. If Stefan von Brandt was injured, could he really be the perpetrator? But then again, who else could it be?

Ted and Mr Knapp shook their heads. 'We can't have this,' Mr Knapp said. 'What are you doing to catch him, Constable Russell? He's helped himself to my stock, he's scared the kids, he's broken into Ted's outhouse and now he's done this!'

'I'm doing everything I can, along with the Home Guard,

and now we have Mr Gastrell here and his men.' The policeman smiled at Gastrell. 'We'll catch him in no time.'

Gastrell nodded. 'My men will get this scrubbed clean, Reverend Hart,' he told Matthew. Matthew listened in silence, but Lottie saw his jaw tighten. 'Constable Russell, I suggest you and me sit down with Captain Spencer and get a plan in place for patrolling the village. We've got an airbase not so far away, we don't want von Brandt getting ideas about mischief over there.'

'I don't need your help,' Matthew told Gastrell, but even he must know, Lottie thought, that Gastrell's team of helpers would get the swastika cleaned away more quickly. Besides, whatever the faults of their leader, the men who worked with him were just like Matthew in their way. No longer able to serve on the battle lines, they served their country in plenty of other ways.

Gastrell reached out and briefly brushed Matthew's arm with his hand before drawing it away. 'Please, Reverend,' he said, his voice gentler now, 'let my lads do this for you.'

'I don't want this in the papers,' Matthew told him, but Lottie suspected there was no chance of stopping it. The nation would know about the missing airman and now they'd know about the swastika too.

The symbol on the side of the church had been paraded about at Hitler's rallies, where his audience screamed and yelled, faces contorted with hatred. But she had seen something of this same hatred beginning to swell in the people of Bramble Heath. If they thought Stefan von Brandt had painted the swastika on the side of the church, their fevered emotions would rise even more.

'Matthew,' Lottie whispered, even though she understood his reluctance to involve Gastrell's men in the clean-up. 'It's best that horrible thing's taken off the church as soon as possible. Gastrell's men could clean it off in a jiffy. We don't want everyone in the village seeing it.'

Matthew looked from Lottie to the painted symbol on the wall, then finally to Gastrell. After a moment he nodded.

'Very well,' he said. His next words, much to Lottie's surprise, were addressed to the reporters: 'I imagine you'll put this in your papers but when you do, make it very clear that the men who scrubbed the church wall are men who are serving their country on the home front. We might not know their names as we know his name' – Matthew nodded towards Gastrell, who bowed his head – 'but I'm grateful to them for their service.'

Lottie heard the soldier in him as he spoke, his respect for the men who, like him, had been injured and could no longer fight. The reporters nodded as they wrote down his words and that made Lottie hopeful. They'd do the right thing, wouldn't they? Surely it was better to focus on the good rather than the bad?

'Thank you, Reverend,' Gastrell replied. Then it was his turn to address the reporters: 'I second Reverend Hart's sentiments. When you write this up, you make sure you include them, eh?'

Matthew took a step back. In a whisper, he told Lottie, 'Come on, let's get you home.'

Lottie gazed up at him. Only then did she realise that they were still holding hands, in front of an audience. But in that moment, she didn't care.

THIRTY-ONE

There was barely any light to be seen as Matthew drove them through the village and out into the lanes towards the farm. His muted headlights scarcely broke the darkness of the blackout, but Lottie felt safe in the passenger seat beside him.

'Imagine having lights on at night,' she said, glancing up at the dark walls of the hedges that lined the sides of the narrow lane. 'It seems crazy now, doesn't it, but we never used to think about it before the war.'

'I keep thinking about the airman,' Matthew murmured, as though he hadn't even heard what Lottie had said. 'Hitler's godson... the son of a monster of a father. What sort of a man might he be?'

'Could he be a good man?' Lottie wondered aloud. 'I suppose it's possible. The longer this goes on without him attacking anyone, the less and less likely it seems that he's a monster. And I can't help thinking, that swastika painted on the wall of your church... he's injured, we know he's been bleeding, and he's been out in the cold without food too, so would he really have been able to do it?'

'Not all sons take after their fathers.' Matthew glanced

towards Lottie and gave her the ghost of a smile. 'And even if this one does, he's one man. One man in the freezing cold, with a whole village looking for him.' She saw his jaw tighten. 'And, when Mr Gastrell starts his no doubt lucrative daily newspaper reports, a whole country. If he's going to come into the village to paint graffiti on the wall, he won't be on the run for much longer.'

'How can Mr Gastrell be allowed to do that?' Lottie shook her head, frustrated with the publicity that she now realised he sought. No doubt he believed it was for the greater good, but wasn't it a dangerous game to play? 'Won't we end up with loads of people descending on the village, baying for blood? Who wouldn't, if they had the chance to catch Hitler's godson?'

Matthew nodded. 'That's my fear,' he admitted. 'So much for careless talk. We need to get him into custody, then it's up to the proper authorities.'

'My friend Alastair knows people in the Ministry,' Lottie said. 'I wonder if he can do anything? They'd want Stefan to be brought in safely. Goodness only knows the secrets he could tell. But then again, Mr Gastrell's on their radar. They'll know what he's up to already. I just wonder if it's too late now, what with the press already in the village. The genie's out of the bottle.'

Despite the darkness, Lottie recognised a large oak tree not far ahead, which stood near to the entrance of the farm. She was nearly home, but she didn't want to say goodbye to Matthew.

Nor did she want to see the wrecked plane. The sooner it was taken away, the better.

As the car turned in at the gate, she swallowed, trying to hold back the despair she felt each time she saw the wreck. She wondered now if the Home Guard would still be there on sentry duty or out looking for the missing man. Would they worry about looters trying to steal the scrap metal of the wreck?

She didn't want to look and yet she turned her head towards it, the pull irresistible.

And she saw a figure in the gloom.

'There's someone there,' she gasped, reaching for Matthew's sleeve. 'That's not one of the Home Guard, surely.'

The shadowy figure, barely more than a phantom, had moved so furtively, Lottie knew at once that whoever it was shouldn't be there.

Matthew slowed the car until it came to a stop, the ghostly haze of the shaded headlights piercing the fog that was beginning to roll in from the fields.

'I think it's him,' he whispered. 'It's von Brandt.'

THIRTY-TWO

Lottie's voice caught as she whispered, 'What should we do?'

She peered out through the mist, repelled and fascinated all at once. Hitler's godson, coming to look at the wreck. Perhaps it was the last place anyone would think to look for him. And yet, this was where his friends had died. Was that why he'd come here?

'Wait here,' Matthew whispered, reaching for the door handle. 'I'm going to try and speak to him. My German's not wonderful, but I know enough.'

'I'm coming with you,' Lottie replied. She didn't like the thought of him going out there alone. Although the German hadn't attacked anyone yet, they didn't really know what he was planning, or what he would do when he was confronted. And if the worst happened, what would become of Daisy?

As they climbed out of the car, the silhouetted figure turned and Lottie knew without a doubt that he was looking at them just as they were watching him. A chill ran through her into the depths of her bones as Matthew called something to him in German. She didn't know what he had said, but his tone was careful and polite, if guarded.

Lottie held up her trembling hands, hoping the airman would understand that they weren't going to hurt him. Was it dangerous to be doing this? But they needed to speak to him. If they could show kindness, even in the face of their terror, perhaps they could encourage him to give himself up.

Moment by moment she could see more of the figure as he came closer. He was tall and slim, and he seemed to be wearing a long coat. She realised now that his furtive-looking gait had in fact been exaggerated as he was dragging his leg and she thought of the blood she'd seen on the pillow.

Matthew called out again, this time asking him, 'Do you speak any English?' Then he took a few steps forward, moving slowly towards the phantom in the mist. Lottie wondered where the Home Guard had gone; maybe they had changed the focus of their patrol. After all, protecting the crashed plane from wreckers ought to take second place to bringing in someone whose family sat at the heart of the Nazi regime.

'We're not going to hurt you,' Matthew said. 'Nobody is.'

'We can help you,' Lottie said, speaking carefully. 'You must be cold out here. Hungry.'

Slowly, as though he was moving through molasses, the slender figure raised both hands in a gesture of surrender. Then, across the field and through the gathering darkness, he spoke. His voice was weak and surprisingly boyish, shaking with cold and perhaps the same fear that had gripped Lottie.

'I don't mean any harm,' he called. Though his accent was strong, his English was confident. His voice was that of a young man. 'Please—'

He fell silent and darted a glance back over his shoulder. Lottie had the sudden instinct that, despite the injury to his leg, he was going to make a run for it, or as good a run as he could manage. If he did, the darkness of the woods would swallow him before she and Matthew could get near.

'We know,' she said with desperation. 'We can help you. Please. No one's going to hurt you.'

But as soon as she said it, the words turned to ashes in her mouth. Because what if Gastrell got his hands on him? Or any of his men – or people from the village, for that matter?

'Don't be afraid.' Matthew held up his free hand too. 'If you hand yourself in—'

'I'm afraid.' It wasn't quite a whisper, because it carried on the bitter air, but it wasn't far off. He glanced over his shoulder again, then took another step backwards and turned, and his limping gait carried him into the darkness.

THIRTY-THREE

Stunned, Lottie stared off into the mist after the airman, her heart racing. She took Matthew's free hand and turned to look at him.

'He just looks like a boy,' she breathed, unable to believe what had just happened. 'Just a scared young lad.'

Matthew nodded, his gaze still fixed on the place where the phantom figure had been.

'If he really is as well connected as Gastrell says, imagine what he might know,' he murmured. 'Even as a lad, if he's as close as all that to the centre.'

'And he's hurt,' Lottie whispered. 'What should we do? Constable Russell needs to be told, but what if Mr Gastrell finds out?'

This time, Matthew's nod of acknowledgement was firm. 'He's the last person I want to tell,' he said, unsurprisingly. 'He'll be up here with a lynch mob if he hears about it.' He turned back towards the car as he told Lottie, 'I'll drive you home, then go and see Constable Russell.'

'Thank you. Then you go home and get some sleep. It's cold

out, I think snow is on the way.' Matthew put everyone above himself; someone needed to care about him.

'I don't know what to think about any of it,' Matthew admitted as he opened the car door for Lottie. 'Somebody painted that disgusting symbol on my church. For now, I can only assume we just met the culprit.'

Lottie climbed in, then looked up at Matthew. 'I know. He may be injured, but I can't imagine anyone in Bramble Heath doing it and he's the one with a swastika on his watch. But we just need to do the right thing, so Constable Russell can hand him over, not take our own justice.'

'I'm glad we don't have to make those judgements,' Matthew admitted. He closed the car door and came round to sit in the driver's seat. Only when the door was closed against the cold and he was settled did he speak again. 'That'll be up to somebody in Whitehall, I expect.'

Lottie rubbed her chilled hands together, trying to warm them. 'How do you know if someone's a Nazi? But then you're a vicar, don't you have to trust people and avoid assuming the worst about them? That must be difficult, though.'

'I'm a man before I'm a vicar, though I don't know if we're supposed to admit that.' Matthew's tone was gentle. 'Honestly, there's a part of me that would tear him limb from limb for what his countrymen have done, what they've taken from all of us. But then what about Daisy and Sarah and the other children like them? We have to teach the next generation that violence can't be the answer. I wouldn't want Daisy to grow up thinking revenge is any sort of solution, even if I've been guilty of wanting it.'

The car bumped along the lane leading up to the farm. Lottie watched Matthew's expression as he drove. A vicar who had wanted revenge, when Lottie had assumed he could simply forgive with pious ease. But the losses to his family had been horrendous and Lottie now understood that even a man like

Matthew could not forgive or let go of a desire for vengeance without considerable effort. It wasn't like flipping a switch.

'I think we've all wanted revenge,' she admitted reluctantly. 'When the plane first came down I was shocked, and I was sad about the airmen dying. But when I knew one of them had survived, all this anger came rushing up inside me and I was just full of hate. Because they took my sister from me – they took her future, her dreams. And they took your sister, too. But he didn't look like a monster, just a scared boy. And yet I don't know if we can trust him.'

'Even if he's the man behind the vandalism, he's not responsible for what happened to the people we love,' murmured Matthew, though Lottie wasn't sure if he was trying to convince himself of that. 'No more than he's responsible for whatever his father did.'

'You're right, he isn't,' Lottie said.

Something struck her as she thought over Matthew's words. He'd said something along those lines before, that the missing man wasn't responsible for what his father had done. And there was something in his tone that convinced Lottie he knew personally what that was like.

'I can scarcely think of anything more petrifying than being a tail-end Charlie,' Matthew said as they drove through the night towards the farm. 'Out there on your own, away from your crewmates, staring out into the darkness. It must be like facing into the abyss.'

He tightened his hands on the steering wheel.

'And he's still on his own now,' Lottie realised, blanching at the thought of Stefan's bleak situation. 'We must be the first people he's spoken to in days. And he wouldn't come near.'

'It's no wonder he's afraid,' Matthew said as they drove into the deserted farmyard. 'But it's hardly the weather to be living outdoors.'

'He must be starving hungry; all he's had to eat are a few

biscuits,' Lottie agreed. The thought of those dark, cold woods made her even more grateful that she was getting home now and Blossom and her friends would be waiting to welcome her. 'Have a safe journey home,' she said.

'And we'll see you tomorrow to help with the Christmas decorations.' Matthew smiled. 'Thank you for being so kind to Daisy. I think I probably get very boring for her sometimes, spoiling all her fun and saying no to exciting clubhouse outings.'

Lottie took his hand again. 'I don't think it's boring at all, caring for somebody. It's a precious thing.' She glanced over her shoulder, into the darkness of the farmyard and the fields beyond. 'We don't know, do we, if he's like his father? Or his godfather? It pays to be cautious.'

'Which is why I'll see you safely to the house,' the young vicar said, still smiling, as he climbed out of the car and came round to open Lottie's door.

Lottie got out. 'You're a gentleman,' she said, smiling up at him.

And there it was, yet again. That spark, that connection. Something she couldn't resist. She looped her arm through his to cross the short distance to the farmhouse's kitchen door. The building was dark and silent in the blackout, the curtains pulled tight against the warmth within, but there was the warmth of friendship here with Matthew, protective and comforting in the winter night.

'Safely delivered,' he said lightly as they reached the door. 'Goodnight, Lottie.'

'Goodnight, Matthew,' she echoed. She paused, her hand on the door handle. Without thinking, drawn to him like a magnet, she leaned towards him and gave him a peck on the cheek. Just a little kiss, the sort a friend would give. 'Goodnight. And take care.'

THIRTY-FOUR

When Lottie came in through the kitchen door, she was surprised to see the other Land Girls sitting round the large wooden table. The oil lamp glowed, the only light in the room, illuminating their blue and white stripy mugs of cocoa. A benefit of working on the farm was the milk that they had in ready supply, and cocoa on tap, as long as Mrs Gosling could find Economy Red Label Drinking Chocolate at Mr Knapp's to make it with.

Blossom hopped out of her basket and came over to Lottie for a fuss, wagging her tail. Lottie picked her up and rested her cheek against the warm fur.

Shona's eyes were red from crying and she held a handkerchief balled in her hand, but she was smiling. She was flanked by Nicola and Frances, who leaned close to her. The table was piled with knitting projects, which none of them seemed interested in tonight.

'Shona, I'm so sorry about Jack,' Lottie began as she took a seat at the table. 'And you are the bravest woman I know, standing up in that village hall and telling everyone about him. You deserve a medal.'

'After you were dragged up onto the stage, I thought, *I can get up and say something, too*,' Shona replied. 'I couldn't bear it, all that anger. When that plane came down, I thought of my brother, and... he's just a boy. My brother could've died, and so could the German airman, but they've both been spared. Imagine if a village in Germany, right now, was full of people ranting and raving about Jack? It'd be awful. We mustn't be like that here.'

'I know, we mustn't,' Lottie replied as she stroked her dog on her lap. She thought of the figure in the mist, the lost boy. But he was Hitler's godson. He could still be dangerous. He might have painted that swastika on the wall of the church. 'And Shona, we're here for you. We all look out for each other, us Land Girls, don't we? We'll listen. It's all right to be scared for Jack. It is.'

Frances nodded and gave Nicola a playful nudge as she went over to the stove, where a pan was waiting. She knew, without having to ask, that Lottie would love some cocoa too. 'We do!'

'Well, my nan'd tell you I talk more than I listen,' Nicola admitted with a smile. 'But I'm here for all my lasses, whatever they need. Unless it's elastic. Can't get elastic for love nor money!' She reached out and patted Shona's hand. 'But anything else, pet, and I'm here.'

'Thank you,' Shona said, and rested her head against Nicola's shoulder. 'They said the Red Cross will pass on letters to us from Jack. Once he's written to us, I'll know he's safe. At least he's not out in the elements like this German lad.'

'That's the spirit.' Lottie smiled. 'Look, I know how strange this will sound, but that German lad... Matthew and I saw him. Just as he was driving me back, we saw him by the wreck.'

Shona nearly dropped her handkerchief and Frances banged the milk pan down loudly on the range.

'Saw him? So he didn't go far after sleeping in our barn, did he?' Frances came back to the table with the cocoa and put it down in front of Lottie.

The steam rose from the surface of the cocoa as Lottie warmed her cold hands round the mug. 'And he's just a slip of a lad. But we don't know for sure, do we, if he's any different from his dad, and his godfather for that matter?'

Nicola's mouth dropped open and she whispered, 'What's he look like? A right radgie? A wrong 'un?'

'It was hard to tell, it's so dark. But there wasn't much to him,' Lottie replied. She took a welcome sip of the warming cocoa. 'And it's so cold out there too. Down in the village – oh, it's dreadful, someone's vandalised the church with a swastika. Stole the paint from someone's shed and daubed it on the wall. It must have been him, right? Stefan von Brandt.'

'I expect so.' Frances nodded as she took her seat again. 'I don't even think there's any silly kids in Bramble Heath who'd do it. They know how wrong that'd be.'

Nicola picked up her mug and took a sip, then shook her head. 'I'll tell youse all this, if little Hitler shows his face round this farm again, he'll get a crack on the napper!' She put her mug down on the table with a firm thud. 'Eyes open, lassies! If he's up to making mischief and he's been round these parts already, he might come back. If he does, he'll wish he hadn't!'

'But Nicola,' Shona said, 'what if he's not making mischief at all? He hasn't done anything to the farm, has he? And we don't know for sure that he painted that swastika. I don't know... I just think how awful it'd be if Jack was hiding out in the woods in this weather. Do you think he's scared to give himself up?'

'Maybe,' Lottie replied, recalling what Stefan had said to them. *I'm afraid.* 'Maybe we need to show him that he doesn't need to cause mischief, that he shouldn't be afraid of giving himself up. And we need him to do that, we need him to be caught properly so he can tell our side what he knows. Maybe...' Her gaze wandered the room, past the racks of herbs hanging from the ceiling, the crockery standing ready on the Welsh dresser, to the door of the pantry. 'What if we gave him some food? We must be able to spare something.'

Nicola was listening with a furrowed brow, looking from girl to girl. She asked, 'Before we lay on a buffet tea, don't we need to tell Mr Gastrell?'

'Matthew's gone back down to the village and he's telling Constable Russell on his way home,' Lottie replied, skipping past the fact that she and Matthew had decided that they didn't want Mr Gastrell to know. 'Then the authorities can come and fetch our visiting German away.'

'How long will that take, though?' Frances wondered. She picked up her knitting, but didn't start to move the needles. 'At least Mr Gastrell's men are here now. They can help Constable Russell.'

'Lottie's right,' Shona said. 'We can show kindness, show who we really are, do what's right. And we can leave the authorities to handle the rest.'

Nicola took another sip of cocoa, then nodded. 'Aye, you're right. A bit of grub and a blanket won't do us no harm.' She smiled towards Shona. 'It's no more than we'd want them to do for your Jack.'

THIRTY-FIVE

The next day, Blossom barked her farewell as Lottie left the farm with Shona and Alastair to go to the village for the funerals. Farmer Gosling had been grudgingly understanding; everyone at the farm knew how much the plane crash had affected Lottie, but perhaps the news of Shona's brother had swung the balance needed for him to give the two Land Girls permission to miss their duties that morning.

The girls wore black armbands on the sleeves of their Women's Land Army uniforms. Although Lottie had spent half the night awake, thinking over and over about the link she felt with Matthew, the prospect of the funerals that morning muted her joy.

There were snowflakes in the freezing air and as they headed towards the wreck, Lottie couldn't help but glance at the woods, wondering how Stefan had passed the night. At least he'd have something to eat now and a warm blanket to wrap himself in. Carefully packed inside the basket that she was carrying was a piece of cheese and half a National Loaf, the government-mandated heavy, wholemeal bread fortified with vitamins. No other was readily available. They had added a couple of squares of chocolate, a slice of Mrs Gosling's ration Christmas cake and a bottle of watered-down ginger beer. It wasn't a feast, but it was enough to keep him going. Over her arm, Shona was carrying a clean horse blanket.

'He won't survive in these temperatures,' Alastair said. 'I left a warm coat out in the barn last night in case he came back, but it's still there this morning. He must've stayed in the woods after seeing you and Matthew.'

People were capable of such kindness, Lottie realised, even Alastair, who had lost his wife to a German bomb. He must have seen things in the navy, too, before being invalided out, that she could scarcely imagine, yet he still wanted to show mercy to Stefan.

'Oh, Alastair, that's so sweet of you,' Lottie said. 'You never know, there might be other people in the village who've left things out for him too, like us. Not everyone's like—'

She stopped. Because up ahead was the very man Lottie least wanted to see. If he knew that Stefan had been here last night, then the chances of the authorities getting to the young German with his potential mine of information about Hitler's inner circle before a lynch mob descended would dwindle rapidly. She gritted her teeth.

'Mr Gastrell's back, I see,' Shona remarked, rolling her eyes.

Lottie hadn't needed to tell her that Mr Gastrell had lost his shine for her. The fact that she had come up with the plan to leave provisions out for the downed enemy airman, which Gastrell would never do, showed her change of heart all too clearly.

Sidney Gastrell was standing by the wreck, the soft snow falling against it a contrast to the brutally twisted metal. But instead of hunting down a Nazi villain, he was posing for photographs. The reporters who'd been at the village hall the day before were aiming their cameras at him and Lottie knew this would be the image on the front pages of all the newspapers the next day. Some of his followers were standing nearby, smiling at Gastrell with admiration.

'He's posing in front of a tomb,' Lottie whispered bitterly. 'And we can't leave the provisions here now. We'll have to hide them in the woods and hope Stefan finds them.'

'It's a delicate path to tread,' observed Alastair, looking over at Gastrell. 'People need to be aware, but panic isn't going to be helpful.'

'I don't think he realises,' Lottie said. 'He thinks he's doing the right thing and there are so many people who agree with him that he's not going to change his mind.'

Captain Spencer stood at the edge of the field in his uniform, his arms folded across his chest and his face set with disapproval. At the sight of Lottie and her friends, he lifted his cap as Alastair said, 'Morning, Captain. Are you going to be on the front pages too?'

'I should coco!' huffed Spencer. 'The wreck's being cleared this morning. I'm sure we'll all be relieved to see it gone.' He lifted his cap to Shona and Lottie. 'Good morning, ladies.'

'Good morning, Captain Spencer. Thank goodness we're going to see the back of the wreck soon,' Lottie replied.

Although she knew that, even when the dead pilots were laid to rest and the wreck taken away, there would still be a scar and broken glass in the field where the stricken plane had crashed and where young lives had ended.

Shona took Lottie's hand and gave it a supportive squeeze. It was hard for her to see the wreck too, Lottie knew; it must remind her of her brother stuck hundreds of miles away in his prisoner-of-war camp. Heaven knew what Alastair must be reminded of every day as he walked past it, but he had his sweetheart Laura to share his concerns with now, at least.

Gastrell held up his hand as a signal to the photographers to pause and called out, 'Good morning to you! Miss Morley, perhaps you and your colleague would care to join me in a photograph for these gents?' The journalists looked towards her expectantly, nodding their agreement. 'Let's show the readers the good work of our Land Girls, eh?'

'That'd be a lovely snap,' said one of the photographers in a thick cockney accent. 'And with the Nazi angle... proper beauty versus the beast stuff!'

Lottie looked from the photographer to Gastrell. She shook her head defiantly. 'No. I won't be a poster girl for hate.'

'And nor me neither,' Shona added, her ponytail whipping round as she shook her head.

Gastrell frowned and asked, 'Hate?' He shook his head. 'We don't stand for hate, quite the opposite.'

Shona set her jaw, clearly too angry to speak. Had Gastrell forgotten her impassioned, spontaneous speech at his meeting?

'I'm no Nazi sympathiser,' Lottie said. 'They're evil, they want nothing but hate and death and destruction. And maybe, for all we know, this Stefan von Brandt is just the same as his father. But we don't know that for sure and you were stirring up vicious, dangerous fear in people at your meeting. Or should I say, your rally!'

'Now, just a minute, Miss Morley—' Gastrell began, but Alastair lifted his hat politely, signalling in his gentlemanly way that the conversation was over.

'If you'll excuse us,' he said. Then he gave Captain Spencer a nod. 'Captain.'

Lottie swallowed. What on earth would people think, a simple Land Girl standing up to Sidney Gastrell? But someone had to. They carried on, leaving Gastrell to his posing. As they walked past the wreck and up to the lane, Shona caught Lottie's gaze and smiled.

Once they were out of sight of the crowd who had gathered around the wreck, Lottie spotted a gap in the trees beyond which a cluster of evergreens stood. 'We could pop in there to leave these things,' she whispered. 'Hang on, Alastair, we won't be a jiffy.'

Shona followed her between the bare trunks to the patch of evergreens. Their waxy, dark green leaves would provide cover from anyone glancing in from the lane but, if Stefan was creeping between the clumps of trees, he'd find the basket. Lottie put it down under a branch and Shona placed the folded blanket beside it.

'He'll need it,' she said, rubbing her arms against the chill.

They emerged from the trees and continued on their way with Alastair down to the village through the ice-laden air. In the lane, the snowflakes were beginning to fall faster, covering the hedgerows and speckling their clothes.

Lottie wondered who would come to the funerals, especially since Gastrell's arrival had riled up so many people in Bramble Heath. Would the villagers who weren't his fans feel too afraid to attend in such a hostile atmosphere?

At the sound of footsteps, she glanced along the road that led into the village from Heath Place, the airbase where Freddy and George and their comrades resided. There she saw a scene that she couldn't have imagined: a dozen men or more in the uniform of the British and Polish air forces, walking through the falling snow towards the church where their foes would be laid to rest. At the head of the men was Group Captain Chambers, who would always bear the scars that marked his own catastrophic encounter with the Luftwaffe. Lottie hardly knew what he must have gone through, but Farmer Gosling had told the girls that the officer had been pulled from the flames of his own Spitfire. His face and body had taken a long time to rebuild and Lottie imagined it must have been a painful process, yet here he was regardless of his scars, bringing some of his men to pay their respects.

Following behind them were the pilots of the Air Transport Auxiliary in their dark blue uniforms. Although they didn't fly in combat, the brave young women knew all too well the dangers of the air. Among the group Lottie noticed Sally, Freddy's fiancée, and among the air force men, George.

'I wish Stefan could see this,' Lottie said. 'Then he'd know that we British are decent sorts, that our boys are paying their respects to his comrades even though they're enemies in the air.'

Group Captain Chambers exchanged a friendly nod with Alastair before taking off his cap and putting it beneath one elbow. He greeted Shona and Lottie with a nod.

'Families have lost their sons,' Chambers told them, glancing towards the churchyard, where snow was falling like fleece on the shoulders of the headstones. 'It's right that they're properly laid to rest.' Then he looked to Shona and added, 'I was sorry to hear your brother was captured, Miss. I'm glad you've received word that he's well, though.'

Shona did her best to smile. 'Thank you, he's in fine fettle. All in one piece – we have his RAF parachute to thank for that, of course. And I'm glad we're doing this in Bramble Heath, for the Luftwaffe. Because if Jack hadn't made it, I hope there's a churchyard in Germany where he'd be at rest now.'

'You'd hope so.' George had stepped forward as he spoke. 'But you start to wonder, don't you? People like von Brandt's dad, butchering folk in Europe... Hitler ranting and raving and telling folks to hate each other. And I think about my girl Martha, who went out into the fields to do her job and never came home.' He shook his head and offered Lottie a sad smile. 'But we've all lost brothers here. We've all seen our mates shot out of the sky, so we came to show respect.'

'I know, poor, poor Martha,' Lottie replied. She remembered Martha poring over a knitting pattern book of baby shoes and bonnets. '*Funny to think that maybe one day I'll be knitting tiny clothes for a little George.*' 'She loved you, George. I'm so sorry Hitler took her from you.'

'From us,' George said gently. 'You and me.'

Group Captain Chambers laid a comforting hand on George's elbow and, with a last nod to the party from the farm, the airmen turned towards the church.

Lottie looked up at the ancient stone walls and grimaced as she recalled the sight of the ugly swastika, its broken arms daubed on the old building only the day before. But there was nothing there now. Not even a shadow of it to show that it had been there. Gastrell's men had done a good job, she couldn't deny it.

The snow went on falling, the soft, white flakes covering the grass between the headstones, and garlanding the dark boughs of the yews and the firs that bordered the churchyard. Snow had settled on the tower and the church roof. All it needed was a robin perched on a branch of the holly tree that leaned over the churchyard wall and it would look like a Christmas card.

Matthew stood at the church door, greeting the attendees as they entered. He looked up at Lottie's approach and gave her the briefest of smiles, a secret shared between them. Then he took Group Captain Chambers' hand and shook it, exchanging a few words with him before he and his party went inside.

Standing by the church porch, waiting to go inside with the other mourners, was a man Lottie didn't think she'd ever seen before. Snowflakes were gathering on his fedora and the wide shoulders of his well-cut overcoat, and he was watching everyone through narrowed eyes as they headed up the path to the church.

'He looks familiar,' Shona said, nodding towards him. 'But I can't remember where I saw him.'

'I wonder who he could be? He looks very official. A man from the Ministry, maybe?' Lottie replied. She looked over at Alastair. As a Ministry man himself, maybe he knew.

'It's to be expected, with German airmen and British vigilantes making the front pages,' Alastair said placidly as he raised his hand to greet his fiancée Laura, who was waiting for him.

'Especially given the atmosphere Mr Gastrell is intent on creating.'

And where were Gastrell's men? A few had been up at the wreck, watching their leader with obvious pride, but most weren't. They were patrolling, Lottie imagined, out looking for Stefan. How she prayed that he would surrender, or be found by the authorities, before they captured him and possibly treated him to their own kind of justice.

Laura looped her arm through Alastair's and smiled gently at him. As they reached Matthew, standing solemnly at the door in his purple robe, Lottie desperately wanted to reach out for his hand and hold it. Performing the service wouldn't be easy for him and the additional pressure of having Gastrell in the village, ramping up people's fears, made it even more difficult. But she couldn't, because no one else knew how close they had become.

'Hello, Reverend Hart,' she said with a friendly smile. 'How are you?'

'Very well,' Matthew replied warmly. 'Thank you for coming, Miss Morley. I hope you're well.'

'Oh, yes, thank you. And I wanted to come,' she replied. 'I wanted to pay my respects. There's nothing sadder than a funeral that nobody goes to.'

'Miss Thewlis, thank you for joining us,' Matthew said to Shona. 'And for speaking out yesterday. How are you feeling today?'

'I feel better now that folk know,' Shona replied, with a determined nod. 'Thank you for listening to me ramble on about my woes, Matthew. This village is lucky to have you.'

'It's a lovely place to live,' Lottie told him. 'And I'm so glad you're here, too.'

Then, with another smile for Matthew, she and her friends continued on into the ancient stone church, where Stefan's crewmates waited in their simple coffins.

THIRTY-SIX

The organist had softly played 'Silent Night' as the mourners arrived, a reminder of what the two countries shared, rather than what tore them apart. Lottie's father had told her that during the first Christmas of the last war, an unofficial ceasefire silenced the guns and shells, and the troops had left their trenches to sing the carol together in No Man's Land.

Ranged along the ancient stone windowsills were candles, some brand new and others burnt down to stubs, brought out especially for Christmas. The figures in the stained-glass windows glowed; Christ as the Good Shepherd with his flock reminded Lottie of the farm. The Good Samaritan in the next window tenderly cared for the brutalised traveller, but, taking quite a different attitude, on an embroidered banner by the time-worn tomb of a long-dead knight was St George, his spear raised, ready to plunge it into the scaly dragon that reared up at him.

The Christmas tree Lottie and her friends had brought down from the woods stood by the altar rails and a nativity crib had been set up, the porcelain figures surrounded by real straw spared by one of the farms. Lottie's gaze wandered over to it and she thought about Stefan sheltering in the barn, like the Holy Family had done all those years before, because there had been nowhere else for them to go.

The pews of the church were filled with young men in RAF blue and young women in the dark blue of the Air Transport Auxiliary. But there was hardly anyone else from the village there. Apart from Lottie's group, the only people out of uniform were those who attended church at least once a week without fail. They were a cross-section of the village; old ladies wearing felt hats and whose lavender perfume scented the church, one of the farmers with his wife, who helped with the collection every Sunday; some of the older farm workers, and a handful of young women born and bred in the village. They were the faithful, who had refused to let Gastrell's words of fear turn them from Matthew's message of love.

She turned back to watch Matthew, a young man presiding over the funerals of four other young men. She saw the pain and sadness in his eyes; inevitably he would be thinking about the sister he had lost, but she hoped too that it would bring him solace, just as it did her to be there. Anger never solved anything; treating the dead airmen with respect, even though they were the enemy who had taken their loved ones, was a powerful act of forgiveness.

Here in the quiet contemplation of St George's, Lottie listened as Matthew read the service. The air was still and peaceful despite the sorrowful occasion and she became aware of how relieved she was that Sidney Gastrell was occupied elsewhere. These would not be the first enemy airmen to find a resting place on British soil; Bramble Heath's churchyard had been dug over for their comrades throughout the years of the war, just as men from Bramble Heath would have been laid to rest in German churchyards. She wondered at what the families of these four men thought, if they even knew what had become of their sons. And what about Stefan von Brandt's mother? Surely she was worried that there was no news about her son since his plane had gone down?

'Glory be to the Father, and to the Son, and to the Holy Ghost...' Matthew intoned, but Lottie didn't hear the rest of the service.

How loaded those words now sounded, *father* and *son*. Stefan's father had nailed his colours to the mast of an evil ideology and his son, who maybe carried the same hatred in his heart, was hiding somewhere in the woods near the village. At the behest of his godfather, millions had died, and many more likely still would. And, because of his comrades, Martha was gone.

Sidney Gastrell thought he was doing the right thing, capturing a dangerous young man, and she understood why. But surely there had to be a better way to do it, without turning themselves over to hate and violence. Just as any film star knew how to show off their favourite angle, Gastrell knew instinctively how to play to the flashbulbs and newsmen. And he understood, just as Hitler did, the devastating power of fear. It was a dangerous game to play and it had cast a shadow over the welcoming village which Lottie had come to love.

The airmen from RAF Bramble Heath lifted the simple coffins onto their shoulders and bore Stefan's crewmates down the aisle of the church and out into the churchyard. Lottie and her friends followed the coffins out, Lottie holding tight to Shona's hand. Although she tried not to, inevitably she kept thinking of Martha's funeral, the bouquet of wild spring flowers on the box that contained all that was left of her in this world. She reached for her handkerchief to wipe away her tears.

As Lottie came outside into the frosty air with her friends, she was aware of figures waiting in the churchyard, a scatter of snowflakes whirling in the breeze around them. She wiped her eyes again and, with a shiver of disgust, saw who it was: Gastrell and his men. And with them, people from the village. Mr and Mrs Knapp must've left their shop in the hands of an assistant in order to come. Lottie recognised farmers and their workers. Older, grey-haired men who'd fought in the Great War, their medals pinned to their overcoats. Wives, and mothers, whose men and boys were away from home, risking their lives in Europe and Asia to fight evil.

And they certainly hadn't come to pay their respects.

'God save the king!' Gastrell barked like an order and suddenly the silent churchyard was filled with the voices of Gastrell's followers and the villagers who had turned out to support them, every one of them joining in to sing the National Anthem.

Lottie was dimly aware of the well-dressed stranger she had seen in the porch at her side and of his jaw tightening. He said nothing, just set his gaze on Gastrell as they passed. Gastrell was singing louder than anyone, his tone one of withering disrespect, as he watched them pass. Matthew, however, didn't even look at him. Instead, he continued to lead the way to the freshly dug graves, refusing to give the interlopers so much as a glance. Lottie wasn't sure what the correct response to such a display as this was, but his dignified silence seemed to say so much.

One by one, the coffins were lowered into the ground as Matthew spoke the words of the service over them. Gastrell and his supporters carried on, now singing 'Land of Hope and Glory'. How dare they disrupt a funeral, of all things, with their misplaced patriotism? If the young men who were still in uniform could show respect, why couldn't Gastrell and the people who followed him?

But Lottie knew that they believed they were doing the right thing, that they felt these young men who had died in

Bramble Heath simply didn't deserve respect. By loudly displaying their patriotism, they were showing that they were making a stand against Hitler; *they* were on the side of goodness.

Lottie watched Group Captain Chambers scatter soil over the coffins as the ceremony came to its end. How Matthew had done it she couldn't imagine, but somehow he had managed to ignore the noisy singing and conduct the dignified service for the dead men. Around him, the airmen of Britain and Poland saluted the fallen Germans and, as they did so, the singing stopped. To her surprise, Gastrell's group stood back as the mourners filed away from the graves.

Lottie held back, not wanting to abandon Matthew to face the singers alone. She hoped he'd understand that she was there for him.

Matthew was the last to leave, following in the wake of those who had come to the church to pay their respects. When he drew level with the group of singers, he stood patiently, his hand resting lightly on his cane, as he waited for the song to finish.

When it did, one of the old men, who Lottie had seen raising his glass in the pub to the airmen, lifted his head proudly. He told Matthew, 'You didn't expect a choir, Reverend, but you got one.'

'Very true on both counts,' said Matthew calmly. Then he drew in a deep breath and nodded as he took in the scene. 'Today I have buried four young men in nameless graves. Four young men who have left their families behind to die on foreign soil. They're fighting for a monstrous regime, nobody denies that, a regime that murders and hates without reason. But we should be better than that. Whatever these men stood for, whatever they've done, they'll be judged by a higher power, but we owe it to ourselves and to this village, which has welcomed everyone who needed a refuge, to give them a peaceful and respectful funeral.'

The old man touched his medals and looked from Matthew to the top of the church spire, where his gaze settled. It seemed to Lottie that that he was mulling over Matthew's words and was perhaps wondering if he'd been right to disturb a funeral after all.

'Do you think they'd do the same for our boys?' a woman challenged, the black netting of her hat casting her face into shadow. Lottie had seen her at the tea room before, gossiping with her friends. 'Do you think those beasts would bury my sons with dignity if they were slaughtered over there? And yet you've done this, in Bramble Heath!'

'I don't know if they would. I hope so, but I don't know,' Matthew replied. 'But that's why we're going to win this war, Mrs Wheeler, because we don't blindly follow where Hitler leads. We do things with respect and humanity. We need to treat them the way we would hope to be treated.'

Mrs Wheeler pursed her lips, but she didn't reply. Instead, she turned her attention to Sidney Gastrell. Lottie wished she knew what the other woman was thinking. Were Matthew's words breaking through the anger and fear that Gastrell had drummed up in the villagers? Maybe, *maybe*, she was asking herself if blasting out patriotic songs at a funeral was the right thing to do after all.

'The men deserve a burial,' said Gastrell. 'But they don't deserve ceremony. When I was in the trenches, no German turned out to mourn the British lads they mowed down in no man's land. No Germans are mourning the Jewish folk they're crowding into trains and camps and slaughtering in their thousands.'

Matthew was calm as he said, 'I know. But we're not in Germany, Mr Gastrell. And that's precisely why we will continue to show proper respect to the dead.' Then he looked to the villagers again. 'Thank you for coming, all of you. I hope when you go back to your homes you'll reflect on what you've done this morning. Good day.'

And Matthew turned and walked away from Gastrell and his supporters without a second glance. In fact, it was as if they weren't there at all.

THIRTY-SEVEN

Daisy, who had been at home during the funerals, skipped her way to the car, holding on to Matthew's hand. Her ever-present toy rabbit swung in her grip and her copy of *The Children of Cherry Tree Farm* poked out of her pocket.

Lottie had said goodbye to Alastair and Laura, who were staying in the village. They had both looked shocked by the actions of Gastrell's mob, yet they reserved smiles for Matthew, who had been so brave in the face of angry provocation.

'I'm going to put holly up in the milking shed. The cows will like that, won't they?' Daisy announced, then she beamed at Lottie and Shona in their Women's Land Army uniforms. '*And* I'm going to be a Land Girl when I grow up!' she told them proudly.

'I'm sure you will!' Lottie replied, as they climbed into the car. She sat next to Daisy and put her arm round her shoulders, holding on to the little girl. She smiled at Matthew. Daisy must give him so much joy, with her innocent chatter. With any luck, by the time Daisy was old enough to be a Land Girl the war would be over and the Women's Land Army would be a thing of the past. But that wouldn't stop the little girl from growing up to work on a farm if it was what she really wanted.

There was a friendly closeness now between Lottie and Matthew, but the memory of the peck she had given him on his cheek came back to her and she blushed. He'd been so brave, earlier, taking a stand against the villagers. He hadn't been angry or rude, he'd merely stood his ground. As Lottie thought back to it, she felt butterflies flit in her stomach.

But it was nothing. She was just proud of her new friend, that was all.

As they drove up to the farm, Daisy was full of excitement at the prospect of being back in what had seemingly become her favourite place in Bramble Heath.

The woods loomed up ahead, just at the turning for the farm, and Lottie peered into the trees as they passed. She hoped Stefan had found the food and was warm in his blanket. But he couldn't go on hiding in the woods, could he? Especially not as the snowflakes kept falling, getting thicker by the hour.

Her gaze roamed to the wreck. But it wasn't there any more. Her heart tugged at the sight of the scarred earth and the fragments of the plane – small pieces of metal, shattered glass – that were too small to be collected. Eventually, the grass would grow over them and there would be little to remind anyone of what had happened there. And yet Lottie knew that, every time she saw this spot, she'd see the shadow of the wreck in her mind.

But her gloomy thoughts soon vanished as Daisy bounced up and down with excitement. Blossom rushed out of the kitchen door into the yard as the car arrived, barking and wagging her tail with glee. Daisy was even more thrilled, and as soon as they climbed out of the car, she was fussing her new friend, energetically rubbing Blossom's tummy.

'Come in, come in!' Mrs Gosling said cheerily from the doorway, beckoning everyone inside. She grinned at Matthew. 'I've never had a vicar trim my house for Christmas before!'

'We're very grateful to be invited,' Matthew told her warmly. He glanced up at the iron-grey sky and added, 'I'll be surprised if we don't have snow for Christmas.'

Farmer Gosling was crossing the yard, a heavy bale of hay carried in both arms. Despite his burden he paused to welcome the visitors and, with a fond look at his wife, said, 'When I was a lad we trimmed on Christmas Eve and not a day before. But Mrs Gosling has chewed my ear right off and won the day. *Trimmings up today*, she said, and who am I to argue? Tradition means not a lot to these ladies, Vicar.'

'But I love Christmas!' Mrs Gosling replied. She pulled a sprig of holly from the pocket of her apron and brandished it at her husband. 'And we need to cheer ourselves up at the moment. If that means decking the halls before Christmas Eve, then so be it!'

'Sadly, Mrs Gosling, I have a farm to run,' said her husband with a chuckle. 'Now get this little lass indoors before she gets frostbite. You make sure they do as they're told, young Miss Daisy. And you too, Vicar, don't put up with any nonsense.'

'Howay!' called Nicola from the open door of the farmhouse. 'You're letting all the heat escape. Come on in and let's get this place looking canny for Christmas!'

Daisy bounded into the farmhouse, Blossom beside her. The little girl's eyes were wide as she took everything in; the treats that Mrs Gosling had baked, and the decorations laid out to trim the farmhouse. Mrs Gosling switched on the radio, filling the house with Christmas songs as everyone busied themselves trimming the house.

Soon, there were paper chains garlanding the walls and Mrs Gosling's precious glass ornaments were nestling among the branches of the tree that stood by the sitting room window. A row of brass angels were ranged along the mantelpiece and every picture frame and mirror got its very own sprig of holly.

Even though the farmhouse was full, each time Lottie

caught Matthew's gaze she felt that connection again. Her heart skipped, and for the briefest moment she felt as if everyone else had disappeared. He felt it too, didn't he?

'Now who's going to put the fairy on top of the Christmas tree?' Mrs Gosling asked, her words breaking in on Lottie's thoughts.

She knew exactly who would get that honour; their guest who had the same mop of golden hair as the tree topper.

'Daisy, I don't suppose you'd like to?' Lottie asked her.

Daisy nodded, then glanced to her uncle as if asking for permission to accept such an honour. 'Can I, Uncle Matthew?'

Matthew made a pantomime of considering the request, then gave a very definite nod. As he told her, 'You're the only girl for the job,' he swooped down to pick up his niece. 'Even Blossom agrees!'

The little dog was at Matthew's feet, eagerly wagging her tail, her gaze fixed on Daisy.

Lottie carefully took the porcelain fairy, in her delicately mended tulle skirt, from her tissue-paper box and passed her to Daisy. The little girl took the fairy in her small hand, then stretched as far as she could towards the top of the tree, where she placed the ornament with great care.

She gasped in awe. The fairy was a little wonky on her post, but it didn't rob her of her magic. Then Daisy giggled. 'It's really Christmas now!'

'About time an' all!' said Nicola and laughed. 'Back home, we'd have the paper chains up in July if our mam would let us. Good work, Daisy, you're a cracker!'

'I'm going to be a Land Girl, too,' Daisy proudly told them all. She pulled her book out of her pocket to show them. 'I've been learning all about farms, you see.'

The girls crowded round the book and Lottie glanced at Matthew, who looked pleased to see that his niece had been so warmly welcomed on the farm.

'Let's have a read together before you go home for your tea?' Nicola asked, casting a glance towards Lottie and Matthew. She gave them a wink and said innocently, 'Why don't youse two go and start shutting the blackouts?'

'Yes, why not?' Lottie chuckled. Nicola could see the spark too, couldn't she? 'Come this way, Matthew, I'll show you the ropes.'

She lightly touched his elbow and in that brief contact felt as if the world had stopped turning. She led the way out of the lounge and into the empty farmhouse kitchen. One of Mrs Gosling's creations was in the oven, filling the room with the scent of sage and rosemary, garnishes she grew in her garden.

'I think, well, I *hope*, that earlier, when you stood up to Mr Gastrell's choir, you were getting through to people,' Lottie told him. She took his hand. 'Or starting to, at least. You were so brave to do that.'

Matthew looked down at their joined hands. 'We've all had to be,' he said simply.

'You especially.' Lottie's gaze fell for a moment on his stick. 'You've kept going, even in the face of so much... so much loss.'

'I had to, for Daisy. I don't know how I would have managed without her.' He glanced towards the door, where his niece's laughter could be heard, dancing on the afternoon air. 'She's the reason for everything I've done since that day.'

'She's so happy, clearly so well cared for,' Lottie observed, holding his hand more tightly. 'And that's all down to you. You're an inspiration, you know. To show compassion for Hitler's godson too, after everything you've been through. Shona and I left some food out for him, and a blanket. We hid it in the woods near the wreck. I hope he's found it. I hope he starts to realise that we're actually not such a bad lot in Blighty. Maybe it'll give him a change of heart?'

She looked up at him. His face was very close to hers when

he said, 'I think we're quite a nice lot on the whole. You, especially.'

He was smiling; just a little smile but, despite everything, it was there. She sensed something change between them.

He likes me. He actually likes me!

'And you're just smashing,' Lottie whispered. Not quite sure of what she was doing, she brought her lips to Matthew's and gave him a gentle kiss. He returned it with unmistakable passion, any trace of tentativeness ebbing away.

How lucky they were to have found this bright, golden moment in a world that had grown so cold.

THIRTY-EIGHT

'I ought to get Daisy home.' Matthew's words were soft and the thought was lost in another kiss.

Lottie kissed him back, not wanting the moment to end. But it had to. She reluctantly drew her lips away from his. At any moment, someone might come in and disturb them in the kitchen and she was sure that Matthew would want to tell Daisy that they were sweethearts before anyone else knew. 'I know. You don't want her to be out in the blackout, or in the cold.'

'She'd stay here all night if she could,' he admitted. 'She loves the farm almost as much as she loves the deer or the idea of that mysterious clubhouse in the woods.'

'I think she might be ready to move in.' Lottie beamed at him, her hand still caught in his. 'You know, perhaps I could come back to the village with you? When we were on paper-chain duty, she was telling me about some books that Sarah's lent her and she wanted to show them to me. I could come and look at her haul of Enid Blytons and help tuck her in, if you like?'

'I won't be able to bring you home,' Matthew explained

regretfully. 'The petrol coupons are getting a little bit stretched. And I don't want you out on your own after dark.'

'The girls were talking about going down to the George and Dragon for a drink,' Lottie told him. 'I can walk back with them. A gang of Land Girls is quite a fearsome sight. Enough to make any German quake in his boots.'

'In that case, Daisy and I would love you to come home with us.' Matthew beamed. 'I don't think even Hitler would tangle with Nicola!'

'She'd soon sort him out!' Lottie chuckled.

After rounding up Daisy and Blossom, Lottie and Matthew headed out to the car. Nicola stood at the door and called, 'Don't forget, Miss Lottie Morley, we'll be in the George and Dragon whenever you're ready. We'll all walk back up to the farm together.' And there was another of those cheeky winks, this one for Matthew. 'Don't you worry, Vicar; if she dinnae show up, we won't grass you up to the bishop!'

'I don't know what you mean,' Matthew said innocently as he opened the car door. 'I'm a stranger to your farming ways!'

They headed down to the village. The snowflakes were still falling in the fading afternoon light, but little of it had settled yet. A white Christmas would be lovely, Lottie thought, but then she reminded herself about Stefan. For his sake, and all the secrets he held about the Third Reich, they couldn't have snow while he remained hiding in the woods. An injured man wouldn't survive the plummeting temperatures for long.

But what if, even now, he'd already gone to the village to give himself up? Lottie hoped so.

'Thanks so much for coming,' she said to Matthew and his niece. 'Daisy, you did an excellent job with the decorating, and Matthew, you weren't too bad either!'

'Oh, high praise indeed!' Matthew chuckled. He glanced towards Daisy, who was bouncing her toy rabbit on the palm of her hand, Blossom sat next to her, watching intently. Seeing

Daisy was occupied, he asked Lottie in a whisper, 'What do Land Girls do in the evening for fun?'

Lottie leaned a little closer to him, enjoying their secret. 'Well, once we've put the sheep to bed and hosed down our muddy boots, we collapse in a heap in front of the radio! Or...' She was sure he was hinting at taking her out, that there would be future evenings together. 'Or, those of us who are lucky enough to have one – we meet up with our boyfriends.'

Matthew beamed. He darted another glance towards Daisy and confided, 'You're always welcome to call by. I don't go far once Miss Daisy is safely tucked up.' Then he gave an innocent sort of shrug. 'Just in case you're ever at a loose end.'

'Oh!' Lottie grinned, pretending to be casual, even though her heart was drumming wildly. *He likes me! He really likes me, and he says I can call by!* 'Well, I might just take you up on—'

A figure on slender legs ran from the woods across the path of the car.

Caught by the muted blackout headlamps, the deer flashed by in a second, then was gone, swallowed by the dark trees on the other side of the frosty lane.

'A deer!' Daisy cheered, hopping up and down on her seat, as Blossom gave an excited bark.

'Just Prancer,' said Matthew. 'Making sure you're still on Santa's nice list.'

'Am I?' Daisy asked hopefully.

'I'm certain of it,' Lottie told her, turning round in her seat to take Daisy's hand and affectionately squeeze it. 'Isn't that right, Matthew?'

Matthew nodded. 'You're at the very top of it!' he announced. 'Blossom and Bunny are second. Do you think Lottie's on there too?'

Daisy nodded. 'Of course, and *all* the other Land Girls are, too. Father Christmas thinks they're marvellous, you see. And you're on there, as well, Uncle Matthew.'

Lottie chuckled. 'I'm glad we've all made it on to his list! I wonder what presents he'll be bringing us on Christmas morning?'

She glanced at Matthew's profile as he drove and her heart leapt. Because she knew that Father Christmas had already brought her the perfect gift.

As they drove down the high street, Lottie saw Constable Russell standing outside the George and Dragon, writing in his notepad. His expression was grave as he talked to Ted, who was in his shirt sleeves even as snowflakes speckled him. The landlord's fists were clenched and he scowled as he looked up and down the street.

Was Constable Russell trying to find out more about the theft of the paint from Ted's outhouse? But why was Ted so angry, scoping everyone who passed as if he was out for revenge?

The policeman looked up from his notepad. Seeing Matthew, he rushed out, raising his arm to flag him down.

What on earth had happened now?

THIRTY-NINE

As Matthew pulled up at the kerb, Lottie flipped open her window and leaned out.

'What's up?' she asked the policeman.

'Our vandal's been busy again,' Constable Russell told her tiredly, tapping his pencil against his notepad. 'He's done in the pub.'

'My pub, the village's pub!' Ted shouted, jabbing his finger at the George and Dragon. 'The place our boys have a drink in before they go off to risk their lives for this bloody war! You know this pub is the last place some of them ever saw before they took one of Jerry's bullets? Mr Gastrell's staying here, too – the Nazi thinks he's clever, thinks he'll have a go, he'll dare to taunt the man who's come to catch him.'

Matthew leaned over and asked, 'What's happened?'

'It's all right, Ted, we'll get to the bottom of this.' Constable Russell laid a calming hand on his shoulder. 'Well, Reverend Hart, it's like this. Someone's smashed the windows in, round the back. And there's another of those awful swastikas painted on the wall. Must have done it last night, after we'd all gone to bed. A right mess they've made, too! It's the Nazi, all right, mark my words, creeping about at night and committing an outrage!'

Lottie glanced back at Daisy, who was playing with Blossom, showing the dog her rabbit. She didn't seem to be listening too much to the adults' conversation.

'Oh, Ted, I'm so sorry,' Lottie said, turning her attention back to the men. 'And after they broke into your outhouse, too. Is there anything we can do to help?'

'Thanks, Miss Morley, but nope,' Ted replied, toning down his anger as he spoke to Lottie. 'We'd been shut today, see, and I hadn't seen it until now. Anyway, Mr Gastrell's men got the buckets and mops again and cleaned up. And one of them was a glazier before the war, so he's made sure it's all tight until we can get it fixed up proper.'

'If you need anything, you'll let me know?' said Matthew.

'What we all need,' said Gastrell as he strode out of the pub, 'is to bring in Adolf's pal. I've got a few ideas up my sleeve though – he won't last long. Not with Bramble Heath joining our search.' He slapped Ted's shoulder. 'Mess with the village pub and you've messed with the wrong folk, eh?'

Lottie had tensed at the sight of Gastrell and she sensed Matthew bristling beside her. Daisy looked up too, staring at him with large, wondering eyes.

Ted's face lit up, reflecting Gastrell's confidence. 'Too right, Mr Gastrell. Mess with a village pub, and you mess with the whole of Britain.'

Gastrell stepped forward and stooped, offering Daisy a friendly wave. 'Are you looking forward to a visit from Father Christmas, young Miss?' he asked her kindly. Matthew's eyes had narrowed, but he said nothing, no doubt in consideration of his little niece's feelings.

'Yes,' Daisy replied, still staring at Gastrell as if she couldn't work out what to make of him. Then, in a teasing tone, she asked him, 'Because I'm on his good list, you see. But I don't know if you are, though. Are *you* good?'

Gastrell looked thoughtful before he said, 'I hope so. I do my very best. Merry Christmas to you, Miss.' Then he lifted his hat and said to Matthew, 'She's a credit to you, Reverend. And to her parents.'

Matthew said nothing, but sat back in his seat, his face ashen. In silence, he started the engine and drove them away from the pub.

Lottie didn't try to start a conversation but she knew what he would be thinking. That the village would be even more stoked with fear and would demand revenge. And who would stand in Gastrell's way now? What his ideas were for bringing Stefan in, she didn't want to guess. And yet she knew what was going through everyone's heads because exactly the same had gone through hers not so long ago. Fear, anger, a desperate urge for retribution after four years of war. Four years of senseless death.

But when they arrived at the vicarage, a lightness filled Lottie. It was home, for a small but loving family. As she sat at the fireside with Matthew, Daisy proudly showing her the Enid Blyton books that Sarah had lent her, Lottie wanted to hold on to the moment for as long as she could. The small hands turning the pages, the warmth of the fire, Blossom curled like a cushion in front of it and Matthew's gentle smile.

It was getting dark outside and Dorothy came in to close the blackout curtains. She paused, staring outside.

'Good heavens!' she called. 'You've got to see this!'

Lottie looked up. There in the gathering dusk, out on the lawn, which was turning white from the snow, was a family of three deer.

Daisy was on her feet at once and ran towards the window, Matthew and Lottie in pursuit. The little girl planted her palms against the glass and gazed outside in wonder.

'It's Prancer again!' she called, as two of the deer cropped the tufts of grass with their soft mouths. The stag, with branching antlers, stood guard, staring straight at his audience behind the window. 'And Dasher and Vixen.'

They stood as long as they could, the light dimming, until, at a sound that no one in the vicarage had heard, the deer turned as one and ran away, melting into the dark edges of the garden. Finally, Dorothy drew the blackout curtains and they went back to Daisy's books. Then, after cocoa, and Dorothy's miniature gingerbread puddings, it was time for Daisy to go to bed.

Lottie hadn't helped put children to bed since her cousins were little, but she stood by Daisy to make sure she brushed her teeth and checked the temperature of the warm water so it wouldn't scald her as she washed her face.

Daisy's bedroom was bright and light, with pink curtains across the window hiding the blackout curtains and a matching pink quilt on the white-painted wooden bed. Multicoloured paper chains garlanded the walls and a small army of soft toys waited at the foot of the bed for their friend. A ragdoll with strands of orange wool for hair sat on a small chair, another of Enid Blyton's books on her lap, as if she'd been interrupted reading it.

It reminded Lottie of the bedroom she'd shared with Martha when they were children. She swallowed down the jabbing sensation of loss and reminded herself instead of how happy they'd been, how cared for, in a space that was just for them.

On top of a chest of drawers, there were two photographs in silver frames. One showed a family at the seaside, leaning against a metal railing with a pier marching out across the water behind them. It was a sunny day and the breeze had caught the young woman's hair, which she had reached up to brush away from her face. Her beau looked smart beside her in his suit and his open-necked shirt, beaming into the camera as he balanced a little, chubby-legged girl in a sun bonnet on his hip. Beside them was an older couple, grandparents on the family holiday. The older man had looped his arm round the woman's waist as she leaned her head playfully against him.

The other photograph showed a woman on her own, taken in a studio against a painted backdrop of a garden. She looked to be around forty and had her head tipped slightly to one side and her hair in the horizontal waves that had been so popular a decade before. At the square neck of her dress she wore two angular sparkly clasps.

And Lottie realised there was something of Matthew and Daisy in her face. Maybe it was her gentle smile or the glitter in her eyes, or just the angle of her head, she wasn't sure, but she looked like an older version of the young woman holidaying in the other photograph.

Lottie knew she was looking at photographs of Daisy's family: her grandparents and her parents, all lost to Nazi bombs. Only the little girl had survived. And in the other frame, alone, was Matthew's mother. Where was his father? Perhaps, she thought, as with so many families, Matthew had lost his father to the trenches, or the cold seas off Jutland where the British Navy had suffered so many losses.

Daisy got into her pyjamas and settled in her bed. She smiled up at Lottie and Matthew in the glow of her nightlight.

'I've had a brilliant day,' she told them with a yawn. 'And it'll be brilliant tomorrow too!'

'Nothing but brilliant days for my Daisy,' Matthew said and smiled, then kissed her cheek tenderly. Blossom sat neatly at his side, wagging her tail as she watched the little girl start to drift. 'Sweet dreams until tomorrow.'

'Uncle Matthew,' Daisy said, her nose wrinkling in a way that Lottie had come to realise heralded a question. She stroked her rabbit's ears as she went on, 'Uncle Matthew, who was the man we saw? The one who asked me about Father Christmas?'

Matthew stroked Daisy's hair from her face and assured her with a softness that Lottie knew concealed his true feelings, 'Nobody. Just someone who's visiting the village.'

'Oh!' Daisy gasped. She smiled up at them. 'Just like Jerry the German!'

Lottie glanced at Matthew. She knew about him then, the downed airman, the man her friends had gone off hunting for in the woods.

Matthew swallowed and asked, 'Jerry the German?' He glanced towards the window, but there was nothing to see but the blackout curtains. It stood to reason that Daisy would have heard, Lottie realised now. All of the children in the village were filled with excitement about the missing Nazi, whether or not Matthew would let Daisy join the hunt. 'Who's that?'

'The German. The Hun!' Daisy giggled, as if she knew she'd said something she shouldn't. 'He crash-landed on the farm and he's creeping about like the bogeyman. He might be hiding under the bed!'

'I don't think he'd hide there,' Lottie promised her, trying to keep her tone level and hide her worry about Daisy having nightmares. 'There's dust under the bed. You'd hear him sneeze.'

Matthew fell to his knees beside the bed and peered beneath it, beckoning for Blossom to do the same. After a few seconds, he and the dog both lifted their heads again and Matthew told his chuckling niece, 'No, nobody there!' He kissed her cheek again. 'And nobody will be. There's nothing outside either, except Santa's reindeer, keeping an eye on you to make sure you stay safe. Just like Mummy and Daddy and all three Gramps, keeping watch from their photos.'

Daisy lifted her head and gazed in the direction of the

photographs. She kissed her fingertips and waved to the sepia figures frozen in time in their silver frames.

'Goodnight, Mummy and Daddy, and Granny and Gramps, and Nana Hart,' she whispered fondly. 'Sleep well.'

Instinctively, Lottie reached out and stroked Daisy's golden hair. She'd been through so much in her short life and yet she could remember her lost family with joy.

She glanced at Matthew, knowing that Daisy's happiness despite such awful loss was down to him. She caught his glance and smiled. His gaze was so warm, so affectionate that Lottie felt her heart leap. Then he whispered, 'Night-night, Daisy-doo,' before he touched Lottie's hand and nodded towards the door.

Daisy's eyelids began to droop and she yawned again, before turning her head to one side and drifting off to sleep.

Lottie took Matthew's hand and they crept across the bedroom as quietly as they could, Blossom padding softly beside them. They went into the corridor, leaving the door ajar behind them. It was quiet in the house, so quiet that the only sound Lottie could hear was the steady tick of the grandfather clock in the hall downstairs, like the house's heartbeat.

Suddenly, there was a sharp knock at the front door.

FORTY

By the time they had reached the bottom of the stairs, Dorothy had appeared and opened the door. Although the light was off to avoid breaching the blackout, the snow outside gave its own glow and Lottie realised it was the strange man she'd seen at the funerals earlier.

The man she had thought might be from the Ministry.

He had the firm jaw of a matinee idol and his watchful eyes were shadowed by his fedora's brim. He wore a wine-coloured scarf, wrapped round his neck with the ends tucked into his overcoat, and leather gloves. Despite the lack of light in the hall, Lottie could tell he was well dressed. He wasn't wearing wellingtons, but polished lace-up shoes. He certainly didn't look like anyone from Bramble Heath.

She curled her hand more tightly round Matthew's, wondering if she should still be there.

'Good evening, Sir,' Dorothy said. 'Is it Reverend Hart you're looking for?'

'Morley and Hart, to be precise,' he replied. 'Not a music hall turn, despite the name.'

Lottie turned to look at Matthew. She could understand

why he'd want to speak to Matthew, but why on earth did he need to talk to her as well?

Matthew barely had time to acknowledge the question before the man spoke again. 'Wyngate, Ministry. Miss Morley, Reverend Hart, show me to the sitting room. Mrs Jenner, you'll excuse us?'

How on earth does he know my name?

She looked up at the square-jawed man. His dark eyes were narrowing as his steely gaze bored into her. He was tall and broad-shouldered, every limb tensed with latent strength.

'Of course, Mr Wyngate,' Dorothy said, standing aside so he could come in.

Wyngate stepped over the threshold as Matthew cleared his throat and said, 'Thank you, Mrs Jenner, I'll deal with our visitor.' He looked Wyngate up and down, clearly stung by the stranger's curt dismissal of the loyal housekeeper. 'Follow us, Mr Wyngate.'

And he turned, touching Lottie's arm briefly before they made their way through into the sitting room. Blossom followed, her bright eyes taking in the stranger with curiosity. Wyngate looked out of place in the soft light cast by the fire and the lamp by the armchair. His black overcoat seemed to have brought the night-time indoors with him, as if he was a man who was far more used to shadows. Although the red of his scarf seemed to be a concession to the season, it was as if he came from a world that was far too serious to have time for trivial things like Christmas trees with strings of fairy lights, or paper chains and piles of gifts.

'I'm sorry, Mr Wyngate, but perhaps you could be a little clearer about who you represent?' Matthew asked. 'Which ministry?'

In reply, Wyngate gave a disbelieving bark of laughter and shook his head. He leaned one elbow against the mantelpiece, his gaze moving slowly across the room.

'Even Churchill wouldn't dare ask that,' he murmured coolly. 'I've come to talk to you about Stefan von Brandt.' And as he said that, he settled his gaze on Lottie again. 'He seems to have taken a shine to the two of you. Nobody else has laid eyes on him.'

Now that Lottie could see him in the light, an odd feeling washed over her. She realised, now, that she'd seen him before the funerals too, but she couldn't place him at once. Where on earth would she have seen someone like him? But then, hadn't Alastair come to the farm with someone from the Ministry before he'd moved in? She'd been busy and hadn't had much time to speak to them. As she looked back at Wyngate, she realised that had to be it.

'Alastair's very well, by the way,' Lottie told him.

'I know,' he replied without a flicker of emotion. Then, to her surprise, he said, 'I'm sorry for your loss, Miss Morley. And yours too, Reverend Hart.'

'Thank you,' Lottie replied. Even though Wyngate had seemed cold, he had expressed his sympathies. And he was, Lottie was sure, friends with Alastair, so he couldn't be all bad.

Matthew nodded and said, 'Thank you,' before adding, 'We saw him for just a minute or two; I reported it to Constable Russell right away.'

Wyngate nodded calmly, looking from Matthew to Lottie and back again. 'Our very own Rudolf Hess, although a good deal less theatrical, I think. And hopefully less of a handful,' he added, though not without the barest hint of good humour in that otherwise emotionless voice.

Rudolf Hess. Hitler's heavy-browed right-hand man, who'd flown to Scotland in a Messerschmitt in a deranged attempt to take Britain out of the war. And for his troubles, he'd ended up with a broken ankle and prison.

'We barely saw him. He's injured,' Matthew told Wyngate.

'My concern is that Gastrell's whipping the villagers up into a mob.'

'So, our young German visitor has made contact,' Wyngate said. 'How's his English? Or your German, Reverend, after your sojourn with our Yorkshire POWs?'

How does he know that? Lottie tried not to let her surprise show. But then he'd known that she and Matthew had both lost family to the war. What else did Wyngate know about them?

'He spoke good English, as far as I could tell, as he didn't say much,' she replied, trying her best to be helpful. 'Only with a very strong accent. I suppose he hasn't had the opportunity to get much practice with British people.'

'It's better than my German,' Matthew said. 'But it was him. He was at the wreck site. The Home Guard—'

'The Home Guard have found their attention diverted,' said Wyngate. 'Because Saint Sidney has ridden into the village on his white charger and tried to whip up a lynch mob along with his book sales. The Home Guard, therefore, have other fish to fry. I'd like the young man brought in before he's strung up, hence them being on increased patrol.' Then he gave a long sigh. 'But our German is annoyingly good at playing the phantom.'

As though he could scarcely tolerate such a perfectly reasonable occurrence as the patrol not being at precisely the same location as the man they were looking for, Wyngate gave another sigh. Then he prowled across the room and settled into an armchair before the fire.

'Shot out of the sky by his own people,' he said. 'Göring sent in one of their aces to be sure of the kill. VIP treatment, Third Reich style.'

Freddy and George had said the same, only they seemed to think that it had been a tragic accident, friendly fire because another German pilot had lost his head for a second. Instead, Göring, who ran the Luftwaffe and was one of the most powerful men in Hitler's camp, had made the order to shoot down a plane filled with his young German countrymen.

'He signed their death warrant!' Lottie exclaimed with disgust. 'But why? What purpose does it serve, trying to murder Hitler's Nazi godson if you're also one of his best mates?'

'He isn't.' And Wyngate, so granite-faced, so steady in tone, said that with all the casual acceptance of a man saying that he didn't take sugar in his tea. He even gave a little shrug, as though to suggest that surely it was obvious, that of course Stefan von Brandt, son of a Third Reich murderer, godson of Hitler himself, wasn't a Nazi and how could anybody who thought otherwise be so utterly absurd as to believe it? 'His father and brother certainly were; the mother might as well grow a little moustache and start wearing jackboots. But von Brandt Junior... no, not him.'

Then Lottie saw the light catch Wyngate's wristwatch. And something occurred to her.

'The watch I found in the woods... the strap wasn't damaged,' she said. 'It didn't fall off. He *took* it off, didn't he? Threw it onto the ground, because he didn't want anyone who found him to know how close he was to Hitler.'

'It was a stupid thing to do,' said Wyngate coolly. 'He's barely eighteen years old, it's a stupid age. The question is...' He steepled his fingers beneath his chin, his tone growing more thoughtful. 'What to do about it?'

'You have no doubts about this?' Matthew asked. 'People are frightened. They think there's a madman on the loose.'

And Wyngate smiled. 'There is,' he replied. 'Saint Sidney can scarcely be called *normal*, can he? One or two excellent collars, but the fame's gone to his head.'

Matthew nodded and gave a shaky breath, then muttered, 'It did a long time ago.'

He had clearly been following Gastrell's career for some time and Lottie wondered why Matthew was drawn to a man he clearly loathed. Perhaps it was just because it was impossible to pick up a newspaper or go to the pictures without Gastrell popping up in articles or in newsreels, smiling at his fans or glowering for the cameras.

'Stefan von Brandt made contact with my section through the Berlin resistance several months ago,' said Wyngate. Suddenly Lottie felt as if she were a million miles away from the sleepy streets of Bramble Heath, with this talk of the Berlin resistance and the German High Command. 'The air war is good as lost. The Luftwaffe are on the run.'

'But we still hear the planes coming over,' she replied. Wyngate knew what he was talking about and she wanted to believe him, but how did it tally with what she saw? 'The siren still goes off and we all run to the shelters. Although it doesn't happen as often now, I suppose.'

'Stefan was the younger of two sons,' Wyngate went on. 'His elder brother was considered the crown prince of the family, Nazi from head to toe. Stefan, however, wasn't quite the Aryan ideal. He was a very sickly child, walked with his legs in braces for the first five years; they considered him intellectually backwards, though there's no evidence of that. His father was...' He furrowed his brow, choosing the word with care. 'Brutal. He began to refer to his youngest son as *der Familienjude*. The family Jew. He was considered the shame of the von Brandts; he seems to have been a rather gentle, quiet sort of lad.'

Lottie thought of Mrs Gastrell, who had taken on so much to help the Kindertransport children. Whatever Lottie might think of her husband, Mrs Gastrell seemed like a genuinely kind, big-hearted woman. The very idea that the name of Jewish people like her could be used as such a nasty insult left Lottie stunned. 'That's just appalling. And I thought Stefan was a Nazi himself. Poor boy, what a horrendous start in life.'

Matthew was shaking his head. 'That poor young man,' he whispered.

'There is a programme of euthanasia in Nazi Germany. It targets children who aren't considered valuable members of society,' said Wyngate in his measured way, but his jaw tightened as he spoke, betraying his disgust at the very idea of it. 'By the time the Third Reich made it a policy, Stefan was too old to be a victim, but his own father mooted the idea of euthanising his son during a conversation with the Führer when Stefan was just seven years old. The little boy was thought so backward that Otto von Brandt didn't even ask him to leave the room. What saved Stefan's life, ironically, was Hitler's ego. He couldn't have his own godson seen to be anything other than a perfect Nazi, so Stefan was sent for re-education.'

Lottie gasped and Matthew took her hand. 'H-how could anyone even *think* of doing that to their own child?' Lottie said. 'What sort of twisted ideology puts that thought into someone's head?'

Lottie thought of Daisy sleeping upstairs and fought the urge to run to her, to hold her tight and protect her from a regime that would do such unspeakable things to children.

Wyngate went on with his story: 'The re-education worked for some, while for others it ended in the concentration camps. For some, including Stefan and the crew of his bomber, it bred cunning. He's anything but slow; he's intelligent, observant – and curious. And curiosity does not a good Nazi make.' And he gave the glimmer of a smile. 'The more the ideology was drummed into Stefan and his friends, the more they learned to play-act until they convinced their families and their tutors that they were loyal to the Third Reich until death.' He nodded with admiration. 'They were brave young men, every one of them. They made contact with the resistance and, through them, me. The crew of that Heinkel was defecting to us. They were bringing with them the sort of information that's going to see those monsters in Berlin on the scaffold one day. Hitler took a personal interest in Stefan when his elder brother and father were killed.' He leaned forward again, drop-ping his voice to say, 'He made Stefan his messenger boy for a few months while he was finishing his Luftwaffe training. Stefan von Brandt, still believed by the Führer to be a little defective in the brain, was a charity case. They talked in his presence as one might a child. And they talked about everything.'

'My God,' Matthew murmured. 'So, he's an informant? Why hasn't he surrendered then?'

Wyngate shook his head. 'Fear,' he said. 'We don't know when, but clearly someone found out about the plan and gave them away. It must've been after the plane had left, because they wouldn't have let it take off if they'd known it was a defec-tion. That's why Hitler had it shot down: he wanted to silence the men on board. And he almost – almost – managed it. Now Stefan is alone, and he's terrified.'

Lottie shook her head sadly. 'I can't imagine Hitler's the sort of chap to take it very well when he's been deceived, especially when he knows what Stefan could tell us. To think he's out there, in the woods, in some old farm building somewhere... We must find a way to show him that we won't hurt him, that he mustn't be afraid.'

She bit her lip, thinking for a moment, then she had an idea. 'We left food and a blanket out for him first thing this morning. I haven't checked yet to see if he's taken it. I'm an idiot, I really should have done. Could we leave some more food out for Stefan, with a note for him?'

'For whatever reason, he chose the two of you to make himself known,' said Wyngate. 'We need to play this softly-softly; I don't want him coming up against the local heavy squad.'

'I wonder if it's because he was at the crash site when we were,' Matthew murmured, almost to himself. Then he told Wyngate, 'The morning after the accident, Lottie and I were at the wreckage and I prayed for the dead crew. Perhaps he heard me.'

Wyngate was watching Matthew very closely indeed, his eyes narrowed slightly. Then he decided something. 'I have a note for him. In German,' he decided. 'I want you both to take it up and leave it, along with some more food. I'll make sure the rations and petrol coupons are reimbursed. Make it unobtrusive, tuck it away. Gastrell's lot aren't looking for anything but a red-eyed devil, they won't notice a note. I want to bring him out. Chances are he's still armed and I have a feeling he'll be carrying a cyanide capsule; he and his friends knew what it'd be like for them if they were unmasked as traitors in Germany and didn't want to take any chances if the Gestapo pulled them in. We need to convince him that he doesn't have anything to fear, that the deal I agreed with him when he was in Germany still stands, regardless of Mr Gastrell. Usually I'd send in my people, but this is *very* delicate, do you understand?'

Lottie turned cold with alarm. It hadn't occurred to her that Stefan might be carrying a cyanide capsule. Such were the uncomfortable realities of war. She hoped that Matthew was right; that Stefan had heard his prayer and knew he could trust them. Was that why he'd slept on the farm, because he thought he might be safe there even though he'd been too scared to approach that night?

And aside from that, Wyngate wanted her and Matthew to act as a bridge to Stefan. His own people were trained, but they didn't have Stefan's trust; she and Matthew did.

They had to get Stefan safely to the authorities – not just so that he could have a proper meal and see a doctor, and to stop Gastrell's mob attacking him, but to ensure that whatever it was he knew from his time in Hitler's circle could be delivered safely to Ministry men like Mr Wyngate.

'I need to be clear; Mr Churchill has taken a personal interest in the wellbeing of von Brandt. And I'll be taking your signatures to guarantee your understanding and your silence,' said Wyngate. '1944 is going to be a pivotal year for the Allied campaign. The messages Stefan carried, the conversations he's been privy to, will inform the planned action on a level we couldn't otherwise hope to achieve. He's come all the way from Berlin, I don't want him hanging from a tree in Bramble Heath. Understood?'

'And you have no doubt about him, Mr Wyngate?' Matthew asked him, though Lottie suspected that Wyngate wasn't the sort of man who was used to his opinion being questioned. 'He's definitely not a Nazi? What about the vandalism?'

And now Wyngate narrowed his gaze again, appraising Lottie and Matthew. But she got the feeling that, if they hadn't already proved satisfactory to him, she wouldn't be part of this plan.

'If he *were* a Nazi, I wouldn't have bothered turning out on a night like this,' he said. 'Does that answer your question? As for the vandalism, think of who might want the village frightened, to keep them on his side. Think of the headlines.' Then, without waiting for a response, he went on in his business-like way. 'He's a harmless young man who had the bad luck to be born to a family of hardened fascists. All you need to do is leave a couple of notes, maybe have a conversation with him, then we'll take over. I can't afford to have him frightened off or torn to pieces. Understand?'

Lottie glanced at Matthew.

'Yes, I understand,' she replied, her breath catching. 'We'll do it. We'll reach him, we'll make this right.'

FORTY-ONE

THREE WEEKS EARLIER

It was chilly in the Bavarian Alps, the snow lying thickly over the peaks. Snowploughs had been busy, keeping the roads open that led up to the Berghof. A fire blazed gaily in the grate. It could have warmed the coldest of hearts.

'Smile, Stefan,' Lina whispered to her son, her voice strained. She toyed with her pearl earring, which her rigid blonde hair was styled to reveal. Stefan glanced towards his mother, a statuesque woman who was as affectionate as a slab of marble, and sat up straighter, folding his hands neatly in his lap. He had to do as they told him, he couldn't risk them seeing behind his mask. Even though the new Luftwaffe uniform he'd had to put on didn't quite fit – his legs and arms were too long and his shoulders too narrow – he had to make them believe that it did.

Then, addressing the man in the armchair, Lina said, 'It is so good to see you. I feared we wouldn't make it up the mountain at all!'

'Then I would've come *down* the mountain to see you,' their host assured her kindly. It was the same tone he always adopted when addressing Stefan too; gentle, cajoling, the same voice

Stefan heard him use whenever he called to his faithful dog. It
was a world away from the bellows and yells he unleashed on
his stage. 'Ever since word reached me of the death of your elder
son, I have thought of nothing but seeing you and expressing my
sympathy in person. He was a fine young man... I was honoured
to be his godfather. Such a terrible, terrible loss.'

Stefan smiled stiffly at the thought of that loss, of the elder
brother who had joined their father in taunting him with nick-
names and the belt buckle. He thought instead of what lay
ahead, of England, and smiled again as he stroked one hand
distractedly down the back of the dog that sat so patiently
between his seat and that of its master. Then their host asked
him, 'And now, Stefan, you are to be the man of the house, eh?
Make your late father and brother proud of you.'

'Yes, Sir,' Stefan replied in that quiet voice that made his
mother so wary. He cleared his throat and spoke again, more
clearly this time. 'Thank you for your letter of condolence,
Sir—'

But their sympathetic host shook his head and told him with
a smile, 'There is no need for such formality here, my young
friend. I am your Uncle Wolf!'

Then he turned to Lina. 'It was your husband's dream for
Stefan to follow his late brother into our Luftwaffe, I believe?'

*No. It was his dream to see me euthanised to preserve the
family honour.*

Lina nodded, her pearl earrings catching the light, smiling
on their host as if he was talking about Stefan being given a
place in a family firm, not hurtled to an early grave. And yet,
Stefan knew it was the perfect cover, the ideal way for him to
defect and tell his godfather's enemies secrets that could end his
hateful, murderous regime.

'And how old is Stefan now?' he enquired, stroking his
fingertip over his small moustache. 'Old enough to do his bit?'
Then he looked at Stefan and gave him an encouraging smile.

'Think of all the young maids who will be knocking at your door with you looking so smart in your uniform, my boy!'

'He is most definitely old enough to do his part,' Lina said with a smile on her lips, her eyes sparkling, almost drunkenly, with patriotic zeal. It was a lie; Stefan was too young to fight for his country, even if he wanted to. But Lina never worried about such things, not when the honour of the glorious Fatherland was at stake. And what they'd done for their Fatherland, these people. Slaughtered millions, murdered children in their so-called special wards, laid waste to lands that they had no right to tread in.

But Stefan could help stop it. There were others like him too, friends and comrades who could try to bring these monsters down.

'And my son is very excited and very proud to step into the shoes of his brother. Are you not, Stefan?'

There was just the slightest note of steel in that question aimed at her seventeen-year-old son; a tone that their host wouldn't notice, but Lina knew Stefan would. And he knew exactly what it meant. He had learned to play dumb, to keep his head down and say yes, Sir, yes, Madam. He had learned to be stupid.

You are to do as you are told. You are to be an obedient son.

Stefan sat up as though to attention, just as he had learned to do at the cost of a thrashing from his father, the husband whom Lina had so adored. The husband she had lost and for whom she would have traded her youngest son's life in the blink of an eye.

The war had stolen the moon and stars from Lina's heaven when it took the lives of her husband and their eldest child, leaving her with nothing but this idiot boy who had less life in his sorry bones than the fox fur she wore round her shoulders.

The idiot boy who was anything but.

'I want to do my bit for the glorious Reich,' Stefan lied, even as the words threatened to choke him. 'To honour the name of my late father, the man who did so much to spread your message. And most of all, Uncle, I want to make you proud.'

Uncle Wolf nodded and shone his smile on Lina. Stefan could see she liked that smile, the smile that said she had raised her child the right way. Then he advised Stefan, 'You will make all of us proud, Stefan. Every mother, every maiden... every hero who has given their life and every babe who slumbers in the cradle. When you fight for the Fatherland, you fight for a better world for all. You fight for a brighter future.'

'I am the proudest of mothers,' Lina said. 'And I am even more proud to see my Stefan in uniform. But I know who will be the proudest of all.' She gestured towards Uncle Wolf, her voice hushed with reverence. 'Our most excellent Führer.'

And again, he smiled that smile Lina clearly so enjoyed. And Stefan smiled too, as he thought of England and the secrets he could share, of the French beach defences and the troop numbers and lines, of all that stood between the Allies and Normandy.

FORTY-TWO

As they went into the kitchen to prepare Stefan's food parcel, Matthew asked Dorothy to watch Daisy upstairs. The housekeeper glanced at Wyngate, nodded and left them in the quiet of the kitchen.

The vicarage's kitchen supplied another piece of a National Loaf and some luncheon meat from a tin. There was a slice of a Lord Woolton pie, a meatless dish of cheese and vegetables conjured up to help the nation get by on rations, and one of Dorothy's delicious miniature gingerbread puddings. Wyngate had assured Matthew that he would make up the rations that had been spent on the parcel.

They placed Wyngate's note in German on top of the food and covered it all with a folded blanket from a cupboard. Before they left, she and Matthew signed the document that Wyngate had produced, swearing them to secrecy from this day to their last.

Lottie held the basket on her lap as Matthew drove them back up to the farm, his windscreen wipers working against the snow. She was still stunned that she had been drawn into this to the extent that she and Matthew had needed to be sworn to silence.

Lottie had already decided that she would tell everyone on the farm that she'd been talking to Matthew and lost track of time. How else could she explain why she was returning home so late?

Blossom, sitting in the footwell leaning against Lottie's legs, gazed up at her expectantly. She knew when Lottie was worried.

'I hope he finds it,' Lottie whispered. 'But then I think he watches us, don't you? Maybe he's trying to work out who he can trust.'

Matthew nodded. The note Wyngate had given them was brief but friendly, explaining that his message had been passed on and that the authorities Stefan hoped to reach were keen to take him in and talk. No names were mentioned, which Lottie was glad of; at least this way, if someone found it neither she nor Matthew would be accused of being traitors. Wyngate had placed a blank piece of paper and a pencil in the envelope, in case the stricken German wanted to reply.

The village had seemed quiet as Matthew drove through it. Perhaps by morning, Stefan would've handed himself in and the village would return to normal.

Something moved in the darkness. A figure in the road.

Stefan? What is he doing so close to the village? Or is it the deer again, heading back to the woods?

But suddenly, Lottie was aware of several figures, not just one man, standing in a line across the lane.

'They're blocking the road!' she gasped, and she suddenly realised who it must be. Gastrell's followers had apparently taken it upon themselves to vet who was on the roads around the village.

'In case a runaway German comes through in a car.'

Matthew sighed as he drew to a halt and wound down his window. 'Good evening, gentlemen!'

Lottie's grip tightened on the basket she held and she peered out at the men who had gathered at the window, with their greatcoats and scars, their canes and eyepatches. She swallowed, her mouth dry. What if they saw the basket? What if they demanded to see inside it and found the note, written in the enemy's language?

'Evening, Sir, Madam,' one of the men said as he poked his head through the window, his eyes narrowed with suspicion. He ran his shielded blackout torch around the interior of the car.

It rested for a moment on the basket and Lottie's heart pounded.

But the beam moved on and the man said, 'You're the vicar, ain't you? And you're the Land Girl what found the watch. What are you about at this time of night for?'

The man wasn't being unfriendly, but nor was he particularly welcoming. And this wasn't even his home or his village; he had arrived in support of Gastrell because he thought he was doing the right thing. No wonder the young airman was so afraid to make himself known.

'I'm just running Miss Morley home,' Matthew said with measured politeness. 'We lost track of time, we know we shouldn't be out in the blackout.' And he smiled, disarming all of a sudden. 'You know how it is for a couple of young folks like us, eh?'

Lottie smiled, too, despite her fear of what Gastrell's gang were capable of if they found the note and decided she and Matthew were traitors. Because it was true, they were courting, although they had spent the evening reading stories and watching deer in a snowy garden rather than what Matthew's cover story suggested.

The man chuckled, revealing yellowed teeth. 'Even a vicar's gotta have his fun, I s'pose! Go on, mate, off you go with your girlfriend. Rest assured, we'll find the Kraut before he bashes anyone's head in!'

Matthew gave a nod of agreement and replied, 'I don't doubt it, friend.' Then with a merry wave he pressed the accelerator and they drove on through the group of men at a stately pace. Nobody else would know it to look at him, but Lottie could see the tension in Matthew's jaw when he said, 'I didn't know what other excuse to give. I should've come up with something that wouldn't have involved your reputation.' His face softened when he glanced at her. 'At least it wasn't a lie though.'

Lottie was glad it was dark, otherwise Matthew would have seen her blush. 'Oh, you don't need to apologise. And besides, there's so many jokes about Land Girls cavorting with pilots – I'm sure a Land Girl dating a vicar would seem very innocent by comparison.' She giggled, all her nerves bubbling up inside her. 'I'm sorry. It's not funny, this situation, is it? But at least Gastrell's men aren't up in the woods. Let them bother the drivers and leave Stefan alone.'

'And hopefully, by this time tomorrow he'll be in Mr Wyngate's custody,' Matthew replied. 'And the village will be peaceful again.'

FORTY-THREE

Matthew drew the car to a halt at the top of the lane that led to the farm. It was so dark, but the snow pattered against the windscreen and was sticking to the road, lending glitter to the night.

Once they had reluctantly left the warmth of the car, Blossom ran ahead of them and abruptly stopped in the lane. She was facing the woods, her nose twitching.

'Let's check the spot where I left the other basket,' Lottie whispered. 'If he's taken it, then he might come back to the same place for more, you never know.'

And then he'll find the note and know it's safe to give himself up.

As they approached the woods, Matthew was peering into the darkness for any sign of life. Of course there was none, not in the pitch darkness. The moon was now and then shrouded by heavy clouds and there was new bitterness in the air, brought with the threat of heavier snow. Stefan had to hand himself in, or he'd freeze.

They went into the trees, where occasional beams of moonlight filtered between the branches with their scatter of snow. Blossom trotted ahead, sniffing the air as the snowflakes tumbled through it. Lottie knew the woods were deceptively deep, even in winter when the leaves had fallen. If the deer could happily hide among the trees, then a slip of a lad like Stefan could easily keep himself from being seen.

Lottie shone her blackout torch left and right until the weak glow alighted on the basket she had left before, slightly obscured by a tree. Her heart sank. He hadn't found it, had he?

But as they drew nearer, Matthew managing with his stick despite the gnarled roots that ran across their path, Lottie realised that Stefan *had* found it after all. Blossom ran up to the basket and eagerly poked her head inside. Lottie caught up and saw that he'd taken the food and had returned the basket neatly to its place, even bringing back the empty ginger beer bottle.

'Thank goodness he found it!' Lottie said, relieved. 'He's had something to eat.'

'Stefan?' Matthew whispered into the blackness. 'It's Matthew and Lottie. We've come to bring you some more food. We'll leave it for you; thanks for leaving us the basket.'

Lottie held out the new basket in her gloved hands. 'We've got something for you,' she said quietly, speaking to the dark expanse of the woods where the injured, terrified young man was hiding. She decided not to mention the note; he'd find it and, she desperately hoped, would give himself up.

The young man stepped out into what little pale moonlight there was, limping heavily on his right leg. His greatcoat was a cloak of darkness around him, but though each new step brought him closer to Lottie and Matthew, Stefan still looked hesitant. It was as though at any moment he might yet turn and flee.

'Matthew and Lottie,' he said in a quiet voice. His heavily accented English was halting as he chose each word. Whether that was because of his physical condition or his lack of confidence with the language, Lottie couldn't say. 'Thank you,' he added.

Forcing herself to stand still, and not rush forward with the basket and frighten him, was one of the hardest things Lottie had ever done. It went against her urge to help and to care. Instead, she held out the basket as far as she could, the weight dragging on her arms. She hoped against hope that he didn't think it was a trap. But the night was utterly silent; there was nobody here but them.

'We've got bread and a piece of pie, another blanket – because you must be freezing,' she told him, hoping he could hear her friendliness. She put the basket down in front of her so that he could take it. Blossom looked up at him, her tail wagging. She wasn't frightened of him at all.

'I'm not a Nazi,' Stefan whispered, his arms still hanging limp by his sides. He moved forward another couple of paces until he was close enough to take the basket. Instead, though, he looked at Matthew and Lottie with hollow, tired eyes. For one so young, he looked so old, old enough to drop down on the spot. 'I want to help, I'm not like them.'

He was tall and must have already been slender, even before he'd been forced to go days without a proper meal. Blond hair poked out from, of all things, a flat tweed cap that had seen better days; Lottie recognised it as Farmer Gosling's old hat that he'd donated to a scarecrow. Stefan's long, fine-boned face was grimy with soot and dirt; dried blood had trickled down one side of his face and his large, frightened eyes were a washed-out blue. The greatcoat was torn and the right leg of his flight suit was ripped and bloodied.

'We know. There's someone you can trust, as well as us,' Lottie told him. 'He told us all about you and wants to speak to you, not hurt you.'

'There were men here,' Stefan said, his voice trembling with fear. 'Not your Home Guard. They knew who my father was. If they catch me— I'm not my father. Let me show you...' And suddenly he was unfastening his flight suit with dirty, bloodied fingers. 'Let me show you what he did.'

'There's no need,' Matthew replied, but Stefan continued. He was fumbling with the buttons beneath the flight suit now. 'Stefan, we believe you. You're not responsible for your fa—'

Lottie looked at Stefan in horror. Even though there was so little light, the pale white of his chest was now visible in the freezing air and it was criss-crossed with angry scars.

'Oh, Stefan, I'm so sorry,' she said, past the sob rising in her throat. 'What a wicked, dreadful man you had for a father. We don't think you're like that. We don't.'

'You *cannot* know,' Stefan said hopelessly, his own voice heavy with despair as he began to fasten his clothes again, hiding the evidence of his father's brutality. 'A son isn't his father.'

'*I* know,' Matthew told him, his gaze settled on Stefan's. He held out his walking cane to the young man, even though Lottie knew he would struggle to make his way back to the car without it, and said, 'This will help you manage on your leg. Come with us, Stefan, we can take you to the man who will help you right now. You'll be looked after and can tell your story.'

Stefan reached out and took the cane from Matthew.

'You can have a nice, warm bath and dinner,' Lottie promised him, relief beginning to take hold. He was going to come with them, wasn't he? He wasn't going to spend another night out here in the freezing cold. 'Please come back with us to the village. You'll be safe from those men that came up here. There's a man who's got the wrong idea about you, he's told them all sorts of things. But *we* believe you, Stefan. *We* know Mr Gastrell's wrong.'

'I will come with you,' Stefan said. 'Lottie and Matth—'

'Is someone out there?' a voice shouted. Not just any voice. It was Sidney Gastrell. 'Is that you, Adolf? Come on, lads, we've got him!'

Lottie froze with terror, her eyes wide with alarm. Just as they were so close to winning Stefan's trust and getting him to safety, Gastrell and his men were making their unwelcome arrival. What on earth would they do to poor Stefan if they caught him? And what if he panicked and put his hand in his pocket, reaching for the cyanide pill? Stefan's life, and the priceless secrets he carried, would be lost for ever.

Matthew glanced over his shoulder in the direction of the shout, then whispered urgently, 'Take the basket, Stefan, and find somewhere to shelter tonight. We'll send them off.' Then he turned and shouted, 'It's Reverend Hart and Miss Morley! We saw someone on the roadside. He took off towards the open fields.'

FORTY-FOUR

Lottie clenched her fists with frustration as Stefan's limping figure disappeared between the trees. She heard Gastrell and his men approach, their feet crunching through the undergrowth towards them. Blossom stood close to her, watchful.

She held Matthew's hand as if they were out for a stroll. Thank goodness she hadn't picked up the empty basket. Unless someone knew where to look, it was safely out of sight. Matthew leaned his weight lightly against her as they listened to Gastrell telling his followers to fan out this way and that and search the fields. It was precisely what Matthew had wanted when he gave them the wrong information about the fleeing man. What neither of them wanted was for Gastrell to approach, but now he was crossing the field towards them, his breath a fog on the air.

'Vicar, Miss Morley,' he said. 'You've seen our rat?'

'No,' replied Matthew, but the muscle in his jaw now tightened again. 'We've seen what looked like a wounded, frightened teenage boy who needs medical help and a hot meal before the weather does for him. He needs help and you're hunting him down. Anyone would run!'

'If he hands himself over, he has nothing to fear,' was Gastrell's reply. 'They never do though – they go down fists flying more often than not.'

And something about that struck Lottie as all too fortunate. She'd seen Gastrell on the front pages with the Germans he'd tracked down, or the escaped convicts he'd apprehended, the captives often boasting black eyes or split lips, and had marvelled at the bravery of Gastrell and his followers, risking their necks to bring in these villains. But now she wondered... had they really *all* come out with their fists flying, or had Gastrell's gang simply enjoyed taking down those who didn't a peg or two?

Lottie tightened her hand around Matthew's. She'd had enough of Gastrell.

'I don't believe you,' she told him. 'Stefan can barely stand, let alone throw punches.'

Gastrell's eyes narrowed and he said archly, 'You got a good look at him considering he was fleeing across the fields, Miss Morley.' Then he folded his arms across his chest and asked, 'What's going on here? What do the pair of you know?'

'You're doing more harm than good,' Matthew said. 'He's not responsible for his father—'

'His father!' scoffed Gastrell. 'Let me tell you about his father, and his brother too, come to that. Thugs and gangsters, the pair of them. The father was at Adolf's side when he came out of the trenches, right there next to him in the beer hall and in prison too, spitting hatred and bile! Murderers and villains together, no matter how many medals they pinned to his chest. The same goes for the eldest brat. He killed dozens of our lads before the RAF shot him down, so don't you tell me that this one's anything but scum! Like father, like son.' He jabbed his finger towards them. 'These people stand for everything that's evil. We can't let them sow their poisonous seeds here.'

'He's a boy, for heaven's sake!' Lottie protested, thinking of everything Stefan had been through. Gastrell was right, Stefan's father *had* been a monster, but why should his son suffer for it? He wanted to rid the world of Hitler and his revolting ideology, just as much as Gastrell did. 'You can't assume that someone must be a bad apple just because their father was.'

Gastrell ignored her. He turned and hurried after his men, shouting, 'Stefan von Brandt, give yourself up and you've nothing to fear! You've run out of luck!'

Matthew watched him hurry away into the shadows, then heaved a heavy sigh. 'He was going to come with us,' he murmured to Lottie. 'He's not a danger to anybody.'

'I know. I'm so afraid for him,' Lottie said. 'I just hope that he can keep himself out of sight, then come down to the village and give himself up.'

'It's too cold to be standing out here,' Matthew said. 'I don't suppose you'd mind helping me back to the car? The ground's a bit difficult without my stick.'

'Of course I don't mind,' Lottie said with a smile and held her arm out for him.

Nothing else was said as the two of them made their way back to the car. Even the short drive up to the farm passed in silence and Lottie didn't want to break it. They had grown so close in such a short time; there was something precious in their shared silence.

When Matthew pulled up in the yard, Lottie turned to him and gently traced his jaw with her fingertips. She leaned closer to him, bringing her lips close to his, and glanced up at him. She saw so much affection in his soft gaze that her heart rushed and she met his lips in a kiss.

He had endured so much and yet his capacity to care and to love hadn't wavered. Lottie drew strength from him; together, they could be invincible. They could help Stefan. They could save him from the freezing woods and the men who wanted to capture him.

Couldn't they?

FORTY-FIVE

The next evening, Lottie decided to drop in on Matthew. She checked her reflection in the large, old mirror in the farmhouse's hallway, the silver speckled with a patina of age. A Father Christmas with a lopsided grin, handmade from felt, perched on the gilt frame.

She'd spent all day working, wondering if Stefan had come out of the woods at daybreak and gone down to the village to give himself up. Maybe he'd decide to come to the farm instead. As she'd worked with the other Land Girls, milking the cows, lugging the milk cans, shovelling hay and pushing her wheelbarrow, she'd glanced round again and again, hoping to see him.

But he'd never materialised and Lottie wondered if it was because he wasn't sure he could trust everyone on the farm. He'd learned to be fearful. And she'd signed Wyngate's papers, so she couldn't open up and tell the others what was happening.

But she'd done what she could, and she was so excited about seeing Matthew again; she'd missed him all day. She couldn't quite believe that her boyfriend was a vicar. Her parents would be amazed, after all their jokes asking her why she'd never brought home a pilot. Of course, it had been Martha who'd been a pilot's girl and as Lottie brushed imaginary lint from her collar, she felt a familiar twinge of sadness.

But I can't bring her back. No matter how much I might want to. No matter how much I miss her.

At her side, as ever, was Blossom, wagging her tail, excited to be going on a walk. She was wrapped up for the cold in her tiny Fair Isle jumper, which Nicola had knitted for her.

Over her shoulder Lottie saw that she'd been joined at the mirror by Shona, who was wrapped up in her coat and boots. She was slightly taller than Lottie and she was examining her reflection too.

'Are you walking down to the village?' Shona asked conversationally as she reached to pat a stray auburn hair back into place. 'Fancy some company? I've got a few last-minute Christmas cards to drop off – I hadn't got round to them with all the worry.'

'I am, yes. I thought I'd drop in on Matthew,' Lottie replied. 'I wouldn't say no to some company, actually. We can share a torch!'

'It feels like Christmas now, doesn't it?' Shona said, as they strolled to the door and out into the freezing-cold air. 'Now the trees are decorated and the paper chains are up. And Daisy looked as though she was having the time of her life; she deserves it, what a lot she's already lost.'

Lottie shivered in the chill and rubbed her gloved hands together, but Blossom didn't seem to mind the cold at all and eagerly trotted ahead through the falling snow.

'Oh, yes, it's definitely Christmas,' Lottie agreed. 'The farmhouse looks so festive and it was lovely to see Daisy. And she was so excited! It's fun spoiling her.' As their footsteps crunched across the yard and onto the lane, she added, 'And she *has* lost a lot. Too much.'

The thought bothered her and as she pictured Matthew, she knew why. She didn't want Daisy to think that she was taking her uncle away from her; the one person she had left in her family.

'She's not the only one.' Shona took Lottie's arm in hers, not needing to say any more. They both knew what Lottie had lost, and Shona's own brother was a prisoner of the Germans even now. 'I was worried sick about Jack and when I found out he was captured, I fretted about how you'd feel, because you lost Martha and I still had Jack. I feel so lucky to be here on the farm with such good friends. I love my Land Girl family.'

Lottie blinked away the snowflakes that were still falling and beamed at her friend. 'I love all of you too. We're like sisters, aren't we? When all of this over, wherever we might end up, I know we'll all still be friends. Gosh, you never know, maybe you'll come down to visit me and Matthew at the vicarage – imagine that!'

Shona chuckled and admitted, 'We thought that was going on! You've thawed out the vicar!'

Lottie laughed. 'And he made me lay down my pitchfork and stop being so angry!'

To her delight, Shona gave a squeal of excitement and clapped her hands together eagerly. 'Oh, that's so sweet! Vicar's wife in the making!' She stooped to give Blossom's ears a scratch. 'And Daisy will be the best sister for Blossom!'

'I know! I think Daisy might be more excited about Blossom than she is about me.' Lottie chuckled, as Blossom wagged her tail. 'But a vicar's wife… I've never organised a tombola in my life, let alone an entire village fete! I don't think about all of that though. I just know that Matthew makes my heart go giddy.'

Suddenly Blossom took off, haring away towards the trees. She vanished between the trunks and into the thick undergrowth.

'Oh, heck.' Lottie tutted. 'She must've smelt a rabbit!'

What if the little dog found Stefan? Her excited bark would carry and anyone out hunting for him would hear. 'We better go in and get her. Blossom! Come back here!'

FORTY-SIX

Once Lottie and Shona were on the path through the woods, they strained to hear any sound that would tell them where Blossom had gone.

'Blossom! Come on, girl!' Lottie called as she ran the beam of her torch from side to side. 'Where are you?'

The towering, bare trees seemed to be full of menace and it was disorientating, the woods rendered unfamiliar by the night-time. They were further into the woods than Lottie had been last night. The trees were closer together, crowding into a wall of darkness in front of them. The cloud was heavier tonight, smothering the moon.

'Blossom!' Shona shouted with what sounded like forced jollity. 'Your mum's worried, come on!'

Lottie called again, and again, and suddenly she heard a bark.

She froze on the spot, glancing at the dark shapes of the trees rearing up all around them, trying to work out what direction the bark had come from.

'That's Blossom, I'm sure of it,' she said. 'That sounded like my little girl.'

The barking carried on and Lottie was convinced. And she was relieved, too, because she was sure that Blossom sounded happy; it wasn't the bark of a dog that was lost and afraid. They just had to find her now.

'Where on earth is it coming from?' Lottie whispered to Shona. It sounded close by, but muffled. A jolt went through her as she wondered if Blossom had gone into a badger's sett or fox's den, but her merry barks seemed too chipper and too loud for that.

They'd wandered off the path in their search for the dog, the undergrowth whipping against their shins, and Lottie had no idea where they were in the woods. But at least Blossom wasn't far away now.

'Blossom!' Lottie called again. 'Blossom, come on now, where are you?'

As the barking went on, Lottie could hear that they were getting closer. She nodded to Shona and they kept going. The brambles that gave their village its name were rampant among the trees, but there seemed to be a path through them, as if someone had recently come this way. Had someone else been through here? Had someone—?

Suddenly, a delighted woof sounded, very close to Lottie.

She blinked, taking in the scene. A tree had grown up in the middle of a thicket of brambles and part of the trunk was hollow. And there, sitting in the hollow like a woodland sprite, was Stefan, with Blossom in his arms.

'Stefan!' she whispered. 'I'm so sorry. Blossom's very friend-ly.' She gestured to her dog, who must've recognised Stefan's scent from the evening before and run off to find him. Then she nodded towards her friend: 'And not forgetting my friend Shona.'

And now Shona would know that Lottie had met the airman before.

Stefan looked up and Blossom followed, covering his face in

affectionate licks. At Lottie's side, Shona had frozen in her tracks and was silently staring at the young man before them. She didn't turn and run though, which Lottie took to be a good sign at least.

'Hello, Stefan,' Shona said after a moment, her voice very careful. Then she glanced towards Lottie, her eyebrows raised in a question.

'Matthew and I came back yesterday,' Lottie admitted. 'We met him. Brought him some food and a blanket. And Matthew gave him his stick.'

She hoped that Mr Wyngate wouldn't mind her telling Shona that, but at least it sounded like the sort of thing a conscientious vicar would do for someone struggling in his parish. The basket she'd carried was sitting beside Stefan and the horse blanket and the one Matthew had donated were wrapped round his shoulders. He was sitting on something that showed up white in her torchlight and she realised it must be his parachute.

The woods were silent and the trees seemed to lean in towards them as if they were listening, their bare branches a mesh above them.

Stefan struggled awkwardly to his feet, holding Blossom in one arm and resting his other hand on the stick Matthew had given him as he did. It struck Lottie as a curiously courtly gesture, as though he was greeting them in a neat drawing room rather than a freezing-cold wood. There was something pathetic in it that was mirrored in his pale skin and tired demeanour. He had to give himself up, she realised, if he was to survive.

'I have decided that, tonight, I will hand myself in at the airbase,' Stefan said. 'You have shown me more kindness in one day than I knew in my mother and father's home in seventeen years and I have to do what I can to help end this war.' He swallowed, his thin throat bobbing. His voice was stronger as he went on, 'We have to stop them. For the good of everything that's right.'

'Oh, yes, we have to, we must,' Lottie said, taking a step nearer to him, the snow crunching underfoot. 'I'm glad you're handing yourself in. There's so much you can do, Stefan, the things you'll be able to tell will wreck your godfather's plans. And there's people who'll look after you, who care. We're going down to the village now. Why don't you come with us? We'll show you the way.'

She knew it was bold to offer, bearing in mind that there were patrols out looking for him, but surely if they saw Stefan flanked by two Land Girls they'd know he didn't mean any harm?

Stefan shook his head and replied, 'I will go when the village is asleep.' He pressed a kiss to the top of Blossom's head. 'And I will go alone. I don't want people to think badly of you for helping me but I am very grateful that you did.'

Blossom licked his cheek affectionately.

'I don't care what they think,' Lottie replied, but she knew, deep down, that he was right. People *would* think the worst of her; they'd call her a collaborator, wouldn't they? Gastrell and his men would, at least. 'I don't want you to be wandering about on your own, not on your bad leg.'

'No,' he said, though not unkindly. 'You have done enough for me already.'

Shona smiled and said, 'They'll look after you. It'll be all right.'

'Can you tell the person who wrote the note to expect me?' Stefan asked Lottie. Then he smiled and added, 'At midnight, I will be at the gates.'

Lottie nodded. 'I will. And you'll take care, won't you? Good luck, Stefan.'

'Thank you.' Stefan smiled again. He set Blossom down on the snow and bowed his head to Shona and Lottie, courtly once more. 'If you will permit, I will write to you and tell you how I am getting on.'

Blossom pawed at his trousers, tail wagging, as if she was saying goodbye, then she came to Lottie's side.

'I'd really like that.' Lottie grinned. 'And I don't know how it works, but if they let you have a day trip, you're welcome to come and visit us on the farm. But we'd better go. If Mr Gastrell's men are around, they might overhear us.'

'Goodbye, Lottie and Shona and Blossom. And please thank Matthew for me too.' Stefan smiled. 'Merry Christmas to you all.'

FORTY-SEVEN

Lottie and Shona carried on through the cold, dark woods, Blossom now on her lead. After fighting their way through more of the brambles, they finally reached the path that wound through the trees.

Lottie wondered what had gone through Stefan's mind when Blossom had found him. Perhaps he'd thought she'd been sent to sniff him out, but then instead he'd been met with one of the friendliest dogs in Bramble Heath, clad in her Christmas jumper. Little moments like that must've helped him as he'd hidden in the cold, making the decision to give himself up. A moment of innocent friendliness.

And thank goodness he was about to turn himself in. Very soon, he'd be safe and Gastrell would have the wind well and truly knocked from his sails.

'I'm glad he's made his choice,' Lottie whispered, deliberately avoiding saying Stefan's name as she glanced about. She hoped none of the patrols were in the woods, but it was hard to know who was there among the dark trees, listening, watching. 'And I'm sorry I didn't tell you before, Shona, that we'd met him. Please don't think I didn't trust you.'

'We all know about careless talk.' Shona smiled. Blossom looked left and right, then gave a low growl and flattened her ears in response to some unseen creature in the woods. On instinct, the two women quickened their pace. 'Look at how quick the village found out about him going on the run, thanks to the gossip, then we've got Sidney Gastrell and his newspaper men spoiling the village before you know it!'

'I thought my ear was itching,' said the unmistakable voice of Gastrell as he stepped out of the trees, two of his men at his shoulder. 'You young ladies should take care. There's been a monster running loose in the woods.'

Lottie nearly tripped as she came to a sudden halt and Blossom growled at the men who were blocking their path.

'I don't think an injured teenager can do much harm,' she retorted. 'Besides, we've got Blossom and she'd bark her head off if anyone tried to harm us.'

But despite her boldness, she quailed inside. Gastrell and his gang were clearly combing the woods on the hunt for their quarry. At least Stefan was well hidden among the brambles; if it hadn't been for Blossom, she would never have known where he was. Hopefully, Gastrell and his men would come away disappointed.

But what would happen once Stefan was on the move? There was no way to warn him, unless their voices carried his way.

'I think you ladies may be lucky and he's gone to ground somewhere,' Gastrell said. 'It wouldn't surprise me if he's found himself a nice cosy barn or hayloft while this snow's falling. But he won't stay free for long, we've caught worse than him.'

Lottie clutched at the chance to throw Gastrell off Stefan's scent. She nodded eagerly. 'Oh, yes, he must've found somewhere on one of the farms. There's plenty of out-of-the-way sheds and whatnot, where no one will look.'

'And that's where we're going at first light. We'll see no

more this evening in the snow,' Gastrell informed them self-importantly. 'It might not be long until Christmas but if Mrs Gastrell and my men have to give up their festive celebrations and share a humble meal at the George and Dragon instead, we'll do it.'

Of course he'd gladly have a humble Christmas dinner at the George and Dragon, because it'd look good in the newspapers.

'We're all away from family this Christmas,' Shona said coolly. She squeezed Lottie's arm. 'And some of us have lost the ones we love to a prison camp or worse, so you're better off than a lot of them, Mr Gastrell, however humble your meal.'

Christmas was only a matter of days away now. All over Bramble Heath, decorations would be going up and presents would be placed under the trees. Even though the decorations might be sparse and the presents few, and families were scattered for the war effort, there was still joy in the darkness of winter.

But how much Christmas spirit was there here, in these dark woods, where Stefan hid, injured and terrified, while Gastrell strode about looking for glory?

FORTY-EIGHT

The snow was falling more thickly now. After saying goodbye to Shona as she went on her way to post her Christmas cards, Lottie turned to head towards the vicarage with Blossom. And there, crawling slowly down the high street, was a dark blue sports car.

Lottie stared. It wasn't the sort of car you saw in Bramble Heath very often. But then through the windscreen she saw a familiar face.

That's Mr Wyngate, the man from the Ministry!

She jogged towards the car over the snowy pavement, Blossom trotting along with her as she waved her arm, trying to attract Wyngate's attention. She needed to pass on what Stefan had told her.

How he could see to safely navigate the snowy roads without headlamps Lottie couldn't imagine, but if the mysterious Mr Wyngate was having any trouble, she saw no sign. He pulled the car in to the side of the road and climbed out, his face shadowed by the brim of the hat that he never seemed to take off.

'Mr Wyngate,' Lottie said, breathlessly. She glanced over

her shoulder, satisfied herself that there was no one close by to overhear, then whispered, 'Midnight, at the airbase. He's giving himself up.'

'Get in the car,' Wyngate said curtly, then turned and did just that himself.

Lottie blinked the snowflakes from her eyelashes. *Get in that?* She'd never been inside a car like Mr Wyngate's in her entire life but she did as she was told. She wasn't going to leave the little dog out in the snow.

The inside of the car smelt of polish and leather, and Lottie knew Blossom would be leaving dog hairs all over it.

'Are we going for a drive?' she asked him, puzzled. Blossom cocked her head to one side, apparently fascinated by Wyngate. Then, with a merry yap, she wriggled free of Lottie's embrace and stepped over the gap between the seats to stand on the immaculate lap of the man from the Ministry. For a second Blossom and Wyngate looked at one another, then the little dog turned in a circle and snuggled down against his coat.

'I didn't introduce you two yesterday. This is Blossom,' Lottie said, hoping Wyngate liked dogs. But how could anyone resist Blossom, especially when she looked so adorable in her Christmas jumper?

'Hello, Blossom, I'm Mr Wyngate,' was his surprising reply, his voice as brisk as ever. He pulled off one of his leather gloves and settled his elegant palm on Blossom's back, stroking her gently as he told Lottie, 'Villagers gossip, Miss Morley. Especially about Germans.'

'They really *will* gossip if they saw me getting into your car,' she mumbled, feeling chastened. But she knew she should've thought before she said anything. *Walls have ears* and *Careless talk costs lives*, as the government information posters said, but Lottie had forgotten about all that and had started telling Wyngate about Stefan in the middle of the street. What a fool she'd been. 'So, you're not the first new friend that Blossom's met today. She ran off into the woods and found Stefan in his hiding place.'

'He must be well hidden,' Wyngate said, with the barest hint of admiration in his tone. 'He's evaded the Home Guard, Gastrell's mob and a few of my men too. How does he look?'

'He's found himself a hollow tree that's quite some way off the path and surrounded by a thicket of brambles,' Lottie explained. Then, as she recalled Stefan's feeble state, she sighed. 'He really needs to see a doctor. He looks so frail, Mr Wyngate. But he's decided to turn himself in, at least. Couldn't we just go back up there now in your car, you and I, and collect him, so he doesn't have to get to the airbase under his own steam? Matthew's given him his walking stick, but every step he takes must be agony. Blossom will show us the way.'

It wasn't what Stefan wanted, of course; he wanted to walk in and hold his head high, to surrender on his own terms. But if they went and got him safely into this luxurious car and took him to the airbase, he would be safe. Safe from the cold, safe from his injuries, and safe from Sidney Gastrell.

'We could,' Wyngate replied, though Lottie already knew there would be a but. 'But this is delicate. He trusts you. Through you, he trusts us. *England*. If we break that trust now, we might never get it back.'

'Oh...' Lottie breathed, taking in what Wyngate had said. 'He did say he wants to hand himself in. And if I turn up with you, and he doesn't know you, of course, he might think I've tricked him and he might bolt, or do something stupid.' With a shiver, she remembered what the man from the Ministry had said about Stefan potentially having a cyanide pill on him. 'Poor boy, his family were just so awful to him. It must've been difficult for him to decide he could trust me and Matthew, or anyone. And you're right, we can't do anything to risk breaking that trust.'

Wyngate was still stroking Blossom, his fingers moving

softly against the top of her head as she slept. He seemed thoughtful for a moment, then said, 'Families are complicated.' Then the thought, whatever it was, was gone and he nodded. 'I'll make sure he's properly looked after.'

'I should mention, by the way, we bumped into Mr Gastrell in the woods,' Lottie told him, and glanced out through the windscreen. The view of the dark street was steadily vanishing behind a feathery layer of snow. 'He's planning to visit some farms tomorrow, so he won't be able to intercept Stefan before he can get to the airbase.'

'I'll be heading up to Heath Place later,' Wyngate said. 'Do you want a lift to the farm? It's not a night for walking.'

Lottie smiled at him. 'Mr Wyngate, you're a very kind man to offer but I'm on my way to visit Matthew.'

'I'll come by in a couple of hours or so,' he replied. Then he looked down at Blossom and told the little dog as she blinked up at him, 'I'll even give your mistress a lift too, eh?'

Lottie chuckled as she adjusted her scarf, readying herself to go out into the snow. 'Thank you, Mr Wyngate. And I promise to get better at being a spy!'

'You've done your bit,' Wyngate assured her. 'Good job, Miss Morley. Very good job.'

Lottie couldn't help but smile at his words. She'd planned to do her bit for the war effort by joining the Land Army, helping to keep the nation fed. Somehow, she'd ended up gaining the trust of a stricken enemy airman who knew the secrets of the Nazis' innermost circle.

FORTY-NINE

Lottie carefully made her way up to Matthew's front door, Blossom trotting ahead. The path was covered over with a layer of snow. The bare branches of the wisteria that clutched the front of the house were laden with snow and the wreath on the door looked even more ready for Christmas with the soft flakes nestled on its shiny holly leaves and flecking its ribbons.

She knocked on the door and Blossom gave a woof. It was only a few seconds before the door opened and in the hallway, where no light was lit in deference to the blackout, stood Matthew. He greeted her with a warm smile of welcome.

'Hello Lottie – and Blossom, who's wearing a nicer sweater than any of mine,' he said brightly. 'The fire's lit and we've got Mrs J's ration book Christmas cake waiting; come on in.'

'Evening, Matthew.' Lottie beamed as she stepped into the hallway, Blossom sniffing the air. He wasn't Reverend Hart tonight, as his dog collar wasn't in evidence. Instead, he was wearing an open-necked shirt under his jacket. Something in Lottie relaxed at that; she really wasn't sure about being a vicar's wife, but she liked being Matthew's girlfriend.

'The snow's getting heavier and heavier,' she told him. 'And there's something I need to tell you. But first of all...'

She rose up on her tiptoes and gave Matthew a kiss on his cheek.

'This is already more fun than the WI coffee morning,' he teased as he kissed her cheek in return. 'All I get from them is rock buns.'

Lottie chuckled. 'Well, my rock buns do actually taste like rocks, so you're much better off getting kisses from me instead!' She gave him another one, then whispered, 'By the way, I've got news. About our friend.'

'Come through in front of the fire and tell me.' Matthew slipped his arm through Lottie's, his walking cane tapping on the floor as they walked along the hallway. She was glad he had a spare cane after giving his other one to Stefan. 'Because I'm a vicar, I even have sherry. Or beer, courtesy of a very generous parishioner. Which would you prefer?'

'Sherry?' Lottie was amazed. 'It's not bad being a vicar, is it? I'd love a small glass of sherry, if you wouldn't mind!'

They went into the lounge, where the fire glowed in the grate and the Christmas decorations glittered. An Enid Blyton book and some crayons sat on the sofa, no doubt left by Daisy. Slices of Christmas cake were waiting for them on the coffee table, fanned out with care on a plate decorated with robins.

It was so warm and friendly, and the chill in Lottie's bones disappeared. She let Blossom jump down from her arms and the little dog made a beeline for the rug in front of the fire, where she turned in circles before settling for a snooze.

'Make yourself at home,' Matthew said, smiling, as he went over to the dresser. 'Daisy's still determined to be a Land Girl one day. Or maybe a farmer. She hasn't decided yet. She was halfway through telling me when she put her head on the pillow and went out like a candle.'

Lottie sat down on the edge of the sofa and turned to watch

Matthew at the dresser. He was nothing like the lads she'd once danced with back in East Grinstead; he was so much more mature than them, even though he wasn't much older.

'I hope we won't need Land Girls by the time she's old enough to join,' she said. 'It's funny, isn't it, how the war's something we've had to get used to but little ones like Daisy don't know any different? But I'm sure she'll find a way to work on a farm one day. She has such a deep love for the countryside, doesn't she? It's so lovely to see.'

Matthew had leaned his stick against the dresser as he poured the drinks and when he came over to the sofa, he left it there. His gait seemed easier here at home than it had in the freezing-cold night when he had surrendered his other cane to Stefan, but Lottie still knew that he must be aware of it. There were a lot of men like Matthew now, left with permanent reminders of the war that was still raging. Group Captain Chambers bore his scars and Matthew his limp, yet as far as their loved ones were concerned they were lucky: they were home.

Martha would've loved this homely room and she would've teased Lottie for dating a vicar. She smiled and in her head she told her sister, *Tease me all you like, I don't mind at all*.

'This is a lovely treat,' she said as Matthew sat down beside her. 'You've made the vicarage such a delightful home, you know.'

'Reverend Ellis is a tough act to follow,' he admitted, offering Lottie the plate of cake. 'But Daisy and I want to make a home here. It is a lovely village; there are plenty of places that wouldn't suffer a German aircrew in their churchyard.'

Lottie took a slice of cake with a smile. It was dotted with dried fruit and smelt of nutmeg and cinnamon.

'He was a very kind man,' she replied, and took a small bite of the cake before continuing. 'He was so supportive after Martha... and you're quite right, he allowed German airmen to be buried in his churchyard, just as you have; he wouldn't have had it any other way. *I* think you're doing a very good job, Matthew. I think the village likes you.'

Matthew smiled. 'I hope so. A few of them have told me they're glad I spoke up against Gastrell. They don't want to be front-page news every day.' He selected a piece of the cake too. 'So, you've got something to tell me?'

Lottie was relieved to hear that there were people in the village who had told Matthew their feelings about Gastrell. And for every one who had spoken to him, there would be several more who felt the same way too. Not everyone in Bramble Heath was under the *humble hero's* spell.

'I have,' she said. 'Shona and I found Stefan's hiding place. Or at least, Blossom did, on the way down to the village just now.' The little dog twitched in her sleep at the sound of her name. 'He told us he's turning himself in. Tonight, at midnight, he's going to go to the airbase. Isn't that wonderful news?'

Matthew let out a long sigh of relief. 'Then it's over,' he said, glancing up at the ceiling as if to check that Daisy still slept safely in her bed. 'The Gastrells will leave and Stefan will be safe. And Bramble Heath will go back to being the happy village it was before the mob arrived and brought the photographers with them.'

Lottie took Matthew's hand and gently squeezed it. They could get to know one another better, spend time just being together, without the village on the hunt for a man who wasn't their enemy at all.

'Everything will go back to normal,' she said confidently. 'I only wish I could see the look on Mr Gastrell's face when someone tells him at breakfast tomorrow that the hunt's all over! I just wonder... Stefan's definitely not the vandal. So is it really Mr Gastrell painting swastikas on walls, or smashing windows?'

'It has to be Gastrell,' said Matthew. 'He had to do it, because Stefan wasn't doing anything except hiding. A scared

Nazi hiding out isn't as good for the headlines as one who's terrorising a village. It's just like Mr Wyngate said.'

Lottie frowned. 'He's such a hypocrite. Banging on about protecting our nation from tyranny, while *he's* vandalising it. I hope he pays for someone to fix Ted's windows. But how can we ever forgive him for graffitiing your church?'

'Because it's the only thing we can do. He committed the damage and he put the damage right, because it looks good in the papers,' said Matthew. He shook his head and took a sip of sherry. 'What a fool he is.'

'I suppose we can't even force him to apologise, can we?' Lottie sighed as she picked up her glass. 'He's too popular, and everything around Stefan is so secretive – and for good reason. Maybe it's better if people think he really is a dangerous, vandalising Nazi, rather than the truth.'

'Anyway, let's drink to getting things back to normal,' Matthew said, signalling an end to such serious talk. 'And toast tomorrow, Christmas Eve!'

FIFTY

Lottie was in the middle of a dream. She was in a lovely, cosy room, with a sweet, handsome man, and his hand was on her shoulder. But then, the dream changed; his hand tightened and he was saying her name, again and again.

'Lottie, Lottie, wake up!'

She blinked away her dream and woke in her bed on the farm. She'd had such a wonderful evening with Matthew and had drifted back to the farm through the snow in Wyngate's car barely registering the journey home. Her heart was full of happiness. A snowy Christmas was coming, and she was wondering if she was falling in love, and Gastrell and his men would leave now that Stefan had given himself up and was safe.

Why was Mrs Gosling shaking her awake with such urgency? There was no siren shrieking to send them all to the shelter.

Blossom, who was still wearing her Christmas jumper, had leapt down to the floor where she was barking, running in circles. Something had put her on the alert.

'Lottie, there's a Mr Wyngate here,' Mrs Gosling told her,

looking alarmed. 'He says you're to dress for the cold and come with him at once – and bring Blossom!'

Mr Wyngate?

That name made any trace left of sleep flee. He wouldn't come up here in the middle of the night for nothing. And why did she need to dress for the cold if they were going in his fancy car?

'All right, tell him I'll be down in a second,' Lottie said, pushing back the covers. 'I'll just get dressed.'

Mrs Gosling left, and Lottie hurriedly threw on some clothes. Land Girls knew very well how to dress for the cold and Lottie put on two pairs of socks and extra underwear, her thickest jumper and a scarf and gloves. As soon as she was ready, she picked up Blossom and carried her down the stairs to the kitchen, where the light was on, glowing against the darkness of the winter's night.

'Mr Wyngate?' she asked, as she entered the room, where he was waiting for her. 'We're ready.'

The contrast between the immaculately dressed man from the Ministry and the simple farmhouse kitchen couldn't have been more marked. He was standing at the door, one gloved hand already on the handle as though he had been poised to leave since before Lottie came downstairs.

'Come on,' he said, opening the door. A blast of freezing air filled the kitchen and Lottie could see that the snow was falling again, steadily landing upon that which already lay on the ground. He stepped out into the yard. 'We're going to the woods.'

'The woods?' Lottie grabbed one of the blackout torches from beside the door and followed him out into the freezing night, Blossom by her side. She closed the farmhouse door behind her. 'Why? Oh, no... it's Stefan, isn't it? Did he leave something in his hiding place?'

'He didn't come,' Wyngate replied, striding ahead. 'I need to see where he's been hiding.'

Wyngate's news hit Lottie like a brick wall.

'Didn't come?' she repeated, the cold air catching her breath. She trembled with fear as she walked, the weak beam from her torch dancing as she did her best to keep up with Wyngate. 'Something's happened to him, hasn't it? Or not... no, maybe it's all right, maybe he was resting and he's slept through. That's all it is... *surely* it is!'

But what if Gastrell *had* intercepted him after all? What if his men had seen the shambling figure, struggling through the falling snow, and had pounced?

'Somebody's been busy tonight,' Wyngate told her. 'Supposedly, our limping German somehow made it all the way to the airbase, only to set a meagre fire on the wrong side of the wire. We found a snapped walking cane not far from the gate. Very odd for a man who was going to hand himself in, don't you think?'

Lottie was cold with shock. *A snapped walking stick?*

'Matthew gave him his stick, because Stefan can barely stand. He wouldn't have just left it. And how on earth could it be snapped?' Her voice was rising with panic. 'It's that bloody Mr Gastrell, isn't it? He's trying to make everyone even more scared of Stefan!'

Lottie never swore, but she couldn't help herself this time.

All she could hope, as they quickly made their way up the lane towards the woods through the ever-deepening snow, was that Stefan had been scared off, lost the stick and had managed to return to his den. Then they could take him down to the airbase in Wyngate's car. The thought that Gastrell's men had found him made her feel sick with fear for the injured, terrified boy.

'And no footprints to follow,' Wyngate said bitterly. 'Covered by fresh snow.'

'Oh, this is terrible.' Lottie sighed, not that she needed to tell Wyngate that. They were close to the treeline now and she carefully put Blossom down on the ground; the dog's nose was already twitching. 'Blossom, I want you to go and find your friend. You remember, the nice boy in the woods?'

Blossom, on her lead this time, tugged at it with an impatient woof. That was a good sign. She knew the way and was keen to head off.

'You ought to watch out for your suit, Mr Wyngate,' Lottie warned him as she followed Blossom into the woods. 'There's a lot of brambles.'

'Brambles wouldn't dare,' he replied dryly.

Snow had fallen between the bare branches of the trees, the white carpet lending the woods a ghostly light. Lottie let Blossom run on ahead and hurried to keep up with the busy little dog as she nosed her way back to Stefan's den. Squeezing between tight tree trunks, and wincing her way through clusters of brambles, Lottie followed in her dog's wake, the man from the Ministry not far behind.

Finally, they pushed through a large patch of brambles. Blossom wagged her tail eagerly as they reached the tree in the middle. Lottie recognised the place.

'It's just here,' she whispered as she turned back to Wyngate. 'This is where he's been hiding. Stefan?' she called.

Was he still there?

Wyngate stepped forward, saying something in German that no doubt was intended to set Stefan at ease if he heard. But there was no reply, no sound at all other than the crunch of their feet on the snow.

When no answer came, Wyngate took another few steps towards the tree. From his coat he took a shielded torch, which he shone down on Stefan's humble den. But there was no one there.

All they could see was the horse blanket from the farm, folded neatly, and the silken parachute, grey with mud and dirt. Stefan had tidied his den before setting off to give himself in. And yet he'd never arrived.

'Oh, no...' Lottie gasped. 'Mr Gastrell's got him.'

FIFTY-ONE

Lottie and Blossom climbed into Wyngate's car, bringing the snow with them, and headed down to the vicarage.

'And people think that Mr Gastrell's such a good man!' She sighed with frustration.

'Every side has its cranks,' Wyngate replied. 'He wouldn't be the first to start out with good intentions.'

'Who does he think he is?' Lottie fumed as they drove down the lane towards the village. Blossom knew that she was upset and nuzzled her affectionately. 'He's risking so much. Stefan doesn't deserve to be beaten to a pulp and what about all those things he might know?'

'Winston quite likes Gastrell in his way.' Wyngate's gaze slid over to Lottie for a moment, then returned to the snowy road. The car was going at a crawl, but it was warmer than walking through the darkness. At least the snow had stopped falling now, though the clouds around the moon still looked heavy with it. 'Bullish. Good at inspiring people. Too much of a loose cannon in the end.'

'The prime minister likes Mr Gastrell?' Lottie mused. 'I suppose at least he's on our side. But you're right, he *is* a loose cannon. To start with, I rather admired him, and then he had me up on his stage, and I thought to myself, *he's using me*. And it was a horrible feeling.'

Wasn't it interesting, though, that Churchill liked the way that Gastrell inspired people? Matthew wasn't so different; both men weren't afraid to get up on their feet and inspire their audiences. Only Matthew preached forgiveness and love, while Gastrell preached fear.

'He's going to be trouble one day,' murmured her companion as they drove into the village. 'Perhaps that day is here.'

The snow was still falling, and the clouds glowed, turning the world to twilight even though it should have been dark. The small village green on the high street was thronged with people. They were wrapped in their warmest woolly hats and scarves, their overcoats and boots. The Christmas tree stood above them, its evergreen boughs heavy with snow. Constable Russell was there, running his blackout lantern over the growing crowd, and the Home Guard, with their rifles, were standing by, but they weren't sending anyone back to bed.

As they got closer, Lottie saw reporters in scarves and heavy overcoats, scribbling in their notebooks to record the sight. Gastrell's ex-military men were among the villagers and Lottie gasped as she realised that some of the crowd were armed. Some carried spades, as if they were innocently digging out the snow, but others had garden rakes and hoes, and snooker cues.

Whatever was going on, it was clearly considered more important than everyone staying indoors during the blackout. And then Lottie saw Mr Gastrell, standing in front of the crowd, one arm raised as he addressed his audience.

'What do you think he's done with Stefan?' she whispered. 'Mr Gastrell should be up at the airbase, posing for the cameras, if he's handed him in. But all these people are armed! Are they going to break into the airbase to carry out their own justice? Mr Wyngate, we've got to stop them!'

'The mystery deepens,' deadpanned Wyngate as he pulled in to the kerb in the shadows thrown by the little row of shops that looked out over the street. Amid the spectacle, few people bothered to look at the new arrival. 'Keep in touch.'

'Will do. I'll keep my eyes and ears open,' she replied, wondering how he could stay so composed. But she liked Mr Wyngate, she decided, and it amused her how he'd taken to Blossom. Faced with a village armed with pitchforks, she clutched for a little bit of joy. She held Blossom's paw, waving it at him, just as she and Martha used to do with the dogs they'd had when they were small. 'Blossom says goodbye.'

'Au revoir,' Wyngate replied. And Lottie wasn't certain, but she thought she heard the bare hint of a smile in his voice.

She smiled at Wyngate, then opened the car door and climbed out, her feet crunching on the snow.

FIFTY-TWO

'It's time to show him that we've had enough!' Gastrell told the audience, who roared their agreement. 'We're going to search every inch of the woods until we find the blighter! He's had his fun, tonight we drag him out of his lair!'

A raucous cheer went up, and the spades and rakes were held high.

Her heartbeat drumming in her ears, Lottie hurriedly made her way over the snow, Blossom at her side, following the weak beam of her torch. Then she looked up from her path and saw him: Matthew. She rushed to his side, slipping on the snow in her haste but managing not to lose her footing. She rose up on tiptoe and urgently whispered, 'Stefan hasn't handed himself in, but he's not in the woods any more. Someone's taken him!'

Matthew touched Lottie's hand in acknowledgement, then said as loudly as Gastrell, 'I have something to say to the people of Bramble Heath!'

Faces turned to look at Matthew. A couple of the weapons were lowered, just a little. Just enough for Lottie to have hope.

'I've met Stefan von Brandt,' Matthew said. 'I've spoken to him and I can tell you, he isn't a danger to this community. He isn't a danger to anybody. Believe me, he hates the Nazis as much as anybody here. All we've succeeded in doing is frightening him so much that he daren't even hand himself in. And we tell ourselves that we're the civilised ones!'

A gasp of shock ran through the crowd. Some of them shook their heads, disbelieving the vicar, and looked over at Gastrell, evidently taking his word over Matthew's. But others whispered to one another and didn't look so sure. They edged, a fraction of a step, away from Gastrell.

They believed Matthew.

'He's just a boy!' Lottie told them, her voice cracking in the cold. Somehow, she had found her voice. She'd never liked speaking in front of a crowd and yet Matthew's courage to stand in front of their makeshift weapons had lit something inside her. 'Listen to Reverend Hart, he'd never mislead you.'

'And when this is all over, Sidney Gastrell goes home!' Matthew reminded them. 'Bramble Heath is our home. Please, *please*, think about what you're doing! Von Brandt didn't commit any of the vandalism and the fire at the base tonight can't have been his doing. He was going to hand himself in. Go back to your homes and let that happen. Let this end peacefully!' Matthew swept his gaze across the crowd, then turned to Gastrell. 'You've done some honourable deeds, Mr Gastrell, and I don't deny it. But what you've done in this village isn't among them.'

Captain Spencer lifted his swagger stick to catch the attention of the audience before he said, 'I don't know if Reverend Hart is right about this young man being harmless, but this is a civilised nation. If you want to do your bit, go home and leave the patrols to the Home Guard and the chaps from the airbase. Mr Gastrell, your men are welcome to join us, but we won't have any of you carrying weapons of any sort!'

'It's one thing waving them around on the village green, but you'll stand in a dock if anyone's hurt,' Constable Russell added.

Some of the villagers looked sheepishly at their weapons, but others seemed to hold on more tightly to theirs. They wanted revenge for four years of death and hardship, of going without and being afraid.

Lottie looked over at Gastrell expectantly. Was he going to do the right thing now? One of his men must've found Stefan, just as he'd nearly made it to the safety of the airbase. They had him now, somewhere in the village. But if Gastrell told his followers to leave it to the authorities, then they'd have to give Stefan up, and soon.

'Mr Gastrell, please,' Matthew said. Through the frigid moonlit night and the swirling snowflakes, he and Gastrell watched one another. 'I know you've made this your life's work, this mission to keep the country safe. Please think twice. You don't want to have blood on your hands tonight.'

Gastrell opened his mouth as if to speak, but instead paused for a moment. Then, to Lottie's surprise, he nodded. He bowed his head to Matthew for a second, then told the crowd, 'It's because of villages like this and people like all of you that we'll win this war. Go home tonight, leave this to Captain Spencer and Constable Russell.' Then he looked to Matthew again. 'You won't go far wrong with this young man looking out for you; you're lucky to have him.'

Even Gastrell's most enthusiastic supporters lowered their weapons. And Matthew had his endorsement; they would listen to the young vicar now. The injured servicemen who followed Gastrell nodded towards Matthew with respect.

Lottie gave him an encouraging smile as the Christmas tree standing above them shivered in a sudden blast of wind. The snowflakes were falling faster and more heavily.

'It'll be all right,' she whispered. 'It will.'

She watched as a figure in a fedora and dark overcoat smoothly made his way through the snow, heading for Captain

Spencer. Wyngate would steer them right; he'd make sure that Stefan came in safely.

The crowd shuddered in the freezing wind and in pairs and in little groups they began to make their way home along the snowy paths. Lottie suspected they were no longer holding their weapons with fire and pride, but maybe with just a little shame.

'We have to leave it to the authorities now; I pray that they find Stefan safe and well,' Matthew said, watching Spencer and Wyngate. Gastrell was addressing his own men quietly, no longer shouting to his adoring audience. 'Dorothy came over to watch Daisy; I'm sure she won't mind waiting while we have a hot drink and I run you home.'

'I'm freezing,' Lottie replied, 'and you must be too. And poor Stefan... but the authorities will find him soon. Whichever of Gastrell's men have taken him, they'll soon be handing him over. And I'd love a hot drink to warm me up, and a lift back to the farm would be marvellous, although Blossom and I don't mind kipping on your sofa. I don't want you driving around in this weather.'

Arm in arm, they made their careful way across the village green as the wind buffeted them with stinging snow. They leaned close to each other, holding tight, trying to shield each other from the cold. Blossom was far braver, jumping up as she tried to catch the heavy, tumbling flakes.

'Gosh, what a night,' Lottie whispered as they headed up the garden path towards the vicarage's front door. 'But doesn't your house look lovely? Just like a Christmas card!'

The old house looked beautiful, glowing almost with the reflected light from the snow that had settled across the lawn and on its roof and windowsills. Even the bare branches of the wisteria were covered in snow, leaving a lacy net across the front of Matthew and Daisy's home.

'We'll have a cup of cocoa to warm up, then bed,' Matthew said. He flushed and added quickly, 'Your bed and my bed, obviously. Sorry!' Then he said, no doubt to fill any awkward silence, 'Would you like to come up with me to look in on Daisy?'

Lottie chuckled affectionately. The fact that he blushed so readily told her that she had nothing to worry about. He was a man she could trust. 'It's all right, I know you meant we'd have separate beds! And I'd love to come and look in on Daisy, bless her. She must be the only person in the village who's still asleep.'

Just as Matthew was about to unlock the door, it was flung open.

Dorothy was standing in the doorway, her face whiter than the snow that was falling outside.

'Oh, Matthew, what are we going to do? It's Daisy – she's gone!'

FIFTY-THREE

Lottie's mind whirled, her heart lurched. She tightened her arm round Matthew's. All the colour had drained from his face and she felt him grow suddenly cold.

'I-I went up to check on her and – and she wasn't there,' Dorothy told them, wringing her hands.

'She's not there?' Matthew said, his voice tight. 'She must be there, Mrs Jenner. Or— or she's somewhere else in the house.'

Dorothy stepped aside as he went through the front door like a man in a trance, Lottie's arm still looped through his to stop him from falling. He looked up at the stairs, as if he'd see Daisy there, and when he saw no one he shook his head, snow falling from his hair.

'I've looked all over the house,' Dorothy told him. 'Every room. I called and called. She's not here. All I could find was this, on the stairs.'

She held out the toy rabbit that Daisy had been so excited to receive from Father Christmas. Matthew gently took the little toy, his hand trembling as he looked down at it.

'She never wanders,' he said, each word falling with effort

from his lips. Lottie stroked his arm. 'Even when she had the nightmares, she never wandered.'

'I can't find her scarf or her bobble hat,' Dorothy said. 'Or her coat or her wellington boots. They were by the back door earlier, but they've gone.'

Matthew put the rabbit in his pocket as gently as though it was a holy relic, then moved suddenly, as if awoken from his daze. Lottie hurried to keep up with him as he swept out of the hallway, through the house to the back door, moving fast despite his limp.

Coats and hats hung on hooks, Matthew's dark overcoats and handknitted scarves on the highest ones, and Daisy's anorak and cardigans on a lower row. But there was no overcoat, no hat or scarf for the little girl. Shoes and boots stood on a rack below, Matthew's brogue lace-ups and Daisy's buckle-up shoes side by side, but there was no sign of any child-sized wellingtons.

'She's wrapped up warm,' Lottie said. With mounting horror, she looked up at Matthew. 'She went outside into the snowstorm.'

Blossom purposefully walked a track back and forth, her nose close to the ground. Then she was up on her back legs, scratching at the panels of the back door.

Matthew pulled it open and the icy wind sent heavy snowflakes rushing in. Without pausing, he strode outside, running his torchlight across the garden. Lottie stood beside him, the muted beam of her torch trailing his. It was astonishing how thickly the snow had covered the garden; the air-raid shelter was almost entirely buried under the weight of it.

Then they saw it, right in the middle of the garden. The freshly falling snow was rapidly filling the holes, leaving only shallow dents, but the deer had been there. And trotting up the path away from the back door were a small pair of human footprints.

Daisy's.

'The deer,' Matthew said, his voice hushed as realisation dawned. 'She came out into the garden to look at the deer. Daisy!' he shouted, 'Daisy, where are you?'

They pursued the small footprints, the torchlight glancing off the glittering snow, the larger flakes casting shadows across the path of the beams. There was a rushing in Lottie's ears as Blossom hurried ahead. Moment by moment the footprints were filling with snow.

The gate at the back of the garden was open a crack, the snow banking up against it. Matthew had to shoulder it so that they could get past. Blossom ran ahead and stopped. Her head was up, her tail rigid. She barked and when Lottie ran her torch over her, she knew why.

There were now two sets of footprints.

Daisy had met someone out here. Someone whose feet were large.

Side by side, the little girl and the stranger had walked away from the vicarage, through the snowstorm.

Matthew turned and called back through the gate across the garden to Dorothy, who was standing in the doorway.

'Telephone Constable Russell! Someone's taken Daisy!'

FIFTY-FOUR

There was no time to lose. It was freezing cold; no weather for a child to be out in who should've been warm and snug in bed.

Lottie thought of the presents under Matthew's Christmas tree. Would they find Daisy in time for Christmas? Would she ever open them?

Who had taken her? Surely not one of Gastrell's men. But then, hadn't they intercepted Stefan before he could reach the airbase? If they were capable of grabbing a terrified, injured young man, who was to say they couldn't snatch a child as well? But why would they? Lottie recalled their stories from Gastrell's book, the bullets that had torn them, the bombs that had ripped their skin. Would any of them really take a little girl?

But who else could it be? Surely nobody in Bramble Heath would do such a thing?

The tracks of footsteps were already blurring under the heavy snowflakes that were still whirling from the sky. Blossom tugged on her lead, barking impatiently as Lottie and Matthew trudged through the snow.

Every second that passed was a second too long.

'We'll find her, don't worry,' Lottie whispered to Matthew

through the freezing air, trying to sound hopeful for his sake even as her heart thudded heavily. She glanced this way and that, shining the feeble light of her blackout torch. She'd not had much sleep and yet any tiredness she'd felt had long gone.

They called the little girl's name, over and over, but nothing stirred in the world turned white. If she heard, she'd reply. And maybe the man who had taken her, led her away through the snow, would realise they were coming. He'd stop, bring her back. The nightmare would be over.

'I'm all she's got, Lottie,' Matthew said, his voice panicked. 'I swore I'd look after her!'

'I know you're all she's got and you love her more than anything in the world,' Lottie soothed him gently. She was terrified for Daisy and she couldn't begin to imagine how Matthew felt. 'We'll find her. You haven't let her down, Matthew. You've never, ever let that little girl down.'

'Who would do this?' Matthew asked helplessly. Then he paused, looking left and right into the snow. 'Someone must've stopped Stefan handing himself in. It must be Gastrell or one of his men. What if they've taken Daisy too?' he said with conviction, speaking Lottie's thoughts aloud.

'I was thinking the same thing,' she admitted. 'But why take Daisy? Unless someone saw her and decided to take her home with them, out of the cold?'

Matthew swallowed, considering her words.

Couldn't that be it? Couldn't it be innocent, a local who wanted to help but had gone about it the wrong way? And yet surely any local would know to take her to the vicarage.

But it was hope. One tiny scrap of hope.

They kept going, their eyes fixed on the path of the footprints: Daisy's and the man who had led her away. They shouted her name, pausing after each call, just in case there was a reply.

But none came.

'Reverend Hart, Miss Morley!' a voice called and Lottie turned to see a figure coming along the pavement, the snowflakes dancing in the weak beam of their blackout torch. It was Captain Spencer, leading his platoon. 'Please return home. My men will apprehend the German.'

'Someone's snatched Daisy!' Matthew told him urgently. He pointed the torch at the pair of fast-disappearing footprints. 'They led her away.'

'That dashed Bosch!' the older man exclaimed. 'Mark my words, Vicar, we'll track—'

'No!' Matthew snapped. 'Stefan was going to hand himself in tonight. Instead, he disappeared and now Daisy's vanished too.'

'Reverend Hart's right,' Lottie told Captain Spencer. 'Stefan von Brandt is injured and frail from being outside, half-starved, for days in this terribly cold weather. He couldn't have kidnapped Daisy. But what about Mr Gastrell's men? They could.'

'These are very serious allegations, Miss,' said Captain Spencer. He turned to his platoon and commanded, 'Fan out, men, and look for any sign of that little girl; don't disturb the footprints. Sergeant, take the van and liaise with Constable Russell. We'll get the whole village out if we must. We'll find your little lass, Vicar, don't you worry.'

As Spencer and his men dispersed about their duty, Lottie and Matthew trudged through the settling snow, following the weakening trail. Step by step, the footprints were harder and harder to see. They went on calling, their throats raw with the cold. There was no reply.

Blossom, on her short legs, was sometimes barely visible as she plunged through the snow. It was hard going, even more so for Matthew with his walking stick; in places the snow was so deep that it spilled into Lottie's boots and melted inside them. The track took them past one house after another without changing direction. Lottie's heart sank. The trail was leading them out of the village.

Matthew paused for a moment, bracing his arm against a lamppost. Lottie lifted her head, despite the blast of Arctic wind that rasped her face with pellets of snow, and looked along the road ahead. The pair of footprints had almost vanished.

She knew this route. She knew it well; she'd walked it often enough.

She gasped.

'Oh, no. He's taking her to the woods.'

FIFTY-FIVE

Matthew abandoned the few seconds of rest he'd given himself. With Lottie's arm through his, he was walking again, forging his way through the snow.

'What sort of monster would take a child into pitch-black woods in a snowstorm?' he demanded, the panic gone from his voice, replaced with iron resolve. His arm tightened against Lottie's. 'What could anyone gain from this?'

'There's a phone box just along here,' Lottie told him, wiping snow away from her face. 'I'll ring the farm, tell them to start looking in the woods, tell them to ring down to the village.'

Each slow, wading step through the snow felt like minutes as Lottie pushed on towards the phone box. She pulled Matthew inside with her, to get him some precious respite from the punishing blasts of the freezing wind and the incessant snow. Blossom wouldn't come in and instead marched up and down, sniffing the snow-covered road.

Lottie tried to keep her voice steady as she told the operator the number for the farm. The calm, careful voice on the other end of the telephone and the pale, drawn face of Matthew right in front of her sent her into a panic.

Do something! For heaven's sake, it's urgent!

'A little girl's missing, she's been taken up to the woods behind Bramble Heath!' The words spilled from her in a rush. 'Once you've put me through, tell the police, tell anyone you can!'

'I will, Madam,' the operator said, and Lottie found herself on the line to Goslings' farm.

A bleary-voiced Shona picked up. 'Lottie? But it's the middle of the night, love. Where are you? Has something happened?'

'I'm in the phone box, halfway down the road to the village,' Lottie told her. 'Someone's taken Daisy to the woods. Telephone down to the village, tell them, then get everyone on the farm out to look!'

'Taken Daisy?' Shona was suddenly awake. 'Don't worry, we'll get out there and find her! And the swine who's taken her.'

Back out in the snow again, Blossom led the way and they followed.

The grey snow clouds hung heavily overhead as they forced themselves to go on, step by trudging step, up the hill towards the woods. The muscles in Lottie's legs ached and she knew Matthew must be struggling too; he put down his stick more heavily with every step.

As they came round a bend in the road, the dark bulk of the woods suddenly reared up against the grey clouds. Even with the snow blanketing the top branches, it was a wall of darkness.

And somewhere among the tall, shadowy trees and the sharp, scratching brambles was Daisy.

FIFTY-SIX

The woods that Lottie remembered from the day she and the Land Girls had gone to choose their Christmas tree, with their shiny holly, mistletoe and robins, were a world away from the woods she and Matthew now found themselves in. The gnarled branches and looming trunks crowded out the little light afforded by the brightness of the snow and the air was still, as if every creature in the trees was holding its breath.

At least the trees provided some protection from the vicious, whipping wind and only a scattering of snow could penetrate the canopy of branches overhead.

'Daisy! Daisy, love, come home!' Lottie called into the darkness.

'Where are you, Daisy?' Matthew shouted. He swallowed down a sob.

'He brought her here, he must have done, the footprints came this way,' Lottie reassured him. 'We're close, I know we are.'

Then somewhere, several yards away – it was hard to tell exactly how far – a voice called, 'Daisy! Daisy!'

Lottie knew that voice. She glanced up at Matthew. A deep frown carved his forehead.

'Gastrell?' he spat with angry resignation. 'Very convenient.'

'Who's there? Show yourself!' came Gastrell's voice through the freezing air. Lottie and Matthew stopped as the sound of branches swishing back and footsteps on the cold earth came towards them.

Lottie ran her blackout torch over him and Gastrell shaded his eyes with his arm. Beside him were two of his men, a former soldier with a hunched back and an airman with a puckered scar running down the side of his face.

'Why did you take her?' Matthew demanded and took a shaky step towards him. Lottie held his arm tighter and Matthew stopped, his chest rising and falling with each urgent breath.

'Take her?' Gastrell shook his head. 'No, I wouldn't have – I want to help.'

'Help?' Matthew clenched his jaw. 'You only ever helped yourself.'

Gastrell didn't reply at once. He seemed to be choosing his words with care.

'All I've ever tried to do was help. Perhaps not in the best way, I know that now,' he replied. 'But please, Matthew, believe me when I say I wouldn't harm a hair on her head.'

'But you just happen to be here, where someone brought Daisy?' Matthew demanded. 'And on the night Stefan disappeared before he had a chance to surrender!'

'He was going to hand himself in and you made sure he couldn't!' Lottie stated. 'What have you done with him, for heaven's sake? And what have you done with Daisy?'

Gastrell held Matthew's gaze as he said, 'I've seen neither; I've no reason to lie.'

'But you're here!' Matthew replied. 'Where is she?'

Gastrell raised his empty hands, palms facing up, towards

Matthew, as if trying to show that he had nothing to hide. 'Captain Spencer told us to head up here to the woods in Ted's car and search for the German. For the first time in a long while, I'm just doing as I'm told.'

They must have driven up the other road, Lottie realised, the long way round that nobody walking this way would take. And suddenly, she heard other voices, men and women, calling through the woods, calling for the little girl who had crept out of bed for the wonder of seeing the deer in the garden, only to be lured away to the woods by a stranger.

Matthew glanced around, as if trying to place the voices. Lottie knew the Land Girls would be among them. She desperately peered into the darkness and the more she did, the more figures she saw among the trees.

'It sounds as though you've got all of Bramble Heath out for her,' Gastrell told him. 'They're good folk and they'll find Daisy. We won't go home until she's safe and sound.' He turned to his men and said, 'You get on, gents, I'll stay with the vicar and Miss Morley.'

For a moment Matthew tensed, then he nodded. 'Come on,' was all he said.

It might be dark and snowing and cold, but the villagers had spilled from house after house, and cottage after cottage, as soon as they knew that Daisy was missing. Wrapped up warm, they pushed through the trunks and branches, walking over the snow that lay between the trees and their twisted roots.

They carried on, a group of three now, fanning out, while Lottie refused to let go of Matthew's hand. Blossom hurried along, head low, her nose questing the frozen ground.

Through the cold air, Lottie heard trudging boots and calls of 'Daisy! Daisy, where are you?' She heard a Geordie accent, a Yorkshire accent, a cockney accent. Nicola and Shona and Frances were here with her. The Land Girls never let each other down, even an honorary Land Girl like Daisy.

But for all the cries of his niece's name, there was no answering call from the little girl. Lottie glanced at Matthew. He looked pained; drawn and terrified, and there was nothing more she could do than stay at his side, holding his hand, searching with him.

'We'll find her,' Lottie told him again, 'I swear we—'

With a sudden, sharp bark, Blossom shot ahead, hurried into the darkness and vanished through a tangle of brambles.

'Blossom!' Lottie shouted, 'Come back here.'

But Matthew started forward. 'There's something there,' he said, his voice a mixture of anguish and desperation.

Lottie held her breath in anticipation and Gastrell paused, listening, as Blossom's bark carried through the woodland towards them. Matthew held his cane under his arm and dipped into his pocket to retrieve Daisy's rabbit. He looked down at it, then lifted his head to listen once more.

'Wait, did you hear that?' Lottie whispered urgently. She didn't want to drown out the sound, coming from somewhere through the trees ahead, but she was sure she knew what it was.

A high-pitched call. A little girl's voice.

'Daisy!' Matthew exclaimed. He returned the rabbit to his pocket and strode on with renewed vigour. 'Daisy! We're here, keep calling!'

She was alive, and she was close by.

But they couldn't relax yet. They had no idea who had taken her. No idea what they wanted.

Blossom's barks and the distant sounds of Daisy's calls drew the other searchers towards them through the trees. Lottie was only aware of the shapes of people, the sounds of their steps, the clouds of steam from their breath. The dancing beam of her torch either side of her picked out RAF greatcoats and Home Guard caps, home-knitted bobble hats and stout boots. Everyone was here.

'Miss Morley!'

Lottie looked up to see that George was there, his face pale with concern. He was doing his best to keep up with the vicar's determined pace.

'I heard about the fire at the base,' he said, rubbing his gloved hands together. 'And then the Kraut takes little Daisy? It's a bad do all round.'

'It wasn't him,' Lottie told him, forging ahead, Daisy's cries getting louder. 'It couldn't have been him.'

'But how do you *know*? For sure?' George pressed her.

'He's barely able to stand, let alone hare around the village kidnapping children,' Matthew snapped. 'Daisy!'

Then, suddenly, from the mass of darkness ahead of them, Lottie saw a tiny pinprick of weak, flickering light. And she heard it; they all heard it.

'Uncle Matthew!' the missing girl cried.

Lottie lifted her torch and it picked up the children's club-house. That eccentric hand-built shelter, that had brought together the local children and ones who had come from London and further afield, stood only a few feet ahead. The curtain hanging over the doorway swayed in the cold breeze, the quivering light of a weak candle glowing through its tears and thin patches.

Blossom barked from inside and Daisy called for her uncle again. But there was no fear in her voice, Lottie realised. It was as if she was merely pleased that he'd come to join her in the woods. In the clubhouse that she'd been so desperate to see.

'Oh, thank God,' Matthew gasped and surged forward.

Captain Spencer and Constable Russell had got to the front of the crowd, but they didn't stop him.

And they didn't stop Lottie, either. She went with him, her heart in her mouth.

Matthew dragged open the curtain and they hurried in, shining their torches inside.

FIFTY-SEVEN

Behind the curtain, caught in the torchlight and the guttering flame of a near-spent candle was Daisy, wide-eyed, her winter coat, boots and knitted hat and gloves thrown on over her pyjamas. Round her shoulders was the warm blanket that Lottie and Matthew had given Stefan. She was stroking Blossom, who had stopped barking now.

The little girl was kneeling beside a figure so crumpled and still that Lottie thought she'd been looking at a pile of old sacks. But, she realised now, it was Stefan. His eyes were closed. He wasn't moving. His lip was split and he had a black eye and bruises on his cheek. A thin thread of congealing blood ran down from his nose. It had to be the work of whoever had snatched him.

On the earthen floor, drawn in a thin layer of snow that had made it through the tree canopy and the gaps in the clubhouse roof, Lottie saw a game of noughts and crosses. Evidently, despite how ill he was, Stefan had tried to look after Daisy and had come up with something to pass the time until they were rescued.

But were they too late for the stricken airman and the secrets he held?

'Daisy? Oh, thank goodness!' she gasped.

Matthew knelt beside his niece and drew her into his arms, holding her tight as he asked, 'Are you all right?' He took the bunny from his pocket with a trembling hand and pressed it to her in their embrace.

Daisy clutched her rabbit, then pressed her cheek against Matthew's chest. She was still stroking Blossom.

Lottie glanced over her shoulder to see people crowding around the doorway, peering in over each other's shoulders. Constable Russell and Captain Spencer were trying to hold them back, but they let Gastrell step inside, past the villagers. He gazed down at Daisy, caught in Matthew's caring embrace, before his glance shifted to Stefan. He swallowed as he took in the sight of Hitler's injured, helpless godson.

'Come on, the game's up. Time to face the music,' he said.

'Don't you touch him!' Lottie protested. She didn't know how to do first aid, but she leaned down to Stefan and put her hand on his clammy forehead. He was alive, but he seemed barely conscious. 'We need to get him help.'

'We played noughts and crosses, and hide-and-seek. He said he was tired from our games,' Daisy told Matthew, with a nod towards Stefan. Evidently she could see that he was injured and she seemed a little doubtful as she glanced towards him. 'But he's asleep now.'

Gastrell nodded knowingly. 'He'll have told her it was a game of hide-and-seek when he snatched her, to stop the little one crying out.'

'Why would he do that?' Lottie demanded as she carefully wiped at Stefan's face with her handkerchief, trying to remove the grime of days spent hiding in the woods and the blood from his wounds. 'He was giving himself up. He couldn't have walked all the way from the vicarage without a walking stick, through the snow.'

Gastrell was about to reply when Matthew blinked up at him. Whatever he was going to say, he held back. Instead, tenderly running his hand over Daisy's hair, he asked her in a gentle voice, 'How did you get here to play your games with Stefan?'

'The pilot brought me,' she replied.

Lottie couldn't believe it. Stefan couldn't have walked all that way, especially through the snow, and he'd been determined to hand himself in. But could she have been wrong to trust him, in the end? Could Wyngate have been wrong, too?

'What do you mean, sweetie?' she asked, as calmly as she could, while Matthew went on stroking Daisy's hair. 'Are you sure it was the pilot?'

'Yes, the pilot found me looking at the deer,' Daisy replied, as plainly as if she was relating what she had been doing at school. 'I told him they live in the woods and he said he'd take me up here to see where they live. And I said the clubhouse is up in the woods, too, but I've never been allowed to go, so he said he'd show me that, too.'

She nodded, glancing around the simple room with its earthen floor, its walls and roof made of the bits and pieces that even the scrapmen wouldn't take.

There was a flurry of whispers beyond the curtain where the impromptu search party were waiting, listening to Daisy's story.

A raised voice declared, 'The pilot? She'll mean the damn Nazi.'

Stefan was still unmoving, but something seemed to change in his shallow breathing. It was as if the very last bit of fight was going out of him at the sound of the word Nazi.

'That'll be it,' Gastrell said. 'He's all yours, Constable Russell. Snatching kiddies from their own garden! Dear me.'

'No, it can't be Stefan,' Matthew told him. 'But you've never listened to anyone but yourself, have you?'

'The pilot took her. The Nazi. Who else could it be?' George said, peering in over Constable Russell's shoulder. He was glaring at Stefan as if he'd never seen such a hateful figure in all his life. 'He needs to be behind bars before the sun comes up – Hitler's godson leading a little kid away from home. Bloody disgrace!'

But Daisy shook her head. 'No, it wasn't him, silly,' she said, looking up at George. 'It was you.'

FIFTY-EIGHT

Lottie froze as Daisy's words revolved in her mind like a speeding carousel. She slowly turned to look up at George.

George, the ace in a day, shooting down five Luftwaffe planes in one flight. George, handsome and boyish, with his blond hair and attractive blue eyes, which Martha had said were like sapphires. George, who Martha had adored, with a depth of love that had taken Lottie entirely by surprise. George, who was so nearly Martha's husband, until fate had intervened and taken her away from him, and everyone else who had loved her.

'Of course it wasn't me!' George snapped, his eyes narrowed, his fists clenched. 'Of all the stupid— she said *the pilot*. The pilot's that bag of rubbish sitting there in the corner!'

Matthew watched him for a long moment, then shook his head. 'No,' he said. 'Daisy wouldn't lie. Was it this gentleman who brought you up to see the clubhouse, Daisy?'

She nodded, but she was leaning into her uncle's embrace now, as if she was beginning to feel afraid.

'You snatched this little kiddie?' Gastrell asked fiercely, jabbing his finger at George. 'Did you drag this little mite through a blizzard and all the way up here when you should've taken her safely home?'

'I've just told you, I damn well didn't,' George replied, his voice too loud in the cramped space of the clubhouse. 'It was *him*.'

In a split second, he ceased to look like George. The good-looking boyishness had vanished, replaced by someone older, exhausted and gaunt. Lottie had got to her feet and was heading towards him when he suddenly made a lunge into the club-house, shoving Constable Russell aside, and nearly knocked her flying. It was only because Gastrell grabbed her by the shoulder that she didn't fall.

'It was *him*!' George bellowed, and Lottie gasped as she saw he'd grabbed Stefan and had the shining barrel of his service revolver pressed against the German's temple. The safety catch clicked as Stefan's terrified eyes flickered open for the first time. 'And I'll bloody kill him!'

FIFTY-NINE

Matthew pulled Daisy away, his hand shielding her eyes as he whispered, 'Let's leave them to play their game, shall we? We'll take Blossom to look for the deer.'

She clung on to her uncle, her rabbit still tight in her grip.

'Lottie,' Matthew whispered, but she shook her head.

'I need to stay,' she murmured. 'For Martha's sake.'

Matthew paused for a moment, his gaze so full of concern that something inside Lottie melted. Then he nodded. 'Don't do anything— please be careful,' he said, as he led Daisy through the curtain. 'Please.'

Beyond the doorway of the clubhouse, Lottie was dimly aware that Captain Spencer was trying to make the search party go home. But her focus was on George and the gun he was holding to the Luftwaffe gunner's head. Stefan was so weak that he couldn't hope to struggle against him and he wouldn't have dared even if he had had the strength. The gun could go off at any second.

'George, don't, for God's sake, don't,' Lottie whispered. She took a step towards him, the guttering candle casting dancing shadows against the haphazard walls. He pressed the gun closer to Stefan's temple, digging the barrel into the German's ashen skin. 'What about Martha? Do you think she'd want to see you doing this? She didn't love a murderer. Where's the George she loved?'

His fingers relaxed, just slightly. He glared at Stefan, the man he was moments from killing, before turning to look up at Lottie. She didn't dare take another step closer.

'Please,' Stefan gasped. 'Please don't. I have information, things I need to tell you. It can't all have been for nothing. Please.'

Lottie felt a hand on her elbow and realised it was Constable Russell. 'We'll take over, Miss,' he murmured.

But she shook her head. She needed to do this. She could get through to George, she was sure. Constable Russell knew that charging in with handcuffs would only make it worse. He'd been there the night Martha was killed; he knew that Lottie and George were linked by her sister's sudden, tragic end and that their shared connection might be what it took to reach George's bruised heart.

'I'll be here if you need me,' he replied as he stepped back to stand by the door.

'I'm not that man any more.' George bit out the words. 'When they killed her, the bloody Nazis, they ripped my heart out of my chest. They killed me, too.'

Lottie knelt on the earthen floor, bringing herself level with him, and wiped her sleeve across her face.

'They didn't kill you,' she told him, trying to stop her tears from choking her voice. 'You're still alive. We're all still alive. Martha's death was the worst thing that has ever happened to me. And to you, too, I know it. But we can't let ourselves be eaten up by hate because of it. We can't let it turn us into monsters. And George, Stefan isn't a monster. He's not a Nazi. He was defecting, him and all the other young men in his plane.

That's why the Luftwaffe shot them down. Please don't blame Stefan for Martha's death, it's not his fault.'

For a second, Lottie saw a flash of humanity through the mask of hate that had become George's face. But as soon as it had appeared, it vanished again, as if he couldn't process what Lottie had told him. 'And on top of her death, there's been all the mates I've lost,' he added, through clenched teeth. 'One minute, it's cricket beside the runway. The scramble bell clangs, we get up into the air and I'm watching these bastards fly in.'

Stefan closed his eyes again, squeezing them tight shut as he waited for the inevitable bullet. Lottie saw his thin throat bob as he swallowed. Then he opened his exhausted eyes again, blinking as though pleading with her to help.

'And they pick them off,' George told her. 'One by bloody one, you see a wing shot off and the plane keels over and goes into a death-spin. That's my mate Smitty, he's done for, and I pray for a parachute. Then there's the next chap, that's Pavel, and if it's not enough the Nazis have ripped his own country out of his hands, the gunfire bursts, they hit his fuel tank and I hear him screaming through the radio. Then silence. He's gone in a ball of flames. I'm flying through the smoke, can barely see through my windscreen through the soot, and am I next? Am I? I never bloody know!'

'I can't begin to imagine what it's like for you,' Lottie said gently. 'But Martha told me, she said you'd tell her that you weren't a killer at heart. That you had to think you were just shooting planes. That you couldn't for a moment let yourself think about the man in the cockpit, who's just like you. And Stefan's even more like you, George. He *isn't* a Nazi. You've got to trust me.'

George cried out, an animal sound that came from the depths. The sound of a man who'd had everything stolen away from him. The love of his life, his friends, his very humanity had gone.

'Believe me, George, I know what you're feeling now. I've felt it too, back in the trenches,' Gastrell told him. To Lottie's surprise, he knelt down on the earthen floor beside her. 'You're looking at the football scores with your mates at breakfast, by dinner they're dead. Lad minding his own business when Jerry sticks a clean one between his eyes... next day it's Jerry's turn and you're putting one through him instead. Day after day, always the same.'

George didn't move the muzzle of his gun away, but he turned to Gastrell. He was listening. Stefan was so still that for a moment Lottie feared they'd lost him. But then she saw that his chest was still rising and falling with each shallow breath.

'My dad was in the trenches, too,' George replied in a small voice. 'He never said a word about it until... until I came home on leave, after the Battle of Britain. He found me at the bottom of the garden. I was crying. He didn't even ask me what was wrong. He just... he just put his hand on my shoulder, and he cried too. I'd never seen him cry before. Never.'

Gastrell's gaze was filled with sympathy. 'It takes a real man to admit that. A real hero.' He nodded, then reached out and put his hand on George's shoulder. 'Your dad won't want to hear that his lad put a bullet through someone's head, George. He's proud of you; don't give him reason not to be.'

George swallowed and looked down at the gun. His finger relaxed on the trigger, but he didn't take it away. He didn't reply. Lottie wished she could reach across and lift the gun away, but she couldn't risk surprising him.

'I came out of the trenches filled with anger; all that grief with nowhere to go. That's how I came to this job of mine, bringing in wrong 'uns year after year,' Gastrell went on. 'But I lost something very precious when I decided to make this my life. Don't you do the same, George.'

'It doesn't matter now,' George whispered. 'I've lost every-thing. I'm so alone. Do I care if they stick me on the scaffold?'

'*Martha* would care,' Lottie reminded him. 'And somewhere out there, there's a woman you'll love just as much. You just need to find her.'

'I had a lovely little family when I went off to fight; bonny little boy and girl, a wife who'd do anything for me,' Gastrell said. 'And that's what I was fighting for. For them and every family like them. I loved the three of them more than I'd ever loved anything in all my sorry days.'

Lottie didn't remember reading about him having a family in his book. Why had he kept it a secret?

'But when we won and came home, what was there to find?' Gastrell sighed and shook his head. 'Good men dead or crippled, kiddies without a dad... wives without husbands. Just tears among all the talk of victory. And men thrown on the scrapheap, who'd given their good health for a country that had no use for them when they came home. And I had to do something. I had to give those lads a purpose again. We don't only bring in criminals and that sort; we rattle tins on the high street, we clear the rubble and build shelters. We try to keep this world safe.'

George nodded.

'I was never much good in school, but I could get folks listening and I could turn my mind to catching the criminals who the law couldn't seem to hold on to. The same sort who managed to dodge the gas and the shells and come home, while decent lads were dead in the mud.' Gastrell blinked and shook his head. 'My dad was a wrong 'un. We never had much of anything, but when I tracked down that first escapee... well, suddenly I was famous. And I had some money from the reward and I could say to everybody that I wasn't like him. I was bringing in criminals. And I could buy my kids what I never had.' He passed his gloved hand over his face, then admitted, 'And the more of them I could catch and bring in, the more books I sold and the more money I made. And when folks are calling you a hero everywhere you go it gets to be like the booze or the horses. There's women chucking themselves at you too, until you don't think too much about that wife you left at home. And before you know it, you've forgotten why you started.'

George's grip relaxed, but he was still holding the gun close to Stefan's head.

'And my wife and kids got forgotten along the way too,' Gastrell admitted. 'Because I chased the limelight and I chased the girls and, one day, I didn't bother going home. I deserve locking up for that.'

'But they should be proud of you,' George said.

'I'm nobody to be proud of,' Gastrell murmured. 'My wife passed away and I was too much of a coward to get in touch with the kids. Too ashamed. My son hates me and I can't say I blame him. My lass got wed and had a little girl of her own. She wrote to me when her daughter came along and I've never been so happy as I was when I opened that letter. We wrote back and forth, but I didn't have the nerve to ask if I could come and meet the kiddie. I wish I had. My daughter was killed just like your Martha. By a Nazi bomb.'

'I'm so sorry,' Lottie whispered.

'Thank you, Miss,' Gastrell told her. Then he turned to George. 'I'm not surprised you're furious, George. Was it you behind all the vandalism?'

'I hated that they were going to be buried in the church-yard,' George admitted. There was a click as he put the safety catch back on and some of the tautness in the room dissipated. But he was still holding the gun. 'Nazis lying in good, English soil. I knew where Ted kept his paint so I took it, I painted the swastika on the church, and you all thought the Kraut had done it. So I had another go, did the windows in on the pub, painted another swastika, so you'd all start to hate him just as much as I do.'

'And *then* you decided to kidnap Daisy,' Lottie said, trying to make sense of how George's traumas, his hatred, could have shattered his mind to such an extent. 'How could you snatch a little girl?'

'I started the fire at the airbase, too,' George confessed. He ran his tongue over his lips before his words tumbled out in a confused rush. 'Then I saw him, right in front of me. I battered him, I dragged him back up here to the woods, to finish him off. I thought he was done for, then I came back down to the village in a daze. Little Daisy was just *there*, and I knew what I had to do. I brought her up here too, told her a nice story – I wasn't going to hurt her, of course not. I was going to tell everyone he'd snatched her and that I killed him to save her. But then I heard all the shouting and I had to come out.'

'Let Stefan go,' Lottie said gently. 'You're not a murderer.'

'Come on, lad, let young Stefan go,' Gastrell said, holding his hand out to him. George, trembling, passed the gun to Gastrell, who handed it over to Constable Russell. As soon as the weapon was safely out of George's reach, Stefan slumped, shivering deeply. 'That's the way; we'll get you some help. It's not too late,' Gastrell said.

'It's never too late,' Matthew said. Lottie turned to see him in the doorway and she wondered how long he'd been standing there. 'I'm proud of you tonight, Dad.'

SIXTY

Gastrell looked up at Matthew. 'Oh, son,' was all he could say, his words choked with emotion. 'My Matthew.'

The similarity between them wasn't immediately obvious, but Lottie could see it now she knew. Gastrell's hair was darker, his face fuller, but there was their shared height, and there was something about the glitter in their eyes, too, and the determined line of their jaws. How had she not seen it before? But then, she hadn't thought to look. She never would have assumed that the kind, quiet vicar could be the son of the flamboyant Gastrell, hunting down convicts and traitors, and popping up constantly on newsreels.

'Emily told me she was thinking of writing to you, but I said I never wanted to know if she did,' Matthew admitted. 'We've wasted a lot of time.'

'When I saw you here, I hoped you and me might put things right. I've always been a daft old sod,' Gastrell murmured. For a few seconds, neither man spoke, then Gastrell raised his eyes to Matthew and said, 'I'm so sorry, Matthew, for all the rotten things I've done. And you did right, taking your mum's name. You're a credit to that woman.'

Matthew swallowed, then gave his father the ghost of a smile.

'We all make mistakes,' he said. 'But maybe we can put them right too.'

Stefan, his eyes rolling under his half-closed lids, suddenly shuddered. His arms flailed and his legs kicked out, beating against the old tin panel of the wall.

George reached out for the German, but there was no hate left in his expression, only concern. He put his arms around Stefan and held him tight. 'Hold on, mate. Don't die on us. I'm sorry. God, I'm so sorry.'

'I'll take him to the vicarage and get some help,' Matthew said urgently. He came forward and George relinquished Stefan so that Matthew could lift him. As he did, Matthew told them, 'He's freezing; we'll need Nurse Russell.'

Constable Russell nodded to Matthew, then gripped George's arm and pulled him to his feet. 'Captain Spencer's men are taking you down to the airbase. Group Captain Chambers will know what to do with you.' Then he led him out through the door.

Lottie came outside, her arm round Matthew's, holding his stick as he carried Stefan to safety. Gastrell was helping him, placing his hand between the doorframe and Stefan's head, protecting him now even though he'd called for blood not long before.

Daisy, wrapped in the blanket, was waiting with the Land Girls. Nicola's arm was round her shoulders, while Shona held Blossom and Frances knelt beside the little girl, admiring her toy rabbit. The girls looked exhausted, but they all smiled at Lottie.

Alastair stood with them, his arm round his fiancée Laura. They were both wrapped up against the cold. As Lottie left the clubhouse, Alastair shone a proud smile on her.

Daisy held out her hand, catching a snowflake that had made it down through the tree canopy.

'It's nearly Christmas!' she told Lottie.

But Lottie couldn't feel any joy at the thought as she glanced at Matthew, struggling with Stefan in his arms. Would that damaged young lad live to see Christmas morning? He was clinging to life by the thinnest of threads.

'It's Christmas Eve,' Matthew said. Lottie could hear the worry in his voice, even as he tried to cover it with good humour for Daisy's sake. 'Father Christmas will be loading up his sleigh soon, so we'd better get home!'

'Hooray!' Daisy cheered. 'Are we bringing Stefan too?'

'We are,' Matthew said, then whispered to Constable Russell, 'He needs medical help urgently, I think he has hypothermia.'

'Don't worry,' the policeman replied. 'Ted left us his car up here – you head back in that, and I'll go back with the Home Guard boys and hop out to fetch my girl on the way.'

His daughter, the district nurse, would know what to do.

But would they be in time?

SIXTY-ONE

Dorothy was waiting anxiously for them at the vicarage. As Matthew and Lottie came through the front door with Blossom, the housekeeper stared in amazement.

'Is that— that's him, isn't it? The German! He's in a bad way, isn't he?' she whispered. 'And Mr Gastrell! I never expected to see you here again. Come in, come in, everyone, let's get Daisy back to bed.'

Lottie was relieved to be out of the cold at last, with Daisy safely home. But the night was far from over. Stefan was still unconscious and if he had hypothermia, as Matthew suspected, could he survive?

'I'll let Stefan have my bed,' Matthew said. But at the bottom of the stairs he paused and drew in a deep breath. He rested his hand on the newel post and looked up the flight of stairs like a man about to ascend Everest. Then, with another deep breath, he put his foot on the riser and began the slow climb.

'Can you make a couple of hot-water bottles, Dorothy?' Lottie asked as she followed Matthew up, Daisy in her arms and Blossom trotting alongside her. She couldn't begin to imagine how exhausted Matthew was. He'd battled through the snow with his walking stick to find his missing niece, witnessed one man try to shoot another and was now trying to forgive his father.

The housekeeper nodded. 'Of course. I'll bring them up just as soon as I can.'

Gastrell stood in the hallway, holding his hat. 'Is there anything I can do? I want to help.'

Dorothy nodded and led him away.

'Stefan's my friend,' Daisy told them as they reached the top of the stairs. 'He'll get better soon, won't he, so we can play noughts and crosses again? He's very tired.'

'We're looking after him,' Lottie said, trying to reassure her, but she couldn't make any promises.

Lottie held back a sob. Daisy was so innocent. She hadn't seen Stefan and instantly feared him as the enemy. Instead, she'd seen a young man who, despite his own afflictions, had done his best to keep the little girl warm and entertained while they waited – hoped – for help to come. Before George could take out his pain on a brave young man who didn't deserve it.

'If Constable Russell wants to talk to you, you just tell him what happened,' Matthew said gently. 'And if Stefan was kind, you can tell him that too. You've been very brave and you've told the truth.' He smiled at Daisy despite his fatigue. 'I love you, Daisy.'

'I love you, Uncle Matthew,' she replied, smiling back at him. 'I knew you'd come, I told Stefan you would.'

Lottie couldn't help but smile, too. Because Matthew had raised her well, this sweet, honest little girl who he hadn't chosen to have, but who fate had given to him.

'I'll settle her, don't worry,' Lottie told Matthew as Daisy lolled her head against her. 'You've done a good job, Uncle Matthew.'

'So has Daisy,' Matthew said, gazing at his niece tenderly. 'She gave me a reason to keep going when I wanted to give up.'

The uncle and his little niece were such a tight unit and yet, as they headed down the corridor to the bedrooms, Lottie felt as if she had become part of their lives.

'I'll come and help as soon as I've got Daisy back to sleep,' she whispered, her gaze moving towards Stefan. He looked so pale. His lips were split from the cold and his cheekbones were more prominent than ever in his narrow face. The bruises George had inflicted were livid and sore.

Please, God, spare him.

Lottie took Daisy into her room, which was lit by the soft glow of the nightlight. She'd not had a lot of experience with small children, yet she seemed instinctively to know what to do. Using her handkerchief, she wiped a smudge of dirt from Daisy's cheek, then found some clean pyjamas for the little girl in the chest of drawers. Daisy smiled through her tiredness at Lottie and it warmed her heart to know that the little girl, who'd had such an eventful night, trusted her.

She tenderly helped Daisy into her pyjamas, then settled her under the blankets with her rabbit. She knelt beside the bed and kissed her cheek, before gently stroking the little girl's hair until her eyelids were heavy. It was so quiet in the room, so peaceful, as if the spectre of George had been nothing but a bad dream.

'Goodnight, little Daisy,' Lottie said softly, her words catching in her throat as she watched her long eyelashes come to rest on her soft, round cheeks.

Blossom settled on the rug beside Lottie, watching Daisy as she drifted into sleep. The little dog's tail wagged lazily when the door opened to admit Matthew and he knelt at Lottie's side, reaching for her hand as he placed a gentle kiss on Daisy's cheek.

'Sleep tight,' he whispered. 'You're safe now.' Then Matthew looked at Lottie and whispered softly, 'I've prayed for a miracle tonight. We're all due one.'

SIXTY-TWO

Matthew and Lottie stayed there, hand in hand, beside Daisy's bed until a knock at the door heralded the arrival of Annie, Bramble Heath's district nurse. Only then did they finally end their vigil, as Matthew kissed his niece's cheek and then gently lifted the sleeping Blossom up onto the little girl's blankets.

As he stood and offered his hand to Lottie, she could see again how much effort it must have taken him to search for Daisy, and afterwards to carry Stefan through the woods to the waiting car. He looked exhausted; but he hadn't faltered.

Lottie took his hand, linking her fingers through his. He'd been through one awful night, but shown such unwavering bravery in the face of his own fears.

Dorothy opened the bedroom door and stepped aside to reveal their visitor. 'Nurse Russell's here.'

Despite having rushed through the snow to get to them, Annie looked neat as a pin. Her expression was gentle as she glanced over to the bed where Daisy was sleeping. 'What an evening you've all had,' she said sympathetically. 'I'll look Daisy over tomorrow once she's awake, if you like. Right now, I think the best thing for her is to sleep. And the young airman…?'

There was worry in her expression now and Lottie wondered how hard it would be for her to look after Stefan, just as it had been so difficult for Lottie to put aside her hatred and fear because of what had happened to Martha. The Luftwaffe had shot Annie's fiancé out of the sky and the burns had left him with a scarred mask of a face. And yet she had battled through the snow tonight to care for a man who had worn the same uniform as the pilot who'd nearly killed the man she loved.

'Stefan,' said Matthew. 'He's in my room.'

And, still holding Lottie's hand, he made his way across the landing to a door that stood ajar.

The cottage-style bedroom was simple, with a patchwork quilt over the bed, under which Stefan lay. On the chest of drawers, Lottie noticed a cluster of framed photographs. A picture from the 1920s showed a woman holding a wide hat and smiling into the sunshine. She was a younger version of the solitary woman in the photograph in Daisy's room.

Matthew's mother, the woman who Gastrell had abandoned.

She spotted next to that a studio portrait of a baby with her parents. In the low light from the lamp beside the bed, she recognised Daisy's parents, two more people who had lost their lives to the war. And now, they were gazing out of the picture frame, out of the past, at a young man whose godfather was responsible for cruelly cutting their lives so short and making Daisy an orphan.

Annie went over to the bed. 'Stefan, my name's Annie. I'm here to help you. You're very cold, aren't you? Let's warm you up, let's get you better.'

Lottie held back a sob, watching Annie tend so gently to Stefan as if he was just another patient in Bramble Heath.

Stefan stirred on the pillow, then opened his eyes weakly. He blinked up at her and murmured, 'I'm sorry to be a burden, Ma'am.'

A look of surprise fleetingly crossed Annie's features. She shook her head. 'You're not a burden to anyone, Stefan. Besides, it's my job to look after people. Now, I just want you to relax. Don't worry, you're in safe hands.'

She smiled as she looked up at Matthew and Lottie. 'Lottie, could you and Dorothy get some more hot-water bottles, some more blankets – and we need some sweet tea as well. Sorry about your rations, Reverend Hart. We need to warm this young fellow up.'

Lottie met Dorothy on the landing and the two women hurried downstairs.

'That young man, he will live to see morning, won't he?' Dorothy asked in a whisper as they went into the kitchen together. 'I don't like the Germans, but he's only a boy, isn't he?'

'We'll look after him the best we can,' Lottie assured her as she took the teapot off the dresser. 'And hope that it's enough.'

It didn't seem like Christmas Eve, but Lottie was determined that it would, once Daisy was awake and the dawn had come. Life was precious and for Daisy and all the other children like her who had lost so much, Christmas was more than ever a time to be filled with hope, gratitude and love.

She could hear the light sounds of Annie and Matthew's tread on the boards above, but other than that the vicarage was silent. The village was silent too, sleeping now beneath its blanket of snow, whiling away the hours until daylight.

Dorothy was busy at the sink, filling the kettle, while Gastrell cut a strange figure, the man from the newsreels taking cups and saucers down from the Welsh dresser.

'I went too far stirring up the villagers,' he admitted to Lottie. 'And because of me, something terrible could've happened, Miss Morley. If I'd known—'

He fell silent as the mournful wail of the air-raid siren sounded, cutting through the silent night.

SIXTY-THREE

Lottie's hands were suddenly clammy with fear, her heart hammering.

We need to get Daisy to safety, right away!

She heard Matthew's footsteps on the staircase and rushed out of the kitchen with Gastrell following behind. Daisy was in Matthew's arms and Blossom at his heels. The little girl was sleeping soundly, wrapped in a colourful blanket, still clutching her toy rabbit to her chest. For a moment the vicar and his father simply looked at each other, then Matthew spoke.

'We can't move Stefan,' he told Lottie. 'And I don't think that we'd be able to get into the shelter through the snow without digging it out. We'll have to stay here in the house. Lottie, you take Daisy and Dorothy and get under the stairs.'

Lottie couldn't reply at once; her mouth was suddenly dry. Staying inside the house went against her every instinct to keep safe in an air raid. But she knew Matthew was right. Stefan was too ill and the shelter was piled under the snow. Sheltering under the stairs was the only option they had. And, for all that she was terrified of remaining inside the house during a raid, she knew that Matthew would be even more frightened. Memories would be flooding back to him that no one should ever have to remember.

'I could dig out the shelter?' offered Gastrell, but Matthew shook his head.

'There's no time,' he said, his voice hushed. 'I'll stay with Annie and Stefan. The best I can offer you is the kitchen table; there won't be room for all of you beneath the stairs.'

'You can have my space under the stairs,' Lottie told Gastrell. She wanted to stay with Matthew anyway. She knew he would be terrified, being in the house as the siren wailed and the sound of planes began to fill the air. She needed to be there for him.

Gastrell shook his head. 'I'll take my chances,' he said.

'I'm going to stay with you, Matthew,' Lottie told him, determined, as Dorothy appeared.

The housekeeper gently took the sleeping Daisy in her arms and headed for the cupboard under the stairs. 'Lottie, the kettle's nearly boiled. Everything's ready.' She smiled down at the little girl. 'Look at her, she's out like a light! I'll take good care of her, Matthew.'

'I know you will,' he said fondly. 'It'll be over before we know it.'

Her hands shaking, Lottie opened the cupboard door. Blossom sniffed around it but didn't follow Dorothy and Daisy inside. Lottie tried to urge her in with her toe, but Blossom retreated and gazed up at her instead.

'All right, come with us,' she said reluctantly. She wanted Blossom to be safe too, but the little dog gave her such comfort, especially during the raids. And Blossom must have known that.

She picked up the dog and held her close, shutting her eyes as she tried to block out the racket of the siren.

Matthew put his arm round Lottie and said gently, 'Won't you go with Mrs J and Daisy?'

'No, Matthew,' Lottie replied in a whisper as she leaned into his welcome embrace and opened her eyes, meeting his gaze. 'I'm staying with you.'

SIXTY-FOUR

After a few minutes, time for everyone to get to their shelters, the siren stopped wailing. Now came the long wait for the all-clear.

Lottie wondered how many of Bramble Heath's residents had braved the snow and managed to dig out their shelters in time. Not many, she was sure. Most of the village would be sheltering under their stairs right now, sitting in the darkness with their brooms and dusters, or under a table, waiting in the taut silence for the ominous rumble of the aeroplanes above them.

Matthew had gone back upstairs to help Annie look after Stefan. Lottie went back into the kitchen to make the hot-water bottles and tea for their patient. And Sidney Gastrell went with her.

'Could you pass me the tea caddy, please, Mr Gastrell?' she asked him as she swilled the boiling water in the pot to warm it. She tried to still the tremble in her hand.

'The cellar at the pub... it's safe down there, isn't it?' Gastrell asked fretfully as he reached for the caddy and handed it over to Lottie. 'I don't like being away from my wife when the siren goes.'

Lottie levered the lid off the caddy with a spoon. 'She'll be safe,' she assured him. 'I've been down there loads of times during raids. And it's comfortable, too.'

'I'm glad to know that,' he replied. 'She put me back on the straight and narrow; she's a good woman.'

Lottie spooned the leaves into the pot before pouring in the water. Talking to Gastrell was distracting her, helping her to push away her fear.

As she stirred the leaves in the pot, she looked up at him.

'You started with the best intentions,' she observed kindly. 'Providing for Matthew and his sister. But you should never have left them, Mr Gastrell.' She felt defensive of her boyfriend; she cared about him and she'd seen the pain that his father's choice had caused.

'I know that,' Gastrell admitted. 'I wish I could've seen my Emily again, Miss Morley. But that little girl... she's the image of her mum.'

Lottie held out her trembling hand and gingerly laid it on Gastrell's sleeve. Her voice catching, she said, 'I'm so, so sorry that she was taken from you. You could've patched things up, couldn't you?'

'I hope we could.' He took a handkerchief from his pocket and dabbed his eyes. 'I wanted to. I've still got the letters she sent me...'

Lottie tried to smile, holding back her tears. She knew how precious such mementos were.

Gastrell blinked rapidly, then dabbed his eyes again and asked, 'Do you think there's any hope for me and Matthew? I've been a bloody idiot.'

'He's a vicar,' Lottie reminded him. 'And they always talk about forgiveness, don't they? I don't think he'd have let you come back here with us if he wasn't already starting to forgive you.'

'Daisy needs her family.' And there in the doorway was

Matthew, unseen by Lottie or Gastrell until now. 'And all this time she's only had me, but she should have her granddad too, just like Em would've wanted. The women were always the ones with sense in our family.'

The room was silent for a moment, then Lottie heard something, a regular beating sound. There was Blossom, by Gastrell's feet, looking up at him, her wagging tail tapping against the floor. The little dog had decided that she liked him, then. Matthew squeezed Lottie's hand as Gastrell knelt to fuss Blossom.

Just then, the quiet of the snowy night was broken by the throb of aeroplane engines in the sky above them.

Martha, Martha, come into the shelter. But she hadn't. She'd stayed outside and she'd been killed.

Lottie had no idea if the sound was coming from aeroplanes taking off from the airbase nearby or from enemy planes, bombers preparing to drop their lethal loads. The urge to get to safety pulled at her again, but it was overruled by something else: her sense of duty, to be there for Matthew, and Daisy, and even Stefan.

Martha felt the same sense of duty the night she was killed.

'Let's take these things upstairs and look after Stefan,' she said, fear in every word. 'Mr Gastrell, will you help?'

Gastrell nodded. 'I'd love to,' he said. Then he added, 'When I said I was sorry about your sister, Miss Morley, that wasn't for the papers. I lost my daughter to those bombs. I really am sorry.'

'Thank you, Mr Gastrell,' Lottie replied. 'I know. It's an awful thing, this bloody war. There's been so much death. Let's pray we don't lose another life in this house tonight.'

SIXTY-FIVE

As they headed back upstairs, carrying a tea tray and the hot-water bottles, they paused by the cupboard under the stairs.

'I hope the planes haven't woken Daisy,' Lottie whispered, as the whole house seemed to throb and vibrate.

Matthew opened the door and peered inside, then closed it gently.

'Both sleeping like logs.' He smiled. 'Annie can't go home with the raid going on, but there's room for her with Daisy and Mrs J. She can take shelter there.'

Lottie wondered how often Annie had had to brave the siren in order to care for others, sometimes strangers. 'Yes, of course. We can sit up with him, I wouldn't be able to sleep anyway.'

They carried on up the stairs and to Matthew's bedroom, where Stefan, still pale and tired, was now sitting up against a pile of pillows. Annie was gently stroking his hair, just as Lottie had stroked Daisy's as she'd fallen asleep. It was an oddly peaceful scene, despite the sound of the planes overhead.

She looked up at them as they came in and smiled tiredly. 'He's going to be all right. Aren't you, Stefan? You're going to be fine. I've bathed and dressed his cuts. We just need to keep him warm and get him eating again, and if he can keep off his sprained ankle too then it'll heal all the faster.'

Lottie sighed with relief. Stefan wasn't going to die; he'd been spared. Hadn't she asked God to do just that, and hadn't Matthew? He'd listened to them. He'd heard their prayer.

Blossom leapt up onto the bed, turned in a circle and settled beside Stefan's feet, resting her head against his leg.

Stefan shook his head and said, 'My father always said I wasn't an outdoor sort of boy. One of the few things he was right about.'

'You and me both,' Matthew told him kindly. 'The first time I climbed a tree, I fell out of it and cracked my head.'

Gastrell had paused in the doorway and settled his gaze on the photograph of Daisy and her parents. He reached into his pocket and took out his wallet.

'You did. Landed right on your noggin,' he admitted gently. Then he showed his wallet to Matthew and Lottie. 'Emily sent me a copy of that photo. I've never been without it. Nor this one.'

The photograph had been carefully looked after, even though it had to be at least twenty years old. It showed two children, standing for their picture in a sunny garden. The little boy looked like Christopher Robin, with a bowl cut and a tunic, his arm round the shoulder of his sister. With her blonde hair and broad smile, she was almost identical to Daisy.

'Matthew and Emily!' Lottie gasped. She grinned at Matthew, squeezing his hand affectionately as she teased, 'You haven't changed a bit. My goodness, doesn't Daisy take after her mum? And you kept it all this time, Mr Gastrell?'

He nodded. 'I did,' he said. 'It's precious as gold to me.'

Annie rose from her chair with a swish of her starched uniform. 'I'd better go, I've done all I can here. Is there space under the stairs for one more?'

'Plenty of space.' Matthew smiled. 'And plenty of blankets too.'

'Wonderful,' Annie said, and picked up her bag. 'Keep him warm and help him drink, just little sips to start with. Gute Nacht, Stefan,' she added, and waved to her patient as she left the room.

'I'm sorry, lad,' Gastrell told Stefan. 'Not much of a welcome to our country, was it?'

Stefan regarded him through tired eyes, then held out his hand to the man who had hunted him. Gastrell took it and shook with care, as though the young man might break in two.

'It's all right,' Stefan said. Then he smiled and added, as so many Britons had said these past years, 'There is a war on, yes?'

SIXTY-SIX

The throbbing sound of the planes overhead grew louder, thicker somehow.

'Yes, there's a war on,' Lottie replied. Somewhere, bombs were dropping and people were dying; like Martha, like Emily.

She sat down on the chair and felt Martha at her shoulder as she looked at the young man. Guilt washed through her at how angry and scared she'd been and she wished that she'd been kinder from the start. She was just relieved that she'd been able, in the end, to understand that he was young and frightened, forced into a situation he had never chosen for himself. She was glad she hadn't become George.

Stefan stared up at the ceiling, as though tracing the paths of the planes soaring through the winter skies. And hadn't he been a victim of a German airman too? Shot down by his own side because Berlin knew the crewmen of his Heinkel had surrender rather than slaughter in mind. Matthew came to sit on the edge of the bed. He reached out and put his hand over Lottie's as Gastrell stood at the foot, his head bowed.

'I'm sorry,' Stefan said quietly. He settled his gaze on Lottie, though he couldn't know what she and Matthew had both lost to the Nazi bombs. 'For what my godfather has done.'

Lottie entwined her fingers with Matthew's. She needed his closeness, just as she knew he needed hers.

'Why should you have to apologise?' she said. 'I won't lie to you, Stefan. I lost my sister. She... she was on the farm, and a bomb fell. Your crewmates died near where she did. And... well, that links us, doesn't it? And Matthew, and Mr Gastrell...' She paused, wrestling with tears that wanted to fall. 'They lost people to a bomb sent over here by your godfather, too. The little girl you looked after in the woods, she lost her mum. But that's not your fault, Stefan. It's not.'

'I am sorry on behalf of all of us. Every decent German,' he said in a small voice. 'I know what my countrymen have done.' Then he gave a tiny, gentle smile. 'I will remember the kindness you have shown me.'

'It's the least we could do,' Lottie replied.

'I'll let you all settle,' Gastrell whispered to Matthew. 'And after Christmas, perhaps you and me could have a cup of tea?'

'Why don't you have some time with Daisy tomorrow?' asked Matthew. 'Emily would want you to. And so do I.'

'That would be lovely, wouldn't it?' Lottie said. 'Christmas Eve with the family.'

As she spoke, she realised that the sound of the planes had stopped. There was a moment, a breath of silence, which was suddenly filled by the sound of the all-clear from the sirens.

SIXTY-SEVEN

Gastrell could have settled on the sofa to sleep, but he hadn't. Instead, while Lottie and Matthew stayed at Stefan's bedside, the young man dozing with Blossom sleeping against his leg, Gastrell had gallantly gone out into the thick snow. He waded through the icy depths to escort Dorothy to her nearby cottage and Annie back home. The reporters would not have seen any of his good deeds, but Lottie knew that Gastrell wouldn't have wanted them to.

He returned with Mrs Gastrell on his arm and the reunited family settled by the Christmas tree, the fire blazing in the hearth. Lottie was sitting beside Matthew on the sofa, and so was Stefan, wearing Matthew's clothes, which were far too big for him, a blanket wrapped round him.

Daisy sat on the rug with Blossom at her side, beaming at her family. She didn't seem at all the worse for wear considering her ordeal the night before. When she had awoken that morning, Matthew had explained to her that he had a very special gift for her. And she was still trying to take it in.

'I got a grandma *and* granddad for Christmas!' she announced. '*And* a new friend, too!'

'A new friend who cannot beat you at noughts and crosses,' Stefan lamented merrily, as a knock sounded at the door.

'I'll get it!' Lottie said, rising from the sofa. She recognised the knock. 'I'll be back in a second.'

Although she'd had hardly any sleep last night, the joy of Christmas Eve's dawn had woken her up. She felt refreshed. She hurried to the front door and pulled it open. The freezing air rushed in and she squinted in the face of the glittering white blanket of snow and the light grey clouds that hung overhead. The garden was unrecognisable, the thick snow pierced only by the few footprints that had struggled back and forth that morning.

There on the step was Shona, wrapped up warm.

'Morning, Shona!' Lottie gave her a hug.

'Morning, you!' she replied, hugging Lottie back. She peered in over her shoulder, then dropped her voice to a whisper: 'How is he?'

'Recovering,' Lottie told her. 'He had hypothermia, poor lad, but he's getting better. He's out of bed, actually. Why don't you come in and say hello? And Mr and Mrs Gastrell are here, too.'

The Land Girls, who had patiently waited outside the club-house while Gastrell and Lottie had talked George down, had by now all heard that Matthew was Gastrell's son.

Shona kicked the snow off her wellies and stepped into the vicarage. As she bent to remove her boots, she called, 'Morning, all! Land Girl bearing gifts!'

Blossom started barking, and Lottie and Shona laughed.

'It's just through here,' Lottie told her, and led the way into the lounge.

Mr Gastrell didn't look like he was posing for the papers any more. He looked rather normal, a man enjoying Christmas Eve morning with his family.

'Shona's come down from the farm,' Lottie explained,

showing her in. 'You know Matthew and Daisy, and this is Mr and Mrs Gastrell. Blossom, calm down! And Stefan you've met before.'

Shona made a round of the room, shaking everyone's hands.

'Lovely to see you all!' she said. 'It took me ages to get here through the snow, but here I am. I suppose I should've come on a sleigh, like Father Christmas. Especially as I've got some pressies.'

Daisy's eyes shone with delight.

'We like knitting, up at the farm,' Shona explained with a warm smile. 'We were kept awake by all those planes last night, so we got busy with our needles.'

She reached into the deep pockets of her coat and pulled out a parcel wrapped in Christmas paper. It had a simple design of triangular green trees with red ribbon looping between them. She went over to Stefan and held it out to him.

'I know you do presents on Christmas Eve in Germany, so I'd say you're allowed to open it now, if you like,' she said.

Stefan looked momentarily bewildered, as though he didn't quite understand that the gift Shona was holding was for him. Then he reached out and took it, saying, 'Thank you,' in a voice that was thick with emotion.

'Open it!' Daisy exclaimed excitedly, as Stefan carefully undid the wrapping with a trembling hand.

A pair of warm, stripy mittens emerged from the wrapping paper. Lottie knew what a gesture this was; it had cost the Land Girls some of their precious wool that they'd managed to find in the face of so many shortages. And they had knitted it up for a young man who had worn the enemy's uniform.

'Oh, don't those look smart!' Mrs Gastrell said, smiling at Stefan. 'What a lovely present.'

'Before you ask, Father Christmas visits English girls tonight,' Matthew told Daisy. 'No presents for you just yet!'

Daisy poked out her bottom lip, but Shona laughed. 'There

might be something else in my pocket, actually. Something for a small Land Girl?'

Lottie leaned her head against Matthew's shoulder. 'She can have just a little present, can't she, Uncle Matthew?'

Matthew kissed Daisy's cheek and said, 'Go on then, just this once.'

The little girl eagerly opened her parcel from Shona. Inside it was a miniature version of Stefan's mittens. She put them on at once and proudly held out her hands.

Shona turned to Stefan and said, 'It's lovely to meet you again. And... my brother's an airman, too. He's in a camp in Germany. They're looking after him, and I know you'll be all right here too.'

Stefan nodded, then smiled. 'Thank you,' he said. 'I hope he will be home with you soon.'

'And we'll keep in touch,' Matthew assured Stefan. 'So when the war's over, you can come back to Bramble Heath and see us all again.'

Wouldn't that be something? No more war, and a man like Stefan free to walk into Bramble Heath without fear.

From outside, Lottie suddenly heard the rumble of an engine and for a moment she tensed, gripping Matthew's hand. It wasn't another raid? Surely not, in broad daylight? But her panic subsided as she realised it was only a tractor.

'They must be clearing the roads,' she said as Daisy raced over to the window.

Lottie followed, and lifted Daisy so she could see over the high sill. The little girl waved her mittened hand at the tractor.

Behind the wheel, recognisable even though she was wrapped up, was Nicola from the farm. And – Lottie could barely grasp what she was seeing – standing behind Nicola's seat, like a footman on a carriage, was a figure in a fedora and a wide-shouldered, tailored overcoat, his red scarf wrapped warmly round his neck.

That's Mr Wyngate! What on earth is he doing on a tractor?

She supposed he must have come down to see Stefan and how else would he get through the snow but on one of the tractors? This wasn't the sort of weather for a sports car, after all.

The tractor drew to a halt and Nicola turned and clearly addressed her passenger in her usual cheery manner. Wyngate nodded, then hopped nimbly down into the snow and offered Nicola another nod of thanks, before he strode through the gate and up the path to the vicarage.

SIXTY-EIGHT

'We've got another visitor!' Lottie announced, and went through to the hallway, Daisy following her. She opened the door onto the snow-covered garden. 'Mr Wyngate!'

'Merry Christmas Eve,' Wyngate said, straight-faced. Then he dropped his gaze to Daisy. 'Nice mittens.'

Daisy waved at him and said, 'I like your hat.'

'Come in, Mr Wyngate,' Lottie said, stepping aside so that he could enter. She wondered what he would make of the unexpected family circle in the lounge. 'We've got a full house. Stefan's here, and the Gastrells too.'

'The players gather in one room,' said the visitor as he took off his hat and put it on Daisy's head. Then he swept past Lottie and headed for the gathering. 'Very Agatha Christie.'

Lottie hurried after him, with Daisy holding on to what was now *her* hat, and was just in time to see the effect his arrival had on everyone in the room. The amiable chatter ceased and they all stared up at him.

'Mr Wyngate,' she announced. He was the sort of person whose presence made an instant impact. His briskness made it clear that he was here for business, and Mrs Gastrell got to her feet.

'Shona, why don't you and I take Daisy into the kitchen?' she suggested. 'Maybe we could look for some Christmas treats?'

Shona nodded and the two women left the room with Daisy, who was still lopsidedly wearing Wyngate's hat. Lottie closed the door after them and steeling herself, settled beside Matthew again.

Wyngate addressed Stefan first, speaking to him in German. It was rapid and, she sensed, far more proficient than Matthew's hesitating efforts. The two men only exchanged a few words, but Stefan seemed to visibly relax as he nodded in reply. With a nod of his own that evidently signalled that an accord had been reached, Wyngate told Gastrell, 'Wyngate, Ministry.' Then he added with relish, 'You should see the file I have on you, Mr Gastrell.'

'I'm not surprised,' Gastrell admitted. 'If I have to speak for young George, I will. I'm the one drove him to lose his head.'

Matthew cleared his throat. 'Mr Gastrell— my father knows he's made mistakes, Mr Wyngate, but I ask you not to forget all the good he's done too. Those criminals he's tracked down, the traitors and their like too. The men who help him wanted to fight for their country and, when they couldn't, they did what they could at home. My father gave them that.'

'Be kind to him, Mr Wyngate. It was George who took Stefan and Daisy, not Mr Gastrell,' Lottie said, joining forces with Matthew. He had forgiven his father; or, at least, he had started the journey.

Wyngate raised one eyebrow, then said, 'Sidney Gastrell. A history of questionable decisions, proven results and a masterful eye for the public mood. People have ruled countries with less.' He tapped his chin with one finger. 'Mr Gastrell, you and I need to have a long and serious conversation; I think the Ministry could make good use of your talents.'

'O-of course, Mr Wyngate,' Gastrell stammered, blinking in surprise.

'Then we come to Flight Lieutenant Harvey.' Wyngate's expression was unreadable. George would be going to prison, wouldn't he? He'd kidnapped a child and come close to committing murder. 'The Ministry feels that criminal proceedings will unfairly besmirch an otherwise exemplary record. Flight Lieutenant Harvey will be taking an extended period of sickness absence in the care of some exceptional physicians who have made combat stress their business. He'll heal, in time.'

'Thank you, Mr Wyngate,' Lottie said, relieved. 'I've been so worried about what would happen to him. He's not a monster, he's just been broken by the war. Losing Martha was awful and I will never know how men like him can take to the skies day after day, risking their lives. He needs to be looked after and I'm so glad that he will be.' Then she smiled, as she thought of Daisy. 'And you've made a little girl very happy too, giving her your hat.'

'You won't get it back now.' Matthew smiled.

Wyngate's lips twitched very slightly, just enough to suggest a smile. Then he said, 'I'll be taking Stefan with me when I leave Bramble Heath; I'll make sure he's properly cared for.' He glanced towards Stefan, who smiled. 'But the roads are impassable so if you have room at the inn, Mr von Brandt would be glad of it.'

Matthew nodded. 'Of course,' he said. 'Stefan's always welcome here.'

SIXTY-NINE

Christmas Day morning was sunny and bright, but still very cold. The snow was heaped up all around the village still, with only a few tracks carefully carved out around the airbase. But still the villagers, wrapped up in their woollens and their stoutest boots, made it to the church for the Christmas service and the ancient stone building rang to the rafters with the sound of happy carols.

Lottie, sitting in a pew with the Gastrells, beamed up at Matthew in the pulpit. He looked radiant as he reminded the village that, by celebrating the birth of Christ, they were celebrating the power of forgiveness, too.

Stefan had come to the service; rest and food were doing him the power of good. Sarah and the other evacuees moved along their pew so that he could sit with them, along with Daisy and Blossom.

The people who had been cursing Stefan's name now greeted the young man with polite but understandably guarded smiles, but for the children there was no such standing on ceremony. In the minutes before the service started, they clamoured at the airman with questions, desperate to hear how he had survived in the shattered tail of the Heinkel, plummeting through the sky and into the canopy of trees. And Stefan greeted their questions with smiles and answers, holding the children in a fascinated thrall.

Once the service was over, the villagers began to head home for the Christmas dinners they'd been able to put together despite rationing and shortages, and Lottie saw Freddy, in his RAF blue, as he came up to Stefan to shake his hand.

Sarah had got as far as the door of the church before she turned and hurtled back up the aisle to where Stefan was standing.

'What's Adolf actually *like*?' she asked as, in her wake, the other children gathered to await the answer. From within the folds of Sarah's coat her cat, Winnie, peered out.

Stefan frowned, then said heavily, 'He doesn't believe in Christmas. But I do.'

Sarah's eyes grew wide and she murmured, '*Blimey.*'

Nicola had driven to the church on her tractor with a holly wreath secured to its front and now everyone from the vicarage climbed up onto it. There was always room for more at the farm for dinner. Gastrell and Matthew helped Stefan onto the trailer, and Daisy and Blossom leapt up after him. Mrs Gastrell, glamorous as ever, found the whole business of travelling by tractor most amusing and laughed all the way to the farm. As they plunged through the snowy lanes, the sunlight glittering on the unblemished snow, everyone was smiling.

Lottie clasped Matthew's hand tight and snuggled against him. There was a light in his eyes that she'd seen a hint of before, but now it was blazing.

Back at the farm, Mrs Gosling had done her best to make space for everyone around the table, even though it meant unmatched chairs and, in some cases, milking stools. But no one minded at all as they passed around the dishes and enjoyed the spread. Using the recipe books sent out by the Ministry of Food, and making the most of the vegetables that were so plentiful in the countryside, Mrs Gosling had stretched their rations and presented them with a feast.

There was a spicy parsnip soup as a starter and for the main course, she'd managed to find a chicken. Mrs Gosling had made stuffing from stale bread, flavoured with onions and herbs grown in the garden, and she dished out potato and parsley cake too. She'd made a Christmas pudding, rich with the scents of cinnamon and fruit, and there was even fudge that she'd somehow made from carrots.

Martha would've been in her element here, surrounded by laughter and friends, and Lottie felt her closeness once more.

Mrs Gastrell explained to everyone that it was the middle of Hanukkah, the Jewish festival of light, and asked if she could light Mrs Gosling's candelabra. As Mrs Gastrell lit the candles, she sang 'Maoz Tzur', which she told them meant 'The Rock of Ages' in Hebrew. Lottie recognised it as the name of a hymn she'd sung in church and it reminded her that even among the differences between people, there were still things that they shared. Then, in the candlelight, Mrs Gastrell prayed aloud for her people suffering in Europe, saying that she was looking forward to the day when everyone would be free of the hatred and tyranny of the Nazis.

Stefan invited her to sit beside him and the two of them held hands over the table.

Once dinner was over, Lottie helped to carry the plates and dishes to the kitchen, with Blossom trailing after her, hoping for titbits. On her way back to the dining room, she paused to see Matthew standing in the doorway. His gaze seemed far away and Lottie knew he was thinking about Emily.

'Thanks so much for coming to dinner,' she said, her hand resting gently on his sleeve as she looked up affectionately at him. 'It's been lovely spending Christmas Day with you and your family.'

'Thank you for welcoming us into your family,' he replied. And it was true; the residents of the farm *had* become a motley sort of family. 'It's a wonderful way to spend Christmas.' He took her hand in his. 'And there's nobody else I'd rather spend it with.'

Lottie beamed at him, her heart full of warmth. 'You know, there's something I should tell you, and I hope you won't mind. I think – no, I *know* – I'm falling in love with you, Matthew.'

Just as she said that, her gaze darted upwards. There, hanging from the doorframe above them, was a bunch of mistletoe and Lottie couldn't help but smile.

'That's lucky on two counts,' he said innocently. 'Firstly, because it'd be terribly awkward to be under the mistletoe with the vicar if you weren't already his girl. And secondly, because I've fallen in love with you too.' Then Matthew dropped his voice to a mischievous whisper to confide, 'The Women's Institute will be devastated.'

Lottie tenderly brushed her fingertips against his handsome face, running them along his jaw, before rising up on her toes to claim his lips with hers. She slipped her arms round him and held him tight. They'd both been through so much in this war, but now the future lay ahead of them.

Once peace came – and it would – there would be a new world, and a new path paved with love.

EPILOGUE

AUTUMN 1945

Lottie walked up the aisle of the church on her father's arm. She held a bouquet of wildflowers that Daisy had picked for her from the lanes around Bramble Heath. Ahead of her, Matthew, the man she loved, was standing at the altar rail, waiting for her. Just for today, he wasn't the one in the cassock, officiating; because this was *their* wedding day.

They'd planned this day for a long time. There wouldn't be a shop in her future now, but without Martha to run it with her, the dream would've been bittersweet anyway. Instead, she would help Matthew care for his flock in Bramble Heath: she would give back the love that the village had given to her.

The war had ended but there were still shortages, so her dress was made from a silk parachute and she wore her best shoes, with a couple of brooches stitched on for sparkle. Her engagement ring, which she'd worn every day for nearly two years, sparkled on her finger. It was only a little thing, as everything was so hard to get, but she loved it more than she would have done a huge, shiny gem.

She had three bridesmaids behind her as she headed towards Matthew. Daisy was ecstatic, and Sarah had made the trip down from London especially. They wore matching pink dresses, made from fabric that Lottie had, by a miracle, found in a shop. She'd made the dresses herself, tricking them out with extra ribbons and lace. As they walked down the aisle behind Lottie and her father, they were accompanied by Blossom, the third bridesmaid, who had a matching pink bow threaded into her collar.

The long feather on Mrs Gastrell's hat bobbed as she looked up at her husband. Gastrell was standing proudly beside Matthew as his best man, father and son wearing matching buttonholes of local wildflowers. Lottie had watched as time healed the rifts between them. Daisy and Matthew had a family again.

The pews that Lottie passed as she glided by with her father were filled with people from Bramble Heath and beyond. Lottie's mother, dabbing her eyes with a lace-edged handkerchief, was sitting in the front pew with the Land Girls from the farm. Her parents had eventually come to understand why Lottie couldn't leave the village and they were beginning to fall in love with Bramble Heath too.

Shona's brother Jack had returned from Germany and he sat beside Stefan, who was no longer a slip of a lad; during his time at the prisoner-of-war camp, he had turned into a handsome young man. He had decided to make his home in Britain and, in Shona's brother, he had even found a new friend.

Alastair, a large orange flower in his buttonhole, held hands with Laura, beaming. As Lottie passed on her father's arm, Alastair gave her a nod of friendly acknowledgement. Laura smiled too and Lottie knew she had friends for life in the village.

Bramble Heath had changed both their lives for ever. So many stories had been told in this little village, some tragic and some, like that of Matthew and Lottie, filled with joy.

Everyone in Bramble Heath had been through so much in

the years of the war. The village had turned towards fear and hostility when a terrified young man in enemy uniform had been stranded here and a celebrity had swept in to capture him. War had made people vulnerable and afraid, as Lottie knew only too well; the village had forgotten how to be friendly and welcoming. But with Matthew to guide them, they had come to accept the truth and had found it in their hearts to forgive, and Bramble Heath was all the stronger for that. Lottie was proud that she and Matthew would live here together as a family, with Daisy and Blossom. A bright future lay ahead of them all. At last, peace had come.

As Lottie took her place beside Matthew in the dappled light that shimmered through the church's stained glass, she felt that peace like the warmth of an embrace. And when she settled her gaze on Matthew, the man she loved, she knew that she had found her home here in Bramble Heath, the village that opened its arms to all who found their way there.

A LETTER FROM ELLIE CURZON

Dear Reader,

We want to say a huge thank you for choosing to read *Wartime Wishes for the Land Girls*. If you enjoyed it, and want to keep up to date with all our latest releases, just sign up at the following link. Your email address will never be shared and you can unsubscribe at any time.

www.bookouture.com/ellie-curzon

Ellie Curzon is two authors writing as one and we're both so grateful to you for joining us in Bramble Heath for our series, *A Village at War*. Whilst we're sorry to bid farewell to the village and its inhabitants, we're heading into Blitz-torn London for a brand new series in 2025, filled with heart-stopping drama and gripping historical detail. Sign up to our newsletter or follow us on social media to find out more!

Thanks,

Ellie

KEEP IN TOUCH WITH ELLIE CURZON

www.elliecurzon.co.uk

facebook.com/elliecurzonauthor

x.com/MadameGilflurt

goodreads.com/ellie_curzon

ACKNOWLEDGEMENTS

Many thanks to Rhianna, our editor, and everyone at Bookouture, for bringing *A Village at War* to life. Your advice, guidance and trust has really been an inspiration.

Catherine's love and thanks go to her family, who instilled a love of history in her from childhood, and especially to grandad Steve, whose feet didn't reach the Spitfire pedals, and nana Win, who had no truck with airmen. She dedicates this entire series to Pippa and Rick, who have been at her side for every adventure.

Helen would like to thank Gordon for making the tea, and Vincent for the cuddles. And thanks are also due to her family for their stories about ordinary people finding themselves in extraordinary times, whether they were sheltering from bombs in an Underground station, or dodging bullets on D-Day.

This book is in celebration of the Land Girls of both world wars; the thousands of women who joined the Women's Land Army to work on farms far from home and kept the nation fed.

PUBLISHING TEAM

Turning a manuscript into a book requires the efforts of many people. The publishing team at Bookouture would like to acknowledge everyone who contributed to this publication.

Commercial
Lauren Morrissette
Hannah Richmond
Imogen Allport

Cover design
Eileen Carey

Data and analysis
Mark Alder
Mohamed Bussuri

Editorial
Rhianna Louise
Lizzie Brien

Copyeditor
Jacqui Lewis

Proofreader
Jane Donovan

Marketing
Alex Crow
Melanie Price
Occy Carr
Cíara Rosney
Martyna Młynarska

Operations and distribution
Marina Valles
Stephanie Straub

Production
Hannah Snetsinger
Mandy Kullar
Jen Shannon
Ria Clare

Publicity
Kim Nash
Noelle Holten
Jess Readett
Sarah Hardy

Rights and contracts
Peta Nightingale
Richard King
Saidah Graham

Made in the USA
Coppell, TX
03 September 2024